John Doe

By Buz Sawyers

Aignos Publishing

Honolulu, Hawaii

2013

Published in the USA by Aignos Publishing, Inc.
1910 Ala Moana Blvd, #20A
Honolulu, HI 96815
www.aignospublishing.com

Printed in the USA

Edited by Chunghea Oliver
Cover art provided by
Print Layout by:
Cover design by Liang-Han "Kevin" Yu

13-digit ISBN: 978-0-9895191-2-0
10-digit ISBN: 0989519120

Aignos Publishing
Honolulu, Hawaii
2013

Chapter 1

Monday, October 27, 1952
Dallas, Texas

I was trying to finish off the last couple of pages of another Erle Stanley Gardner, Perry Mason novel, when the phone intercom buzzed. Reluctantly, I set down the paperback, punched the button, and picked up the receiver. "Yes, Jenny, and this better be *damned* important. I'm down to the last ten pages of *The Case of the One-Eyed Witness.*"

As usual, she ignored my threat. "Harry, you're not going to believe this, but *Senator* Doe is here to see you," she reported in a controlled whisper.

"*The* Senator Doe?" I asked, thinking to myself, *probably wants me to see if his beautiful, millionaire wife is boffing the estate grounds keeper.*

"Yes," she whispered. "He says it's imperative that he sees you...he says the future of his political and personal life depends on you seeing him."

A little overly dramatic for my taste... "He's a Republican in Texas, Jenny. He hasn't got a future. It's a proven fact. And, why are you whispering?"

"Because, he's standing *right here.* Why would he want to see *you?*"

"You underestimate me, Jenny, but good question. Why don't you ask him while I finish the last ten pages of my book?"

I figured that'd throw her into a panic.

"No! You..."

There seemed to be some kind of wrestling match over the phone, then a new voice, much deeper than Jenny's came on line.

"Mr. Stumbaugh? This is Senator John Doe and it's very important that I see you *now*."

"That's exactly what I've been trying to tell my secretary, Senator Doe. Why don't you come into my office, sir? It'll be easier to talk that way, don't you think?"

I hung up, drumming my fingers across the length of the cradled receiver, contemplating how to handle this unannounced windfall that just fell into my lap. I decided to act professional, since I knew he'd be a *paying* client.

The door opened and Jenny ushered in our distinguished visitor. "Your appointment, Mr. Stumbaugh," she said with a smile and a surprisingly professional tone. She must have been reading my mind.

The Senator removed his hat and politely nodded to my lovely assistant. "Thank you, Miss McClain," he said quietly, bowing his head an inch or two.

Two things surprised me right off the bat. First, I didn't know Jenny knew a word as long as *appointment,* and second, the man walking through the door had no resemblance to the firebrand campaigner that'd been stumping for fresh new votes across the state for the past year.

Jenny gestured, getting my attention. "Could I get you gentlemen some coffee, perhaps?" She said, nodding so I'd know the right thing to say.

Who kidnapped my secretary? "That'd be perfect, Jenny."

Shaking hands, I motioned the Senator to one of the stylish leather, wing-backed chairs in front of the desk. "Have a seat, Senator. If you don't mind me saying so, I think you need to take a load off. You look a little stressed." He took the chair on the right, of course, and I took the chair next to him, instead of sitting behind the desk. More personal. More professional. "What brings you to

Stumbaugh Investigations, Senator? I don't usually see many politicians this time of the day, unless of course it's in a bar at the Adolphus or the Baker."

He gave a short laugh, which seemed out of character with the obvious stress lining his face. "That's what I like, a man who's secure in his own skin."

Now I've recognized the man's appeal. Senator John Doe was a striking figure of a man. He was over six feet tall, a thick head of coal black hair with a smattering of gray at the temples, and built like quarterback: lean and muscular. I was about the same height with that smattering of gray hair thing going for me, but I was built more like a front lineman than a sleek, streamlined quarterback. His suits were expensive, but not over the top. His facial features were sharp and chiseled with a strong square jaw, reminding me of the main character in the *Buz Sawyer* comic strip in the Sunday papers. I had a feeling he'd be more comfortable behind the controls of a bulldozer tearing something up than contending with verbal jousts on the floor of the Senate. "I'm comfortable in my own shoes, if that's what you mean. I put them on the same way you do, Senator."

"So you do, Mr. Stumbaugh," he answered.

"So...now that we've got our chest thumping ceremony out of the way, maybe you'll tell me why you're here," I said, not wanting to play word games for half an hour before getting to the point.

From the news, I had already gleaned that Doe was a self-made man with a reputation as someone who bucked the system and went against the grain regardless of the flak he might have to take. And, of course, he had that whole amnesia thing working for him. I'm not sure if he sided with the Republicans early in his political career because he believed in their causes, or that bump on the head he took twenty years before had something to do with it.

Whatever his reasons, he had made a name for himself at the State Capitol. The fact that he was elected as a Republican State

Senator from Dallas, which was the bastion of democratic ideas, said a lot for his charisma. Hell, I voted for him four years ago, and I'd never swayed from the democratic ticket since I was old enough to vote.

Doe leaned forward in the chair, his usual exuberant, confident features had become drawn, but his dark brown eyes still maintained that well-known intensity. "Do you know me, Mr. Stumbaugh? What I mean is...do you know that much about my past?"

I shrugged. "I know as much as the next man, I guess. Is that what this is about? Your past?"

He nodded. "It is, but before I go into that, some things I'd like to discuss first. I'm well aware of your own reputation, Mr. Stumbaugh, and..."

I held up a hand to keep him from gushing my virtues. "And, you still came to see me? I'm flattered," I said with a smile.

It was all part of my 'warming-up-the-client' routine.

He returned the smile. "Don't underestimate yourself. I won't, Mr. Stumbaugh. That's why I came here instead of somewhere else. Your reputation as an investigator precedes you. You're recognized as someone who is tough, fair, as somebody who gets results. I understand that you hobnob with the rich and famous on occasions and shoot craps with the underbelly of Dallas on others. And, more importantly, you don't care who knows it."

"Kinda like you, I'd say," I noted. "And, I see you've done your research, Senator."

He nodded and said, "I'm a cautious man," he paused, nodding. "As I was saying, I know that you're comfortable on both sides of the tracks. That's why I came to see *you*. I need that kind of diversity in a man to help me in my...situation."

Looking directly at me, Doe shifted back into the recesses of the chair. "You know that I'm a man of means, right?"

I wanted to see how thin-skinned he was. "Yeah, married into it, right?"

He snorted or laughed or something, I wasn't sure. "Damn straight, I did," he said.

That impressed me a little bit. "Well, I'm flattered about *why* you chose me, but how about telling me *what* you want, Senator? Time is money and you've wasted about ten minutes of mine, so far."

Brass tacks.

With his focus momentarily punctured, his eyes shifted down to his feet, before focusing back on me again. "Fair enough, but let me just start at the beginning for you. Then, you can make your own judgment about taking me on as a client."

"I'd make my own judgment, anyway, but go ahead." I grabbed a pack of Lucky Strikes from my shirt pocket, pulled two cigarettes halfway out, offering him one.

"Smoke?"

He looked around the room as if to see if anyone else was with us, then slipped one out. "This, my friend," he said, pointing to the smoke, "is our first confidential secret. Client or not."

"Bad for the image, huh? You've got to be the only guy in Congress that *doesn't* smoke," I joked, but didn't get a grin out of him. "Consider it a freebie and it puts us on a first name basis as far as I'm concerned. Please, call me Harry"

"Consider it done, Harry. Well, as you know - along with everybody else in the state - back in '32, I was walking along Highway 377 on the outskirts of Denton and was run over by a hit-and-run driver. They never found the driver or vehicle. I woke up from a coma a month later in the hospital with a severe head injury…and amnesia."

He let the word hang there in the air like the smoke that should've been smoldering from our unlighted Lucky Strikes. Shaking his head, he continued, "It's a mysterious thing, Harry. Some people don't believe amnesia even exists, but that's because it can't be *absolutely* proven, I guess. Some people say I faked it to get attention or to get out of a bad marriage or something crazy like that, but I can tell you right now, this isn't the kind of thing you can fake and get away with."

"Why's that?" I asked. I didn't want to tell him I was one of those skeptics.

"It's too easy to get tripped up. People try it all the time. It's like telling a lie. You tell one, then you have to tell another to cover-up the first one, and on and on it goes. After time, you forget what the first lie was even about and eventually, even the greatest liar of all would make that fatal slip. Trust me, it's impossible to erase twenty-something years and act like the past never happened."

"Yeah, well, what about those cases where somebody claims amnesia, then sits down at a piano and plays Bach's *Fifth Concerto* without missing a beat." *Was there a fifth?* "What do the doctors say about that?"

Doe nodded. "Good question. They call it retrograde amnesia. That's my diagnosis. A person loses their pre-existing memories, but still maintains learned skills, such as playing a piano, reading and writing, or throwing a ball."

This was already going over my head. "I see," I followed, though coolly recognizing that I had no idea what he had just said.

Retro – whatever…

"It's been exactly twenty years ago today, as a matter of fact, when the accident happened…and I'm sure that's no coincidence either.

"Nice anniversary present, huh?"

He ignored another one of my clever comebacks and the question it implied, too. "Still to this day, Harry, I can't tell you one iota about myself prior to 27th of October 1932. In the hospital, I was tagged as a John Doe, identity unknown. Since it was the only name I had at the time, I kept it. I had no idea who I was or where I'd been. For some reason, I considered it a blessing instead of a curse. Maybe that says something about my past; I don't know. Anyway, I decided to rebuild my life. Went to school, got my degree, then on to law school, had a successful practice as a defense attorney for a few years."

"You crammed in a lot of living in twenty short years, plus you married money," I said, reaching over and firing up my lighter for him. "Rude of me," I said, "offering a cigarette without a light." I lit his, then my own. "You've done a lot in a short period of time," I repeated.

"I'm an ambitious man, Harry. And, marrying money didn't hurt, either," he added, good naturedly. He took a deep drag from the Lucky Strike like somebody getting their first breath of fresh air after staying underwater too long, then blew out a long stream of smoke to the side. "My wife will kill me if she smells smoke on my suit. Can't help myself, though."

"I can't help you either, when it comes to the missus," I said. The cigarette looked comfortable between his fingers, so I assumed it wasn't his first in a long time like he acted. *Interesting. You lie about the little things...*

This might get a little touchy, but I've got to know. "Your little finger," I said, pointing to his right hand, "looks like you lost it at the first knuckle. You a nail biter?"

Doe laughed. "You don't sugarcoat do you, Harry?" He held up the hand, showing off the nub of his right-hand pinkie. "Another injury resulting from the hit and run. Lost my memory and a finger. Does that satisfy you?" Doe added the final question with a little edge.

"Just curious, Senator. I observe; I ask. Anyway...you were saying, before I asked about your anatomy?"

He tapped an ash in my ashtray. "Now where was I? Oh, yes. A new life...got interested in politics. Started in local politics, did some fund-raising, then with my wife's encouragement...and money, of course, I made a successful run as a state senator four years ago. Now, I'm making a symbolic run against the most popular man in Texas for the United States Senate. Only in America, Harry, can a guy with a blank past get into politics."

"Yeah, says a lot about the voting public, doesn't it? Well, glad you recognize your campaign as symbolic, because you're going to get your ass kicked, you know." I took a drag and then pinched away a small tobacco leaf sticking to the end of my tongue. I gave up trying to find out what the hell he wanted. Like all politicians and college professors, he liked hearing himself talk, I guess. The man could talk about a screw-driver for thirty minutes and never mention the handle.

"You think?" He said, the words dripping with sarcasm. "Well, I believe General Eisenhower's going to kick Adlai Stevenson's ass in the election next week. Who'd you rather have running the country with the Soviet Union ramping up their commie rhetoric and the Korean peace talks stalled every other week? A milquetoast intellectual from Illinois or the General of the Armed Forces that kicked Hitler's ass into a Berlin bunker?"

I smiled. "Good point and you must really believe it. You used the word *ass* twice to complete one thought."

He returned a knowing grin. "Sometimes I get on my soap box, and it doesn't take much to get me started, unfortunately. Bad habit, but mark my words, Harry...Eisenhower will take eighty percent of the vote next week. You can call your bookie on that," he said, with a crooked smile, tapping the side of his nose with a forefinger.

"If I had a bookie." *Which I do.* "And you? You think you'll get caught up on Ike's shirttails and get swept into office over ol' Price Daniels?"

"No, he's going to kick *my* ass, but I couldn't let him run unopposed. Somebody had to stand in for the other side."

"Very noble," I said. "You think Daniels has anything to do with this? This...coincidence you mentioned half an hour ago, or whatever it is you're here about?"

He shook his head. "No. He'd have nothing to gain and everything to lose if it blew up in his face. He'll probably take eighty percent of the vote himself. So, what's to gain?"

"Well, you've enlightened me on the medical and political

front, but so far you haven't told me anything I didn't already know about you. I need to know why you're here, if I'm going to save the election...as you told Jenny."

Senator Doe nodded with agreement. "I had a visitor today," he said, gravely. "Man by the name of Petrie, Robert Petrie. He got in to see me on the pretense of being an old high school buddy, but he wasn't, of course. Do you know how often I have crackpots coming to me, saying they know who I was prior to 1932?"

Doe wasn't done, though. I could see it coming.

He punctuated his rhetorical question with, "...And, usually with their hands out wanting some kind of reward."

After that first puff, his cigarette had burned down halfway after the amnesia speech, the political lesson, and now the sob story about hucksters trying to get into his deep pockets. He stubbed it out in the desk ashtray without taking that enjoyable, final drag.

Figures...it's what happens when rich people bum cigarettes...

"A bunch, I imagine. More than...let's say, two?"

"The numbers have slackened off with the passing of time, but two or three a month still...without fail. In the end, though, there's never any proof."

"Did this Petrie character have proof? He must've had something to spook you into coming to see me. I figure coming to me a week before the election had to be the last straw for you. And, you're a senator, after all. There's got to be a lot of people you can reach out to." I got up and went behind my desk for a writing pad and a pen. "Mind if I take a few notes?"

"Not at all. Does that mean you'll help me?"

"Don't know. You haven't told me what you want, yet." I shrugged a shoulder for encouragement. "Leaning that way, though. Sounds intriguing. I think I know where you're going with this, but I still want to hear it from you. I love paying customers, and you married money, you know." I took my seat again. "What were you saying about proof?"

He dodged the marriage taunt thing again. "No, he didn't

have anything concrete *with him,* but he assured me he had irrefutable proof of my past life."

"Irrefutable, you say," I mumbled, scribbling on the notepad. *How do you spell that*? "So, I'm assuming this *irrefutable* proof was good stuff."

"Depends on your point of view, I guess. How does a double murder in the act of an armed robbery sound to you?" He asked.

I stopped taking notes. "Sounds like they'll be firing up Old Sparky on Death Row to me, John," I said, then took a deep drag off my Lucky Strike.

Chapter 2

A knock on the door prevented the senator from responding to *another* clever comeback. I was on a roll.

"Come in, Jenny."

The doorknob turned and I saw her swing the door open the rest of the way with her foot, providing a nice knee shot with a slice of thigh on the side. I noticed that John didn't miss it either.

Classy.

With both hands, she carried a silver tray I'd never seen before, complete with a fresh pot of coffee, silver containers for the cream and sugar, and two porcelain cups with grapevine designs wrapped around them. I recognized most of the paraphernalia from the attorney's office next door. I'd been served from them many times myself.

Nice move, Sweetheart.

"I'll just set these down right here," she said, placing the tray on the corner of my desk. "Senator? Would you like cream and sugar?"

"Just sugar, please." He stretched his neck towards the desk, checking out the tray. "One cube, please."

She extracted one cube with a dainty pair of silver tongs and carefully dropped it into his cup, then stirred it for him. "There you go," she said proudly, handing him the cup.

The whole thing amused me, watching her fawn all over the senator, since Jenny didn't know the first thing about making coffee, let alone serving it. The secretaries next door must've given her a crash course on etiquette. "Black for me, Jenny. Thank you for this," I said it sincerely and meant it.

She nodded. "My pleasure, anything else I can do?"

"Just hold any calls and get rid of anyone that might come in. The senator's visit is private and for all intent and purposes, he's not really here."

"I understand," she said, nodding and closing the door discretely behind her.

Doe took a sip of his coffee. "M-m-m, good. You've got a great girl, there. I bet she really takes care of you."

I tried not to read anything suggestive in his comment. "Yes, she does and she's easy on the eyes, too. One in a million," I answered. "She probably had to knock the dust off from everything here before bringing it in," I said, pointing to the tray. "It's not my everyday serving piece, you know."

"It's the thought," he said standing and retrieved the Perry Mason novel from my desk and checked out the cover. "Read this one. I like Gardner. His courtroom drama is full of shit, but it's a fun read." Returning it to my desk, he said, "Are you my Paul Drake, Harry?"

I took a sip of my own coffee. He was right; it was very good. "M-m-m-m," I said, adding one more *m* for emphasis. "Perhaps, but I don't have the operatives all over the state like he does. I'm a two man, one woman operation."

"Who's your help, besides Jenny?"

"Missed that in your research, huh? A young vet from the war. Good kid." *No need giving out too much info just yet.* I set down my cup of java. "So, according to Petrie, you're a mass murderer. Must've been a big job. Who'd you stick up?"

"Armored truck heist. Supposedly carrying receipts from Santa Fe Railroad."

"Yeah? What happened to the dough?" Then, I held up a hand in a stopping gesture. "Wait, let me guess, he thinks you've got it, and he wants his half or he's going to blow the election, which you can't win anyway, if you don't pony up with the money. Am I close?"

"You're exactly *on* the money, so to speak."

"How much moolah we talking here, Senator?"

"A little over a million."

I whistled a long note. "Definitely worth killing two people for, I guess. Did you recognize this Petrie character?" I asked, already knowing what he'd say. Didn't mean it was the truth, though.

"Of course not. He wasn't any different from the other imposters that have tried to shake me down over the years. But there's something different about him. Something that makes me nervous."

"Yeah, what'd that be?"

The senator's eyes drifted back to his feet, and then he delicately set his coffee cup on the desk. "He said if I didn't come up with half-million cash by five o'clock today, he'd go to the papers and spill his story."

"You must like cutting your deadlines close, John. Not much time to think about things, huh? So he's the first that's ever had the balls to call your bluff? Is that what you're saying?"

I thought I'd see how he reacted to the word *bluff*. That's like asking if you still beat your wife. Which I knew he didn't. He couldn't afford the pay cut. I took another sip of coffee.

"Isn't that like asking me if I *still* beat my wife?" He asked with a grin. "You're good, Harry, that's why I came here. And the answer to your question is, 'yes'. He's the first to attempt blackmail with any degree of success."

"Why? Did you do it? Did it all come back to you in a flash when he said the word *murder*?"

"No, and I don't give a damn about losing the election or even my own reputation, for that matter. But my wife, Hedy…her reputation. The scandal, if it's true…that's what scares me," he said. "She doesn't deserve this." There was even a slight quiver in his voice this time, a nice touch of drama on his part.

I hesitated before saying anything for my own dramatic effect. *Say something intelligent.* "I understand...and actually believe you." I smiled. "To a point, anyway. Nobody's *that* noble, in my humble opinion, John. You have to understand that: in my line of work, it's seldom I get to see the good side of human nature. In fact, I usually see human nature at its worst."

After that little piece of philosophy, I decided to build the drama even more, so, imitating him, I retrieved my cup with grapevine designs and took a prolonged, silent sip, and then delicately replaced it on my desk. "Okay, John, what I believe really doesn't matter. What is it *you* want from *me*?"

"I want to know if this man is on the up and up. If he's telling the truth...then we'll see what happens after that. My whole future changes. *But,* if he's another grifter trying to dig into my pockets, I want to fuck him over *real bad.*

Whoa! The f-bomb! This must be serious.

"Fair enough," I said, calmly, making no mention of the *f* word slip. "So do you want me to take this guy out in the parking lot out back and work him over with some brass knucks or a slapper and beat the truth out of him? I'm getting a little long in the tooth for that kind of work, you know." His answer would determine whether I took the case or not, tempting as it might be to take his money. Even *I* have *some* ethics.

"No, I don't operate that way and neither do you. I could get any thug off the street for fifty dollars to make him disappear. I want to be able to stand up in front of the cameras and reporters and debunk everything he claims. I have to know for myself. I *have* to know, Harry."

"Then, I assume, you're not going to pay him. You're going to let him go to the papers. Am I reading this right?"

"You are, which means you don't have any time to waste."

"Did he say how he'd contact you? Did he give you a meeting place where the exchange was supposed to take place?

Anything like that?"

"He's calling me at four o'clock."

"Where?"

"My place in downtown."

"And where's that?"

"The Adolphus Hotel, across the street."

"Of course, I forgot that you married money."

Chapter 3

I checked my watch; it was three-fifteen. "Okay, John, we've got forty-five minutes before you talk with Petrie. Two questions, then we've got to go."

"We?" Doe asked. "You're going with me? Don't you think...?"

I love interrupting senators, so I stopped him in mid-sentence. "No, I'm not going to be sitting with you, Senator, but I'll be watching. If he comes to the hotel, then I'll tail him. See where he goes. Now, what's the name? Who did he say you were in your past life?"

"Ralph Morris."

"Geez, with a name like that you better hope he's not right about all this. Okay, what's he look like?"

"Well, he was medium height, five-nine maybe. Thin, maybe one-forty-five or one-fifty in weight. Age, mid-to-late-forties like us."

I laughed at that one. "Maybe you're in the mid-forties range, but I'm already checking that decade in my rearview mirror, John."

"Then you wear it well. Anyway, my age then, and he wore a dark, pinstriped, double-breasted suit that was aged and had a shine to it. Probably the only one he owns. Dark, thin hair slicked straight back with a part in the middle and a pencil-thin moustache. He reminded me of a weasel, and had the look of some kind of underworld figure."

"*Very* observant, John. Underworld, huh? You think he's connected?" I asked.

The senator shook his head. "No, but I just think he's the type that wants you to *think* he's connected.

Interesting.

"You figured that on your own, huh? You hob-nob with the underworld types much?"

"If you shake as many hands as I do every year, Harry, you develop a sixth sense about people. Like you, for instance."

That one came out of left field. "Me? What do you mean? You think you've already got me figured out?"

He shrugged. "I do my research like I said before. You've had high and low profile clients, but they're the good guys. The ones that really need a champion. Not the scumbags or scallywags that look for a way *around* the law. That's where your ex-cop background comes into play. And in my humble opinion, you'd probably be some high-ranking muckity-muck in the Dallas PD if you hadn't been forced to retire when you did. How's your leg, by the way?"

I consciously rubbed my left thigh. "My...you do get around, don't you? It's good enough for this job."

I didn't like being the one answering questions.

"You prod and poke and have a tendency to piss off people."

"Now you're talking," I said with pride.

"You've tried to goad me into saying something wrong, tried to get under my skin with references to my rich wife. You're a flippant, smart-ass, son-of-a-bitch who constantly prods for thin-skinned weaknesses, or a slipup in oratory reflection. Those are your assets and part of the act at the same time. You pretend to be an asshole, but you're not."

Oratory reflection? *Jeez...*

"Really? Didn't know that. If that's true, don't let it get out because it'd ruin the image I've tried to build over the past years." I narrowed my eyes for effect. "You should know that I *am* an asshole. I'm not pretending."

Senator Doe stood up and stuck out his hand. "Then, we'll agree to disagree on that point. I've no doubt that I've come to the right man. That's why I came to you instead of using whatever more prominent contacts I may have. I'm not looking for a *yes* man."

I stood and took his hand with a firm grip. "I don't have a dog in this fight, Senator, so I'll just follow the trail and see where it takes me. You do what you want with the results." I finally let go of his hand. "And speaking of fees, how's about five c-notes a day plus expenses?"

Doe reached in his inside coat pocket and pulled out a checkbook. I was hoping for cash. "I was coming to that. I don't believe this will take that long to wrap up, and I'm afraid you wouldn't earn what you deserve. If this comes out the right way, then I'll consider this money well spent. How about a flat fee of ten thousand dollars and you pay your own expenses?"

He leaned over the desk and started writing out the check before I could respond.

"Is this how you do it on the Hill down in Austin? Write a check to get what you want?"

"Sometimes," he said, still writing. "Make it out to you or Stumbaugh Investigations?"

I watched him fill it out. Love those zeroes. "Company name is fine. It's all the same pot."

"That's not good business, Harry. I can help you with that when this is over, if you like." He tore out the check and handed it to me. "So, what now?"

I folded it once and stuck it in my shirt pocket. I didn't acknowledge his offer to help as my financial advisor. "What room are you in?"

"Suite 1449," he said. He dug in his suit pocket again, produced a business card, and wrote a number on the back of it. "This is my private line at the Adolphus on the back. The numbers on the front are home and office. You can reach me at either number, or leave a message and I'll get back to you."

"Suite 1449 *and* a private line, of course. Okay, you wait for his call. I'll be in the lobby wandering around to see if he shows up. If he does, then I'll make sure he's followed. But, you don't worry about that. And, don't try to get in touch with me after he calls you unless something really big happens. I'm going to be busy. I'll call you. Got it?"

"Got it. Simple enough."

"Don't tell him you need more time to get the money or try to string him along. You told me you weren't going to pay, then tell *him* that. Don't get nasty and tell him to fuck off or use threats, just tell him you don't believe him. If he wants to go to the press, tell him to do what he's got to do, but don't argue with him. And don't mention *me*." I watched him closely while I told him what to do. He didn't flinch, squirm, or object.

"That's the way I wanted to play it, too. Good. And confidentiality all the way around." He stuck out his hand again for a final handshake. "I'll be talking to you soon," he said, heading to the door. "And a thank you to Jenny for the coffee, if I don't see her on the way out."

When he turned to leave, I waited until he got to the door before answering. "I'll tell her. Say…one more thing, John."

He turned and faced me. "Yeah?"

I removed the check from my shirt pocket and waved it at him. "Is this check okay to deposit? I just thought I should check if this was from your account or your wife's."

He smiled. "Asshole."

Bingo.

Chapter 4

Sam Wolfkill was having an afternoon drink at the Baker Hotel bar when a waiter came up and told him he had a phone call at the front desk. He gave the messenger a dollar, thanked him, grabbed his beer, and made his way to the front. Harry preferred the Adolphus as his hangout, but Sam liked the digs at the Baker. He thought the waitresses were better looking.

"You got a call for me?" Sam asked at the front desk.

"Yes sir, here you go, Sam," said a young man, sliding the phone towards him.

He took the receiver. "This is Sam."

"Harry, here. We've got a job; I need you over at the Adolphus. You sober?"

Sam laughed, "Yeah, you caught me just in time. What's up?"

"I need you to tail a guy, and it's all gonna go down in just a few minutes. You got your car, or did you walk to the Baker?"

"Drove."

"Perfect. Take your car over to the Adolphus and have Riley keep it for you on the drive. Don't use the parking lot. I'll meet you out front."

"On my way," Sam said, before hanging up.

He got his car from the Baker Hotel parking lot and drove across the street to the Adolphus. When he pulled into the entrance drive, Riley commandeered his Ford almost before he came to a complete stop.

I stood by the hotel front doors and gave him a short wave.

"What's going down?" Sam asked while shaking my hand.

I guided him through the doors by the elbow. "Inside, don't want to be seen out here. The perp'll be here any minute." Once in the lobby, I led the way to the area of the hotel's complimentary phones with outside-lines only.

"I'm covering bases here," I said. "There's a guy, about five-nine, one-fifty, moustache, seedy looking character that might make a call from here. I've got the house phones covered, too. Listen to what he's got to say, remember any names, and then follow him in your car or by foot, whichever he does. I'm thinking he might go to the *Morning News* building when he's done, but don't assume anything. Once you've got his location, have me paged here."

"What're we working on, Harry?"

"Could be something big. I'll fill you in later. Just don't lose this asshole," I said, walking away.

Riley Wilson, the head doorman at the Adolphus, smiled when he saw Harry Stumbaugh pull his partner, that loose cannon Wolfkill, through the door. Riley had been tipped off by Harry earlier and knew something was afoot. These weren't unusual antics for Harry, though. Riley had been involved before in various Stumbaugh investigations. Regardless of the excitement around the hotel, though, Riley always manned his post at the front door of the hotel as though he were on duty at the Tomb of the Unknown Soldier, in Washington, D. C. He was proud of the job he'd performed for the past twenty-five years, and while others might consider it mundane, he considered it *their* loss. After all, how many people can claim to be on a first name basis with presidents and celebrities from all over the world?

Over the years, he'd developed an adept and keen knack at making snap judgments of his hotel guests. Were they rich or poor? Were they pretenders or the real thing? Sneaking out on the wife with a mistress on the arm or a woman indulging in a clandestine rendezvous with a young lover? It was a game he played every day to pass the time. Like the man approaching on the sidewalk from Akard Street. He eyed him critically. *Cheap suit.* The man had a medium, wiry build with a short gait to his walk, a scowl on his face, and both hands stuffed deep inside his double-breasted suit pockets.

"Afternoon, Sir," Riley said, greeting the stranger with a smile and opening one of the oversized, double-doors to the lobby. "Welcome to the Adolphus."

This has to be the guy Harry told me about. Scam artist. Harry had just said to watch for a guy that looked like something you'd scrap off the bottom of your shoe. And, this guy fit the part. Regardless, Riley tipped his hat with a slight dip of the head, as he did to all the guests who entered into the portals of the rich and famous and the decadent opulence of the grandest hotel in the country.

Moving through the door, Robert Petrie didn't acknowledge the doorman in the red marching band uniform with even a grunt. *Fuck 'im.* This was his first trip to The Adolphus Hotel and he hoped his last. He'd heard plenty about it, and now that he'd finally arrived, he decided that he preferred the dark, smoky dens of the Vegas Club. The clown who opened the door got him off on a bad foot to start with.

I can open my own damn door.

He gave disinterested glances to the twenty-foot tapestries on either side of the staircase as he made his way up to the lobby floor. A gold chandelier the size of a Buick hung overhead. Observing the surroundings, he stopped at the head of the stairs and took in the grandeur of the bustling room. People, dripping with money, milled about everywhere. A young man in a white suit and bow tie and a thick shock of blonde hair slicked back like a helmet played a Benny Goodman tune on some ungodly looking grand piano. It had intricate carvings around the body, *Gaudy, if you ask me,* which looked like it was made out of oak or something.

Paintings of people that'd been dead for hundreds of years,

dressed in robes and dresses that bloomed out like a hot air balloon, decorated the walls. The furniture looked like they robbed one of those king's palaces from France, or somewhere. The check-in desk was directly ahead and to his left was the Century Room, another place he'd heard about. Famous stars like Cab Calloway and Sophie Tucker performed there regularly. Not exactly his cup of tea, but it'd give him something to brag about with the boys back at the club.

Petrie checked his watch. Almost five till four. He'd been told where the outside-line phones were, so he moved to his right and found what he was looking for against the opposite wall. Three black phones were situated on a six-foot long table with chairs and fancy wooden dividers providing a minimum of privacy. The middle booth was taken by a man wearing a black, light-weight over coat and fedora. He was hunched forward with his elbows on the table, cradling the phone against his ear with his shoulder, evidently in a deep conversation. Petrie took the phone to the guy's right, sat down, and dialed a number. The other end rang five times before it was answered.

"Yeah," a monotone voice answered.

"I'm here," said Petrie.

"Okay, you know what to do, right?"

"Yeah, yeah. Use the house phones. Room 1449. Make it short and sweet. See if he's got the dough. If he reneges, just hang up. Short and sweet, like I said." Petrie retrieved a crumpled pack of Camels and a book of matches from his shirt pocket and dug out the last butt. *Shit, only one left. Gotta stop and get some at Walgreens next door when I'm done with the senator.*

"Good," said the voice. "Either way, haul your ass back here to the club and make sure you're not followed. Remember, he talked to that private dick, and we don't want him in our business. Got it?"

"Yeah, yeah. Big guy with a cane, I know. This ain't my first time at the State Fair, you know." He checked his watch again.

"Gotta go. It's almost four." The line went dead at the other end and Petrie hung up afterwards. "And goodbye to you too, asshole." He lit the Camel, stood, and looked over the partition to his left.

The man in the coat and hat was still there, finally able to get in a word edgewise, evidently. "Ah, come on, Frances! Don't be that way, honey," he whined. "Just come on down to the hotel. I'll make it up to you. Promise!"

Pussy. Don't ask. Tell the bitch what to do.

Petrie walked away disgusted with the snippet of conversation he'd overheard. "Man's got to know his place in this world," he mumbled, "just like a woman." Next, he headed back in the direction of the entrance and the Century Room. That's where the house phones were supposed to be. As he passed by the check-in desk, he saw a big man in a dark brown suit leaning on a cane that looked like a branch he'd cut off a tree somewhere. He was talking to one of the guys behind the counter. That had to be the guy. *He ain't very smart for a private dick. Standing in plain sight.* Petrie smiled to himself. *I'm pretty sure I can lose a gimp on a cane if he tries to tail me.*

At the other side of the check-in counter were two white phones on a small, fancy desk. One was taken by some old lady with gray hair sticking out from under a bright yellow pillbox hat. She had a mink rug wrapped around her shoulders, covering up some god-awful dress with red and yellow flowers all over it. Petrie thought to himself, *Evidently money and taste in clothes don't always go together.* He stepped over to the available phone and dialed Senator Doe's room number, simultaneously turning towards the check-in desk so he could keep an eye on the guy with the cane.

The senator's line picked up after the first ring, and he identified himself. "This is Senator Doe."

"Afternoon, Senator. How's your day been?" Petrie asked in a friendly voice. He didn't see a need to identify himself.

"Fine, and yours, Mr. Petrie?" The senator answered calmly.

"Fine, just fine, thank you. You got the money?"

"No, Mr. Petrie, I don't. I've chosen not to be a part of your blackmail scheme. I'll take my chances with the press. I'm afraid you'll be the one looking over your shoulder from now on, not me."

Petrie chuckled. "Really, Senator? That a threat? I'm shak-king in my shoes, *Ralph*." He dropped the smoldering cigarette from between his fingers onto the marble floor and twisted it out with the toe of his shoe. "Well, your life as *you* know it just ended, buster. And this ain't nowhere near over, and the price of doing business just went up, my friend. I'll be in touch, Senator. Oh...and tell your lovely wife, *Robert* said hello," he chuckled, hanging up before the senator had a chance to respond.

Standing at the check-in desk doodling circles and squares on an Adolphus writing pad with an Adolphus monogrammed pen just a few steps away, yours truly was not really paying attention to anything in particular. I wanted to get involved, but I knew the weasel had spotted me. From the outside, I knew I looked solid, nondescript. On the inside, one idea kept me focused, directed.

I have other people watching this animal for me.

Teddy Sears, the head checker-inner guy behind the desk excused himself from one of the paying customers wanting a second key to his room and came over my way. "He just left, Harry. He's heading to Walgreen's, it looks like."

I loved freebies, so I stuffed the monogrammed pen and writing tablet in my jacket pocket and then slid a five-dollar bill across the counter to Teddy. I could afford it, since Doe gave me a retainer big enough to live on for the next three years without lifting a finger.

"Thank you!" Teddy exclaimed. "Somebody die and leave you a bundle, Harry?"

"Not yet, kid," I said, stepping away and taking my time as I headed to the hotel door leading into Walgreen's. I didn't make a big deal about being seen. I wanted the little prick to know I was there. I just had the feeling he knew it already. Petrie was paying for a pack Camels when I saddled up behind him, grabbed a pack of Juicy Fruit from the rack, and tossed a nickel on the counter. He didn't give me the time of day, and I returned the courtesy. We were just two customers, wordlessly paying for our goods. I watched him go back in the hotel, instead of taking Walgreen's exit to the street.

The only thing I hated about the Adolphus was those damn stairs at the main entrance. They were hard on a fellow with a .45 slug still embedded in the thigh; otherwise, it was like a second office to me. I did more business here than I did in the Praetorian Building, the international headquarters for Stumbaugh Investigations. An insurance company owned that building, so that meant I was definitely the coolest guy paying rent there.

Jenny met me at the top of the staircase wearing that same god-awful dress and gray wig and dead mink wrapped around her shoulders. "You make that dress out of your grandmother's curtains or something, Jenny? Flower print and a mink stole?" Petrie was already outside. I took her arm by the elbow and led her downstairs. "Come on, we can talk and walk at the same time. At least, I can. Don't worry, baby, I've got hold of you."

She winked at me and then tucked her elbow in tight to her side, giving me support as I hobbled down the stairs. "You're so full of it, Harry," she laughed. "You love my dress and you know it."

"Yeah, baby," I said, giving her elbow a love squeeze.

She adjusted one side of the mink with her free arm. "Worked, didn't it? I took down everything he said in shorthand. See?" She said, holding up the same kind of Adolphus writing pad I stole from the front desk. It had chicken scratches all over it.

"He say anything interesting?"

"Threats. The weasel looking man said this didn't end it and the price of business just went up and asked if something the senator said was a threat. You know, the usual stuff."

"Shit, I told him not to do that. Anything else?" I could tell when Jenny was holding back.

"Yeah, he's a real slime-ball. The weasel, not the senator. And, he called him Ralph. The weasel, not the senator. The weasel called the senator, Ralph. What's that mean?"

"You're giving me a headache, Jenny. That all?"

"He said, *Tell your lovely wife, Robert said hello,*" she said, imitating Petrie in a deep voice. "And then, he laughed. Isn't that creepy to you?"

"Yeah, it is. Listen, I gotta go do my part in this. Go back to the office and translate your notes. I'll be…"

"I just did," she said.

She loves bustin' my chops.

"Then do it in *real* writing. Type it or something. I'll be back here at the hotel in a few minutes. Have me paged when you hear from Sam." I bent down and gave her a peck on the cheek. "See ya." Riley opened the door for me and pointed west.

"He's headed down Commerce there, Harry. I had Sam's car waiting for him. See him?"

"Yeah, Riley, I see him. Kinda hard not to miss that new Ford, huh?" I shook his hand, slipping him a fiver in the process. "I'll be back in a few."

Riley didn't even look at the bill. He just stuffed it in his pants pocket and said, "I'll be here if you need me, Harry."

My kind of guy.

I gave him a quick nod of acknowledgement, spotted Petrie about halfway down the block and followed him at a leisurely pace. I wasn't as crippled as I made out most of the time, but I preferred to let people think what they wanted. I also noticed Petrie didn't seem to be in any kind of a hurry either, pretending to window shop now and then. If he was headed to the *Morning News,* he had quite a walk ahead of him, but us down-towners were used to it. When everything you needed to survive was within a couple of blocks of each other, what was the point in driving? Besides, you might end up parking further away than your original destination.

Sam was the primary here, anyway. Petrie probably spotted

me in the lobby, since I did everything in my power to make sure he did, and figured I'd be the one trying to tail him. That was fine. Exactly what I wanted, as a matter of fact. Then, he wouldn't notice a car following him. Traffic was pretty thick about this time of day, and Sam had a couple of cars between him and the mark for good cover. I was thirty or forty feet behind Petrie and watched him as he finally got to the crosswalk at the corner of Commerce and Field. I expected him to go straight or left towards the newspaper, but the little prick surprised me. Instead, he turned around and faced me with a big grin on his face, stuck his arm up in the air giving me a big exaggerated wave, and then shot me the finger. I'd have to do something about that later. Then, he went to his right and disappeared around the corner towards Main Street.

I just smiled and waved back to an empty corner, watching Sam make a slow and easy right hand turn towards Main Street.

Chapter 5

Sam tossed the black fedora and topcoat into the Ford's back seat after he made his turn off of Commerce and onto Field Street. He observed Petrie's little exhibition at the corner, and that move alone told him the guy was a prick.

Idiot.

The smart ones stayed in the dark unnoticed, and if they had to be exposed to the light, they damn sure didn't make a show of it.

Well, he's not going to the newspaper building, that's for sure. Let's just see what you're up to.

Looking beyond Petrie's strolling figure, he spotted a vacant parking spot to the right on the corner of Field and Main. *Perfect.* Gradually increasing his speed, he cruised by his mark, who didn't give the Ford a second look. Sam slipped into the free spot head first, then backed up as close to the car behind him as he could without touching bumpers.

Petrie got to the corner a minute later, took a step off the curb into the crosswalk, and stood there waiting for the light to turn green. When it finally turned, he crossed the street slowly, letting the crowd pass him by, then made a right on Main. Still, he made no indications of being in a hurry.

Sam kept his place, watching the prey leisurely stroll to mid-block, and then he stopped in front of the Praetorian Building. *Wonder if he knows that's our office building*? Petrie stepped off the curb almost into traffic, waved down a passing cab, and jumped in. Coming back in Sam's direction, the black and white Checker Cab

Co. sedan sped through a yellow light and made a quick right-hand turn back onto Field Street.

Perfect.

Sam's light immediately turned green afterwards and he floored the Ford, darting ahead of a Chevy coming off the light to his left. He followed the cab at a safe distance as it meandered through various streets in a northerly direction from the downtown canyons, and into an area on Oak Lawn Street full of small businesses and beer joints. Sam stayed well back from the cab, keeping enough traffic between him and his mark so as not to be spotted, but still able to keep him in sight at all times.

Evidently, Petrie had instructed the cab driver to make evasive moves in and out of traffic, including quick turns in an attempt to shake off anyone that might be following; but, Sam still maintained the tail, he was sure, without being spotted. After making a roundabout circle of the area, the cab finally pulled to a stop at the corner of Lemmon and Oak Lawn. Sam shot the Ford through the intersection, whipped into the Piggly Wiggly parking lot on the opposite corner, and killed the engine. He had a good view of the intersection and saw Petrie leaning in through the passenger window, probably paying off the cabbie. *The gods are with me today.* When he got a look at the neighborhood businesses located on the street, there was only one establishment that would attract somebody like Petrie. The Vegas Strip Club.

Sam wanted to follow Petrie into the club to see what he was up to, but he needed to call Harry first. He wasn't up to speed on the details of the case or even why he was following the guy, so he didn't want to barge into something unprepared. He held true to his strict Marine training that had been drilled into him during boot camp and the on-the-job training that took place on the islands of Guadalcanal, Guam, and Iwo Jima. Having survived bloody beach landings and Jap suicide attacks, he sure as hell didn't want to get shot for no reason at a titty bar in Dallas, Texas.

Spotting a pay phone by the entrance to the grocery store, he abandoned his car and took off at a brisk pace on foot to call Harry. He wasn't worried about Petrie leaving the bar any time soon, and was sure the guy was probably set for a couple of hours at least. The phone was free so he dropped a nickel in the slot and called the front desk of the Adolphus Hotel.

"Could you page Harry Stumbaugh for me?"

"Yes sir. One moment, please," responded the desk clerk. Sam waited less than a minute before Harry answered at the other end.

"Sam?"

"Yeah," he said. "Your man didn't go to the paper after all. I think he wanted to wet his whistle first."

"Where are you?"

"The Vegas Club, off of Lemmon and Oak Lawn. You know the place?"

Harry hesitated before answering. "Yeah, but not the way you think."

"Want me to go inside and scope it out?" More hesitation. Sam sensed something wrong. "Harry? What's going on? What're we into? Something I need to know about?"

"Not on the phone, Sam. I can't talk here. Yeah, go in and I only want you to see if Petrie meets anybody, and if so, then who. Have a beer. Smoke a cigarette. Shoot the shit with the bartender. You know the routine. Then, meet me back at the office," Harry said, "but I need to talk to the guy that hired us first. I'll have a better handle on things after that."

"Anything I need to know about this club before I go in? I'm not much of a titty bar kind of guy, you know."

"Yeah," Harry said, "the entertainment is lousy and a guy from Chicago owns the place."

"Chicago? You mean mob guys kind of Chicago?" Sam asked, in a tone of curiosity, not concern.

"Says he is."

"What's his name, so I'll know who to watch out for."

"Ruby. Jack Ruby," answered Harry.

After hanging up from Harry, Sam decided to leave his car in the Piggly Wiggly parking lot and walk across the street to the club. That way he'd have better access to his car and no fear of getting jammed in by parking on the street. Before leaving, he retrieved his overcoat and hat from the back seat, popped open the trunk of the Ford, and tossed them inside. He decided to shed his sports jacket and tie, too. Rolling up his shirt sleeves past the elbow and loosening up his shirttails a bit, he headed for the club.

The first thing assaulting Sam's senses when he walked in the door was the smell and then the darkness. The Vegas Club smelled of stale beer, sweat, and cigarettes; at the opposite end of the room, stage lights shined upwards from the floor of the performance stage; and dim, sputtering four-foot fluorescent bulbs behind the bar provided even less light in the place. A fellow could barely see the hand in front of his face. And when Sam saw the bleach-blonde dancer on stage manipulating a long feather boa in unnatural ways to the strained notes of a four-man band, he had a better appreciation for the darkness. The sunset, after work crowd hadn't arrived yet, assuming they even would in this dive. The place was about one-quarter full. Men were scattered at various tables in pairs or alone, but no one really conversed with one another. Probably afraid somebody might recognize them. He waited until his eyes adjusted to the dim light, then pretended to grope his way haplessly through the maze of tables and chairs, heading for the bar.

The bartender was typical of a strip joint of this caliber. Black slacks, black tee shirt, arms the size of hams with a pack of cigarettes roll up in one sleeve, and a face that showed signs of an unsuccessful boxing career. Sam still had the slim, muscular physique from his stint in the Marines. He stood five-ten, weighed, one seventy-five, and was as hard as a rock. He liked to take care of himself and worked out at Gold's Gym everyday. He had a lot of demons to sweat out. Closing in on the bartender, Sam sized him up, as he did every man he met. It was a habit. Especially in strip joints financed by wise guys. The bartender, leaning with his back against a rear counter, arms crossed over a massive chest, eye-balled Sam as he took a seat at the bar. He had twenty pounds and three or four inches on Sam. *All muscle and bluff, but no moves.*

"What've you got on tap?" Sam asked, in a bored voice.

"Bud, Pabst, and Schlitz," the bartender answered, just as bored.

"Pabst'll work," Sam said.

The bartender paused long enough to let Sam know who was in charge, still eyeballing him, then grabbed a beer mug from beneath the counter and filled it to the top. A large head of foam overflowed the mug's rim as he set it down in front of Sam.

"That'll be a buck."

Sam angled his head, watching the bubbly foam flow like lava down the side of the glass, creating a puddle around the base. He pushed it across the bar away from him. "If I'm gonna pay a buck for a beer, I'd like more beer than foam in it."

The bartender shrugged. "Then go somewhere else."

"I'm already here," Sam said.

The two men locked eyes. Sam stretched his arm across the bar and with stiff fingers, nudged the mug another inch towards the opposite edge. He kept his arm in place. "A full beer, if you don't mind," he said.

The bartender examined the face of the man across from him. A weathered, chiseled face with deep creases forming triangles from the outside corners of ice blue eyes, gray short-cropped hair, and a nasty white scar that looped from the base of the left nostril up to the ear lobe. This man was a scrapper. He glanced down at the beer and noticed the Marine emblem tattooed on the man's forearm. "Marine, huh?" He said, in the same bored tone. "You in the war?"

Perfect. Very seldom did Sam let it be known he fought in the big one, and he never talked about it unless pressed or made it work to his advantage. Like now. "Yeah, the Pacific. How about that beer?"

The bartender grabbed Sam's mug by the handle and placed it back out of sight below the bar. "Pacific. The Japs, huh? Man, I heard that was bad news. You know, Jack loves the vets. He's a patriotic fanatic. First beer's always on the house for you guys," he said, grabbing a tall clean glass from the shelves behind him. He opened the beer tap and let it run a second, then tilted the mouth of the glass beneath the spout. There was a half inch of foam this time. "There you go," he said, sliding it across the bar.

"Thanks," Sam said, indicating no grudge against the man and took a deep drink, draining half the glass.

"You kill a bunch of those fuckin' Japs while you were over there?"

Sam winced. "Yeah, there was more than enough to go around."

"I tried to join the day after Pearl, you know, but bad knees kept me out. Pissed me off, too. I had to sit it out here. I would've loved to have been there beside you killing those motherfuckers."

That's what they all say.

"Yeah," Sam said, then swiveled around in his chair, facing the stage. The drummer hit a loud rim shot, thankfully bringing the dancer's routine and the music to a temporary end. Three men in the room clapped with an obvious lack of enthusiasm. Sam pointed at the stage. "Tell me she's not the star act. If I come back later tonight, will there be some prime beef or is it all a bunch of heifers on the hoof?"

The bartender laughed. "Oh yeah, the night shift is prime beef. Jack really likes to put on a show. He's got girls, comedians, there's even a ventriloquist."

"A real Vegas show, huh?" Sam's eyes had completely adjusted to the dark, and he surveyed the room, looking for Petrie. He spotted him in the very back of the club sitting at a table near the stage. Another man, heavy set, was with him.

"You want another beer, fella?" The bartender asked, pointing to Sam's half-empty glass.

Sam drained the last of his drink and handed him the empty. "Sure."

The bartender grabbed another clean glass and filled it to the top. "Be right back," he said, placing the drink on the bar. He didn't ask for a buck. Sam watched him go over to Petrie's table, but he only spoke to the heavyset man, ignoring the weasel. When he returned, he said, "Jack wants to meet you. He'll be here in a second. Told you, he admires you vets."

"Okay," Sam said, taking a small sip this time, "but I've got a call to make and need to go after I finish this beer."

"Here he comes, just hold on a sec, Marine," the bartender said.

Asshole.

Sam faced the bar, but a mirror expanding the width of the bar gave him a clear view of the approaching figure behind him. The guy was about Sam's height, but outweighed him by an extra forty or fifty pounds. Fat. Out of shape. His facial features were pointed with thinning hair slicked straight back from his forehead.

A fat weasel.

He wore a dark suit, probably tailored, and a silver tie with no pattern, and evidently, the man liked jewelry. As he got closer, Sam spotted a big gold watch on one wrist and a diamond pinkie ring on his left hand that could light up the room on its own. When fat man arrived, a hand gave him a friendly pat on the shoulder, and Sam finally turned around.

"I understand you're an ex-Marine," he said. "My name's Jack Ruby. I own this place," he said, waving his hands, "and I'm glad to meet the boys that fought in WWII." Ruby gave Sam his hand.

Sam took it with a firm grip, then let go. "Sam Wolfkill and there's no such thing as an *ex*-Marine."

Ruby's grin disappeared, then returned, with a quick recovery from the blunder. "Of course not, my mistake. Well, you're always welcome here, and your buddies too. First drink is always on the house."

"Thanks, Mr. Ruby. It's appreciated." *Here it comes.* Sam recognized the look and the next question that always followed.

"Jack, call me Jack. No need for formalities around my place." Ruby paused, then asked the expected question, "Wolfkill? You said your name was Wolfkill? What kind of name is *that*? Indian or something?"

"Yeah," said Sam.

"What kind of Indian? I'm from Chicago, you know, so we don't get many Indians up there," Jack said, intending a joke.

"Apache," Sam answered. Actually, Wolfkill was a German name, but since the war was still so fresh in people's minds, Sam had no intention of testing fate. Besides, he enjoyed the game. Everyone assumed it was an American Indian origin just from the way it sounded. Wolf…kill. So he strung them along. "Do you have a pay phone around here I can use? I need to make a call. About a job."

Ruby pointed to the front, by the entrance. "Over there by the door, but you can use the one in my office if you like. No need to waste a nickel."

"Thanks, but no thanks. I can spare the change," Sam replied, getting up from the barstool. "Thanks for the beer, Jack. I'll be sure to tell my friends about your place." He stuck out his hand.

Ruby took it and gave it an enthusiastic shake. "You do that, Sam. By the way, what kind of work do you do?"

Sam shrugged. "A little of this, a little of that. You know." And Ruby *did* know. Sam recognized that look too.

"You know," Ruby said, placing a hand on Sam's shoulder, "I've got three places here in Dallas. The Vegas and I've also got a piece of the Silver Spur Club and the Bob Willis Ranch House. I believe in diversification," he said, grinning. "I can always use somebody that knows a little of *this* and a little of *that*. If that phone call doesn't work out for you, drop by to see me. Maybe we can help each other."

Sam nodded. "I'll keep that in mind, Jack. Nice to meet you." He shook himself free from Ruby and made his way to the phone booth by the entrance. He called the office and Jenny answered.

"Hi Jenny. Harry there yet?"

"Sammy! How are ya' darling!" She exclaimed, in her usual drawl.

She was the only living person that got away with calling him *Sammy*. "I need a shower. Is he there?"

"No, Honey. I think he's talking to the senator, but he said for me to call him if you called in."

"He at the Adolphus still?" Sam asked.

"Yeah, Shug."

"I'll call him. I need to talk to him. What senator are you talking about, Jenny?"

Jenny giggled. "Our client, silly. Senator Doe."

"Oh, that senator," Sam said. "Okay, kiddo. I'll call him. I'll be in the office in twenty or thirty minutes unless Harry comes up with something else for me to do."

"Bye, Hon."

Senator Doe and the mob. Sounds interesting.

Sam turned and checked out the back of the club before leaving and saw Ruby and Petrie hunched over the table talking to each other.

Chapter 6

Sam's report about Petrie's meeting up with Jack Ruby was not what I expected or really wanted to hear. When Senator Doe said he thought Petrie looked like somebody from the mob, well, I thought it might be from an overactive imagination. Too many Bogart movies. Or, like having amnesia or something. But, if there *was* mob involvement in the shakedown, I could be on the edge of a real shit-storm. I knew for a fact that the mob eliminated anybody they even *suspected* of sniffing around in their business. As a cop, I saw the bodies on the streets and in the alleys of Dallas, and I wasn't quite ready to die in a hail of bullets or to try on a pair of cement shoes to explore the bottom of the Trinity River, just yet. I had a plan to avoid that kind of nastiness, of course, but first, I needed to talk to the honorable John Doe and set up a meeting for tonight.

As I lounged in an overstuffed, leather couch in the waiting area outside of the French Room, my second office, I waved to get the waitress's attention for another drink. The waitress, Michelle, pulled double duty at the Adolphus, working long hours schlepping drinks at the bar during the week. On weekends, though, she was a star, dazzling audiences with her prowess as one of the performers at the ice skating rink in the Century Room. Those babes were the hottest ticket in town, and she was the hottest of the hot. It was also the place where I met Jenny McClain, five years earlier. We had a little fling for a while, but before it went too far, we both realized it'd be better to enjoy each other's company without all the attachments and luggage that came with a relationship.

We met at a time in our lives when both of us were wounded and vulnerable. She was fresh off a divorce from a guy that liked using her for a punching bag, and I was fresh off forced retirement from the Dallas PD with a limp and a .45 slug in my thigh. Jenny, who was thirty at the time, knew her days at the skating rink were numbered, since a new breed of younger babes tried out every week for the coveted roll as an Adolphus skater.

When we met, she was on the hunt for a new career that didn't require twirling in circles and showing off her ass. I just happened to need a secretary that could put up with my bullshit and answer a phone at the same time in my newly opened, Stumbaugh Investigations office. She agreed on the condition I made sure her ex-husband never bothered her again. I did; the rest is history. Best move I ever made.

Michelle came to the table, picked up my empty, and laid down a fresh napkin. "Need another beer, Harry?" She asked. "Want something to eat?"

"Nah, sweetie, how 'bout a glass of tea, though? I'm on the job and need to make a call, but if you see Sam come in, bring him to the table, will ya?"

"Sure thing, Harry. Hey, I saw Jenny earlier dressed up like an old lady. Y'all playing dress-up now?" She teased.

"You know it," I said, dropping a nice tip on the table for her. I checked the wad of bills in my hand. I figured I was already down to nine-thousand, nine-hundred, and eighty dollars from the ninety-five hundred, I deposited this morning. *I need to slow down on my spending spree.* I made my way to the phone bank and called Doe. He picked up on the first ring, probably wondering why I hadn't called earlier, since it'd already been over two hours from the time he'd spoken to Petrie.

"This is Senator Doe," he said.

I could hear the anticipation in his voice. "Harry," I said, casually. "How'd the conversation go?"

"Short and sweet, just like you said. I told him no, he threatened me, and said I'd regret my decision. Something along that line. But, Harry...the one disturbing thing he *did* say was, to tell my *wife* hell-o. If that sleazy bastard even thinks about getting close to her I'll..."

"Settle down, John. He's just rattling your cage. He knows better. That'll never happen, and besides, I'll be taking care of that tonight. But, I want to get together later. I'm bringing along my partner for you to meet. There are some links to this case that I'm not real crazy about, and they need to be addressed.

"Okay, but did you follow him? Where'd he go?"

"Yeah, of course, and we'll talk about it tonight. Where will you be? Here, at the hotel?" I asked, firing up another Lucky Strike.

"No, I'm getting Hedy away from here, for now. I don't want her getting upset listening to our conversations. We're going home. We'll have more privacy there."

"And where would *home* be, John, since we don't run in the same circles?"

"Fifty-five hundred Swiss Avenue," he answered. "Know where it is?"

"Of course I do, John. I cruise by there every Christmas to see the lights. I'll find it." I checked my watch, "It's a quarter-to-seven, how 'bout between eight-thirty and nine? Will that work for you?"

"Of course. What did you find out, Harry? I can't just sit around all night waiting to hear from you. I think my ten thousand dollars should at least buy me a hint."

I thought about that for a second before answering, and since I'd already blown twenty dollars with nothing to show for it, except happy employees at the Adolphus Hotel, I decided to give in. "What made you think Petrie was part of the *underworld*, as I think you put it? Anything in particular?" I was fishing.

"No," he answered immediately. "He just had that look. You know what I mean? Seedy, kind of had that gangster look."

"Uh-huh, well let me ask you this...and I need a straight answer on this, John, because I'm meeting with someone who will *know* the answer. Have you had any past or current contact or business dealings with anyone, no matter how remote it might be, that's connected to the mob? Think before you answer, John. I gave you a lot of choices to choose from."

Again, he answered immediately. "I don't even have to think about that one, Harry. The answer is *no.* Emphatically *no.* I've never been approached at any time in my position as a senator *or* as a defense attorney. Why? What are you leading up to? Is Petrie connected to them in some way? Is that what this is about? The mob wants to get me in their back pocket, somehow? The bastards. That'll never happen, I can promise you that."

Emphatically. I've got to start writing these down. Must've hit a sore spot with the mob connection question...interesting. "Not for sure, just yet, but I'll know more tonight. Could be a coincidence. Petrie might know somebody that's connected, but I doubt that, too. Even organized crime has its standards for membership." *Time to push again.* "Or...there's another possible long shot, John."

Senator Doe snapped, the congeniality a sudden thing of the past. "What? That he's telling the truth? That I'm a murderer and thief?"

Touchy.

"I said, *long shot,* John, not shoot the messenger. And unless you're the best liar this side of the Mississippi, neither one of us knows what's true and what's not, at this point. Right?" I added, "But I can guarantee I'll find out one way or the other."

"Who're you meeting tonight that can clear all this up for you, Harry? Maybe I know him."

"If you do, Senator, then the bookies in town will be taking odds two-to-one that you and Petrie knew each other twenty-years-ago."

Chapter 7

The sun was fading behind the horizon and an evening chill was taking over. Sam and I turned up the collars of our long coats as we made the dash from the hotel to his car.

"So, where we going?" Sam asked. "Damn, that heater feels good."

"Get on Mockingbird. You ever been to the Cairo Room?"

"Never heard of it," he said.

"Great Italian food and best pizza in town. Ever heard of a man named Giovanni Gamboa?" I asked.

"Italian food in a restaurant named after a city in Egypt. Makes perfect sense. Nope, never heard of him."

"Well, you know where Mockingbird is, at least, don't you?" I said.

"Yeah, off Highway 75. Want me to go left or right when I get there?"

"Right," I said. I had an offer for him, but I wanted to make sure he was up for it. "I think it's time to start introducing you around, Sam, but first I need to know if you've got any special plans for the future?"

First, mess with him a little bit…see where his head is at...

Sam and I talked every day, but our conversations were more along the line of me giving him instructions and him reporting back. We've never really talked to each other, even though our first meeting had its moments of…interest, let's say. I had a feeling that the Doe case was going to make us either goats or heroes, and it was time to move him up to another notch. A partner, not an employee. I figured now was as good a time as any. I noticed him frowning when I asked about his future, but he kept his eyes on the road.

He finally said something. "I thought it was with you. You firing me? I can drop you off now, if you like, since we're in my car."

I laughed, "No, matter of fact, I think it's time to make you a partner, no more grunt work. Or maybe not as much. Get you back into the real world again. You survive in this business by the people you know. How to work 'em...to get what you want. It's time to...it's time to move on with your life, Sam." This time I got the look. Sam had a drop dead elephant look that could melt steel when he was annoyed or didn't like something, and I just ended up on the receiving end of it.

Good.

He shrugged. "Well, I'm on a first name basis with every county clerk and his staff in the four surrounding counties. I know people. People you don't. Remember, I lived on the streets, too. Not for twenty years like you, though."

"I know, that's why I'm bringing this up now. I'm about to..."

Sam interrupted me, "But, I can tell you the names of everybody in Midland, Texas if that ever comes in handy."

"Probably not," I said, "but tonight I'm going to try to introduce you to a major player in this town. A man few outsiders ever get to meet. If I get to make this introduction..." For the first time I can remember, I wasn't sure how to word what I wanted to say next. "It just means...I'm making an introduction here that I've never done before, and I want to make sure this job isn't something you're just passing time with."

This is awkward shit for me. I'm not used to being this nice about something.

Sam's fingers tapped the steering wheel. "Let me ask you

something, Harry."

"Shoot."

"What was I doing when we first met?"

In the year we'd worked together, we'd never spoken about that day since it happened. "You were in an alley, drunk, pissing all over yourself, with a pistol barrel up against the side of your head, getting ready to blow out your brains, if I remember correctly."

"I wasn't pissing all over myself, by the way. I was in full control of my bladder. As I remember it, we had a pleasant conversation about life, then you rapped my knuckles with that damned hickory stick of yours and kept me from saying goodbye to the world. Then you took me to your place to sleep it off and offered me a job the next day."

"That's about right," I said. "I guess that big stain on the crotch of your pants was the whiskey that missed your mouth."

Once again, one of my great comebacks was ignored.

Sam said, "I don't forget things like getting another chance. If it's true we have nine lives like a cat, I've already used up eight of them, at the very least." Then he said something that really caught me off guard. "I'd take a bullet for you without hesitation. If that ever happened, then maybe I'd get some peace."

I think that was Sam's way of finally saying thanks. "I appreciate the thought, but I don't think it'll come to that, Sam."

"So, yeah, until that day comes around, I'd say you're stuck with me."

"Glad that's settled," I said. And I was.

"Yeah," Sam said, "and Giovanni Gamboa is the mob's lead man in Dallas, by the way. I may not know a lot of people, but I know how to read."

"And sandbag, that's good," I said, keeping the grin to myself.

"So…how much of a partner?" He asked.

"Twenty-five percent." I thought that was very generous of me.

"Sure," he said, his arm stretching across the seat, "that's good for a start." Then he grinned. "Appreciate it."

I shook his hand and said, "Keep both hands on the wheel, please. I'll have Jenny draw up the agreement tomorrow."

"Your hand is good enough for me. Just out of curiosity, what brought on all this generosity on your part? Why now?"

I shrugged. "It's time. I'm fifty-eight and I need someone I can trust to take care of me in my old age."

"Not for twenty-five percent. So tell me, why Gamboa?" Sam asked, making a right-hand turn onto Mockingbird. "Where to?"

"Two blocks down on the right. Okay, here's the deal. I already told you about the shakedown on Senator Doe, but the interesting thing about your surveillance on Petrie was the place he went and the man he met there. The owner of the club, Jack Ruby, has some mob connections out of Chicago, but he's a hanger-on, not a made man. With me so far?"

"Yeah, we call 'em punks in West Texas."

"I call them assholes. Anyway, Giovanni Gamboa is the head Eye-talian, like you said, and nothing goes down in North Texas concerning their organization that he doesn't know about."

"And his hangout is the Cairo Room, I assume."

"Right," I said, "he owns it."

Sam nodded. "So…you're just gonna walk in and ask him if he's involved in shaking down a Texas State Senator." It was a statement, not a question.

"Sure, isn't that what you'd do?" I pointed to the restaurant. "On the right there, I see a spot in the front. Grab it."

Sam pulled into the empty parking space, but he kept the engine running after stopping. "I'd approach it in a round-about-way probably, not directly. But only if I had a special relationship with him. Which I'm guessing you do. Otherwise, I'd rattle Petrie's teeth until he talked. He's the weak link."

"That won't be necessary and I do know Gamboa, otherwise

you're right, we'd grab Petrie by his ankles and shake the truth out of him.

Sam finally killed the engine. "Then let's go," he said, about to get out of the car.

I grabbed his arm. "Just a minute, a few rules. Leave your piece in the car," I said, lifting my .38 from of its shoulder holster. I popped open the glove compartment and put it inside, on top of a stack of papers. "No hardware inside. It's disrespectful and dangerous. We'll both get searched. Especially you."

Sam carried his own .38 on a belt holster on his hip. He slid his under the driver's seat. "Okay, now what?"

"If you get the introduction, Giovanni may ask you some direct questions. Don't lie or play games. Tell him the truth."

"Okay, then what?"

"Just be your usual charming self, and for Christ-sakes, if he asked about your name, don't give him that bullshit story about being some fucking Indian. Just tell him you're a Kraut and be done with it."

"He sounds like a bigger asshole than you, Harry. Didn't know that was possible."

"He's definitely more dangerous, but a good friend to have in your corner if you need him. I wouldn't want him for an enemy."

"I'll try not to make that happen," Sam said. "Can we go now? I'm freezing my ass off in here."

"Pussy," I mumbled, loud enough for him to hear me.

The Cairo Room was a long rectangular affair and the decorations had absolutely nothing to do with Egypt or its capitol city. It was well-lit with plain tables and chairs filling the wide-open space of the room, and pretty, dark-haired waitresses busied themselves taking and picking up orders from a full house. No one in Dallas came to the Cairo Room for the décor; it was the food and notoriety of its owner, Giovanni Gamboa, which brought crowds through the front door.

The walls were scattered with framed 8x10, autographed

photographs of famous athletes, movie stars, and cabaret singers who *wanted* their pictures displayed on the walls of the Cairo Room; however, there were no pictures of the restaurant owner sitting at a table with his arms wrapped around any of his famous customers. Giovanni once told me that he allowed them in his place because they were good for business, but personally, he thought most of the male movie stars were all queers and the females fucked their way to fame. Why should he let them take a picture with *him*? Hard to argue against such logic.

Sam trailed about a half step behind me as we made our way to the bar, which ran half the length of the room to the right side. Without publicly acknowledging him, I spotted Gamboa sitting alone, smoking a cigarette at his usual table in the corner by the end of the bar. I knew he saw me, but there was no acknowledgment from him either. We saddled up to the bar and I waited for Eddy Valachi, Giovanni's personal bodyguard, to greet us at his convenience. Nobody talked to the boss without going through him. It'd be difficult for anyone uninvited to get to Gamboa without first getting a bullet in the back of the head, a knife to the ribs, or brass knucks upside the jaw from Eddy. It all depended on which was available to him at the time.

"If I get to see Giovanni," I said to Sam, "I'll talk with him first. If he wants to meet you, he'll let somebody know. Don't watch us while we're at the table, just stay at the bar, have a drink, and enjoy yourself. Pick up a nice looking girl. Something. But stay available."

"Sounds fun," Sam smirked. "Okay to wave down a bartender to get a beer, or is that against the rules, too?"

I grinned. "Yeah, as long as it's not holding a weapon."

"You want one?"

"Bud," I said.

Sam finally got the attention of a bartender and ordered two Buds. "Aren't you going to let him know you're here, or something?"

"He knows," I said. "He'll send somebody when he's ready."

I was halfway through my second beer and a full bowl of pretzels when Eddy came up behind me. Without a verbal greeting, his hands expertly and lightly ran across my back and waist. To the casual citizen, he was just glad to see me, but it was a profession pat-down if there ever was one. "Must be Eddy," I said, my back to him, "nobody's loved me like that since my second wife."

"I should know," he answered. "I'm the one that taught her."

I turned around with a grin on my face. That was very important for my personal well-being and waited for him to instigate the handshake. He did and then I took his hand with a firm grip. "Good to see you, Eddy, it's been awhile."

"Too long, Mr. Stumbaugh. You here to see the man, or waiting for a table?"

I nodded. "If Mr. Gamboa is available and has the time, I'd like a brief audience with him," I said, then angling my body in Sam's direction, "and this is Sam Wolfkill, Eddy. He's a friend of mine." That's mob talk for, *he's a friend of mine and it's okay for him to be here. I take responsibility if he fucks up.* Which means, if Sam fucks up, I'm either dead or will have severe knee problems the rest of my life.

Eddy didn't offer to shake his hand and neither did Sam. *Good.* Eddy just gave him a nod, and asked. "How are you?"

"I'm good, thanks for asking," answered Sam

That was very good.

"How's the family, Eddy? Everyone's well, I hope," I inquired. Always ask about the family.

"Very good," Eddy said, giving a small smile. "Eddy junior re-upped in the Navy. Think he'll make it a career. I'm really proud of him."

He didn't mention his youngest son, so I didn't ask. Not good protocol. "Glad to hear that. Give him my regards when you hear from him next."

Eddy nodded once in his boss's direction. "Go ahead, Mr.

Stumbaugh. He'll see you now. He's waiting for you."

I thanked him, told Sam to wait for me, then went to see *the man*. To describe Giovanni Gamboa, think of an Italian Santa Claus. If he was completely white-headed and had a full beard down to the middle of his chest, he'd make a perfect Saint Nick. His face and belly were round and jovial, and he had a thick shock of coal black hair with a razor-sharp part to the side, and heavy stubble that gave him a permanent five o'clock shadow around the jowls. He always wore an expensive black suit, a white shirt with no tie, and the top two buttons undone. He also smoked incessantly, lighting one cigarette from the butt of another. Gamboa didn't have a reputation as a loose cannon like some of his peers in Chicago. Instead, he preferred to negotiate the gold from your teeth from a position of strength and then steal you blind, rather than take your life. That's not to say he didn't have blood on his hands. He did.

As I approached the table, the big man stood and greeted me with a bear hug and a kiss on each cheek. I'd officially been stroked and kissed more in the last thirty minutes than the past two weeks.

"Harry, my friend," he said softly, "why do you take so long to come see me?" He gave me a paternal pat on the arm, and then motioned for me to sit down, as he did the same.

"Absence makes the heart grow fonder?" I joked.

Gamboa gave a brief belly-shaking laugh. "Only you, my friend, would say such a thing to such an important man as *me*!"

He pointed to my leg. "I see you still carry your cane, such as it is. Does it still pain you much? The leg?" Gamboa inquired, sincerely.

"No sir, not as much. To be honest," I said, "I've gotten used to carrying it. It comes in handy sometimes, and definitely gives me an air of distinction I never could pull off before. Don't you think?"

A chuckle this time. "Nothing gives *you* a look of distinction!"

I chuckled at his good-humored insult. "And the girls?" I inquired. "They are well?" Always ask about the family.

Gamboa's face lit up like Christmas on Swiss Avenue at the mention of his daughters. His arms and hands said as much as his words. "I am so proud of them, Harry. Ann Marie is in her last year at the University of Texas, before going into medical school, and Sophie," he said, leaning forward as though in confidence, "the baby and light of my life, just started her first year at Southern Methodist University. She wants to be an *attorney,* of all things. Can you imagine? *Me,* with a doctor and a lawyer in the family? What do you think of that, my friend?" He asked, proudly.

Some great one-liners came to mind about the girls' chosen professions and how handy they'd be working in the *family,* but I thought it best to keep them to myself. "I think it's a good thing they take after their beautiful mother," I said, with a self-preserving grin.

This also got a big friendly reaction. "I do miss you, Harry, but I suspect you have come here on business and not just to greet an old friend."

"You know me well, Giovanni," I said. "Not so much business, but a sharing of information. Information that can be helpful to both of us."

"I like sharing; it evens things out," he said.

Might as well test the waters. "A client came to me, a prominent man in the state, and he's being blackmailed. I've come to you with a name. The blackmailer's name, who I'm sure is at the bottom of the food chain in the matter."

"And you think I can help you with this? In what way?"

"There could be a remote connection. The name is Robert Petrie," I said.

The bridge of Giovanni's nose wrinkled, as though somebody passed gas, and his face darkened. "This is the man you speak of? The one who is doing the blackmailing? And you know this how?"

Giovanni is not involved in the shakedown. Otherwise, he wouldn't be asking questions. He'd be giving directives at this point of the conversation.

"I followed him after he made the phone call to my client. He was the one who asked for money," I stated.

"You followed him where." It wasn't a question.

"The Vegas Club." I didn't think I'd need to tell him where it was.

This time, Giovanni began slowly drumming the fingers of his right hand, very lightly, one after the other on the tabletop. Next, he sucked on his cigarette, then looked up to the ceiling, and exhaled a fresh, cloudy stream into the air. "This," he said, "...I do not like." Then his dark eyes tuned in directly on me. "You know who the *Vegas Club* belongs to, I assume?"

"Jack Ruby."

"You know him?"

I shrugged, "By reputation only, which only leads me not to like him."

Giovanni gave me a subtle nod, confirming my opinion. He paused a few seconds, then began, "Ruby *wants* to be a big man, but my cocker spaniel is smarter than he'll ever be. It sounds like something he'd *like* to pull off, but I doubt very seriously he's involved. He knows there'd be repercussions...he'd never try to go around me on something like *this*." Giovanni chuckled, and motioned for me to lean over the table as in confidence. I mean, who in their right mind would even try to listen in on one of Giovanni Gamboa's conversations to begin with. "He just spent six weeks in Chicago, where he had a mental breakdown. He came back to Dallas to recover and to be with his sister, Eva. She owns what used to be the Singapore Supper Club, until she turned it over to her little brother. He changed it into some fucking *cowboy* joint with that whining western music. The man has no taste." He leaned back in his seat, as though satisfied that he'd revealed top secret information to me.

I decided to jump in with my first question. "Why do you think Petrie met up with him right after he blackmailed my client, if you don't think he's in on this?"

"That's a fair question. Neither Ruby, nor Petrie has the brains or resources between the two of them to pull this off. This goes much higher, my friend, but as you've already decided in your own mind..." he spread his arms as in innocence, "I have no knowledge of this. Petrie's first mistake was not informing me he was in town. He's out of Florida, you know. The Miami area. Too many Cubans for my taste. They have no manners and kill too easily." He took another drag from the Camel's stub, burning it almost to his fingers. "How prominent is this citizen?"

"A state senator," I said without hesitation.

Giovanni smiled. "At least it is not Lyndon, this time. All you have to do for his vote is ask how much he wants." The smile was gone as quickly as it appeared. "Which one?"

"John Doe, from Dallas." I watched Giovanni's face closely, looking for a reaction, but there was none.

"This is bad for business," Giovanni said, "but that is for me to worry about, not you. You have done something for me, now what can I do for you?"

I grinned. "Give me forty-eight hours before you take care of *your* business. I need to do some leg work before I make my move. If I could get confirmation that Ruby's not involved, then that will eliminate one hurdle for me, at least."

"This senator is a friend of yours?" Giovanni asked.

I shook my head. "No, just a client. We don't exactly hang out together, you know."

Giovanni waved a dismissive hand. "You underestimate yourself, my friend. And how much is Petrie asking for?"

"Half-a-mill," I said.

He whistled. "Why so much? What kind of information does he claim to have that could be worth so much?" He laughed. "Maybe I should invest in this proposition!"

I waggled my finger in the negative. "Trust me, Giovanni, you want nothing to do with this. Petrie claims to know Doe's real identity, which was not as an upstanding citizen, let's say." I didn't want to go into too much detail.

I noticed a slight, subtle grimace pass across Giovanni's lips. It was a reflex move, not an intended grimace. *The son-of a-bitch knows something! I know he does!*

He nodded, "Once again, my friend, you are correct, and I agree, this is too messy for me, and I don't want to be anywhere near it." The gangster lit another cigarette from the burning butt in his fingers. "I will give you twenty-four hours, though, on the one matter. I cannot allow too much water to pass under the bridge before I take care of this. I will take care of the idiot, Ruby, immediately though, and get word to you. There may be plans for such a man in the future." He winked. "You never know." His eyes turned to the bar in Sam's direction. "And who is the man you brought with you? I don't recognize him." No approval or disapproval in his tone.

This was the touchy part. "He's a friend of mine, Giovanni, and I'd like to introduce him to you."

Giovanni's eyebrows rose. "You surprise me, Harry! You have a friend to meet *me*? He must be special. You've never asked before."

I nodded. "That's because there wasn't anybody. His name is Sam Wolfkill. He's…"

Giovanni waved me off. "I will meet the young man for myself." He looked towards the bar, finding Eddy, and nodded. Less than a minute after Eddy's inconspicuous frisk, Sam stood at Giovanni Gamboa's table. The mob leader stood and stretched out a hand to Sam. "Giovanni Gamboa," he said. "I understand you are a friend of Harry Stumbaugh's."

Sam's hand stretched across the table and took Giovanni's. "Yes sir," he said, as firmly as his handshake with the mob boss. "Sam Wolfkill. An honor to meet you, sir."

Giovanni motioned to an empty chair to his left for Sam to be seated, then took a step forward, giving me a farewell embrace with a kiss on each cheek. *I think I'm being dismissed.* Then, he whispered in my ear, "Eddy will be in touch with you tonight or tomorrow. Good to see you again, and thank you for coming by, my friend."

I didn't need to say anything. It was understood. As I headed back to the bar with Eddy, I saw Giovanni take his seat and I heard him say, "Wolfkill? That's German, isn't it?"

Chapter 8

Sam didn't say anything about his thirty minute gab-session with Giovanni, which was driving me crazy. Giovanni never talked to me that long. I mean, I introduced him to the most powerful crime boss in North Texas…he could at least fill me in on what he said. I watched my new partner reach under the seat, retrieve his .38, and start the Ford without a word. All he said was, "Where to?"

That's it? Where to? Okay, we'll play it his way.

"Swiss Avenue," I said, "we have an appointment with Senator Doe." I got my own .38 from the glove box and holstered it. Sam kept his trap shut, but I had to say *something*. "I thought y'all were going to start swapping spit with all the carrying on that went on between you two," I said with a trace of humor. "All that laughing and shit."

That should get the conversation going nicely.

"He's an interesting fellow," Sam said casually, "and inquisitive. Most of the conversation was one-sided. He'd asked questions and I'd answer them."

"Kinda like now," I said, giving up. "Fifty-five hundred Swiss Avenue is the address. Know how to get there?"

"Yeah," Sam said, "I know where it is. Used to do some panhandling in that area in my street days."

"Really? That must have been profitable."

"Not really."

I gave him my best *you son-of-a-bitch* smile. "You're enjoying this, aren't you?" I growled.

"Don't know what you're talking about, partner," he said innocently, then gave me a sly little grin.

The more I was around Sam, the more I liked him. He reminded me...well, of me. I kept my trap shut and let him drive.

The trees that adorned the front yards of the mansions on Swiss Avenue shed dollar bills in the wintertime instead of leaves. The street was divided by a wide, grass median with perfectly spaced rows of trees down the middle that separated the traffic in either direction. The lawns and shrubbery were perfectly manicured for the castles that were fit only for the captains of industry. This, here, was old Dallas money. The occupants of these monstrosities were the movers and shakers of politics, business, medicine, law, and industry in Dallas and around the state. These were the guys that had streets named after them.

"There it is," I said pointing to a white-stone, two-story affair with columns and statues.

I should have asked for more than the measly ten grand he offered me.

We parked on the street, made our way to a front porch that had enough room for a wedding reception, and rang the doorbell. It sounded like the bells tolling at Notre Dame. "Nice place, huh?" I said, stating the obvious.

"If you like this kind of thing. Yeah, I guess so," Sam answered, unimpressed.

Senator Doe answered the door, a pleasant smile creasing his lips. "Come in," he said, waving us in. "Can I get you something to drink?"

We removed our hats. "I'll pass," I said. "We don't plan to be long, John."

"Same here," said Sam, "but thanks, anyway."

I nodded in Sam's direction. "Senator, this is my partner, Sam Wolfkill. He's fully up to speed on everything we've talked about, and it's perfectly okay for you to talk to him about anything going on, if I'm not available. He's the one that followed Petrie after he left the hotel."

They shook hands. "Nice to meet you, Sam. Call me John; we're beyond formalities around here. Come this way, gentlemen, and make yourself comfortable. I'm afraid Hedy's already turned in for the night. It's been a hectic day, you know. For both of us. That girl's a trooper, I tell you what."

"I'm sure she is," Sam returned.

The house was everything you expected it to be. We stepped into a foyer with a ceiling two stories high, and a grand, winding staircase that led to a balcony overlooking the foyer from the second floor. Dark mahogany panels and lattice woodwork filled the downstairs walls, emphasizing, to mere mortals such as ourselves, that no cost had been spared. To the right was an elegant dining room with a chandelier that was every bit as ostentatious as the one in the lobby of the Adolphus Hotel. To the left, was a formal living room with a fireplace and several seating areas throughout the room, and expensive looking trinkets and lamps that cost more than my car.

I doubted I'd get the upstairs tour, and Doe directed us to a couch facing a fireplace big enough to stand in upright. He seated himself in a red velvet winged back chair to our right. "So? Where are we? What have you learned so far?"

I shrugged. "Well, the total of what we know is far less than the total of what we don't know." Sam checked me out with a, *huh?* look on his face. "Let me clarify that," I said, clearing my throat. "There *might* be a mob connection to the blackmailer and someone Petrie met up with later, but neither one is *really* connected. *Might* is the key word there. It's like you said earlier this afternoon, John. Petrie has the look, but that's probably it."

"Who did he meet up with after he talked to me?" Doe asked, leaning forward in his chair.

I'm not telling you because I don't completely trust you yet, Mr. Senator.

"That's not important, as far as you're concerned, at this

point," I said. I've been told by...let's just say by someone who's in the know, that the man he met up with afterwards, is not involved. Certain things and people are best for you to be kept out of the loop, John. Deniability."

"O-kay, I appreciate that," the senator said, doubtfully. "So what do you have that's firm? That you *can* tell me. So far, all I've heard is double-talk, and we're coming down to the wire on this thing, gentlemen. Anything?"

"Sure," I said. "Sam and I have some more leg work to do tomorrow, but to be honest...for now, we've got to sit back and wait for them to make their next move. If they do, that is."

Doe stood and started pacing back and forth in front of the fireplace in silence, like a seething tiger ready to pounce on somebody. "I was hoping it wouldn't come to this. This is the last week before the election, and I've got a schedule of meetings and campaign rallies across the state to meet. I can't just sit around and wait to be slandered by all this. My reputation," he stopped pacing and turned directly to me, eyes drilling into my own, "and Hedy, what am I going to do about her?"

If he thought he was going to lay some fault to all this at my feet, he had another think coming. "Well, John, you came to me about five or six hours ago, it's not like I've had a lot of time on this. There's actually a good chance this might all end before morning. I'll know exactly who all the players are by then and any intentions they might have."

Sam finally jumped into the fray. "I'd say we've got a fifty-fifty chance of closing this by noon tomorrow."

Doe returned to his seat. "Not very good odds for me. And, on what do you base this analysis. As far as I can tell, you haven't learned anything. It's all speculation."

"You're right, John," I said, "but damn good speculation, I might add."

"Mr...I mean, John," Sam started, "is there anything that struck you as odd or unexpected about your conversation with

Petrie, earlier?"

Doe rubbed his square chin, as though thinking. "Not really, except maybe the part about telling my wife, hell-o. I certainly wasn't expecting that. Why do you ask? I told you that already."

"Would it have anything to do with your wife's family money? Bringing up her wealth to help you out, maybe?"

Doe waved a hand before him like he was shooing away flies. "The whole money issue is so overblown. I have my own, you know. I was a successful defense attorney for many years and made my own small fortune. If I had to come up with a half-million on my own, I could do it. I've never touched one penny of my wife's money." His voice raised an octave. "*I* paid for this house and the cars in the garage, *not* her."

Sam shrugged, not reacting to the senator's defense of his manhood. "I don't know, there's just something that's not right. I'm not sure *what* it is. A couple of losers are trying to pull off a blackmailing scheme with national implications, if what they say is true…or can at least give it legs to run whether it's true or not."

Doe's face reddened. "Well, I can damn well tell you it's not true!"

Sam didn't react to this outburst either. He was a cool cookie, in my opinion.

"But, how do you *know* that, Senator?" Sam asked. "How *could* you if you have amnesia? I'm just asking, that's all."

Doe turned to me instead of Sam, this time. "I don't like the accusations your partner's making towards me, Harry. You need to put him on a leash."

This made me laugh. *Right, the guy killed fifteen Japs in less than ten minutes, half of them in hand-to-hand combat, and he thinks I can put a leash on him.* I gave a light chuckle to lighten the mood. "I'm afraid that won't work, John. If you remember our conversation this afternoon, I practically said the same thing. You didn't take offense then. Listen, maybe we made things sound like we didn't have a clue, but that's not true. Like Sam said, tomorrow will be D-

Day for us. For all of us."

Doe's face started to return to its normal color; it was tan, actually. In the winter. Whatever blows up your skirt, I guess. "Well, perhaps I did overreact. This just has me at odds with everything around me. The election..."

Sam dug in with the questions again. "Was that the only thing you found strange or odd about the conversation? The thing about your wife?"

"He's persistent, isn't he?" Doe said at me.

"A bulldog," I said.

Doe let loose with a patronizing sigh. "That's all I can think of. The rest was pretty much as expected. Short and sweet. Give me the money, or I'll go to the press. That kind of thing."

I just happened to be watching Sam, quietly admiring his tenacity, when I saw the slightest pursing of his lips. *Doe said something that got his attention.* I stood and grabbed my hat from the couch. *It was time to make our exit before Sam pissed him off enough to ask for his ten G's back. That'd put me forty dollars in the hole for the day.* "We should go, John. It's getting late and I have a feeling tomorrow's going to be one hell of a day, one way or the other."

Sam got up after me, grabbed his hat from the couch, and stuck out his free hand to the senator. "No hard feelings, John. These things can get a little rough at times. Our reputation means as much to us as yours does to you, and we want to see you come out a winner when all this is over."

That seemed to console the senator temporarily. Doe took his hand with a firm grip and shook it. "No hard feelings. This whole matter has me stretched out thin, that's all. I appreciate all that you're both doing. Good night, then. We'll talk in the morning, I assume."

I nodded. "Or later. I'm not going to call until something comes down, or I need you to do something. You going to be here or the hotel?"

"The hotel. I can get more done there. I have some

campaign matters to take care of with my Chief of Staff. I'm supposed to make an appearance at the State Fair this week. That's prime hand shaking time, you know. And I don't want Hedy involved in all this."

"Good enough," I said, as the senator closed the door behind us.

We walked side by side down the sidewalk, our hands shoved deep into the pockets of our overcoats as the night's chill settled in. "I don't know what got the burr under your saddle in there Chief, but I liked it," I said.

"He's dirty. I can feel it," Sam said, rounding the front bumper of his car.

"Yeah? I've considered it a possibility. How come you're such a genius that you can figure it out in a fifteen minute meeting? The first time you ever met him. You *that* good, partner?" We stood talking over the roof of his car.

"Not really. I had a bit of advantage, though."

"Like what?"

"Eavesdropping on Petrie's conversation, for one. But first, how did Petrie know you'd be there to follow him from the hotel? He knew exactly who you were. He probably didn't figure on me or Jenny being there, but he sure as hell knew *you* would. He made that spectacle of himself at the street corner, shooting you the finger. It was like he *wanted* you to know. How'd *he* know? Why make a scene?"

"He's an idiot?" I shrugged. "I thought about that, too. I just figured maybe he followed Doe to my office. Put two and two together. Bada-bing, bada-boom. That doesn't make the senator dirty."

"Why didn't you tell Doe about Ruby? Why keep that from him?" Sam asked.

"To be honest, it was a reflex, not something I thought out. I just wanted to keep our cards close to the chest for now. There's no reason to tell a client everything you know. Some things you want to hold on to until you think it's the right time. I've got this little voice in the back of my head telling me something's not completely kosher here. Doe told me he wanted me to find the truth…well, that's what we're going to do, whether he likes the way it ends or not."

Sam said, "Yeah, know what you mean. There was something Doe said tonight that really caught my attention."

"I noticed that. Your poker face melted into the chips. What hit a nerve?"

Sam opened his door, but didn't get in. "He said his conversation with Petrie was short and sweet."

"Yeah, so?"

"When I overheard Petrie talking on the outside lines at the Adolphus, he was talking to a superior. A boss. I could tell by Petrie's end of the call, he was assuring the guy at the other end he knew what to do. The guy giving the orders. Petrie answered back something along the line of, *Yeah, sure, short and sweet. I know what to do.*"

"Son-of-a-bitch!"

"What?" Sam asked. "What's the matter?"

I opened my door. "When I called Doe to ask him about what Petrie said, he said the same damn thing, but I didn't pick up on it like you did." I grinned at my new partner. "I think we just might make a detective of you, yet, Wolfkill," I said, getting in the car.

Sam dropped off Harry at the Adolphus Hotel for his usual nightcap at the French room, and then headed for Oaklawn and Lemmon. He decided to make a visit to the Vegas Club on his own.

Chapter 9

After we left Doe's place at about ten o'clock, Sam dropped me off at the Adolphus for a nightcap. He mentioned making his own stop at the Baker for a drink before turning in, and I told him to take it easy on the booze and to get some rest. I figured tomorrow was going to be a busy day, and I didn't need him falling off the wagon. It was time for us to get down to the grunt work of the private eye business. Tomorrow, I planned on making a phone call to Dallas PD and then, going to the records building to see what I could dig up from some twenty-year old files. Sam needed to go to Denton and see what kind of dirt he could dig up about Doe's accident back in '32. At least that was the original plan for the day. We'd see how it all shook out. After a couple of shooters at the French Room and a hob-knobbing session with the hired help, I finally headed back to the office about eleven to get some shut-eye.

On Tuesday morning, I rolled out of the sack at my usual time, about six o'clock, put a pot of water on the hot plate, and picked up my daily delivery of the *Dallas Morning News*. When I originally leased my office space at the Praetorian, the building management leased me a two room suite with a reception area and its own bathroom, which was almost unheard of. Little did they know, I turned the second office into a bedroom. A place to hang my hat if I didn't feel like going home, which was most of the time. I installed a private shower stall in the bathroom, a single bed, a safe, and filing cabinets for decorations. I forgot to tell management about the shower. A former client, a plumber, suspected his wife was doing the watusi with an electrician, and he was right. I got the goods for him and decided to take what he owed me in the form of a new shower stall. Best investment I ever made. What the powers that be in the front office didn't know, wouldn't hurt them. I don't even know why I bothered to keep an apartment. I hadn't set foot in it for the past two weeks except to get fresh clothes.

After dropping a couple of spoonsful of instant in my cup, I rambled into my office, plopped down in the chair, propped my feet on the desk, and perused the sports page for something interesting. Nothing jumped out at me or grabbed my attention. Pickings were pretty slim since Sugar Ray Robinson kicked Rocky Graziano's ass in three rounds earlier in the year, and the Yanks took the Dodgers in seven games in the Series this month.

I crumpled up the paper and tossed it on the floor. My heart and head weren't into reading the paper this morning. The Doe case was all I could think about. When an investigator thinks his client is blowing smoke up his ass, it's hard to know what to believe and what to take as fact. That's why last night, after leaving the majestic castle on Swiss Avenue, I decided to start doing some serious background digging. Digging deep into everything I could about Doe, the hit and run twenty years ago, and the armored truck robbery. But first, I needed some fuel to charge my battery.

After my usual breakfast of eggs, bacon, and pan fries with hot homemade biscuits at Walgreen's, I felt great and ready to tackle the world. My first order of business was to check in with the boss, Jenny, then touch base with Sam, and finally make the call to the Dallas PD. In order to find out about the robbery part of it, there was only one person still on the force that might have a memory of the Santa Fe armored truck heist as far back as '32. That would be my nemesis, Homicide Detective Carl Cochran. I wasn't looking forward to it. He was a racist pig who didn't mind getting his knuckles bloody on a perp's face, probably hadn't paid for a meal in twenty-five years on the force, and thought that taking money under the table for protection was just part of the job description.

His nickname was Phonebook Carl. That name came from the fact that he used telephone books during interrogation sessions more than call operators did to find a phone number. Needless to say, Carl and I didn't see eye to eye on many things. Consorting with the guy responsible for getting me kicked off the force...well, desperate. The man was a walking encyclopedia when it came to case histories. What the hell. Sometimes investigation takes a person to strange, uncharted waters. Doubtful he'd be happy to hear from me either, but when duty calls...

Jenny was behind her desk reading a *Photoplay* magazine and polishing her nails at the same time. She looked up when I walked in, but didn't make a move to hide her extra-curricular activities. "You busy, Doll Face?" I asked, closing the door behind me.

"Kinda," she said, holding up a freshly polished nail and blowing on it. "You need something, Hon'?"

I tried to maintain my, *this is a place of business,* face. "Heard from Sam, yet?"

She put the finishing touches on her pinkie nail. "No, it's not even nine o'clock yet. Want me to try him at home?"

I thought about that for a second. The fingernail polish smell was getting to me. "Nah, wait until nine." I checked my watch and it was about eight-thirty. "Give it another thirty minutes. I've got to make a call." I started for my office and decided to give her one more instruction. "Jen…if *anybody* calls…Sam or anybody else, check with me before you blow them off. You can interrupt me, but come in, don't use that damn buzzer."

She took the nail polish brush thing, switched it to her left hand, and started painting the other hand. *I didn't know she was ambidextrous.* Without looking up she said, "Gotcha."

I closed the office door behind me, boiled another pot of water and made myself a cup of java before making the call. I had a feeling it was going to be a contentious, torturous conversation reviving bad memories. Cochran could talk the numbers off a ruler.

I settled in, got comfy, and dialed the Homicide Department's number from memory. It rang four times before somebody finally picked up.

"Cochran...Homicide. What can I do for you today," he answered dryly.

Cochran's gravel, whinny voice was like fingernails on a chalkboard.

Be nice.

"Well, for one thing, cocksucker, you can get off your fat ass and go solve some murders." Did I mention that Phonebook Carl weighed about two-hundred-eighty pounds and had the foulest mouth on the force? There was about a three second hesitation before he responded.

"Is that you, Gimp Leg? You still buddy-fucking Gamboa, the King Wop?"

I laughed, playing the game. "You still got your balls?"

He actually laughed in turn. "So, to what do I owe the honor, Stumbaugh? By the way, since your *retirement,* I've enjoyed the last six years around here without you stepping on my toes."

At least he's still talking to me.

"I'm sure you are, but I need to bury the hatchet, at least for a few minutes, Carl. Investigator to investigator."

Man, this was difficult.

"You still in the private dick biz?" Cochran asked, "fuckin' those desperate housewives on the side there, buddy?" He laughed, almost coughing up a lung. Cochran always thought his jokes were the funniest in the house.

"Just yours, Carl." The laughter stopped short, but you had to play fire with fire to get any respect from Carl, otherwise he'd run all over you.

"Good one, asshole. What 'cha need? I know you're not calling to check in on my health."

Good, made a break-through. "Listen Carl, since you have the reputation as the force's know-all historian, I wanted to ask you about something that happened twenty- years ago." *Stroke, stroke.*

"Love talkin' 'bout the old days. Even with a do-gooder like you. What is it?" he asked.

"The Santa Fe Railroad armored truck robbery back in '32." There were a few seconds of silence from his end. Not a good sign. When Cochran finally answered, I noticed a change in tone. The friendly banter was gone.

"Why do you ask, Harry? Something to do with a case you're working on?"

Mmm. Now why would he ask me that?

"Well, kinda. Is that a problem?"

"Depends," he said, "on what you want to know."

"Oh, things like...what happened? Who was involved? Things like that. You know, Carl, I'm not sure if this has anything to do with what I'm working on or not. It's just one of those loose strings that's hanging loose out there and I want to pull it in. You know how that works. I called you, because I figured you're the only one still around that would know anything." Flattery always worked on Carl back in the day. His ego was bigger than his stomach.

Another moment of silence. "Okay, I'll fill you in, but after I show you mine, you have to show me yours."

This time *I* hesitated. *Something's up and I need to know what it is.* "Deal," I agreed.

Phonebook started. "I was there, at the crime scene, Harry. I was still on the beat, wearing the blues and on the job for only five years. The department paid shit for salaries, so a bunch of us guys moonlighted. Me and a buddy, Mark DeBusk, did evening shifts as security guards with Santa Fe Rail Road for extra dough. That night, I was scheduled to work, but I got called on a big-ass pile up on Highway 80 that night and couldn't make it. I called Mark to see if he could fill in for me."

"Shit, Carl," I injected, "I never knew."

"It was after you came on board. Wasn't the kind of thing I

talked about, but I can tell you this...it changed my mind around what kind of cop I wanted to be. How to operate." Silence. "Anyway...I got the call right after it happened and went to the scene. Mark was spread-eagle, face down on the ground with a hole the size of a grapefruit in the back of his head. He was executed. Never saw it coming, Stumbaugh."

"And the other guard? There was another one, right? Two were killed?"

"So you do know something about it, after all," said Cochran.

"Not as much as you, Carl. Go on."

"Executed. Not killed. There's a difference, you know. Luis Rodriguez, he was in the passenger seat. He was one of the few spics we had on the job, but he was a good kid. Knew his place. Only on the job six months. He had a houseful of little spics running around. Four, I think. Worked three jobs to keep tacos in their bellies. One shot upside the head. He was still in the passenger seat. Didn't even get a chance to unholster his weapon. He was a moonlighter like me and Mark."

This was beyond anything I visualized about the robbery. You hear, *Oh, two people were killed and somebody got away with a million dollars,* and you don't visualize the facts. The brutality of the crime. I'd forgotten. My thoughts about Doe and Petrie were getting darker and darker. "I didn't know," I said, repeating myself. "Isn't there usually a third man? One in the back with the money?"

"Fucking right there was. Best we could determine at the time, he's the cocksucker that wasted Rodriguez. Evidently, he was in on it from the beginning. Easy for a security guard on the payroll to know the ins and outs. Schedule, so forth. The mastermind of the operation, in my opinion."

I wanted to wait before I started asking names. "How'd it go down?"

"That's the hell of it all. Two fuckin' blocks from the Santa Fe station on Jackson. The truck loaded up the night's receipts, stopped at a red light two blocks from the station. Car pulls up behind and blocks them there, then another slides in front, cutting off any avenue of escape. One of the guys had a fuckin' Tommy gun. Those were big back in the day, you know. Sprayed the fuckin' truck. Must've been a hundred fuckin' holes in the mother fucker."

"Did all three get away? The bad guys?" I asked.

"Fuck no. The asshole in the back got shot. Close as we could figure, Mark must've got off a shot, but it had to be after Rodriquez got popped. One of the other guys in one of the cars that block them in had to be the one that killed DeBusk. Just took one in the back of the head to finish him off. His revolver was on the ground beside him, and it had one spent shell in the chamber. His bullet grazed the motherfucker. If Mark hadn't got off a shot and hit the perp, they'd all got away clean. The asshole Mark shot was out cold on the ground when the cops got there. At first they thought he was a victim like Mark and Luis because of the uniform, but his gun had been fired and the bag of money with Santa Fe Railroad stamped on it was a dead giveaway. He never copped to it, but we figured he's the one that popped the spic when he wasn't looking. His revolver wouldn't have made that big hole in Mark's head. When they dug out the slug in Luis's head, it matched the assholes's gun. One of the other guys got Mark from behind."

"That asshole got a name?" I asked.

"Yeah, Pete Strong."

"He got sent up, right?"

"Damn straight. He had a date with Old Sparky. I went and watched his ass sizzle like a steak on a grill when they pushed the button on him."

I was working up to the million dollar question. "The other two, did you get names out of him?"

"Fuck no. And the homicide/robbery guys let me go at him for fifteen minutes on my own, since Mark was my partner. One of the old-timers told me about using the phone book." He laughed. "I was one worn-out mother fucker, I can tell you. But I'll give Strong his kudos. He never broke. Never said a word. He took his punishment."

That was a bust. Now for the second million dollar question.

"So the other two, did you ever get any kind of a line on them?" I asked, crossing my fingers.

"Oh, sure," said Cochran. "We interviewed Strong's old man. He lived in one of the decent neighborhoods in Oak Cliff, but he kept his mouth shut. Wouldn't offer a fuckin' thing, but his old lady, she was a real doosy. A real bitch. She cussed us out the whole time. That lady had one fuckin' foul mouth. But she slipped. She didn't know when to shut up and said that Pete and his *step-brother, Robert,* would never do something like that. Hell, we checked later and they both had rap sheets as long as my dick."

"That long, huh? Robert has a last name?" I asked, my palms started to sweat.

"Yeah, Petrie. A wop."

Now for the third million dollar question. "And the other guy? Get a name on him?"

"That one's a little sketchy," answered Cochran. "Strong's parents wouldn't give up any names of Robert or Pete's friends. Man, we all worked the shit out of every informant out there on the streets and threatened their asses with jail time if they didn't produce. I miss those old days, know what I mean?"

"Yeah, I do," I said, placating his sorry ass. *Just give me the name!* "And, the name?"

"All we ever came up with was a first name. A guy named Ralph. No last name. Now it's your turn, Harry. What's this all about? Why the history lesson on a twenty-year-old cold case? You got something? I'd love a piece of that action."

I had to think of the best way to play this. "Well, I can't tell you how just yet, but I've got a line on Robert Petrie for you." I figured that one would make his day.

"You'll have to do better than that, Stumbaugh. I've already got him."

What! "What do you mean, you've already got him?" I asked, my thunder stolen right out from under me.

"Don't you read the fuckin' paper anymore, Harry? You were always fuckin' religious about reading that crap every day."

"Didn't this morning. What happened?"

"They found the little prick Petrie in an alley behind the Vegas Strip Club about three o'clock this morning. Somebody beat the shit out of him. Only way we could identify him was his prints."

Chapter 10

After hanging up from Cochran, I needed to wash my mouth out with soap and take another shower, but I didn't have time. He was almost friendly. Too friendly. And free with the information. *Beware of assholes bearing gifts.* I grabbed a Dallas phonebook from the bottom drawer of my desk and checked for the name *Strong*, with an Oak Cliff address. I found an Abner Strong on Colorado Avenue and a J. B. Strong on Illinois Avenue. There were a few more Strongs listed, but these two looked like my best bet. I decided to try the Colorado address first since it was the nicer of the two neighborhoods. Abner it was.

I should've asked Cochran for the first name, but I felt like I'd gone far enough with him for the time being. I didn't especially feel like letting him in on my future plans, and I intentionally withheld any knowledge on my part about the possible identity of the mysterious Ralph. After all, *Ralph* gave me a ten thousand dollar retainer. I jotted down both addresses and headed to the outer office for another brain-teasing dialogue with Jenny. "No word from Sam, yet?" I asked, checking my watch. It was five till nine.

She was checking each individual fingernail for flaws, I assumed. "No, I didn't hear the phone ring, did you?" She asked with a straight face.

I decided not to take the bait this time. "Listen, Jen, I've got to run out for a bit. Get hold of him and tell him to go to the hospital in Denton, it's the only one there. I need him to get a look at Doe's medical records when he was there twenty years ago. See if he can find a doc or nurse that was there and treated him, if possible."

"You looking for anything in particular, Harry?" Jenny asked, taking notes.

"Yeah, there is Doll Face, that's why I love you so much. I want everything he can find, but in particular I want to know about the pinkie finger on his right hand. Did he loose part of it in the accident, or was it missing *before* the hit and run. Got it?"

"Gotcha. I noticed that too, Harry, but of course I wasn't going to say anything about it to his face. That'd be rude," she said.

"Yeah, can't imagine anybody doing something that stupid and uncaring, can you?" I said.

"You would, Harry."

"Thanks Doll Face. I'm not done yet. If Sam gets time after that, he needs to get with the Sheriff there, too. His name's Roscoe...Roscoe Banter. Tell him to use my name as an intro and see what he can dig up about the hit and run from that angle. Got it?"

"Gotcha," she said. "Are you going to be where I can reach you?"

"No, but I'll stay in touch," I said, grabbing my fedora from the hat rack and cocking it at an angle on my head. "If you can't catch Sam at his place, then try the Baker. He might be having breakfast," I added, giving my last instruction to Jenny and giving the black fedora's brim one final tug.

"Be careful, Harry," Jenny said.

"I'm meeting a guy named Abner, Doll Face. What could possibly go wrong?" I quipped, walking out the door. I rushed to my car thinking that the Vegas Club, Petrie's death, and Sam's tardiness just didn't add up. That boy worries me...

At his apartment, Sam woke up face down on his couch with a mean headache, his body hanging half on and half off. One arm and one leg dangled just above the floor. His mind was in the wakening nether world of fog and numbness. He was conscious, but his body was immobile. He tried to think, but there was nothing but a big blank. He stretched open the fingers of the dangling arm and a sharp pain rushed through his hand and up to the elbow. The pain forced open his eyes. He remained still and prone on the couch, staring at the opposite wall, trying to get his bearings. Where am I? He tried to think again. Still blank. He forced his body to move and managed to slowly get himself into a sitting position. His head spun, his vision went dark and bright white dots flashed in the darkness. He closed his eyes shut, squinting, then opened them slowly and the room, the walls, the furniture slowly came into focus one layer at a time. When his vision finally became normal, he glanced at the clock; it was six twenty.

He flexed his fist again to see if the pain he'd experienced before was his imagination. It wasn't. Not wanting to look down in fear of getting dizzy again, he brought the back of his hand up to his face and saw that the knuckles on his right hand were scraped and bloody. Reflexes forced him to glance down at his left hand. The same…scraped and bloody. He was fully clothed. Jacket, tie, shirt. Torn shirt and jacket. It was covered with red specs, as though someone flicked a freshly dipped paint brush at him. He examined the shirt closer. It wasn't paint. It was blood.

Chapter 11

The weather here in Dallas was beautiful, at least Gordy McClendon on KLIF radio station said it was. The temperature was already sixty-eight degrees and expected to reach the high seventies today. Sounded like the perfect time to put the top down on the Nash Healey. The roadster was my one splurge of dough I treated myself to since retirement from the force. No wife, no kids. I had the money. Why not drive in style? It set me back almost five grand, even more than Sam's new Ford, but I looked *go-o-od* in it. That's the important thing.

I added a little strut to my limp and swung Old Hickory with a casual flair as I strolled down the canyons of downtown to the parking garage. The limp didn't bother me that much knowing that the SOB that put the .45 slug in my leg was burning in hell for his sins. Sometimes it's worth taking the bullet. Walking and driving was when I was at my best when it came to thinking things out. It took too much work when Jenny was in the office. *God love her.* At the garage, I folded back the top, secured it, tossed my hat in the passenger seat, and fired up my baby. I left downtown and hit Highway 67 for the great metropolis of Oak Cliff. Actually, it was just an extension of Dallas and housed some of the most exclusive neighborhoods in Dallas, but that wasn't the neighborhood I expected to find Abner Strong. Gordy had Johnnie Ray's *Cry* on the turntable and my foot tapped in rhythm, but my brain rocked like the roller coaster at the Texas State Fair.

There were too many holes in this caper that needed a plug.

I started ticking them off in my head. First, if Doe really *is* Ralph Morris, then why would he throw down ten grand to the best damn private eye in North Texas? Does that mean he's *not* afraid of what I might find? Or does he think his over-payment is hush money to keep my mouth shut if I find out he's really a cop killer? If so, then he misjudged me. Second, there's that pesky mob connection. I *know* Doe's got to be tied into it somehow. But how? Was he into them for some dough? Dirty politics? I saw it in Gamboa's face, and I don't believe in coincidences. Third, there's that dead body matter. Not that Robert Petrie's demise should trouble anybody but his mother, but it still complicates things. Who killed him and why? I knew it wasn't Giovanni. He promised me twenty-four hours, and he was always good to his word. Had Petrie bit off more than he could chew? What about Ruby? It was his joint where Petrie got knocked off. Giovanni seemed damn sure that Ruby didn't have the balls for this kind of thing. Evidently, they wanted him for something else later whatever that's about. And fourth, who followed Doe to my place? Why follow him at all? Too many questions and no answers. Yet.

I wasn't expecting much from Abner either, but every lead had to be chased down. I exited the highway and turned onto Colorado Avenue. It was a mixture of mom and pop businesses and residential areas that looked like something out of a picture book.

I found Abner's place and was pleasantly surprised. The house was a neat, white-framed affair with trimmed shrubs and flowers that thrived in the winter. A white picket fence framed the front yard and extended down the sides to the backyard. Not exactly what I had pictured as the hideout for cop-killing desperadoes. I was beginning to have doubts about making Abner first on my list. I parked anyway and went to the front door and knocked.

"Go away!" yelled a gruff, graveled voice from inside.

Might be the right place after all.

I ignored the instructions and knocked again, this time with a little more power between knuckles and door.

"Go away!" the voice repeated, even louder this time.

I tried the door knob and it turned. Maybe it's an invalid old man, and he can't get up to let me in. I should check to make sure the elderly gentleman is okay. I gave the knob another twist and opened the door wide enough to stick in my head. "Mr. Strong! Are you okay?" I yelled, trying to sound sincere. "It's me, Harry Stumbaugh."

"Don't know a Stumbaugh," the voice yelled back. "Go away, I said!"

Nobody was shooting at me yet, so I made a decision to go for it. I stepped in closing the door behind me and removed my hat. Manners, you know. The house was built in the old shotgun style. Two rooms in the front, a dining room to my right, and a small den to my left. Both were neat and tidy. A hall ran through the middle of the house from front to back, with closed doors on either side of the hallway. I knew the kitchen would be in the back. That's where I figured the kind old gentleman was stationed, probably in a wheelchair, coughing up phlegm. "Mr. Strong," I called, "I'm Harry Stumbaugh, and I've come about your son...Robert Petrie."

There was momentary silence before the voice called out to me, "I'm in the kitchen...come on back, but wipe your feet before you do!"

Bingo. I shuffled the bottom of my shoes on the hardwoods and took off in the direction of Mr. Friendly. The closer I got to the kitchen, the stronger the aroma of recently fried eggs and bacon hit me. With hat in hand, I stepped into the kitchen and, sure enough, in a wheelchair pulled up to the kitchen table was a man that looked like he was pushing eighty. No doubt, a handful in his prime. If he'd been able to stand on two feet, he would've stretched well over six foot. He looked like someone who'd worked with his hands all his life, could lift a pick-up over his head, and didn't take any shit off anyone. Then or now. Abner's big hands pushed away a breakfast plate that had been wiped clean with a slice of toast; he took a sip of coffee, eyes focused on me over the rim. He set down the cup. "Get yourself a mug and put a head on mine, too," he said, sliding his cup across the table in my direction. "Clean ones are in the cupboards to the right of the sink."

Without a word of conversation, I took his cup, got a clean one for myself, and filled them both to the rim with steaming black coffee from a pot on the stove. I wasn't about to insult him by asking if he wanted cream or sugar. I gave him his coffee and took the opposite seat, setting my cane on the table. He gave it a quick glance, then the eyes went back to me. Twisting my head around nonchalantly, I checked out the room like I was interested. Nothing was out of place and the only dirty dishes were the ones on the table. "Place looks nice, Mr. Strong. You live here alone?"

He took a sip of coffee. "What's it to you? You from *Good Housekeeping* or something?"

I smiled. "No," I said, "I was just wondering how a crippled, old fucker like yourself kept the place so neat."

Abner set down his cup slowly, eye-balled me again, then cut loose with a short, deep baritone snort, then he passed gas. When he finally got control of himself, he said, "Don't know who the hell you are, young man, but it's nice to have a visitor with a real set between his legs, for a change." He wrapped his hands around the mug of coffee in front of him and twisted it back and forth. "Nurse slash maid, every other day." He rolled back his chair and pointed to a withered pair of legs that had been dormant for years. "Broke my spine on the job. Sued the bastards and I've got more money than Bing Crosby."

"Harry Stumbaugh. I'm a private detective. I stay broke most the time."

He stared at me hard. His eyes were such a dark colored brown, they looked almost black. They were definitely his most intimidating feature, and he used them well. He didn't scare me, though. I knew I could out run him if it came down to a fight.

A sad smile creased his lips, surprising me. "I'd rather be broke and have two good legs."

"I hear you," I said.

"Detective, huh? You think you're Sam Spade or something?" Abner said.

"No," I said, enjoying the back and forth with the old man, "I think I'm Harry Stumbaugh." I reached across the table, offering my hand.

Abner responded by leaning forward in his wheelchair, offering his own. His hand engulfed mine like it was a child's. He shook it once and let go. "Private dick, huh? What *about* Robert? What's he done now?"

Damn.

"So you haven't been notified by anyone...the police, about Robert?"

"Notified. That means the fucker's dead. Right?"

"Right," I confirmed. I was glad we carried the same opinion about his step-son. "Somebody beat him to death in an alley outside a strip club in Dallas. Sorry to be the bearer of bad news, Mr. Strong. I figured you'd already been notified by the police."

"Probably got offed by one of the strippers. He was a weasel and pussy. He's no blood of mine. He belonged to my wife, God bless her wicked soul. She passed on nine years ago, and I haven't seen Robert since her funeral. Good riddance, if you ask me. You still haven't answered my question, Mr. Stumbaugh. Why are you here? I know it's not to offer condolences for Robert."

"Call me, Harry. And no I'm not here for that. I didn't think any more of Robert than you did. *Let's see what you've got to offer, old man.* "I've got some questions about *your* son...Pete, and one of his associates. A guy named Ralph."

"That tells me *what* you want to know, not *why*."

He's quick.

I shrugged. "Obviously, I can't tell you who my client is, but I've been hired to do some background on somebody. Part of that background check goes back to the robbery. Information is kinda thin, as you can imagine." *I didn't think bringing up Cochran's name would be a good idea.* "Since Pete was the only one caught, you're the next best person to talk to."

Abner stared down at his coffee, and then looked up. "Fair enough...for now. Ask your question."

I jumped right in. I didn't want to give him time to change his mind. "About the robbery, first. I think we can agree, without argument, that Pete was involved. Agreed?"

A few seconds of silence, then, "Agreed. Not something I want to talk about, though."

I decided to avoid talking about the killings and the robbery, then. "I'm not here to pass judgment, Mr. Strong. I..."

He interrupted me. "That's already been done. Don't you think, *Harry*? Call me Abner and get to the point."

Okay, I will if you'll just let me.

"I'm interested in the third man. He---"

The old fart interrupted me again. "I don't know anything about that. I told you...I'm not talking about the robbery."

"I'm not either, but there's *some* justice I'm looking for in all this. I want to know about *Ralph*. Not Pete, not Robert, and not the robbery. Did you ever meet him? Ralph, that is."

Say, yes.

Abner's eyes squinted and bored into mine as though he were trying to drill a hole through both of them. I could tell, he was making a judgment about *me*.

"Met him a couple of times. He was a slick one. A fast talker. Had a nice car, I know that. Brand new '32 coupe. He sure as hell didn't look like somebody named, *Ralph*. Had to'uv been a family name. Who'd name their son *Ralph* on purpose?

"Yeah," I added, "imagine that, *Abner*."

He gave a small, very small smile. "Family name, can't help it. Anyway, he wore nice suits. Rugged looking face, but clean and well-groomed. Would've made a good politician, in my opinion."

Headlines.

I tried to contain my excitement. Or dread. "Did you ever catch a last name for Ralph?" I asked.

Say, yes.

"Let me think." He took a sip of coffee. I did the same. "Morris," he said.

Bingo!

"One more thing," I said. "Have you by chance ever seen him again? Pictures? Anything like that?"

Abner took another sip. "Can't say that I have."

Strike one.

"Well…if I were to bring by a picture of a man, do you think you'd recognize it if it *was* Ralph Morris?"

"I'm crippled, not blind, Stumbaugh."

I gave him a small, very small grin. "So I can bring back a picture for you to check out this afternoon?"

Abner took a pack of Pall Mall's from his pocket, lit one, and tossed the pack my way. "Help yourself." The eyes squinted again. No conversation, just the look. "You're not very good at this detective stuff, are you young man? How long have you been doing this line of work?"

That came out of left field.

I fired up one of his Pall Malls. "I think I'm pretty damn good at my job, Abner. I was with the Dallas PD for nineteen years, before that I was with the Houston PD for five. I've been a private investigator for five. I've learned a thing or two, and I've seen things I'd rather forget about in that time. I've been around the block, Abner, believe me. Why do you ask?"

Abner shrugged a shoulder. "You ever listen to the radio young man?"

"Of course. All the time."

He took a drag from the butt. "This morning?"

"Yeah, I got the weather report and listened to Johnnie Ray on the way here. It's gonna be sunny and seventy-eight degrees. I put the top down on my car. Great day to be outside to take a drive…and a walk later on. What's it to you?"

I'm being set up. I can feel it coming and it's not gonna feel good, either.

He grinned, and then mashed the cigarette butt out on his breakfast plate before even taking a second drag from it. "My nursemaid, Sissy, hates it when I do that," he said, nodding at his plate. "I like you, Stumbaugh, so I'm going to try to make this as painless as possible."

"Is this where I reach over and grab my ankles, Abner?"

"No, this is for when you take me for a ride in your convertible. What kind of wheels you got?"

"Healey Roadster." I said.

Abner smiled again. "Heard a man on the radio this morning that reminded me of Ralph."

"Really? After all these years? That's amazing, Abner."

Here comes the punch line.

"I'm crippled, not deaf, Stumbaugh." Leaning forward in the wheelchair, elbows on the arm rests, Abner's face darkened. I hadn't seen this look before and it was a bit scary. His lips barely moved when he spoke. "You think I'd ever forget the voice of the man that got my boy sent to the chair to die, Mr. Stumbaugh?"

"No," I conceded, "probably not. I wouldn't. Who was it, Abner?"

"Been hearing it for years now, but couldn't ever do a thing about it. Now that you're here, maybe I'll get some justice."

"Who is it, Abner?" I asked the old man again.

"Ever heard of Senator John Doe?"

I stubbed out my Pall Mall in Abner's breakfast plate. Sissy wasn't going to be happy with me.

After the detective left his house, Abner Strong rolled his wheelchair to the phone on the kitchen wall, and dialed the all too familiar number. "He just left," Abner said, recognizing the man's voice when he answered.

"What'd you say?" The man said.

"What I was supposed to say, what do you think?"

"Good, let's see how it plays out. The ball's rolling now, and Doe will be sucking hind wind before the day's over. Short and sweet. That's the way I like it."

"And the rest of my money?" Abner inquired.

"You've waited this long, Strong, don't get greedy on me," the voice said.

Abner said, "You do what you promised…or else. I ain't got nothing to lose anymore, you know."

The man at the other end of the line hung up.

Chapter 12

I merged onto Highway 67 from Colorado Avenue, winding out the Healey's V-8 to the max in all three gears. I was pissed. I didn't like being played for a fool by anyone, especially a cop-killer. The fact that I didn't know DeBusk or Rodriguez personally, or the fact that I didn't know the twenty-two year old rookie, Johnny W. Sides, that'd been with the Dallas PD for only six weeks and got blown away by an ex-con he stopped for running a stop sign earlier this year, didn't matter either. They were family. They were one of us. That made it personal.

I promised Abner that I'd take him for a ride tomorrow with the top down and left him a business card so he could call me for a time to go. It was the least I could do since the old fart busted this case wide open for me. His boys might have been scum, but he seemed like an alright Joe. There was no need for Sam to make the run to Denton now. I had what I needed. I glanced down at the speedometer, seventy-five and my foot was still heavy on the pedal. I backed off a tad and noticed that the gas needle was bouncing on the big E. I needed gas and to make a call. Coming up on downtown, I got off on Cortez and skidded into Luck's gas station in grand fashion. I got out and headed inside to use the phone.

"Fill 'er up, Mr. Stumbaugh?" Jimmy asked, greeting me halfway on the drive, wiping his hands on a stained, red grease rag.

"Yeah, Jimmy and check the oil. I need to use the phone, too."

"Help yourself," he said, "it's still on the desk. Great day to have the top down, eh?"

I waved, acknowledging the comment and location of the phone, but I wasn't in the mood to chit-chat. The gas station office smelled like oil and grease and cigarettes. Jimmy always kept an ice box full of Pabst on hand, and I needed one, even though it was only a little after ten. I grabbed one and used the opener hanging by a string on the fridge's door handle. I punched two holes in the top and gulped down half of it in one swig.

Calm down, big guy. Calm down.

I had two calls to make, Jenny and Doe. I dialed the office first.

Jenny picked up on the first ring. Her nails must be done. "Stumbaugh Investigations, how may I help you?" She answered.

"Very efficient, Doll Face. Any calls this morning?" I asked.

"Oh, hi, Harry. I thought it might be the senator. I wanted to sound businesslike, you know. And no, I haven't heard from a soul, and I'm worried about Sam. He usually calls in by now, Harry."

I admitted that it was a bit unusual, but no reason to go into the panic mode. "I wouldn't worry about it, Jen. Probably overslept. I've got some time this morning…I'll stop by his place. Listen, if the senator does call, tell him we need to meet. Maybe for lunch. Just have him leave a message with you, and I'll get back with him. Okay?"

"Gotcha, but I'm still worried about Sam. Will you call me if you hear from him before I do?"

Was this Jen's untapped, motherly instincts kicking in? "Sure, Doll Face, I will. I'll be in touch." I hung up before the conversation could go any further. Since there'd been no word from Sam, I decided to hold off on the call to Doe.

Jimmy stepped inside right after I hung up, and I finished off the beer. "Filled 'er up, Mr. Stumbaugh. That'll be three dollars. Oil and tire pressure's okay. Man, love that car. You ever want to sell 'er, let me know first, okay?"

"You'll be the first, Jimmy." I peeled a five dollar bill from my wad of cash and handed it to him. "Keep the change, Jimmy. That's for the Pabst and use of the phone."

"Geez, Mr. Stumbaugh! Thanks! But, you don't have to do that."

"Never know, might need a favor some day on a case. You'll be the first I come to."

I like throwing a bone to the hired help now and again.

"Wow, well…you can count on me!"

I laid down some rubber on the station's drive as I took off from the pumps and stuck my arm in the air with a final wave. I was a man on a mission, and the first item of business was Sam. His apartment was less than fifteen minutes away, as long as I didn't get caught in the Texas State Fair traffic. How could so many people afford to take off in the middle of a working day? Never figured that out, and it looked like my plans to indulge in the fair's car show, corny dogs, and beer was put on hold. Maybe next year.

I merged from Highway 67 onto 75, and as the Healey's wheels turned, so did the ones in my head. New questions were popping up again. The visit with Abner. As good as it was, it was almost *too* damn good. I couldn't remember the last time something that easy and juicy fell into my lap. Experience told me to be wary of Trojan Horses, but my gut told me the old man was okay and being straight with me. There was another question that had nagged at me from the beginning, too. Who was Petrie talking to before he called Doe for the extortion money? I wanted the identity of Mr. Short and Sweet. I knew I'd find out one way or another...but *now* would be even better. And another thing, something Doe said at our first meeting. He said he could hire any thug off the street for fifty dollars to kill somebody. Is that what he did to Petrie? Was Petrie getting cold feet or did the senator just want to take care of loose ends? *Or* did Doe decide to keep all the money for himself? This too would come to light.

Sam's apartment complex was a four-story rectangular, red brick affair built during the war. His place was on the second floor, and naturally, the elevator was out of order. I was forced to limp my way up two flights of stairs, which was a chore for a man with one good leg, one gimpy, and a stick. By the time I got to the second floor landing, I dropped any personal concern I had for Sam and had moved on to a full-blown pissed-off mode. I peg-legged along a narrow, hollow hallway and listened to the step, step, clop rhythm of my footsteps and cane as I looked for Sam's apartment. Midway, I found it, knocked on his door, and stepped to the side. A habit I developed on the force. Bullets and shotgun blasts have a tendency to go through plywood and particle board with the greatest of ease. There was no answer.

"Sam!" I yelled. "It's me, Harry! Open up!" Still no answer, but I had a gut feeling he was inside. He *could* be gone, but I doubted it. I reached over and twisted the knob. It wasn't locked. Seemed like I'd already done this once today. "Sam, I'm coming in! Don't shoot, for

Chrissakes!" Still standing to the side, behind the door jam, I twisted the knob again, pushed open the door with my foot, and paused before stepping out into the open.

What I saw wasn't a pretty sight, by any means. Sam's big hulk was slumped down in a brown stuffed chair facing the doorway. All he had on were his boxers, which was more than I wanted to see, and he was in the process of slowly returning a .45 onto the nightstand beside him. Beside the gun was a half-empty bottle of Jack Daniel Whiskey. He looked like shit, and I told him so.

"You look like shit, Sam," I said, motioning for him to keep his seat. "I've already let myself in." I was re-pissed-off again. "Please tell me that you were up all night doing the la bamba with four beauties from the Baker Hotel last night." Sam's legs were crossed, arms stretched out on the chair's arms, and his eyes were as red and blood shot as a stop sign.

"I wish *I could,* but that, I think I'd remember."

I pointed to the whiskey bottle and the gun. "You trying to figure out which would be the best way to off yourself? One takes longer and gets more depressing and it's over in a flash with the other, in case you didn't know."

Sam frowned and glanced at the nightstand. "You got it wrong. Haven't touched the booze, and I keep the .45 close to me when I'm home."

I saw the skinned knuckles and remnants of blood on his hands. It looked like he tried to wash them clean, but did a poor job. "What happened to your hands?"

He lifted up his right hand and checked it out. "Don't know."

"Where'd you go last night after dropping me off?" I asked.

Very slowly and methodically, Sam shook his head once in either direction. "Don't know…I think I…ended back at the Vegas Club, but I'm not sure."

The wheels started turning again, and I didn't like the direction they were taking. *Vegas Club. Robert Petrie. Not good.* The man in front of me had a history of killing with his hands before, and now his hands looked to be bloody with somebody else's.

Shit.

I was stunned. "Why would you…"

"Not much of a partner." Sam said. There was no shame in his voice. Just a stated fact.

I reached into my shirt pocket and pulled out a folded check I'd made out to Sam this morning. I tossed it in his lap. "That's twenty-five percent of a ten grand retainer Doe gave me when he hired the firm yesterday. I took out your part of the office rent and Jenny's salary. You've still got twenty-four hundred dollars there to play with. It's yours. You can blow it on booze or bullets, or you can get off your ass, quit feeling sorry for yourself, and get back to work. If you decide to work, call Jenny. She's got your instructions. We'll talk later, when we're both in a better humor."

This was a broken man in front of me, and I didn't know what to do. But, I sure as hell wasn't in the mood to babysit a shell-shock drunk. This was beyond my…getting out was all I could think of. I turned to leave and spotted a pile of clothes on the floor by the kitchen table. A bloody dress shirt lay on top. I was sure he didn't cut himself shaving. I went over and picked them up. The shirt and jacket were torn, smelled like booze and cigarettes, blood, and something else, but it didn't register just now. I checked the pockets of his suit jacket and pants, which turned out to be empty. I took them over to the kitchen and stuffed them in the trash can and carried it to the door. Looking back, I noticed that Sam hadn't budged an inch, and the check was still in his lap untouched.

I pointed to the clothes. "You could've done this, you know. It's gonna be hard for an old man like me to go down two flights of stairs with a cane in one hand and bloody evidence in the other." He didn't move. "Buy yourself a new suit and trash can. You can afford it." I didn't bother closing the door when I left.

Chapter 13

I was back on the road again, and after the confrontation with Sam, I was numb. I knew Sam was a man on the edge, but what I witnessed today was a man who had returned to a deep, dark hole with no chance of coming out. One night, on his invitation, I joined him at the Baker Hotel for a drink. He'd never asked before, it was his turf, so it seemed like a good idea. It turned into one of those sloppy drunk-fests where you drink too much and talk too much. The more we chewed the fat, the more we drank. It was like two old vets that hadn't seen each other in twenty years swapping lies about the past. Only problem was, the liquor loosened up our tongues and we started telling the truth. About ourselves. It was like two warriors that fought different wars, sharing the horrors. I talked about the low side of being a cop and dealing with the dredges of mankind on a daily basis, getting shot, getting fucked over by the powers that be, and staying drunk for three months before deciding to get off my ass and do something about it; Sam talked about the war.

He was a twenty-three year old roughneck, fresh off the oil fields of Crane, Texas and joined the Marines at the Midland recruitment center the day after Pearl. When he was done with boot camp, he was "volunteered" to train attack dogs as scouts for the troops in the Pacific. This duty put him directly into the belly of the beast. Guadalcanal, Iwo Jima, Tarawa, Guam. He wasn't attached to any specific group or company.

Wherever Sam and his dog were needed, that's where he went. The war dogs unit was a small, tight group who were deployed as island hopping units to all the hot spots, either performing cleanup duty after an invasion, ferreting out the Japs that refused to surrender from the jungles and caves, or he was at the forefront of the invasion doing recon. His job was to scout out the jungles with his dog, find the Japs, and radio back to the American lines with enemy coordinates. Sometimes, it was just him and his Doberman, Clancy; sometimes the two of them accompanied a patrol; but he didn't go to the john without Clancy at his side. That night in the hotel bar, he recalled the stories in a dull, monotone voice, except when that Doberman was the subject, then his face lit up like I've never seen before or since. He recalled dozens of stories about the many times Clancy saved his ass, and I'll admit, I was mesmerized, not by the stories, but the bond between that man and his dog. This was a side of the war I knew nothing about. This was the bowels of hell he was regurgitating.

Towards the end of our drunken confessions, he got down to the nut-cuttin'. The first was about when he and a fellow dog trainer were out on patrol together scouting recon on Guam. They came to the proverbial fork in the road. Sam said he'd go left. The path was rough and gradually dipped into a ravine that had *ambush* written all over it, but the dogs hadn't alerted to anything yet. The path to the right afforded more protection and a better view of what lay ahead.

His partner, Hank Abnernathy, who'd been with him since boot camp, said they should flip a coin to see who took which path. Hank won the toss and without hesitation, chose the left-handed fork and took his German shepherd, Fritz, with him. *See you in a bit* were his last words to Sam. Sam said he was uneasy about it, but knew there was nothing gained in arguing with his partner when he made up his mind about something. The dogs had saved their asses more than once, and their confidence in their ability to protect them was never doubted. But less than fifteen minutes after the two men separated, Sam heard a firefight break out that sounded like two companies going at each other. He recognized the rapid staccato firing of Hank's sub-machine gun and the returning fire of the Arisaka 44's. Sam said he got to where he could tell what kind of rifle the Japs were using just by the sound of the report.

Clancy led and Sam followed as they cut across the field at a dead run to help their partners. Sam knew it was going to be bad just by the sound of it all, and the only thing he could think about before he even got there was…it was supposed to be him. Not Hank. Hank had a wife and two daughters. He had nobody. *It should have been me.* He kept saying.

It was over in a matter of minutes. Sam said the spot where he found their bodies was rancid with the smell of cordite and blood and the air was still thick with smoke from the heavy gunfire that took place in a small, bowl shaped area. He said it was a scene of carnage, unlike anything he'd ever seen before. The two had been ambushed at the mouth of the ravine, the same ravine that had *ambush* written all over it, and a ring of grotesque bodies encircled Hank and Fritz. Man and dog were dead; their bodies had been hacked to pieces, but Fritz's jaws were still locked around the throat of one of their ambushers.

I got the impression that this was the beginning of the end for Sam. The guilt of him being alive and his friend dead was too much. He said the rage became unbridled, and he threw caution out the door. He described himself as reckless when it came to his own safety, but relentless when it came to saving others. But, it was one of many midnight attacks on Jima that really broke him. A force of Japs crept up on the American lines in the dead of night, and then cut loose with their banzai attack that ended up in a hand-to-hand combat which tested every man to his limits. Including Sam. All he told me was that after he ran out of ammunition from his machine gun and .45, he grabbed up a samurai sword off a dead Jap and charged into their lines hacking away at anything in his way. This wasn't bragging he was doing. It was…re-living hell. That's when his face got slashed from nose to ear, fighting against another Jap that had his own sword. The other guy was more skilled, but Sam had rage on his side. It wasn't until after they'd repelled the Japs, that he found Clancy's body afterwards with a bullet hole in his head. He never knew when it happened. Each was fighting their own battle to survive.

As Sam told his story, I never said a word. Matter of fact, I remember just staring at my drink the whole time. I couldn't bear to look him in the face. When he abruptly stopped, I looked up, and he was throwing back another shot of Jack. "Now you know," he said. "It'll never come up again." And he left the table, leaving me with the tab, and a bad taste in my mouth.

That's what I had now. A bad taste in my mouth. Even with Abner's confirmation about Doe, I still needed backup information from Denton. I wasn't going to depend solely on the word of vindictive old cripple. Sending Sam to Denton seemed like an even better idea to get him off his ass. It was the best way I knew of to see if he was going to fight or give in. I wanted to give him something to make him busy. Something to focus on besides getting drunk and blacking out, unless that's what he *wanted* to do. I glanced down at the clothes in the trash can on my floor board. *What's that smell?* If he did kill Petrie, nobody was going to give a shit. Me least of all, since I didn't think it'd matter.

As for me, my own desire to do anything was pissing away. If I went to the Adolphus, I'd probably end up drinking myself into oblivion like Sam. I had my own demons to bear, like the serial killer that put the .45 slug in my leg and got away. But I'd learned to stomp 'em down when their ugly heads rose up. I'd been where Sam is, and I didn't want to go back. What I needed was…Jenny.

Chapter 14

Sam showered, shaved, put on a fresh suit, and made his mind up about the day. He called Jenny to see what Harry had in mind for him, assured her that he was okay, and jotted down his instructions. He holstered the .38 on his belt, grabbed the .45 from the end table, and stuck it in the waist band in the small of his back. He'd head out to Denton...after a return visit to the Vegas Club. He didn't like blank spots and intended on finding out what happened to him the night before. That was the priority. He didn't give a shit what Harry said about it, and he didn't care about whose head he busted either. Before leaving, he reached down and took a swig from the half-empty bottle of Jack Daniels. He saw the folded check from Harry still lying in the seat of the chair; he didn't give it a second thought as he closed the apartment door behind him.

Sam stopped in the Piggly Wiggly parking lot and backed into a free space in front of the store. He kept the motor running and just sat still, drumming his fingers lightly on the steering wheel, thinking.

I was here last night. I remember that much.

He watched the traffic on Lemmon Avenue pass by, retracing in his head what he *did* remember. Dropping off Harry at the Adolphus. Parking here. Remembering *why* he came back to the Vegas Club. Jack Ruby had so much as offered him a job on his first visit to the club, and the original intention was to take him up on it. In his way of thinking, if Ruby was chatting it up with Petrie like he was, he doubted it was a coincidence. If he could get in on the inside, then maybe he could help bust the case wide open. Should he have said something to Harry? Probably, but there was something in his gut that told him the Vegas Club was the hub of the operation, and he wanted to move on it quickly.

He killed the engine, grabbed his hat, and decided to make one more move before going back into the lion's den. He called Jenny back.

"Stumbaugh Investigations, how may I help you?" She answered, picking up on the first ring.

"Hey Jenny, Harry in the office yet?"

"Sammy! How are ya' darlin'? No, he's not back yet, but I expect him soon. Want me to give him another message?"

Sam thought about what to say. "Yeah…look, tell him I'm back at the Vegas Club, sorting out some things. Tell him I'll call the office as soon as I'm done, then I'll head out to Denton. Can you do that for me, kiddo?"

"Of course. You sound funny, Sam. You doing okay?" Jenny asked.

"Yeah, kid, I'm doing okay. Just a little beat down, that's all. I'll call when I'm done. Talk to you later, Jenny."

"Sam, are you…?"

He hung up, not wanting to explain himself any further, and no, he wasn't okay. As he crossed the parking lot in the direction of the Vegas Club, he lightly touched a goose egg on the crown of his head that made his head ache. The knot was just another mystery to add to the skinned knuckles and bloody clothes. *Think!* But, he couldn't make it happen. His mind was like the double-blank domino. Nothing there. No points.

Just take it slow and easy. Don't go in like a charging bull.

He stepped into the club and the familiar stale odor hit him instantly, along with the bad music, and the sad sight of another bored dancer shuffling her feet and staring at the ceiling while on stage. He stepped inside and let his eyes adjust to the darkness. It was just past lunchtime, and he spotted a handful of customers in the entire joint. That was good. No crowds. He went to the bar, but didn't recognize the bartender who was wiping down beer mugs with a dingy rag. He looked to be barely twenty-one, and Sam had the impression he was a college kid picking up some extra bucks.

When he stepped up to the bar, the kid asked, "What can I get you, fella?"

"A beer," Sam said, putting a dollar bill on the bar. A gallon of water would've been better, but he didn't want to argue with the kid about why he didn't want to drink. He just wanted information. "Is Jack here?" He asked, glancing around, checking out the room for Ruby.

The bartender slid across his beer. "Jack who?"

"Ruby," Sam said. "The owner of the place."

Shrugging, the bartender went back to drying his mugs. "Don't know him. I'm just filling in for the rest of the week."

"Where's the regular guy? The one with all the muscles."

He shrugged again. "Took the week off, I guess. I got a call from the employment service this morning to come in. It's my first time at this place. Not much action, is there?"

"What about the girls?" Sam asked. "Any of them here today that worked last night?"

"I told you," he said, "I'm new here. Couldn't tell you."

"Thanks anyway," Sam said, picking up his beer and moving to a table close to the stage. *Well, this is a big zero.* He tuned-out the band as best he could, and set his hat on the table along with the beer. Sam checked out the room. Something, someone, somewhere around here had to spark a memory from last night. The girls, the bartender, the customers, none of them meant anything to him. More blanks. After scanning the room, his eyes moved to the stage, and then something *did* spark. A brief flash. A face. *That girl, the dancer. Something…think!* Why did *this* girl catch his attention; she was different from the other dancers. Not so long in the tooth. She actually had a good figure…and, she was so much younger than the others. Is that what it is? She's just prettier?

What's a girl like you doing in a gin-joint like this, Sweetheart?

She looked to be in her early twenties and didn't look like she belonged here at all. Her moves on stage were awkward and untrained as she went through the motions of a dance. Sam focused on her face, and then caught her staring down at *him* with a look of recognition, *of panic. She recognizes me!* Customers weren't allowed to go up to the stage, so he had to find a way to communicate that he wanted to talk to her. He gave her a brief wave of the hand and a nod of the head acknowledging her. She nodded once in return and finished her dance without looking at him again.

The bartender came by the table and asked if Sam wanted another beer. Evidently, he didn't notice the full one on the table. When the song finally came to a life-saving end, the young dancer left the stage through a side exit, and another, not so young *woman* took her place. She stood center stage in a two-piece sequenced outfit that exposed too many rolls of skin, hands resting on cocked hips, staring at the band impatiently waiting for them to start again. Sam was ready for them to take a break.

Fifteen minutes later, with a pink terrycloth robe thrown over her dancing costume, her hand clutching the robe shut across her breast, the young dancer took a seat at Sam's table. Now that she was closer, even in the dim light, he saw that the caked makeup and thick black eyeliner trimming ice-blue eyes that had lost their luster, couldn't hide the frightened little girl underneath it all. Her face had a look that reminded him of men that fought beside him in the war. Men that had given up and lost hope. Underneath all the paste and the hard look was a girl that had landed on the wrong island and couldn't get off. She put a pack of cigarettes and matches on the table, then waved, getting the bartender's attention to bring her a drink. Neither spoke or even acknowledged each other as they waited for him to serve them.

The bartender approached the table with drinks in each hand. "Coke and rum and another beer. That'll be three-fifty," he said looking at Sam.

Sam laid four dollars on the table and said, "Keep it." He didn't say anything about the mug of beer he hadn't touched.

"I'm sorry about that," she said, nodding at the drinks. "I have to get a drink when I sit with a customer. If you don't pay for it, I do."

"It's not a problem." Hesitating for a second, he finally said, "Do you…recognize me from last night? On stage…I just had the feeling…"

She leaned forward, elbows on the table, and in a harsh whisper said, "*What* are you doing *here*? Are you crazy, Mister?"

Sam moved forward, too, and just as intensely, returned, "That's what I came to find out. Look…I've got a knot on my head the size of a golf ball, I woke up with the skin knocked off my knuckles, blood on my shirt, and the last thing I remember is walking into this place. I just want to fill in the blanks and then I'm gone. I'm not looking for any trouble or payback."

She looked around to see if anyone was close by listening. "Mister, if you don't get out of here, you might get trouble *and* payback. You really don't remember anything from last night?"

Sam shook his head. "Nope."

She stared at her drink, lit up a cigarette, kept her eyes cast down, and said, "You got all that helping me. It's not safe for you to be here." Then, her eyes lifted up to Sam's face. "This is a bad place, Mister...what's your name, anyway."

"Sam," he said. "What do you mean, helping you?" Normally, he would have extended a hand to her, but he didn't think it'd be a good idea just now.

"Kate," she said.

Sam needed to gain her confidence; he didn't want her to get cold feet and completely shut down on him. Something about him had this girl scared out of her wits. He wanted to know everything she knew. *Be patient.* "That's a nice name," he said. "Let me guess, you're a West Texas girl, right?" The surprised look on her face confirmed the statement. Sam shrugged and gave her a small grin. "I can tell by your *drawl*. Me, too. I'm a Midland boy. And you?"

The fear momentarily switched to genuine surprise, but she still hesitated, as though reluctant to give out information about herself. Then, finally, she said, "Pecos."

Sam grinned again. "Deep West Texas girl from the cantaloupe capitol of the world, huh? That's one desolate, God-forsaken place. Can't blame you for wanting to get away from there. But how'd you end up in this hole?"

The front door opened and her head quickly twisted around to see who it was. Two more customers that looked like laborers came in, stumbled around in the dark a bit, and then took a table on the other side of the stage. "Listen," she said, nervously, "I've got to get back to work. Maybe we can meet when my shift is over and we can talk then."

She started to get up, but Sam laid a massive hand across hers. He didn't grab her, but gently applied pressure to a small, trembling thing. "Kate, I can't leave here without knowing two things, and the first one is the most important to me."

Once again, her eyes checked the room in the direction of the bar and then the stage. Another dancer had replaced the last one. "I---I'm on next...I've got to..."

"Just sit for another minute."

She did, and then reluctantly, slowly, asked, "You want to know what happened to you, is that what you want?"

"Yes," Sam said, softly, "but first, I want to know what the hell you're doing in this dump. I just can't imagine a Pecos girl coming to Dallas and ending up *here*, of all places. I'm guessing that you're barely out of high school, and I know you weren't raised this way."

The mention of home seemed to have broken the dam and her eyes teared-up. "Last night...you were sitting at the bar, talking to Louis, the bartender. I was delivering drinks to a table...I don't know...somebody hit my arm...I spilled the drinks on a customer,

Louis came from behind the bar yelling…"

The tears flowed easily now, and Sam patted her hand, saying, "It's okay, you don't have to…"

"No, it's alright," she said, dabbing her eyes with a handkerchief that appeared from nowhere, and she withdrew her hand from Sam's. She bucked up in an effort to sound stronger. "Louis ran over yelling at me and then…he slapped me…and called me a stupid bitch."

Sam's fists automatically clenched and so did his jaw. "That son-of-a---"

Kate grinned for the first time. "That's exactly what you said last night." The smile turned into a full smile. "You decked him good, boy. He tried to fight back, but you were all over him. *You beat the shit out of him!*"

Sam glanced down at his knuckles, and then relaxed his fists. "Good. So that's how I got these?" He said, spreading his hands out on the table.

Her eyes diverted to the scarred hands, then back to him. "Yes, and that's when all hell broke loose. Some men from other tables jumped on you, and you…you were like a madman, Sam." She finally just laughed out loud, her confidence building. "You were chunking 'em over tables, and into each other…it was…*great*!"

Even Sam smiled this time. "And the knot on my head?"

"One guy busted an empty beer bottle over your head, but it didn't slow you down. Matter of fact, you just turned around, grabbed his wrist, and bent it backwards until there was a loud pop. You broke his wrist!"

Sam had heard enough, at least for now. He held up a hand to stop her from saying anymore. "Go in the back, wash that makeup from your face, and put on some decent clothes. You're coming with me. Tell the bartender, you quit."

A panicked expression formed and her mouth flew open, but she had trouble getting out the words. I…I…can't! They…they own me!"

"Bullshit," Sam spat out in anger. "Who? These assholes? Nobody owns you, Kate. Come on, we're..."

Kate reached across the table to grab his arm, but missed. "You don't understand. They loaned me money. Louis found me on the streets downtown, not long after I got off the Greyhound. He loaned me money, and said I could work it off as a waitress. Then, he brought me here...I can't leave. They'll hunt me down! I've seen them do it to other girls."

"Bastards," Sam growled tightly. "How much?"

Her eyes diverted from Sam's to the table. "Twenty dollars."

Sam stood, grabbed his hat, and looked down on the frightened figure seated across from him. "You don't worry, Kate. Do as I told you and clean yourself up. I'll take care of your debt with interest. I'll be right here waiting for you."

"Oh, I..." she jumped out of her seat and unabashedly rushed around the table to Sam, throwing her arms around his waist.

He gently pushed her away. "Go, I'll be right here."

Before leaving, she said, "There's more about last night, Sam. It's really bad."

"We'll worry about that later. Now hurry."

"A man got killed last night, Sam. After they dragged you outside."

"Tell me in the car, Kate. Now go...quickly. Time's wasting."

Kate literally ran past the stage to the dressing rooms in the rear, and Sam made his way to the bar. The young bartender didn't say a word and didn't act as though anything was wrong. He reached in his pocket and peeled off fifty dollars. "I need an envelope, a piece of paper, and something to write with."

The bartender shrugged. "I don't know if..."

Sam took out another five and put it on the bar. "This fiver's for you."

"Let me see what I can find," the bartender said with new

enthusiasm, scrambling around behind the bar looking for paper and pen.

Sam turned around to keep his eye on the room, leaning his back against the bar. He was reassured with the .45 pressing against his back. Now, *he* was getting nervous. Denton would just have to wait a little longer.

Chapter 15

When I got Sam's message about returning to the Vegas Club, all I could think about was the twenty-four hundred dollars I pissed down the drain when I gave him that check this morning. I really misjudged him. And, while I was still wallowing in my self-pity soup and brewing about that, he called the office and gave Jenny a message saying, *Tell Daddy I'm bringing a new girl home for him to meet.* Sounded awful damned *perky* for somebody that blacked-out for twelve hours *and* probably killed another man with his bare hands. Which I needed to tell him about. Well, I was going to take care of his shit as soon as he hit the door. I stashed the trash can of bloody clothes in the spare office, and still hadn't made up my mind about what to do with them. As an ex-cop, I knew that tampering with evidence, especially in regards to a homicide, was serious business.

Luckily, Jen came in, broke my train of thought, and, as usual, led me down into another galaxy. It was okay though, I needed something else to occupy my mind anyway, and she always keeps me on my toes. Conversations with Jenny are like chess games. One bad move, the game can be over, and she'll roll all over you like a steamroller pressing pavement.

Carefully closing the door behind her, she had that flushed, red-faced look like she did the first time Doe came in the office. I had intended on calling the fine senator when I got back here at the office, but I thought it'd be best to wait until I'd cooled off from the encounter with Sam. Dealing with too many deadbeats before noon was too depressing.

"Harry!" Jen blurted out, in that loud, controlled whisper thing she does.

"I'm here Doll Face, calm down, now. What's got you so excited? Let me see you take a deep breath and tell me what's going on."

She took a deep breath. "You'll never guess who's in the front office waiting to see you!"

"Calm down, Jen," I said, "you're losing oxygen." I leaned back and propped my feet on the desk corner. "Let me guess. Yesterday, it was a state senator, so I'm guessing…we've moved up the social ladder of politics and…Lyndon Johnson, our *United States* Senator, has come by for a visit today."

"No! It's even bigger than that, Harry! It's Mrs. Doe! *Hedy Doe*…the Senator's wife!"

I had to admit, I was more impressed with Mrs. Doe's unannounced arrival than if Lyndon had stopped by. I stood, made sure my tie was properly straight, and motioned towards the door. "Then, let's not keep the lady waiting," I said. "Let's bring her in."

This should be interesting.

"You first, I'll follow." I always enjoyed the view walking behind Jenny.

In the past, I'd seen pictures of Hedy Doe in the newspapers, standing with her husband at campaign and social events, but never gave them more than a casual glance, if that; but, the second I laid eyes on the lady sitting in the front room, the word *class* immediately came to mind. She rose from her seat as we entered the room.

"Mrs. Doe," Jenny said first, in her new professional tone, "this is Harry Stumbaugh."

I stepped forward, extending my hand and she took it with a firm grip. "It's nice to meet you, Mrs. Doe. This is quite a surprise. I…"

"I should have called first, I know," she said, interrupting, "but John is a wreck about all this, and I know he's just trying to shield me from what's going on…I just felt…"

I interrupted her this time, "I understand." I motioned her towards my office. "Mrs. Doe, if you don't mind, please have a seat in my office, and I'll be right there. Would you like some coffee? Something to drink?" I asked.

"No, I'm fine, thank you," she said, pointing to my office, "I'll just wait for you inside."

Class.

I had instructions for Jen, and I needed to make it quick. "Hold my calls and take messages, Jenny. If Senator Doe calls, don't tell him she's here. If he indicates he's on his way or something, stall him. Buzz me when Sam gets here, but keep him and his new girlfriend out here in the front until I'm ready for him. Be prepared to ad-lib if things get too crowded in here. Got all that, Doll Face?"

"Gotcha," she said, taking her shorthand notes. "Are you mad at Sam, or something, Harry?" She said, looking back up at me as though I'd done something to him. "You seem like it."

She was very intuitive for a blonde. I leaned down and gave her a quick peck on the forehead. "No, just…working a strategy thing, that's all." I left before she could ask more questions, and I went to see why Hedy Doe was making a surprise visit to yours truly.

The Senator's wife rose to her feet once again when I came in, and I closed the door, taking advantage of the moment to fully take in the classy broad standing in front of me. I took her to be in her mid-thirties and she stood maybe five-foot-six or seven, no more; probably one-twenty to twenty-five; petite, but sturdy, I'd say. She wore a black pleated skirt, a black turtleneck sweater, and a wine red leather jacket cut like a man's suit coat, tapered to fit her like a glove. My suits never fitted that good.

Class, real class.

Her hair was auburn, cut short and straight in a pageboy style, but the eyes…that's what caught my attention. Round and hazel, they were her most outstanding feature, and it was hard to take my eyes from them. And, she knew it. "Please, sit down, Mrs. Doe," I said, taking the seat next to her. I didn't want a desk separating us. "What can I do for you?"

"My husband is innocent, Mr. Stumbaugh. I was with him when that ugly little man first called, demanding money…blackmailing him."

"The first time?" I asked.

Interesting. I didn't know he called twice.

"Yes, you know, when he called John yesterday morning. At first, John just took it as another crank call. He gets them all the time. It's quite disturbing, you know."

You're contradicting what your husband told me yesterday, lady. Not good.

Her eyes didn't shift around the room or go to her feet during the conversation, as most people I meet in the office do. Those big hazel orbs stayed on me with every word she said. I didn't want to get into a staring contest with her, but that's what it was coming down to. "I can imagine. What made him change his mind, do you think? That this wasn't just another crank call."

"I'm sure you discussed that with him, already. There's no need for me to put words in his mouth."

"Right."

Good dodge. You should have spoken to him before coming to see me.

"So, were you with John when the blackmailer called back the *second* time, too? Demanding money?"

"Of course. And, he told me all about the meeting with you." She gave a small smile. "He's quite taken with you, you know. He likes your tough-guy image. He also likes the results you get with your clients."

I had to be careful navigating the minefield ahead of me. "I didn't know my results were published material."

"Don't be coy, Mr. Stumbaugh. You've had several clients of

means. You don't think they can really keep a secret, do you? We gather frequently. Social and sporting events. Gin rummy at the club. The rich love to brag, Mr. Stumbaugh. You should know that." She crossed her legs and tugged her skirt down over the knee. "I hate that kind of thing, really. I'm more up for grilling burgers on the patio and a good game of touch football in the backyard, instead. The country club scene and people are all so phony, you know. But, necessary."

That was a lot of unsolicited information.

"Necessary. I'm sure. You're right, phony socialites are an important contribution to our society. Then, you don't like to play gin rummy? Is that what you're saying?"

A small grin. "You're very astute, aren't you, Mr. Stumbaugh? Not really, I prefer poker and smoky rooms. Same as you, I suspect."

This is almost like sparring with Jenny, except on a different level.

"Maybe," I said. "But for some reason, I'm having trouble picturing you in a pair of jeans and a sweatshirt dodging tacklers or smoking a cigar and bluffing with a pair of deuces."

"I like to play quarterback, Mr. Stumbaugh," she said, "and do the dealing."

"Interesting. I'm sure you do. So why are you here, Mrs. Doe? I can't tell you anything, really. Your husband is my client. Not you. Did you just come by to tell me your husband is innocent? That you're behind your man, no matter what? If that's the case, I'll tell you the same thing I told him. I don't care if he's innocent or not. I'll follow the evidence and where it leads me. I'll report that to him and let him deal with the fallout, if there is any. I don't go to the authorities or anyone else. I report only to John. I'm not hired to make judgments, but to get results."

That small, tight lipped smile again. "I see why he likes you. No, I'm not here to sway any opinions, Mr. Stumbaugh, and I'm sorry if I gave that impression. I just want you to know..." She finally broke eye contact. It was brief and just a quick glance out of the office window, but it also gave me a chance to blink. "You don't live with a man and not know who he is as a person. Even one with amnesia. At least, I don't," she added.

"I'm not like some of these bubble-headed socialites that latches onto a pretty face just to get taken to the cleaners later. I worked for my money, Mr. Stumbaugh. My daddy had me working in the oil fields by the time I was fourteen-years-old, and he taught me the business from the ground up. Being a woman in a man's world is not an easy thing, even if daddy owns the company. You still have to pay your dues. And, if I thought there was any truth to this entire matter, I'd drop John Doe like a hot potato and spend my last dime to make sure he paid for it."

"That's a nice speech, but like I said, it has nothing to do with me and how I work the case."

I wonder if Doe sent her here to deliver this speech. I doubt it.

"Mainly, for myself, Mr. Stumbaugh, I just wanted to meet the man John hired. And, I didn't want you to have any false impressions about me. Society pages are so…fake."

"Really? And, I always thought that stuff was true. You can probably guess that I'm not real big on reading the society section of the paper every day, but I'll start looking for you in the sports section." I knew the meeting, for whatever the real purpose was about, was over. We'd both marked out territory. "Well, I'm glad you came by, Mrs. Doe. Is there anything else?"

She stood to leave, extending a hand to me. "No, I guess not. I wanted to make sure I wasn't spending good money after bad, and I wanted to meet the famous, Harry Stumbaugh, private eye."

Your money? The senator must have his bank accounts mixed up. Or the facts.

"Investigator, ma'am. Sam Spade and Nick Charles are private eyes," I corrected. I stood and cupped her hand, holding on to it in a friendly, cordial manner. She didn't resist. "And, I'm not sure about the famous part."

"You should come by the club someday, you'd be surprised,"

she said with a sly grin and a wink.

I decided to throw in one passing shot before she left. "Had you ever met or seen Robert Petrie before, Mrs. Doe?" Our parting hand holding ceremony came to an abrupt end when she jerked her hand free.

"I beg your pardon? Why do you ask such a thing, Mr. Stumbaugh? No. Of course not," she answered indignantly.

"Well…this is just the detective in me. People say things and they catch my ear and make me wonder."

"And, what could I have possibly said to make you think I'd ever met the blackmailer?"

Here we go, tip-toeing through the minefield. "You referred to Petrie as an *ugly little man*."

"So? He was," she said, "figuratively speaking."

Nice recovery. "Figuratively speaking," I repeated, "as opposed to literally, I assume."

"Of course. Why would *that* peak your interest?"

I shrugged. "Well, he was…literally, an ugly, little man. I saw him after he called John demanding the money."

She smiled and gave a short laugh. "You just keep doing what you do, Mr. Stumbaugh. You're very good at it."

As she started to leave, my phone buzzed. I stretched across the desk to answer it, but before I did, I said, "Mrs. Doe, could you wait just a moment before leaving? This is my secretary." She didn't answer, but she didn't move to the door either. I picked up the receiver. "Yes, Jenny, what is it?"

"Sam's here," she said. "You want him to wait for you out here?"

"Is he alone?"

"No, Miss Culpepper is with him. She's very sweet, Harry."

I pictured Jenny winking at Miss Culpepper when she declared her *sweetness*. "I'm sure she is. Tell them to…wait, let's do this…go ahead and send in Sam. Keep Miss Culpepper with you and entertain her for a few minutes."

"Gotcha," Jenny said.

"I'd like you to meet my partner before you go, Mrs. Doe."

"The veteran with the strange name John told me about?"

Sam was already through the door with an unusual glow of energy and a smile on his face. "Sam Wolfkill, half-breed Comanche at your service ma'am," he said, arm outstretched as he spoke.

Jenny must have identified our guest. I thought the suddenness of Sam's entrance might put her off, it sure caught me off guard, but her reaction was to the contrary. A genuine, open smile lit up her face and her posture relaxed. For some reason, I could now picture her chunking a football in the backyard.

I think she likes him. Maybe she prefers war torn faces over bullets in the leg kind of guys.

She shook his hand, and I noticed how she let it linger a second longer than necessary before withdrawing it. "Sam, this is Hedy Doe, Senator Doe's wife. She came by to meet us…I think."

She either didn't hear me, chose to ignore me, or was too smitten with Sam to care about what I just said. "Well, a pleasure to meet you, Mr. Wolfkill. Such an unusual name. Are you really half Comanche?" She asked.

"Call me, Sam. And no…I'm not half anything. Just full-blooded American."

Her eyes zeroed in on mine like a ray gun. *I think she heard me.* "You two are quite the pair, aren't you?"

I think I blushed and Sam started shuffling his feet, as she faced Sam and said, "Nice to meet you, *Sam*, but I must go now."

"You too, ma'am," Sam said, stepping aside for her exit.

And, she took off without another word to either of us. I heard her say goodbye to Jenny as she passed through the front office, and then she was gone. *Interesting meeting. Not sure what it was about, but it sure as hell wasn't to test my competence. Maybe to let me know who was pulling the purse strings.* For some reason now, I felt better about spending the ten-thousand dollar retainer, knowing it was hers.

The door barely closed behind her and Sam said, "I think I just shook hands with the devil."

"Very observant," I said. "Now..."

Sam said, "I've got somebody you need to meet, Harry."

I shook my head. "No, we've got to talk first. There're some serious shit going on and this little happy act..." Sam walked out on me like I wasn't even there, cutting off the great speech I had planned. "Hey!" I yelled to his back, "you can't do that!" But, he did.

I stood there, ready to draw my .38 and just put an end to all this with two to his chest, when he came back in leading a young girl in her early twenties by the hand into my office. I changed my mind about plugging him full of holes...I didn't want the girl to be in the line of fire.

"Harry, this is Kate Culpepper. She used to work at the Vegas Club, and she's got an interesting story to tell. About Ruby, Petrie, and the racket they've got going, and what happened to me last night."

I flopped down in my chair and motioned to the empty ones across from my desk. "By all means," I said, with no humor, "and exactly how long has it been since you quit working at the Vegas Club, Miss Culpepper?"

She looked at Sam before answering, then said, "About thirty minutes ago."

I took a breath and I'm sure my impatience showed. Matter of fact, I wanted it to. "Sam," I said, attempting to keep a semblance of control in my words and temper, "can we talk in private before we go into Miss Culpepper's story? Her and Jenny can go over to Walgreen's and grab a sandwich and bring something back for us. That'll give us some time to talk first."

I glanced back at Miss Kate Culpepper with a tight smile, but I noticed that her facial features had changed. At first, she seemed a bit timid and unsure, but now I was looking at a scared little girl who acted like she was about to be thrown back onto the street after being promised a hot meal. I needed to reverse engines. "What I meant to say is…Miss Culpepper…is Sam and I need to discuss some important developments that occurred this morning in regards to the very case you're talking about. And…and I need to discuss it privately with him, first. I'm not minimizing your contribution, believe me. I'm anxious to hear what you have to say. Do you understand?"

She nodded, and then turned back to Sam. "I don't want to leave though. I'll wait in the other office with Jenny. Okay?"

Sam patted her hand. "Look, Harry and I really do need to talk…and we could all use something to eat. Trust me, Jenny won't let anything happen to you. I'd rather go down a dark alley with her for protection than Harry, any day of the week."

"Me, too," I added. *Time to bring in the reinforcements.* "Jen!" I yelled. "Come here a sec!"

A level voice that sounded similar to my secretary and didn't sound very pleased with me, said, "The door's open and I'm ten feet away from you Harry, you don't have to scream." She waited a full ten seconds before making an appearance, and then stood framed in the doorway, arms crossed tight over ample breasts.

Perhaps, it was my unprofessionalism in front of guests. I wasn't going to apologize, though. "Uh, Jen, it's about lunch time, so why don't you and Miss Culpepper go over to Walgreen's and grab some lunch and bring back the usual for me and Sam." I stood, handed her some cash, and gave her my *do as I say and don't argue with me* look. In return, she reached out and snatched another ten-dollar bill from the wad of bills in my hand before I could stick it back in my pocket.

I think I just apologized.

She reached out a hand for Kate. "Come on, Doll. We'll freshen up a little bit first, and then I'm taking you to the French Room at the Adolphus for lunch. The *boys* can get their own sandwiches. Us girls gotta be pampered now and then, don't cha' think?" And with that, Jenny, Kate Culpepper, and twenty dollars of my money marched out the door.

Yep, that was an apology.

Sam watched the pair leave. He swiveled around in his chair to face me. He held up both hands and dipped his chin down to his chest. "I know…I know." Then that familiar look of steel came back on me. "I fucked up. You're pissed and ready to kick my ass out. I don't blame you. I was about ready to call it quits myself, but…I'm okay. Just let me talk first."

I wasn't going to be that generous just yet. "No, I'm doing the talking. Did you know that Petrie got murdered last night? He was beat to death outside the Vegas Club, and they found his body about three o'clock this morning."

"I know."

I got up without acknowledging his answer and went into the adjoining office, and returned with the trash can full of bloody clothes. I set it on top of the desk in front of him. "Those are yours," I said, pointing at the trash can and then the hands in his lap. "You beat the hell out of *somebody* last night, *and* this morning, I find you hung-over with a .45 and a half empty bottle of Jack by your side and a brain full of mush. And to top it off, what do *I* do?" I reached over, lifted the trash a couple of inches off the desk and let it drop. "I tampered with evidence to save your sorry ass." I flopped down in my chair and leaned back, letting my emotions calm and the silence do its work.

"I know," Sam started, "but…"

Okay, long enough.

"I give you a chance…send you to Denton for background work on Doe, *important* background imperative to the case, I might add…hoping to salvage something from you…and what do you do? You go back to the fucking club! There's information in Denton *we* need in our hand *now,* not later when you think you'll get around to it. Now you tell me…what do I do, now?" I started rocking slowly, back and forth in my chair. I stayed silent again, waiting on him. That scarred up face had that look of his that could drop an elephant to its knees.

"Can I talk now?" Sam said, calmly. "First off, I wasn't drunk, and I hadn't been drinking the Jack. I told you that this morning. And I wasn't hungover, at least from alcohol. I had one beer last night. I was drugged, Harry. Kate saw it all go down last night. And I know about Petrie, even though you managed to leave that out when we talked this morning."

"You didn't look like somebody ready to handle the fact that you might have murdered somebody. What do you mean, drugged? How the hell did somebody drug *you*?" I asked, not hiding my surprise or skepticism.

"Are you going to listen or judge?"

"Talk. And I'll make a judgment on…that."

"Bits and pieces are coming back, thanks to Kate, but…look, you know I've had blackouts before, but it's been from drinking binges and nightmares, but not this time. The first time I went to the club was when I followed Petrie. When I met Ruby, he offered me a job. He likes vets and I led him on to think I was a tough guy that did muscle work."

"That's good," I said, interrupting. "You played him."

I taught him well.

"Right. So last night, after dropping you off, I thought I'd play him some more. Get on the inside. But, it never got that far. My chivalry got the best of me."

"Chivalry? What the hell are you talking about, *chivalry*?"

"It goes all over me if I see a man mistreating a woman. Especially if he lays a hand on her. It's the way I was raised. Anyway, Kate spilled some drinks on a customer and the bartender, Louis somebody, starts smacking her around."

"And you jumped in?"

"Yeah, and evidently I worked him over pretty good. Then some other guys jumped me…and I worked them over too, I guess. I can get in a rage like that…things kinda flashback sometimes, you know." Sam held up his hands in front of him and turned the skinned knuckles towards me.

"Skinned knuckles from a bar fight. Chivalry," I said, again. "Okay, so it sounds like you were winning. How'd you get drugged?

"Kate said that Ruby was the one that busted things up. Evidently, he's not bad with his fists either, and he was taking my side, or at least trying to peel off the pile of bodies on top of me. During the commotion, Kate said she saw two guys come in through the back door. She said they were pretty big and wore suits. She said they looked *official*."

"Official? You mean like mob guys, you think?"

Sam shook his head. "I asked her that and she didn't think so. She said they wore store bought suits and they didn't fit that good. She said her first impression was that these guys were cops."

"Cops? You think she knows a wise guy from a cop? She looks like she's fresh off the farm to me, Sam."

He nodded. "She is. Pecos girl, but that's another story. Anyway, the two big guys came in, start shouting orders and Ruby snaps to like he was in the army. I'm still on the ground, flat on my back, and Kate says one guy fingered me as private dick, and she said people started getting nervous. Ruby and especially Petrie."

"Private *dick*. Were those her words or the one that fingered you?

Sam frowned. "I didn't ask, but she keeps calling me a private eye. Must've been the other guy's words. Why?"

"Just curious. Could be something. Maybe not. And so Petrie was there, too?" I asked. "How'd she know him?"

"I asked her. She said he'd been there a lot the last two weeks. Always chatting it up with Ruby. Anyway, I'm still flat on my back, trying to shake off the cobwebs, and Kate said she saw Louis go back behind the bar and came back with a rag in his hand. She said he was pretty pissed because I'd busted him up pretty good. The two big guys held me down with some others and she saw Louis put the rag over my face. She said I fought like a devil, but in a matter of seconds I was out cold."

The smell on Sam's clothes. Now I knew what it was. I got up, pulled out Sam's shirt from the trash can, and took a quick sniff. The odor was faint, but traces from the rag still lingered around the collar. "You were knocked out with chloroform." I tossed the shirt back in the can and set it on the floor next to me. "Any idea how you got home?"

Sam shook his head. "Chloroform? No, but somebody had to drive me. They had to know where I lived, too."

"The blood. Yours or Petrie's you think?" I asked, already knowing the answer.

"From the fight, I guess. But, I didn't kill Petrie, Harry. There's no way I could have. He was alive and well when they turned out my lights. It wasn't me, Harry."

"It makes a nice frame job, though, doesn't it? No idea who the two guys were? And how they fingered you as an investigator?"

"No," Sam said. "But, it's an even bet that Petrie might have recognized me from the Adolphus yesterday, when he called his boss before he moved to the other phone to call Doe. He was there right beside me, and I'm sure he saw me. Wouldn't be hard to put two and two together. I showed up at the club minutes after he did. He recognized me, perhaps. Petrie and Ruby got nervous. Maybe, they called in the two enforcers."

"I wonder why they didn't just kill you. Be done with it."

"Like you said, Harry, a frame job. Kill two birds with one stone."

"Yeah," I said, scratching my head, "or you're a protected guy like me."

"Protected? What's that mean?" Sam asked.

"Giovanni could have put out the word on you. You're a friend of his, now. Hands off." As the words passed through my lips, I saw the slightest, subtle grin crease Sam's mouth.

What's with that?

"So what now? What do you want me to do? If anything," Sam asked unsure.

"Get your ass to Denton," I said, void of expression, "and don't make any pit stops on the way this time."

We both heard the front office door open at the same time. I looked over Sam's shoulder as he turned around. At first I thought it might be Jenny and Kate returning from lunch, but I knew it was a little early if they really went to the French Room.

"Hey Stumbaugh!" A course voice called out. "You open for business?" Detective Carl Cochran shouted, entering the reception area.

Chapter 16

I had less than three seconds before Detective Cochran and his sidekick, Frank Megs, made it to my desk. I kept my eyes on the approaching pair and told my new partner in a low, even voice, "Don't say a word, Sam. These guys are cops and bad news. Let me do the talking and don't even give your name. Just act like you're not in the room." I saw him button his coat, covering up his .38, and he gave a short nod acknowledging me. I hooked my leg around the trash can full of incriminating evidence next to my chair, and slid it out of sight under my desk. I wasn't sure why they were here, but it probably had something to do with Sam and last night. The whole thing stunk to high heaven, and I hoped Cochran and his lackey weren't packing a search warrant.

Cochran came through my door first, arms spread wide in a friendly greeting. "What? No beautiful blond at the front desk to greet us, Harry? What kind of private dick office is this?" Sam's eyes quickly shifted to me, as he stepped up to the desk. Sam was seated to his right, and the detective gave him a nonchalant glance as though he was a bug on the floor. "What? You don't have anything to say, like hello or something, Harry?"

Frank came up from behind Cochran's left with a shit-eating grin on his face and fat thumbs hooked in his suspenders. He made a show of letting me see the .32 holstered under his arm. I nodded at the gun. "Hi, Frank. I see you still carry a gun the size of your dick. What's the matter, won't your daddy there let you carry a big gun like the rest of us big boys?"

The grin dropped like an anvil and he took a step forward. "Why you son-of-a---"

Cochran stretched out his arm, halting his partner's progress, and then he gave me a big smile. "Now boys, let's play nice." He pointed to the empty chair next to him. "Have a seat, Frank, relax and take a load off. I've got this." Frank sat down slowly, keeping his eyes on me as he did.

I gave him my best shit-eating grin. "Glad to see you learned to sit without looking down first, Frank." He didn't react, but I could tell it took all his will power. I got my cane off the desk, where it normally stayed, and rested it across the arms of my chair, then I looked over at Sam. "You see *Luther,* Frank and I have a history. We don't like each other."

Cochran jumped in, "Cut the shit, Harry, this is an official visit. We've got some business to discuss. Serious shit."

"Serious shit. *Sounds* official. "What's..." The phone rang and I wasn't going to wait for Jenny to get back to answer it, and I didn't care who it was. I just needed to stall and gather my wits. "Sorry, gotta get this, Carl. The beautiful blond isn't here to answer it." I snatched the receiver from its cradle before it could ring again. "Stumbaugh Investigations, Stumbaugh speaking," I said in my official tone.

"I was hoping the irresistible Jenny would answer the phone," Giovanni Gamboa said. "If I wasn't married, I'd steal her from you, you know."

"Seems to be a lot of requests for her this afternoon, how are you?"

"You and Sam are in trouble, Harry. The police will be paying you a visit soon, and I suggest you disappear for a few days."

"Well, *Mom,* it's good to hear your voice, too," I said. "Dinner sounds nice, do you want me to pick you up?" I asked, obviously speaking in a secret code. I covered the mouthpiece with my hand, "It's Mom," I whispered to Frank, who was sitting directly across from me, "I'll be right with you."

"I see that I've called too late. Listen to me, Harry. Is it that pig, Cochran?"

I coughed into the phone, and I saw Cochran the pig staring me down and pointing at his watch. I guess he wanted me to get off. "Yes, I'll come by about seven, Mom."

"Then time is short," Giovanni said, urgently. "They want to arrest Sam for Petrie's murder, which I'm sure you're aware of by now. Cover yourself, my friend, and call when it's safe. We need to talk. Trust no one, Harry," Giovanni laughed, "except me, of course." Giovanni was gone.

"Okay, Mom, seven-thirty it is," I said to the dial tone. "Bye, love you, too."

Shit.

I hung up and smiled at Cochran. "What can you do? When your mother calls…what can you do? I'm her favorite, you know."

"Really?" Cochran said, smiling and glancing down at his partner. "Frank, I would have sworn Harry's mother died about…oh, what's it been…ten years now?"

"Yeah, at least," said Frank, the shit-eating grin returning.

"It was a long distance call, Cochran," I said, "now what do you want?"

Megs snapped, "You always were a smartass, Stumbaugh, but I'm gonna get the last laugh on you this time."

"Smartass, Frank? That'd be a step up for you from *dumbass,* wouldn't it?" Megs leaned forward, glaring at me, but it didn't go anywhere.

"Okay, you two. Enough," Cochran spat. He finally acknowledged Sam. "What's *your* name, cowboy? Can you talk?"

"Luther." Sam said.

"Right." Cochran's finger pointed back and forth between me and Sam. "You two should be in the movies. You're regular Abbott and Costellos, aren't you? Well, how about a couple of murder raps? Think that'll take the starch out of your shirts, boys?"

He pointed back at me. "You first, Harry."

Me? I thought they were here for Sam. Shit. This could ruin my day.

"Me? A *couple* of murders?"

Double shit.

"I haven't murdered anybody today, Carl." I checked my watch. "It's only one o'clock. Too early for me, especially for a double homicide." I leaned back in my chair, drumming the fingers from both hands on the cane across my lap. Detective Cochran remained standing between the sitting bookends of Sam and Frank, with his hands jammed into his pockets. His oversized gut spilled over his belt, putting a heavy strain on a set of stretch suspenders that looked like they'd unravel any second.

Asshole.

The two most corrupt cops in Dallas came into *my* office to accuse *me* of murder. Paybacks were going to come down hard. Real hard. I gave one of my *really concerned* looks for Cochran. "What's this about, Carl? I've got work to do."

"Good, me too," the detective growled, "and so far you've done nothing but pull on my dick and waste my time. You called me for some information this morning. And in spite of our past history, I was willing to let bygones be bygones, and I obliged you with my knowledge. You wanted to know about the armored truck robbery in '32, and I told you. Didn't even ask why and gave you some names. Damn good names, I might add."

"And I appreciate that, Carl," I said. "What's that got to do with me and a couple of murders?"

"I'll tell you what it's got to fucking do with murder, *numerro uno,* my friend. Abner-fucking-Strong. That's what. Did you go see him this morning after we talked?"

Abner? I wasn't ready for that. I gave an innocent shrug. "Of course, I did. You gave me a lead and I followed up, like any good detective would do." I winked at bookend number two. "Right, Frank?" Back to pig number one. "What about it?"

"What time this morning?" Cochran persisted.

Another innocent shrug, and I knew exactly where this was going, and I didn't like it. "Ten-ish, maybe. Not for sure. Why?"

"He's fucking dead, Harry. Some hired nurse showed up at his house about noon and found him dead in the kitchen. Shot in the head. Still sitting in his fucking wheelchair. For a nurse, she didn't act like she'd ever seen a dead body before."

"No shit, imagine that," I said. "What kind of gun was it?"

"A .38," Cochran answered.

"Of course it was. You sure it wasn't a .32?" I gave Frank another friendly wink.

"Fuck you, Stumbaugh," Frank snapped. "Keep it up, asshole."

"No thank you, and it'd be my pleasure." I turned back to the fat detective. "And *Detective* Cochran...you think *I* did it? Really, Carl. And what would be my motive? He was a lead. He was helping me. I'm not in the habit of rewarding people that help me solve a case by shooting them in the head."

"Funny guy," said Frank.

I gave him a smile. "Keep contributing to the conversation, Frank. You're doing good." I redirected my conversation back to the other fatso. "You didn't answer my question, Carl. Motive?"

He shrugged this time. "Don't know for sure, yet. But don't need a motive when I've got evidence. We canvassed the neighborhood and several neighbors verified seeing your little pussy wagon with the top down, parked in front of his house."

"I already told you I was there, but that's great investigative work on your part. What else do you have?"

He grinned as though the final gavel was about to convict me. "He had *your* business card clutched in his hand when he died. Maybe telling the cops who did it, you think? Fingering the guy that killed him? Coroner said he'd know for sure later, but according to the decease's liver temp, he died about *ten-ish*."

I laughed and I didn't have to fake it this time. "First of all, that's called *cir-cum-stan-shul* evidence, Carl. It doesn't mean shit. Except maybe to you and Frank." I looked back and forth between the two cops.

If this was a setup, it wasn't even a good one. It could be a strong message from somebody higher up the food chain that wants me to butt out, though. But how do Twiddle- Dee and Dum fit into the picture?

"You're shitting me, right? That's what you're wasting *my* time with? You're jerking on *my* dick, now. A fucking business card. Let me see, Carl...maybe it went down like this. Abner sees that I'm about to shoot him in the head, and he's thinking, *I'll take Stumbaugh's card and keep it in my hand while he shoots me in the head and that way the cops...especially my favorite cop, Detective Cochran, who beat the shit out of my only son during an interrogation and then watched him die in the electric chair...I'll leave him a clue to my killer!* Please! This sounds like something *Frank* would come up with!" I stretched out my arms, wrists together. "Here, cuff me, Carl. Take me downtown, and you can bet that my lawyer will be there waiting for us, and I'll be out before my fingerprints dry on the paper. I *love* publicity. Even bad publicity is good in my kind of business, Carl." I moved my arms over in Frank's direction. "Frank? You want the honors? Believe me, I'll be sure to mention your name on the news, too."

"Relax, Harry," Cochran said with a satisfying grin, "nobody's cuffing or taking you in, but until we get more leads on this, don't leave town."

"Right. Did you hear that line at the movies, Carl? Okay, if that's it, I've got work to do, especially now that *somebody's* killed one of my major leads. Nice seeing you," I said, using my cane to point at the door. "You can let yourself out." I knew I was pissing in the wind.

"Well...not just yet," Cochran said, directing his attention to Sam, now. "There's one more matter to take care of in regards to your silent friend here, and I'm afraid the evidence is a little more compelling on him." Cochran reached under his coat and pulled a pair of handcuffs off his belt and tossed them on the desk. "I'll be using *these,* now."

Frank finally got up off his ass and strutted over behind Sam's chair. Sam crossed his legs, reached in his shirt pocket, pulled out a pack of cigarettes, and lit one up. "Stand up, pretty boy," Frank said, "you're under arrest for the murder Robert Petrie."

Sam kept his seat, but I didn't. I walked around the desk and put myself between Sam and Frank. "Whoa, not so fast. Where's your evidence, Carl? If it's as laughable as the shit you were throwing at me, I'm afraid you and dip-shit here are going to be the laughing stock of homicide." I glanced to the nimrod sitting across from me. "Frank already is, of course."

"You always were a pain in the ass, Stumbaugh," Detective Cochran said. "Okay, just for you. First, there's a warrant out for Mr. Samuel Wolfkill for assault and battery, public disturbance, and property damage at the Vegas Club." He pulled a folded sheet of paper from his inside pocket and waved it in front of my face. "Wanna read it, Harry?"

"Yeah," I said, snatching it from his hand. I skimmed it and verified what he said. "This is bullshit. I've got witnesses that will testify that Sam was provoked and defending himself. The ones that started the fight are the ones liable for any property damage that may have occurred, which should amount to about fifty cents from what I've seen of the décor in the Vegas Club. Besides, you're homicide, and nothing on this warrant says anything about a murder."

"Fuck you and your witnesses." He pulled out another folded sheet and handed it to me. "Here's your warrant for Petrie's murder, and I've already got a search warrant for Wolfkill's place, and it's getting tossed as we speak."

"As we speak, asshole," repeated Frank. The shit-eating grin was back.

"Well that's reassuring. I'm sure whatever evidence is missing you'll be sure to provide. That's how you do things, isn't it

Cock-ran." I went back behind my desk and grabbed the phone with one hand and pointed at Cochran with the other. "You just hold it." I turned to Sam. "Don't move; keep your seat." I dialed a number and it answered immediately. "This is Harry. I need to speak to Cameron; it's an emergency. Yes, I'll hold."

"Jesus H. Christ, Harry. Epperson, huh? Bringing in the big gun? You must be worried." Cochran waved the two warrants in my face again. "No high-dollar shyster's gonna help your buddy this time. I've got the *facts* on my side."

I gave him the finger. "Cameron? Hey, Harry here. Yeah, good to talk to you, too. Listen, I've got a couple of corrupt cops here in my office…how'd you guess? Yeah, it's that pig Cochran and his lap dog. I know, I know…" I gave a hearty laugh for effect. "…anyway, they've done a frame job on Sam. Yeah, I'm the pretty one. They've got warrants for his arrest and they say they have a search warrant for his apartment…murder. Yeah, and they're about to take him down to the precinct. Could you come over before they get out the door? Yeah, I don't trust 'em either. Thanks buddy, I owe you one." I hung up and smiled. "He'll be right over."

Cochran stepped up to Sam, "Stand up, Wolfkill," he ordered, waving a hand up, "and put your hands behind your head while Frank frisks you. I'm not waiting on some fucking lawyer to get here; I've got things to do." He grinned at Sam and said, "You can go easy or hard, Wolfkill, your choice."

"*Please* make it the hard way, *Mr.* Wolfkill," mimicked Frank.

Sam looked my way and I nodded. He stood and placed his hands behind his head, and the first thing Frank found was the .45 tucked in his waistband. "Well looky here," he said, holding up the automatic for Cochran to see. "Now where'd you get a piece like this, Wolfkill?"

"Uncle Sam," I said, "something you wouldn't know about, Frank. Give it to me, I'll hold it."

Frank said, "Fuck you, cripple. It's evidence." He edged closer to Sam. "What's the matter, Wolfkill, cat got your tongue?

Well, don't worry. We'll have you singing like a bird once we get you back to headquarters. Won't take no time at all. Short and sweet."

My partner's eyes and mine met midway between *short* and *sweet*.

"Leave it," Cochran said. "This is the one I'm interested in." He reached inside Sam's jacket and pulled the .38 from the holster. "Well, what do you know, a .38, just like yours, eh Harry?" I'm going to need your .38 too, so I can match the bullets against the ballistics of the one that's in Abner's head."

"Fine," I said, "I've got more." I unloaded my .38, set it on the desk, then I shoved the bullets across the desk to Frank, but handed the gun to Cochran. "We don't want the children playing with guns," I said, grinning at the nimrod.

The front door opened with a flourish and three suits marched in with Jenny and Kate Culpepper trailing behind in step.

"The cavalry's arrived, Cochran. Did I forget to mention their offices are next door?"

They all came through the reception room and into my office, which filled up quicker than the First Baptist Church on a Sunday morning. Cameron and two of his associates formed a small semi-circle around Sam, Cochran, and Frank, while the girls stayed back by the office door. Jen made eye contact with me, and I could tell she was concerned, but she also wanted to talk to me. I wish I could say it was great telepathic powers on my part, but she mouthed the words so that anybody standing in the building across the street could have figured out what she said. I just nodded once. That was our secret code.

There was no doubt about who took over once Cameron was in the room. He stood about a head taller and a hundred and fifty pounds lighter than Detective Cochran. I considered him a health nut since he worked out in a gym every day and trimmed the fat off his T-bone steaks. His suit, tie, and shoes costs more than three-months rent on my office, and he was the most ruthless, smooth-talking son-of-a-bitch that ever hit a courtroom in the state of Texas. When he smiled, sparkles of light reflected off his teeth. He was also my biggest employer since I did all the investigative work for his firm. Thus, my high-end clients.

Epperson patted Cochran one time, with affection, on the back. "Well, Detective Cochran, such a pleasure to see you again. How have you been? Beaten any old ladies or children with a phonebook, lately?" He inquired.

"Fuck you, Epperson," Cochran answered, shrugging his shoulder away from the lawyer's hand, "I don't have time for this bullshit. Let's get you booked, Wolfkill. Off we go."

"Oh, no, Detective Cochran," Epperson said stepping in between the detective and Sam, "fuck *you*. I'd like to see all the warrants, and I need an opportunity to speak to my client privately before you take him to police headquarters. And, by the way, I'd like to see the arrest warrants *and* the search warrant for his apartment." He turned to Sam and shook his hand. "Hi, Sam. Missed you at the gym this morning." He nodded at his two associates. "Randy, Simon, if the two of you don't mind escorting the detectives into the reception area and keeping them company, I need a little time with my client to get the *real* facts of the case."

Cochran handed over the warrants and said, "This is a professional courtesy on my part gentlemen. You've got five minutes, counselor, then we're coming to get him."

Epperson smiled and said, "I'll take whatever time I need, detective. You wouldn't want this thrown out of court just because you didn't afford the proper due process of law to my client, would you?"

The girls stayed behind with the three of us, making a cozy little group, while Epperson examined the warrants. I informed him that we were working on a high profile case and couldn't go into details or names, but I did let him know that at some point, it might be necessary for him to get involved. Then, Sam started things off telling his side of the story about the events from last night and leading up to his visit and conversation with Kate Culpepper today. I threw in my two-bits about my visit to Sam's this morning and then I slid out the trash can for Epperson to see. He tossed the warrants on the desk with a grunt, then took a whiff of the chloroform from the shirt and wrinkled his nose.

"That's nasty stuff," he said. "Now, Miss Culpepper could you fill in the blanks in your own words for us?"

The girls now occupied the two wing-back chairs, and Jenny leaned over and patted Kate's hand, giving her reassurance. "Go ahead, sweetie, tell them everything. Including what you whispered to me when we came in the office with Mr. Epperson's associates."

Kate nodded, and with confidence and without hesitation, she recalled her own rendition of the night's events, plus how she ended up working at the club. It disgusted me and pissed me off to no end. Regardless of how this case ended, I was going to add the Vegas Club to my things to take care of in the future list.

Epperson never interrupted and waited until she was completely done before questioning her. "Very good, and lastly, would you please reveal the confidential contents of your final conversation with the beautiful Miss McClain? The lawyer asked with a smile. "I have a feeling this will be our coupe d'tat---after we shut down that irreputible strip joint."

"I'm with you on that, counselor," I tossed in.

Kate said, "The two men in the suits that came in and held Sam down…the one's I told you about. It was them."

"Be more specific, please," Epperson instructed.

Kate nodded in the direction of the reception room. "It was Detective Cochran and the other man that's with him that came in and took control of things."

"Bastards," I said, "I knew it."

"Yes, they are," added Epperson quietly. "But there's still some unsolved mysteries here. What happened to Sam afterwards? How did he get home? Who drove him to his apartment? It wasn't

Cochran, was it, Miss Culpepper?"

Kate shook her head. "No, but there were two other men that stepped out from the crowd that I hadn't noticed before. They came out of nowhere. Both took an arm and dragged Sam outside without anybody saying a word. Through the front door."

"And no one stopped them?" I asked.

"No," she answered. "Matter of fact, no one even tried. "It was almost like everyone knew not to mess with them."

"How'd they look? You don't think they were with Cochran?" Epperson asked. "How were they dressed?"

"No, not with the police at all. Suits, well cut. Expensive. They were good sized men, too."

I asked, "Did you follow them outside?"

"No, I wish I would have, though. If I had..."

"Nothing would be different, my girl. Not to worry." Epperson glanced my way. "Harry? Any ideas? Friend or foe?"

I thought about the phone call I received after Cochran and Frank got here. "*Yes,*" I said, delivering the non-answer with a grin. There was no way I was going to bring Epperson into this circle. "For your own protection on this deal, Cameron, this is where *deniability* will do you more good than harm."

"Okay, then I assume we're talking *friends*, unless you say otherwise," Epperson said.

I stayed quiet.

"Very good. Sam? Anything to add to all this?" Epperson asked.

He shook his head at first, then said, "Shit, you're not going to like this Harry. That check you gave me...I left it in my chair, and if Cochran's men are searching my place..."

Epperson held up a hand, "Not to worry. How much was the check for?"

"Twenty-four hundred," stated Sam.

Epperson whistled. "Jesus, Harry, what kind of client have you got here?"

"Well," I said, popping my knuckles to make a point, "you're not the only paying customer that hires me, you know, Cameron."

"Perhaps you should start shoving business my way, then," he answered good-naturedly. "Which bank?"

"Republic," I answered.

He nodded at the phone, "Call and stop the payment. I'll send Randy and Simon over to Sam's place after Cochran leaves. Sam, write down your address and give me the key to your apartment. Anything else of value there we need to check on?"

"Just my Silver Star," he said, "it's in the nightstand drawer next to the bed. I don't want them putting their hands on it."

There was a knock on the door and then Cochran barged in. "Time's up, Epperson. Cuff him, Frank," he ordered.

Epperson said, "Before we go, and yes I'll be coming with you, I need to remind you of a few..."

"Fuck you, counselor, I don't need you to remind me about anything that has to do with my job. Come on, hurry up Frank."

Epperson stepped up unafraid, nose to nose with Cochran. "Well, since we have a room full of witnesses, I'll add this anyway. I'm fully aware of your reputation, Detective Cochran, and I see no cuts or bruises on my client." He smiled. "So there should be none that occur while in your custody. As his attorney, I've advised him, and I'm telling you now, he will not talk to you so there's no reason for interrogation. I'll have him out on bail before the day is done."

"Is that all, *counselor*? Cochran said, while Frank finished cuffing Sam's hands behind his back.

"No it's not," Epperson said, "thank you for asking, Detective Cochran."

"What the hell is it, then? Not that it's going to matter."

"Inventory of Mr. Wolfkill's apartment. He left a check for a rather large amount in his chair, and he has the prestigious Silver Star Medal for heroism that he was awarded while defending our country in the Pacific. Both of those items better be in his apartment when my associates arrive there in a matter of minutes. If they are not…well, I'll leave it to your limited imagination."

I wish I could talk like that. I thought I saw steam spewing from Cochran's ears.

Chapter 17

I was enjoying the peace and quiet of my office, knowing it was going to be short-lived. I fired up a Lucky, filled my lungs with sweet smoke, propped my feet on the desk, and reveled in the moment. I checked my watch and realized it had been only twenty-four hours since the honorable Senator John Doe had graced the portals of my humble abode and enhanced my life. In that short period of time, I'd dropped ten g's in the old bank account, created, dissolved, and gave life again to a newly formed partnership, which I think would be a good thing to talk to Sam about as soon as he got out of jail. I've talked to the head of the Dallas mob; consorted with the two most corrupted cops in the city; watched my on-again partner hauled off in cuffs for murder; dallied with a socialite that hates gin rummy, but probably deals underhanded poker games, and to top it off, I've got two dead bodies hanging around my neck. Not a bad day's work, if I do say so myself. And, oh yeah, I wasn't any closer to finding out if my client was a cop-killer or a walking miracle. What the hell, it took God seven days to create the birds and the bees and man. I've still got six left.

Deciding I'd done enough commiserating over the good old days, it was time to get some things sorted out, and I needed to put my lovely assistant back to work. So instead of yelling this time, I picked up the phone and buzzed Jenny; I didn't need to be told twice about improper etiquette. "Miss McClain, could you and Miss Culpepper please come into my office?"

"*Much* better," Jenny said, "I can't believe you yelled at me that way, and in front of clients, of all things. It was so *rude.*"

I wonder how long this is going to perpetuate itself.

"Just get your sweet ass in here, Doll Face. We've got work to do," I said. As far as I remembered, I was still the boss around here.

They came in together with Jenny leading the way, notepad in hand, both taking the wingbacks across from me. "Have you heard from Sam, yet?" Kate asked, before she even got settled in.

I nodded. "Uh, not from Sam, but Cameron called me. He said Cochran was trying to squeeze him out of the loop, and he wanted to know if I still had any pull left at HQ. So I called an old friend, the Captain of Detectives, Dan DeRita. He has the same love for Cochran as I do."

"And?" Kate asked.

"And…he's going to get back with me and Epperson as soon as he finds out what's going on. Now you don't worry Miss Culpepper, with ol' Cam and Captain DeRita there, it'll be okay. Trust me, Sam can take care of himself."

She didn't look very assured by my words and to be honest, there was some concern on my side too. It would be no problem for Cochran to have Sam disappear into a broom closet somewhere while the pencil pushers got lost in their own maze of bureaucratic paperwork. Did it myself when the need arose. But in the meantime, Cochran and Megs could be getting their jollies working Sam over with a phonebook.

I also saw that Kate was a mess and needed some of Jenny's mothering. I still had questions for her, but knew this wasn't the right time. Her knight in shining armor was in the pokey, and I was sure she had nowhere else to go and was worried about where she would be when we closed up shop for the night. I took it upon myself to reassure her. "Kate, first off, I don't want you to worry your pretty little head about what's going to happen to you or to Sam. I've already got both bases covered."

Jenny smiled and laid a hand across Kate's. "See, I told you

Harry would take care of things."

"Sam's got the best attorney money can buy in his corner, and you've got…well, me and Jenny." I snubbed out a smoldering butt and fired up another. "So, how are you at a real waitressing job, Kate?" I asked. I started to add, *with your clothes on*, but didn't think she was ready for my sense of humor yet. She's still a little fragile from what I can detect.

She smiled weakly. "My family owns a restaurant in Pecos. I worked in it since I was tall enough to swipe down a table. Why?"

"Perfect," I said, "I got in touch with the counter manager at Walgreen's just a little bit ago. I called in a favor and he's agreed to give you a try. Working the morning/afternoon shift, kiddo. You up for it? It doesn't pay much, but with your looks and smile the tips will compensate your hourly wage. You start at five A. M. in the morning, and…" Before I could finish the sentence, she'd already jumped up from her chair, ran around the desk, and wrapped her arms around my neck, applying a choke hold that left me short of breath.

"Oh, thank you, thank you! Thank you, Mr. Stumbaugh! This is all happening so…so fast!"

"It's okay," I mumbled, unlocking her arms from around my neck and taking a healthy intake of desperately needed oxygen. I patted her on the back with one hand and eased her away from my chair with the other. "No problem, just don't let me down. I eat breakfast there every morning, you know."

"Oh, I won't! I won't!" She exclaimed.

Jenny's eyes were starting to mist up and she mouthed, *thank you*. "And, you'll stay with me," she said, "until we find you a decent place to stay. We can go apartment shopping tomorrow!"

I mouthed back, *oh, goody-goody*. "Okay, okay," I said, "enough of all this. We've got work to do. Since Sam is vacationing on the city's dime, the two of you are gonna have to fill the void." I gave Jenny another one of my looks. "Apartment hunting is not on the priority list until after I get Sam back on the job. Agreed?"

"Agreed," they both sang in unison.

I checked my watch again. Suddenly, I was running out of time. Funny how that happens so quickly. I nodded to Jen. "Jen, I need the two of you to go over the court house before they shut down for the day. It's after three, and they think they're on banker's hours over there. Do whatever it takes with the clerks to get the info. If you need to cut in line, do that pouty-mouth thing you do when you want something. It always works on me."

"What *exactly* do you want, Harry?" Jen asked, suspiciously.

"I want background on Doe when he was a lawyer, before he started serving the public for the greater good. I want to know his batting average. What kind of clients did he have and who they were. Anything unusual with his cases. Red flags. Something that jumps out at you. You know the routine. Did he get the same judge too often? Is this guy as squeaky clean as he wants me to believe? Got the drift?"

"Gotcha," she said, scribbling and keeping up. "Anything else?"

"Yeah, if a name shows up more than once, I want the name and address."

"And?" Jenny probed, pencil poised for action again.

I smiled. The girl knows me like a book. "*The Dallas Morning News.* Get with Albert Day, one of the editors up there. He'll help you out. Tell him you want to knock the dust off the archives. I want everything you can pull about the Santa Fe payroll heist that took place on October 27th, 1932."

With Jenny and Kate out of the office, once again there was peace in the valley, but I was about to start stirring the waters. Calls to make. Doe, Gamboa, DeRita, Epperson. Time to tie up some loose ends.

Doe first. I called his number at the Adolphus, but he wasn't Johnny-on-the-spot this time. I almost hung up after the fifth ring before he came on the other end.

"Senator Doe," he said.

"Private Investigator Stumbaugh. How's it going, Senator?"

"Harry!" He exclaimed. "What the hell's going on? I haven't heard from you all day. *You* tell me what's going on?"

"We need to have another face to face tonight, Senator. There have been some…well, let's just say *interesting* events have taken place today. Are you good to meet around seven tonight?"

"I…well, I'm supposed to meet with my campaign manager at six-thirty here at the hotel…maybe I can be done by then…" he answered, as though unsure.

"Well, I suggest you make it happen. If we don't get some things ironed out, you're not going to have a campaign to worry about…or a job for that matter," I said, letting him know that there was some urgency.

There was hesitation on the senator's part, then, "Doesn't sound good, Harry. What have you got?"

"Not now, tonight, John."

He didn't push it. "I'll delay the meeting. Seven o'clock, here in my suite if that's okay?" Doe said. "You remember the number?"

I noticed that his tone was less cocky, with an added dash of concern.

Good.

"Yeah, gotta mind like a steel trap, 1449. Order bourbon and some steaks and all the trimmings. We'll eat and dine-in. I'm not sure if Sam will join us, but he might. Order a steak for him, too. We both like 'em well-done," I said.

"Where is he? Working a lead?"

"Kinda. Depends on how soon he gets out of jail."

"W-what?"

"See you at seven," I said quickly, and hung up. I didn't want to give explanations or start giving him any hints about the meeting. Ten grand or not.

Gamboa was next. There was no way to call him directly. Everything went through Eddy, if you could find him. I called the

Cairo Room and talked to the receptionist first, giving her my name and who I wanted to talk to. She put me on hold for almost five minutes before coming back. I waited, of course. She told me to leave a number and she'd have Eddy call me. Glad this wasn't life or death. Since I'm an upscale investigator, I've got *two* outside lines. I gave her my private number so I could use the office line to keep making calls.

I called DeRita next. "Hey Dan, any luck locating my boy, yet?"

He answered with a boom. "That son-of-a-bitch, Cochran! I swear, I'm gonna have his balls this time," DeRita said, obviously pissed to the max.

"Then that's a yes, I assume," I said.

"You won't believe this, Harry. It's like something out of the movies. They had him in an interrogation room upstairs in Vice, of all places. Cochran told them he needed a place to interrogate a possible cop-killer from Houston, and he wanted to take a run at him before the HPD boys got into town. Of course, they obliged him."

"Is he hurt?" I asked, pretty sure of what came next.

"Yeah, Harry, they worked him over pretty good. Messed his face up a bit, and he might have some cracked ribs. But, he must be one tough guy."

I grinned. "How bad did he hurt *them*?"

DeRita laughed. "I'd have given anything to see it. Megs was switching his cuffs from front to back. Your boy snatched his arm when he was free and did some jujitsu shit on him. Twisted his arm up behind his back till he was scratching the top of his head," DeRita chuckled, "tore his shoulder out of joint and broke the mother-fucker's elbow. They said you could hear the pop and Meg's screaming to high heaven down the block. Took six guys to pull your man off Megs. They thought they had a cop killer, of course, so they worked him over good."

"Where is he now?" I asked.

"We patched him up some here, but he needs to get his ribs checked out at the hospital. That'll be on our dime, courtesy of the city. He's sitting in my office with Cameron Epperson," he laughed again. "I love it."

"Shit could roll downhill on this one, Dan. Cochran's under your jurisdiction, you know," I cautioned.

"I'm not worried. This is it for Cochran. He shit in his own birthday cake this time. The boys upstairs have wanted his ass for a long time, and he's got some serious charges coming his way, finally. In legalese that'd be..." DeRita grabbed a sheet of paper from his desk, "you'll like this...if a public servant acting under color of his office or employment commits what is called *Official Oppression*," he read, "which is to intentionally subject another to mistreatment or to arrest, detention, search, seizure, dispossession, assessment, or lien that he knows is unlawful, his ass is grass. I added that last part." He tossed the document back on the desk. "I think that'll cover it, don't you? And by the way, your boy did get in one good punch on Cochran. Flattened his nose like pancake. Lots of blood. It was great."

"Don't know what you just said, but works for me. What kind of punishment goes with official oppression?" I asked, hoping it was the electric chair.

"Indefinite suspension for starters, then the D. A. will get in on the picture and drop the hammer. What have you got to offer?"

"Whatever it takes to get him off the streets." I didn't want to give too much away, but I needed to throw Dan a bone for watching after Sam. "There's more to all this, Dan. If this plays out right, the charges you've got against him won't amount to squat compared to what might be in the pipeline. I might have something that'll send him to Old Sparky."

"I'm listening," DeRita said. "What've you got, Harry?"

"Nothing solid yet, but hold on to your nuts, buddy. Shit's gonna start flying and you don't want to get caught standing in front of the fan. I'll give you a heads up, don't worry. So...Cochran and Megs, what happens next?"

"They're both suspended for now, but we'll be keeping an eye on them. Megs isn't going anywhere. He's laid up at the hospital in a body cast with his arm sticking straight out to his side like a railroad guard rail. He's messed up bad. I think they're trying to mash Cochran's nose back into place at Parkland's emergency room now. I'm looking forward to slappin' the cuffs on both of them."

"What about Sam? You droppin' the charges on the murder rap?"

"No, can't just yet, but considering the source and all that happened today, we're going to kick him out on bail, and take a much closer look at the case. From what Epperson says, it's all smoke and mirrors. No real evidence. I tend to agree if everything he says is true. I'm gonna need to talk to the Culpepper girl, too. Sam didn't want to involve her in anything, but Epperson reasoned with him."

"Oh, he's good alright. No doubt about that," I said. "You want me to come down with bail?"

"Nah, Epperson said he's got it covered," DeRita said. "Listen, Harry, I don't know what you've got cooking, but keep me in the loop, you hear?"

"I will, Dan, and I owe one. Big time."

"This one is my pleasure. Wanna talk to Sam? I can go get him," DeRita asked.

"No, just tell him and Epperson to meet me at the Adolphus about six-thirty if they can. If not, I'll see them at the office in the morning."

What I needed now was a call from Gamboa. I was hoping for some answers from him and Jenny before I met with Doe tonight. A picture of things was beginning to form in my head, but it still didn't put me any closer to knowing if Doe was for real or blowing smoke up my ass. Gamboa always has to be handled with kid gloves. Talking in circles. He gives you a round-about answer and you connect the dots. I didn't want to burn him as a source or a friend, but it might be time to throw out the rule book and just ask what I wanted to know. "Come on, Giovanni, call," I said to the phone.

I fired up another cigarette and the phone rang, but it wasn't the private line. *Shit.* "Stumbaugh Investigations," I answered.

"Harry! You're not going to believe this!" Jenny exclaimed. We're down at the courthouse going through Senator Doe's cases…really boring stuff if you ask me, but I think we found what you were looking for. Well, maybe you didn't…"

"Jenny, Jenny stop! You're driving me crazy here, girl. Just tell me what you've got," I ordered with a dash of pleading and whining together for effect.

Silence. "We've really got to talk about your manners, Harry. You've turned into this…"

I didn't know how much I could take of this. Retirement was beginning to look very good at this point. "Jen, please, just tell me. I don't have time for this. What do you have?"

Jenny giggled. "You should pay *me* to be the detective, Harry. You wanted to know if we found any names that we recognized or showed up more than once."

"And you're going to tell me, right? Today?"

No build up this time. "Harry, Doe worked for the law firm of Henshaw, Dozier, and Epps."

"Yeah? And?"

"And…Senator Doe was the attorney on record for one Robert Petrie. *Twice in 1943.*"

Chapter 18

Before hanging up from Jenny, I told her to go ahead and check in with Albert Day at the newspaper. I still wanted as much dope on the Santa Fe heist as possible, and if I had time, I even thought about dropping by their offices tomorrow. Just go straight to the horse's mouth. Why not? As far as the gold mine of information she gave me about the previous relationship between Doe and Petrie...well, I don't like being lied to and I don't like anybody trying to make a fool of me. Doe's been playing me like a well-tuned piano; however, $7500 dollars of *his* money in *my* bank account helps to ease the pain.

Gamboa still hadn't called, so he was either ignoring me, out of town, or breaking somebody's arm. I wasn't going to sit around doing nothing while I waited on him, so I decided it was time to untwist the circles of the past twenty-four hours. Since I was meeting with the senator tonight, I needed to have all my facts down pat. It was going to be a very uncomfortable visit for the amnesiac, and I was expecting a full ten-pucker-factor reaction from him by the time I was done saying my piece.

I love this job.

If he fessed-up and laid out the real facts, I'd consider keeping him as a client; but if he continued his lying ways, I was going to cut his ass loose. I planned to get to the end of this fractured mess whether it was on my dime or his. Actually, it'd still be his dime supporting my bad habits; he just won't be a client...whatever.

From the top desk drawer, I grabbed a notepad from the illegally obtained stockpile of Adolphus writing pads, one of their fine monogrammed pens, and started my list. That's how I do things. Make lists and see what fits where. It helps me focus through all the noise in my head.

After jotting it down, I fired up a Lucky and went over the list three more times, added more notes, a few answers, and question marks; but, I still didn't know any more than when I started. I had guesses and theories, but no real answers. At least I had something to go by. Something to mark off as time ticked away. Then, my private line finally rang. I waited until after the third ring and picked up. "This is Harry," I said, nonchalant as can be.

"My friend," Gamboa said, "I'm guessing you're as busy as the whores on Harry Hines on a Saturday night."

"Good analogy, Giovanni, except they're getting laid and I'm not, but good for *your* business, I assume."

Giovanni chuckled. "Only you, Harry. Only you. And, Sam?" Giovanni asked. "He is well?"

"He's not getting laid either, but I'm guessing you probably already know about his day."

"You give me too much credit, Harry. But, let me ask you this, my friend. The past twenty-four hours, have you any idea of what you've been doing? What I mean is, do you appreciate the hornets' nest you've stirred up?"

I doodled interchanging circles in the margins of my list. "You know me, Giovanni. If I see a nest, I'm gonna poke a stick at it…and I always have an appreciation for what gets stirred up. Sometimes, you get stung. Sometimes, you kill the wasps. But, I have a feeling you could give me a bigger stick. How about saving me some time and shoe leather, Giovanni?"

Small laughter. "You disappoint me, Harry. You've only been in this game for a day. I've been playing for twenty years."

Bingo. At the bottom of the list, I jotted down *20 yrs. + Doe +*

Giovanni and circled it. "Then, enlighten me, my friend," I said.

"No-o-o, *you* enlighten *me,*" returned Giovanni.

"Okay, then," I said, quietly.

I'll play the game you old fox.

"Cochran and Megs are involved in this extortion scam up to their necks. There's not a whole brain between the two of them, so there's no way they're the masterminds. Whoever's behind this has got brains and balls. It's no secret that they're dirty cops, and that makes them easy targets. Muscle. They're expendable. They're just not smart enough to know it."

"That's not bad, Harry, but way too easy," Giovanni said. "My youngest, Sophie, could have deduced that much. You know that."

Confirmed.

"Okay, let's move on to Abner Strong, then. Both of his boys, Moe and Curly, were involved in the heist. One got fried in Huntsville, the other most recently in an alley. Logic tells you ol' Abner was involved to a degree. I'm not sure about how much just yet, but I'll find out. Once again, he was expendable. Now you've got Abner, and both of his boys, all out of the picture. And, I doubt Cochran and Megs will make it to the weekend. Do you?"

"Leaving you where?" Giovanni asked, avoiding the last question.

More confirmation.

"Doe...and, of course, *you,* my friend. Or we wouldn't be having this conversation. Playing the game."

Hearty laughter this time. "Only you...is *that* all you have, Harry?"

Are you probing for information, you old fox, or leading me to the next square?

"No, I've got a little bit more. Doe and Petrie are connected. Doe was his attorney in '43. Which creates questions and adds spice to the game."

"Now *that's* good information! One worthwhile, my

investigator friend," Giovanni said, as though praising a child for good grades. "But, there's so much more, Harry. You've only just begun to scratch the surface."

I was growing tired of this. *Time to make my own move.*

"Then, Doe *doesn't* have amnesia, and somebody else is pulling the strings, I'm guessing. Doe or Mr. Big, whoever he or *she* is, is removing the expendable...*constituents*, so to speak."

Gamboa laughed, "Not a bad guess, but I'll neither confirm nor deny on any of what you just said. As I said, you've just begun. Let me ask you something, though. What drives people like Senator Doe, even table scraps like Cochran and Megs, to do the things they do?"

Confirmation.

"Power. Money," I answered without hesitation and enjoying the grin on my face he couldn't see. I scribbled the two words in the margins.

"Then, follow the power and the money. You keep doing what you do, Harry. I knew you were the right man for this. And by the way, Mr. Ruby has found his way back to Chicago for the time being, and his club will be closed by tomorrow. Certain things cannot be tolerated. You can mark him off your list, too. You still make lists, don't you? How many times was I on your list this time, Harry?"

What's in it for Gamboa? Sure as hell something. Sounds like he's either pulling the strings or finding a way out of the picture when it all goes down.

I was scrambling, writing as quick as I could, *keep doing what you do?* Who said that to me earlier today? I added two question marks. Then wrote, *knew you were the right man for this???* That deserved three question marks and a box around it. "Numbers six, seven, and eight," I said.

"I can visualize you writing frantically as we speak, Harry, but I'm disappointed. I thought I would be higher on the number scale."

I added checks to those three numbers. "Oh, you are now, my friend. I assure you," I said.

"Just continue to watch your back, as you always do, Harry. Perhaps, it is time to take the offensive position."

Shit, running out of space.

Another thing to add, *offensive position?*

What the hell?

I knew those were his parting words and the game for now was over, but I wanted to play just a little bit longer. "Thanks for taking care of Sam…back at the Vegas Club," I said casually, but anxious to hear his response.

That small, quiet laugh again. "I think you like the game, Harry." Silence. "He's a good man. I wish he would come work for me, but I'm afraid his scrupulous sense of patriotism would get in the way of business. And, he needs to take care of that little girl he's rescued and latched on to. Tell him he has my blessings…and Harry, go ahead and remove that one from your list too, my friend."

"You know me too well, Giovanni. That's what worries me."

Again with the small, quiet laugh… "Most people say that's what *scares* them. Only you, Harry. Only you."

I wrote, *Sam? Giovanni?*

Chapter 19

Time to take the offense, Gamboa said. Thought that's what I was doing. Cameron Epperson once told me I was *proactive,* attorney's jargon. The Chief of Dallas Police, Beck Minniweather, called it the *kick-ass mode.* I liked his term better. I ran back over the list again, the whole time thinking...offense, offense...kick-ass. Doe...kick-ass. *Tonight!* I wrote next to his name.

Now to be *proactive.* I dialed DeRita's number at police HQ, hoping he was available. Not only was he available, he picked up before the first ring was finished.

"Captain DeRita," he answered.

"Checking in, Dan. Anything new on Sam?" I asked, flipping to a clean sheet of paper on my writing pad and started doodling again. More intertwining circles.

"You know, normally I don't care much for attorneys, especially defense attorneys, but I kinda like ol' Epperson. Especially since we have the same affection for Cochran and Megs. I certainly wouldn't want to be the one opposing him in court."

"He's an alright Joe, as long as you're on the same side as him," I added. "And Sam?"

"Yeah, Epperson posted a five-hundred dollar bail for him just a few minutes ago. He gave me a call from downstairs. Probably walking out the front door now. I'm sure you'll hear from him soon, but I wouldn't plan on them meeting you tonight, though. Sam needs a few stitches and needs to get his ribs x-rayed. He's going to be one sore puppy, come tomorrow. I think Epperson's taking him to his personal doctor at Parkland. What bothers me is, with Epperson as Sam's new best friend, I smell a lawsuit in the air over the beating he took." There was some hesitation on DeRita's part to let that sink in. "Any help waylaying that idea would sure be appreciated," he added.

That caught me as funny. Suing the police department.

What for? Wrongful arrest? Police brutality? Used to be SOP. I thought I'd let that one hang for a bit, just for fun. "You got a pen and paper handy, Dan?" I said, instead. "I'm about to increase your caseload."

"You're going to make my life even more miserable than it already is, aren't you, Harry? You were right about shit rolling downhill." He chuckled, "It hasn't hit my front door yet, but I sure as hell can smell it coming. That fucker Cochran and his asshole buddy…well, never mind. Yeah, I'm ready. Shoot."

"Hell…I'm gonna make you a hero before this whole thing is done, DeRita. You remember earlier I told you I had some things working…well, I'm gonna unload some, not all, but some of it on you now."

"You gonna start dictating or keep jerking me off, Harry?"

"No foreplay? You've changed, DeRita. You're not as fun as you used to be."

"I didn't always wear captain's bars, either."

"Better you than me, pal. Okay, first off, word on the street is somebody's put hits out on your two buddies, Cochran and Megs. *They,* whoever they are, want them completely out of the picture. Don't want them singing the blues to the cops or anybody else about what they know."

"What the hell are you talking about, Harry? Singing about what? What street talk?"

"Just listen, while I talk." I fired up a Lucky. This had to be played just right. "And no, I don't know who sanctioned the hit, but my source is reliable enough. You can take that to the bank. Those two won't see the end of the week or get to church on Sunday if you don't put some kind of protective detail on them. Better yet, lock 'em up in isolation or some undisclosed location. The fingers on this are long and go mighty deep, I suspect."

"Shit. You talking about more department corruption, Harry?" DeRita asked, hoping he was wrong. "I don't like the way this is sounding. We're not gonna play word games, are we Harry.

I don't have the time or patience for that kind of bullshit anymore," DeRita said.

Keep to the facts.

"They're involved in the extortion of a...prominent citizen, let's say, and probably on the hook for at least two murders that I'm aware of. All in the last twenty-four hours."

"Shit. Like who? What *prominent citizen* are we talking about? What murder? Petrie? The one they tried to hang on your boy?"

"Yeah, for starters," I said, avoiding the prominent citizen part of the question.

"Figures. That's a weak-ass case if I've ever seen one. Who else?"

"Abner Strong. Name ring a bell?" I asked.

"Of course. The DOA from this morning. Cochran thought you and Sam were involved, told me he actually took your .38's down to ballistics to be tested against the bullet in Strong's head. I haven't received any paper work on it yet, since the two detectives on the case are...out of pocket right now. What's that all about? You laying that one off on Cochran and Megs too?

"The dots all connect, Dan, just listen. Does the name mean anything to you besides that?"

"We're playing word games, Harry, but I'll string along for now. Let me think...Strong...it's...uh...hey...an old case, right?"

I was impressed. The heist happened before DeRita came on board in Dallas. From El Paso, I think. "Yeah, very old. He had two sons that held up a Santa Fe armored truck..."

"Yeah, back in the thirties, wasn't it?" DeRita injected. "I remember. What do you mean *two* sons? They caught one...Strong...shit, Pete *Strong*, wasn't it? And sent him up-river to Old Sparky, right?"

"Right, and Cochran's the one that filled me in on all the details when I talked to him earlier this morning. Now Papa Strong's dead, and you'll love this, Dan. Robert Petrie and Pete

Strong were step-brothers." I stopped talking to let that little tidbit of information sink in.

"Shit."

"That's what I thought you'd say," I said. "There's more. Robert was suspected in the robbery, but Pete never gave him up in interrogation or in the pen. There was never any hard evidence against Petrie, so…he disappeared out of Dallas and hadn't surfaced around here until now. Not a good move on his part, wouldn't you say? Pete took the rap for killing two cops and Robert walked."

DeRita snapped his fingers. "DeBusk and Rodriquez…you don't mean…so you're telling me the old man, Pete, and Robert were all in on it? Holy cow, Harry! This is big stuff you've got here. This extortion racket you mentioned, that you're avoiding giving me a name on, Petrie and Papa Strong in on this, too?"

"More than likely, Dan. The dots are painting that picture," I confirmed.

"What's the connection with Cochran and Megs?"

I smiled. Every now and then I enjoyed doing something nice for the coppers. "Working on it. You might have better luck than me, though. That's why I'm telling you all this, Dan. Two heads cooperating on the same case makes sense to me. As long as we keep each other in the loop, that is."

"I'll show you mine, if you show me yours. I'd have come out looking like a fool letting all this get by me without a clue knowing what was going on. What else can you share?" DeRita ask, enthusiasm rising in his voice.

Best to have you as an ally, than opponent, old buddy. Having the resources of the Dallas PD behind me sure as hell wasn't going to hurt.

"I don't think old man Strong was ever considered a suspect in the heist itself, but there was a third man involved. Name's Ralph Morris. Might want to see what you can run down on him. I've hit a blank wall so far."

Kinda. This was as far as I was taking the captain on this line of information, for now.

"Okay," said DeRita. "I'll see what I can come up with. This is going back a long ways, though."

"And Dan...Curly and Moe are in this sewer pit up to their necks. Probably not the murders of DeBusk and Rodriquez, but after the fact. You know, that was a million dollar purse those boys high-jacked from Santa Fe, and the money's never been recovered, as far as I know. Pete never got his share, since spending ill-gotten gains in prison is frowned upon, and from what I've seen of Petrie, he sure as hell wasn't living the life of a millionaire, so..."

"So that leaves Ralph Morris living the high life," DeRita injected.

"Right, and I've still got some digging to do on that."

Time to bring this to an end.

"That enough for you to feed on for a while? Tying your two fair-haired boys to Strong and Petrie? A little extortion here, a little murder there." I asked, feeling a bit smug and proud of myself.

"It should fill my calendar for the rest of the day, at least. Probably all I have to do is twist the pinkie on Meg's broken arm, and he'll sing like a bird," DeRita said chuckling.

"Can I watch?" I asked. "I'd love to be there."

"No, I'm saving this for myself. You got any leads on this Morris character you'd like to share before I get started? You know anything about him?"

"Maybe, but I've got to keep it close to the chest right now. You work your end and I'll work mine. We'll see what turns up in the middle," I repeated, ready to get off the phone. "I think you've got enough on your plate for the time being. I'll be in touch, Dan."

"Do that, I'll do the same."

"And Dan," I added, "don't fret the lawsuit. Finalizing this case will separate the goats from the heroes. It'll never happen."

Normally, involving the cops on anything in my line of work is taboo, unless it is to my advantage, of course. The boys in blue usually gum up the works more than help and are reluctant to share their toys. I trusted DeRita, though. He was one of the few that stuck with me and had my back…before I was forced out of the department. I needed some inside help now, especially since this case was growing like a spider web and getting more complicated than my personal life. Of which there didn't seem to be much of lately.

My eyes drifted back to the list on my desk again. It was becoming like an old girlfriend I couldn't shake loose. The words and circles and squares were talking to me.

Gamboa. It keeps coming back to you and Doe, old friend.

I glanced up from the list and spotted the empty holster for my .38 hanging on one of the wingbacks across the desk, and it motivated me to take care of something I should have done earlier. I went into the adjoining office and opened the top drawer of the filing cabinet. I only kept two things in that drawer. Guns 'n' whiskey.

Good name for a country western band.

I grabbed the bottle of Jack Daniels by the neck, an extra .38, along with a small .25 caliber, and ankle holster I kept in there, and then returned to my office. I holstered the .38, looped it around my shoulders, and wrapped the .25 on my ankle.

All snug now.

Sam liked the freedom of keeping his gun on his hip, but I was old school. I liked the feel of the holster against my side. I liked the pressure against the inside of my arm. Reassurance. I checked the time. Still plenty of time before meeting Doe. Pouring myself a shot, I settled back with my feet on the desk, closed my eyes, and took myself back. Six years ago…*Gamboa.*

With WWII one for the history books, the fall of 1946 had the air of fresh victory, new found world dominance for the U. S., and new life for the cities. Dallas was alive with returning vets ready to fall back into a normal lifestyle at home and searching the job market. I'd no doubt that the country was about to experience a baby boom unlike anything the nation had never experienced before. If I'd been the one schlepping over the hedges of Germany or island hopping on Pacific Ocean beaches for years, it'd be six months before I let my old lady out of bed. If I had an old lady, which I didn't. While the boys were overseas doing their part, I was fighting my own war against crime in the canyons and alleys of the Dallas metropolis as a homicide detective. With half the male population in Europe and the Solomon Islands, you'd think the crime rate would be down, but no such luck. Just a lack of manpower to enforce it.

My shift was done for the day, and I'd just wrapped up a double homicide in the "M" district of town, and decided I deserved to treat myself with a Jack and Coke at the Adolphus Hotel. Of course, this was nothing new. I treated myself to a Jack and Coke at the Adolphus every night, so it wasn't really all that special. At least not until the fat man showed up.

I settled in at my favorite table in the bar outside the French Room and ordered my drink, when I saw him approach. He was heavy set, but carried himself well. He wore an expensive black suit, white shirt with no tie, and black loafers with tassels. He needed a shave. I didn't know him, but he looked like a wiseguy to me. The muscle walking lock-step two feet behind him and the large lump beneath his armpit, covered by his coat, were my first clues.

Probably a .45.

My .38 had a smoother fit. Fat Man wasn't packing any heat from what I could see, but his eyes were on me. Watching me, watching him. Slowly, I straightened up in my chair and unbuttoned my coat.

Fat man stepped up to my table, hands opening the flaps of his jacket showing me he was clean. He nodded to the muscle and said, "Wait for me at the bar, Eddy. I'll be fine." The muscle left for the bar, but he gave me a glancing look, as though to say,

Don't fuck this up.

"May I sit down, Detective Stumbaugh?" Fat Man asked,

pointing to an empty chair across from me.

"It's a free country," I said.

Fat Man settled his bulk into the chair; he didn't offer his hand and neither did I. "Yes it is," he said, "and I'm thankful for that."

The waitress I ordered from returned with my Jack and Coke and turned to my new friend. "A drink for you, sir?" She asked.

"He won't be here long enough for that," I said, my eyes on Fat Man as I spoke.

"No, my dear, thank you," he answered politely for himself.

"Wave if you want a refill, Harry," she said and left.

"My name is Giovanni Gamboa, and I realize this is awkward for you, Detective Stumbaugh. However, I've made some inquiries about who I should speak to about a certain matter, and your name came up frequently."

The Kingpin of the Dallas mob is checking me out? What the hell?

"I'm flattered. Was it from some of your former associates I put behind bars?" No response, just a grin. "And what kind of matter could you possibly have to discuss with me?" I asked, with obvious disinterest.

"Detective Stumbaugh, I've learned that you are a man who is respected by your peers, and yes, even the criminals you've arrested in the past have spoken highly of your fairness...but they also include your bulldog investigations and determination to nail the bad guy...but most important to me, you're *untouchable.* You're not on the take, unlike some of your fellow officers. And I understand your proficiency with a weapon is outstanding...and deadly."

I was unimpressed. "What do you *want,* Mr. Gamboa? I know you're not here just to blow smoke up my ass, and I hope I don't offend you by telling you right now that I'm not interested in whatever it is you're selling," I said. "Like you said, I don't have my hand in anybody else's pocket, but my own and an occasional girlfriend or two."

"And colorful. May I ask you a question then? And I'll get to the point of my visit, Detective."

I nodded. "If it'll hurry things along, sure. The ice in my drink is melting, so make it fast. I'm particular about who's at the table when I drink."

"Very good," Gamboa said smiling. "What would you do if you were threatened...subtly, by an *opponent*, let's say?"

"I get that every day, Gamboa. Every time I put the cuffs on an *opponent*. Most of the time, it's some asshole blowing off steam, trying to show off for the other losers within ear shot. Letting his mouth charge more than his ass can backup. But I'm always watching my back, Mr. Gamboa. Always."

"Are you married, Detective?"

"No, and you probably know that much about me already, but I'm not interested in discussing my personal life with *you*. Word games bore me," I said, getting impatient with this guy. "Are we close to the goal line on this conversation, yet?"

"Indulge me a moment, Detective Stumbaugh, and I don't mean to get personal. Let's assume that you are married and have children. If someone threatened your *family* to get to you. Then what would you do?"

"Cut off his balls and feed them to him." I didn't see any reason to elaborate.

"Exactly as I would do. And if it were your *daughters* that were threatened?" The mobster said softly.

"Feed them to him one at a time, cut off his pecker, and give it to him for dessert." No further elaboration needed for that statement either. "Have you been threatened, Mr. Gamboa? Do you wish to file an official complaint with the police? Is that what this is about? I thought that a man in...your line of work...took care of your own problems," I said, wanting this conversation to be done. Sitting across the table from the head of organized crime in Dallas was not a way to enhance my career.

Gamboa nodded. "I'm a simple man who owns a restaurant, Detective. However, there is a code among us...Italians. No retaliation against another man's family. Regardless of how heinous of a crime may have been committed among us. That is the cardinal sin and to my knowledge it has never been broken, but..."

"Very honorable," I injected. The look on Gamboa's face told me he wasn't a man accustomed to being interrupted.

"In its way, yes. However, when my family is threatened by one of *your* fellow detectives, it becomes another matter. It is not good..." Gamboa hesitated as though considering the right word, "to...let me put it this way. We have the same code about law enforcement, believe it or not. This is not the old days of Al Capone and such animals. Those days are past. Inflicting pain or death to the police is not good business. To the point Detective Stumbaugh, I wish for you to pass along a story to a Detective Carl Cochran for me."

Cochran, I should have known.

"Is he the cockroach that threatened your girls?" Unfortunately, he finally had my attention. And I think he knew it.

"Yes, he and his friend came to my establishment to eat this past week. He had too much to drink, began talking loud, and became very brave. Some of my associates had to remove him from the restaurant. Quite embarrassing, but his final words out the door referred to my daughter's...heritage. The implication was that he'd hate to see them picked up on prostitution charges off Harry Hines one night soon. I take such threats seriously, Detective."

I shook my head, tightening my jaw. I took a drink from my Jack and Coke. No need letting good whiskey get watered down. Gamboa watched me with a slight grin. "Mr. Gamboa, in spite of our differences...we too have a code among our *family*. We don't deliver messages to another cop from...other families. I could take steps with my superiors to..."

Gamboa waved me off. "No, Detective Stumbaugh, that won't be necessary." He stood from the table and before he had time to adjust his coat, the muscle stood behind him. "A pleasure to meet you, Harry Stumbaugh. I appreciate your time."

"Can I ask, how old are your girls, Mr. Gamboa?" His face lit up like a Christmas tree and I knew it was the right question.

"Sophie, my youngest and biggest heartache is a freshman at Highland Park High School. My oldest is a senior and has a full scholarship to UT. I'm very proud of both of them. They are my life, Detective Stumbaugh. Children are a wonderful thing."

Gamboa nodded towards the muscle. "My friend here has sons, two of them. His oldest, Eddy Jr. returned from doing his service in the Pacific. Constant worries for the past two years as you can imagine."

I was afraid that the pair was going to pull out their wallets and start showing me family pictures. "I understand," I said. "Thank your son for his service, for me," I said to the muscle. I got a nod and that was it. Must be mute.

"Come, Eddy. We need to let Detective Stumbaugh finish his Jack and Coke." And with that, they were gone.

A week had almost passed and Cochran was still living and breathing, to my surprise. I really expected to hear about him being found in a ditch somewhere smoking his pecker like it was a cigar, but no such luck. I was juggling four homicide cases at the same time, so Cochran's fate wasn't a top priority with me; but every time I saw him in the squad room, I knew I was looking at a dead man walking.

Then, on a Thursday afternoon of the same week, Cochran hauled in a young Italian looking kid into the squad room, maybe seventeen or eighteen max, one hand under the armpit guiding him along at a quick clip so that the boy's tiptoes barely touched the ground. He snatched a phonebook off a nearby desk with the other hand and marched his suspect towards an interrogation room. Megs was on Cochran's heels, mimicking his partner by grabbing a phonebook from another desk.

I stared at the interrogation room door for a full minute and then, made my decision. I walked in unannounced and my timing was perfect, for the perp, that is. The kid was handcuffed to the chair, totally defenseless, and Cochran and Megs stood over him on either side of his chair, phonebooks poised to rain down.

"Put the phonebooks down," I ordered. "*Now.*"

Cochran displayed no surprise or alarm at my sudden appearance, matter of fact, he smiled. "Fuck you, Stumbaugh. You tend to your business and I'll tend to mine. So either take your pansy ass outside or grab a phonebook, either way don't' make a shit to me."

"Me either," repeated Cochran's parrot, "don't make a shit either way."

The kid looked like he was about to piss all over himself, and his eyes were all over me, wide and pleading for help. "This kid a mass murderer or something, Carl? He looks pretty mean to me, too. Must be, for somebody as important as you to give him all this attention. Megs has the yellow pages, appropriately so, and you've got the white. Color coordinating?"

"He's *connected,*" Cochran spat. "He's related to the king wop in town. Start with the little fish, work your way up to the top. Work your way up the ladder one rung at a time. That's how you have to do it sometimes, Stumbaugh."

Shit. Sometimes doing something stupid is the right thing to do.

"Wow. That's original, Carl. What are the charges? You had to have a reason to bring him in. Manslaughter? Bank robbery? Wait, let me guess, kidnapping."

"Shoplifting," Megs said, as though solving the major crime of the day.

"Wow," I repeated. "On a roll, huh? Jackin' up your arrest numbers again, I see." I turned my attention to the kid. "Did you shoplift, like he said? Best tell me the truth," I said, nodding, trying to get a message to the kid that he needed to be honest with me if he wanted to walk out of here in one piece.

"You trying to take over my investigation, Stumbaugh?"

Cochran growled. "You want me to start steppin' on *your* toes? Your cases? I've got this and I don't need your fuckin' help."

"You couldn't handle my cases, Carl. They're real crimes...like *homicide,* remember? That's what it says on the office door. *Homicide Department.* I must have missed the small print that said *Shoplifting Too.*" I glanced over in Megs's direction. "That's *too,* with two o's, Frank, in case you were confused."

He's so easy. Say something besides, "fuck you, Stumbaugh."

"Fuck you, Stumbaugh," Megs snapped.

Ignoring the parrot, I returned to the boy. "Did you?"

"Yes sir," he said softly."

"What'd you take?" I asked.

"Two packs of cigarettes."

"Wow. Master criminal, huh? What kind?" I asked, close to wrapping up the interrogation.

"Camels. And I told *him* that, too. There's nothing left to confess about!"

Back to Cochran, "Connected? To who, to what, Carl? A shoplifting ring?" I asked.

"*Conneted,* asshole." He turned on the kid, "Tell the *detective* your name, kid," Cochran ordered, eyes still on me.

"Gamboa. Alexis Gamboa," the kid answered.

Cochran grinned. "Now tell him the name of your *uncle,* Alexis."

The kid hesitated, as though afraid to utter the name. Then, "Giovanni Gamboa."

Oh shit, Carl, what have you done?

"So, let me get this right, Carl. You've hauled into interrogation the nephew of the biggest crime boss in Dallas on a C Class misdemeanor. And you and your sidekick here, are going to work over a teenager with phonebooks to progress up a mythical ladder of crime you've dreamed up. Do I have this right?" I asked with amazement.

"Right," answered Megs.

I shook my head. "If I were you boys…I'd hold on to my balls."

"What do you mean, Stumbaugh? Fuck you. You think you're so high and mighty and know everything," Megs spat. "Like Carl said, take your pansy ass outside and let the big boys handle this."

I grinned. "Hold on to your nuts, Frank." I retrieved the handcuff key from my pocket and walked around the table to cut loose the kid. The kid's mouth slipped into a slight grin. He knew exactly what I was talking about.

Cochran shook a threatening finger at me. "You touch that kid, Stumbaugh, and I swear I'll beat you down like you've never had before."

I unlatched the left-hand cuff, ignoring Cochran. "I'm not cuffed to a chair like the others you beat on Cochran. I can fight back."

The detective took a step forward. "I'm warning you, Stumbaugh," he threatened again.

I finally looked up, giving the fool my attention and made a point of checking him up and down from head to toe. "Okay Carl. Let's make a comparison here." "You're an overweight fat-ass with short stubby arms that starts breathing heavy when you start shoving donuts down your throat. I'm younger, fitter, and can whip your ass any day of the week and you know it. Hell, you and your idiot partner both know it, so waylay with the threats. Believe it or not, I'm trying to save your sorry ass. *And* for your information, *I'm* the one looking at a dead man, not you. Want me to tell you why, Carl? *I* got sidelined by *the* Giovanni Gamboa about a week ago."

That was a stupid thing to say.

"Yeah, that's right. Approached me right on the street. Him and his *associate*. Know what that's like, Carl? Very uncomfortable, that's what. Want me to tell you *why*, Carl?"

Shouldn't have said that either.

I stopped, but there was no backing down now. I let the foot-in-the-mouth-syndrome take its natural course.

"You what?" Cochran said with no attempt to hide his surprise. "You *talked* to a wiseguy? About what?"

"You," I said, letting that sink in.

"M-me? What the hell are you talking about?"

"Getting drunk in his restaurant. Trash-talking his daughters. Calling them whores." I walked around to the other side of the kid's chair and unlocked the other cuff. "Don't move," I snapped.

"I didn't!" Cochran started.

"He wanted me to give you a message, but I refused because that would be crossing the line, *unethical*. Know what that means, Carl?" I was pissed and words rolled off my tongue like a downhill skier. "He wanted me to tell you a story about a man that threatened his family once..."

Cochran hitched up his pants, an obvious move of false bravado. "Yeah, so what, he don't scare me. You go back and tell your wop friend that he don't scare me. He's the one that should be scared of *me*," Cochran bragged.

"He cut the guy's balls off and shoved them down his throat until he swallowed them, one at a time, Carl. In front of the wife. Then, he called the ambulance so he wouldn't bleed to death. He wanted him alive...to remember. You're married aren't you Carl? Think your wife would enjoy watching that?"

"Probably," the kid whispered.

I cuffed him on the shoulder. "Shut up and get up," I told the kid, "and come with me. I'm not done with you, yet. I'm not forgetting that you're a thief. I've got something in mind for you that's going to be a lot worse than what you were facing." I jabbed a finger at Cochran and Megs. "You two better drop this little campaign you're on, or you'll be sitting on a toilet like your old ladies when you need to take a piss."

I led Alexis Gamboa out of interrogation, slamming the door

behind me. Detectives' heads jerked up, but they didn't say anything. I took him into the squad room pointed to a chair beside my desk. "Sit down." I saddled into my own chair and shoved the phone to his side of the desk. "You know how to get hold of your uncle?"

At the mention of his uncle, young Alexis looked scared. He pleaded, "I-I'd rather call my father, he-he'll come get me. He won't make any problems. Please don't make me call Uncle Giovanni."

"No," I said, "you're not getting off that easy." I picked up the receiver and handed it to him. "Call him. Tell him we'll be waiting on the front steps on the Harwood side of the police station."

I listened to Alexis's side of the conversation, which was short, pitiful, and full of sobs. The kid was obviously scared out of his wits. I don't know about the other side of the conversation, but it was very short. Afterwards, I took him outside and we stood at the bottom of the steps of HQ, waiting on his ride.

"You tell your uncle what happened here. If you lie about anything...the shoplifting, where it happened, what you took...I'll know about it."

Alexis nodded. "No way I'd lie to Uncle Giovanni."

I knew he was telling the truth about that. In less than fifteen minutes, a black Caddie pulled up to the curb, and Giovanni's muscle got out from the driver's side, walked around to the back door on curbside, and opened it for Alexis. The kid's eyes were cast downward at the street, not making any eye contact with his chauffer. The muscle closed the door once he was inside. He gave me a single nod of the head, got back in the car and drove off.

Recall of the past cleared away a portion of the fog encasing my thoughts about the case. About Gamboa. The word games. The innuendos. The clues and advice. Gamboa wasn't involved. He knew things. Why he knew them wasn't important. This was payback. Giovanni Gamboa was repaying a six-year-old favor. I marked him off my list of suspects.

Chapter 20

I had some time to kill before the meeting with Doe, so I fired up the Healey and went to El Fenix, off Field Street, for the best damn Mexican food in North Texas. The crowd was big, my margarita had a kick to it, the enchiladas were steaming, and the jalapeños set your mouth on fire, just the way I like 'em. Life was good. After polishing off the meal, I ordered one more drink, fired up a Lucky, and pulled out the list again. I ticked off the items I intended to confront Doe with, preparing for battle.

As far as I was concerned, this was a make it or break it time for the senator. If he wasn't straight with me about everything I asked, then I was giving him the boot as a client. And, keeping the money, of course. I tried to give him an out with a daily rate, but he wanted to buy me off with a big retainer. With his wife's money, that is. Finally satisfied with the game plan I had in mind, I put away the list and sipped on my margarita until it was time to go. I left a generous tip and prepared for battle at the hotel.

Time to fish or cut bait, Senator Doe.

When I pulled into the drive at the Adolphus, Riley was on duty manning his usual post. I got out and flipped him the keys, then peeled a couple of bills from the diminishing wad of dough I started with yesterday. "Go ahead and park it in the garage for me, Riley. I may be a while." I handed him the tip.

"Will do, Mr. Stumbaugh. If you need your wheels in a hurry for anything, just let the concierge know, and he'll pass word on to me. I'll take care of it," Riley said, pocketing the tip.

"I'll let you know, thanks, Riley. You're a good man," I said, not really sure about what the night held for me. I limped upstairs to the lobby, acknowledged some familiar faces, and rode the elevator up to the fourteenth floor. This was my first visit to the senator's Adolphus digs, and I strolled the trademark crooked hallways at a leisurely pace, following room numbers like a map, and searching out the king's castle. I found it midway down on the left and knocked on the door of room 1449. When Doe opened up, I glanced over his shoulder and noticed his babe of a wife and some other mug, wearing a five-hundred dollar suit and slicked-back silver hair, sitting on a small sofa just as pretty as you please. I also noticed that Doe neglected to order the steaks. That meant a short meeting.

Shit.

Two more words popped into my head. *Lawye*r…actually, *rich* lawyer and *ambush*. That'd be three words.

I took a couple of steps inside, and from what I could see of the place, the suite was bigger than my apartment. The entry room where I stood was an office/sitting room kind of thing with a fancy, French looking desk, two stuffed chairs, and a small matching sofa. And a television set against the far wall. This was high dollar. To the right was a small kitchen and bar combo connected to a nice sized dining area with a long table and chairs for chow time. Beyond that was what looked to be a small bedroom. To my left was another bedroom, and checking out the size of it, it was definitely the master. "Nice digs, Senator," I said, nodding my head as though I was impressed. "Need to get one of these for myself."

"You should be able to afford it with what I'm paying you. Come on in, Harry," he said with a friendly smile, patting me on the back like we were old college buddies.

Said the spider to the fly.

"Thanks," I answered, shaking a pro-offered hand. I made a big deal about looking over his shoulder, pretending I hadn't noticed the sofa-sitters as I entered. "I see you brought company.

You didn't tell me we were having a party. I would've left my gun at home, if I'd known." I stepped around Doe and went to the doll on the couch first. She had on a pair of tight-fitting, black slacks that stopped at the shinbone, a black turtleneck that fit…well, very tight, and some black heels. She definitely reminded me of Cyd Charisse in that devil dance thing she did with Gene Kelly in *Singin' in the Rain.*

The doll kept her seat, but offered her hand, palm down; I guess she wanted me to kiss her ring. I gave it a firm grip and a steady shake instead. She gave me a crooked, mischievous little grin in return. "Mrs. Doe, I assume," I said, tipping the front brim of my hat. I didn't know if the senator knew about our secret rendezvous earlier or not. Hell, the way things were working with him, he probably set it up…or not.

"Mr. Stumbaugh," she said, "nice to finally meet you."

That answered that question.

Silver Hair stood, at least I thought he was standing, he was maybe five-two in height, offered his hand, and gave me one of those dazzling smiles with perfect teeth that was only possible through good genes or a high-dollar dentist. I'm guessing the latter.

Napoleon complex. Lawyer for sure.

"Mr. Stumbaugh, I've heard many interesting things about you, and I'm pleased to finally meet you face to face," he said, all the while shaking my hand. "Garland Henshaw, of Henshaw, Dozier, and Epps. I'm Senator Doe's attorney."

"How's Josephine?" I asked.

His brow knitted. I wasn't sure if he got it or not, but the look told me he probably did.

Good.

Hedy Doe got it for sure, snickered, then coughed lightly covering her mouth and attempted to hide a smile, but she didn't do a very good job of it.

Garland glanced her way after the cough, then back at me, "What? I…"

"Just kidding, pal," I said, giving him a friendly pat on the arm. "So, you got first billing on the front door, huh? Good for you," I said, returning a less than dazzling smile for him.

Doe stepped in to save the day, evidently recognizing my sarcastic humor as a bad omen for the things to come. "Harry, I thought it best to involve Garland in all this. I'd like you to fill us in on where everything stands at this point, so he can advise me on my next move."

I smiled. "I think that's a good idea, John, but *Garland* won't be advising me on anything. I've got my own lawyer.

Henshaw gave an appropriate cough, *he must have something in his throat again,* then he stepped into the conversation. "Well, of course, I'm not here to advise *you,* but I'm here to represent the senator's best interest in this unfortunate and malicious attempt at extortion. He's filled me in, with not much information at this point, as best he can. But *his* interests are foremost, as far as I'm concerned."

"Would anyone like something to drink before we get started?" Doe said, changing the subject. "Hedy, darling, anything for you?"

"No, I'm fine for now," she said, intentionally dipping a finger into her martini glass and then sucking off the moisture.

Oh my.

Doe ignored the gesture, "Uh, Harry? How about you?" He said, moving towards the kitchen.

"I'm fine too, John, thanks."

Garland Henshaw strode behind Doe, joining his client at the bar. "I could use a whiskey," he said. "Don't bother, John, I know where everything is."

I'm sure you do.

"Can we get this little party started?" I said, wanting to move things along. "We've got a lot to cover."

Henshaw nodded, "Of course."

Henshaw abandoned his seat on the sofa for one of the

chairs, and Doe followed suit, leaving me sitting next to Hedy Doe on the pint-sized couch. Reluctantly, I tossed my fedora on the coffee table and took a seat, keeping as much distance between me and the babe as possible, but I was too big and the furniture was too small. I scrunched against the arm on my side, crossed my legs, and pulled out the list and a pen for notes. I think it amused the missus.

I started things off, "Well, I'm going to give the short version of the last forty-eight hours, and the events that've happened since." I nodded at the senator, "I'm going to explain how it's connected to you, John, along with some tough questions."

"I'm up for it," responded Doe. "Nothing to hide here."

Henshaw cleared his throat. "Uh, I doubt that..."

I decided to cut the shyster off at the knees now, so he wouldn't think he could inject his opinion anytime he wanted. "Listen Mr. Henshaw, I appreciate the fact that you're here to represent the senator, but that don't mean shit to me. I wasn't hired to exonerate him in any way. I was hired to find the facts, not find a way around them. This isn't a courtroom, so you need to stay quiet unless spoken to. Got it?"

That should do it.

"Now just a minute, Stumbaugh. You can't..."

"That didn't require an answer, Henshaw. Now where was I? Oh yes..."

Hedy gave another muffled giggle and Doe jumped into the fray, taking control, a tad of impatience in his tone. "Now, just a minute boys, we're not going to get in a pissing match here." He jabbed at his chest saying, "This is *my* fucking life on the line here," he said, "not either of *yours*. I'm not going to have this schoolyard bickering. This isn't Congress." He nodded at me. "Go, let's hear it." He shot a *shutup* look at Henshaw.

Balls. I like it.

"It looks like two Dallas PD detectives *might* be involved in all this. The extortion, even the heist back in '32."

Henshaw raised his hand, "Who are they, *if* I could ask."

"No, you can't," I said. "Now, we've got two murders in the last," I checked my watch, "twelve hours approximately. Robert Petrie and Abner Strong. Abner was the father of Pete Strong, who got caught at the heist scene in '32 and was executed later for murdering the two security guards. Petrie was Strong's step-brother, so you can see the tie-in there. "Obviously, he wasn't caught at the time, but they found his body outside a strip joint alley at three o'clock this morning. He was beat to death."

"My God, I had no idea this was all so...," Henshaw said quietly. Then, "Sorry, continue please." He leaned forward in his seat, arms resting on his knees.

Got his attention now.

"No problem," I said, cutting him some slack. "At first, we thought there might be a mob connection, but there's not. Don't ask me how I know. You'll just have to take my word for it." Henshaw shot a quick glance Doe's way, as if to say, *I know.* He just took two steps backwards in my book, and I directed my attention to the shyster at that point. "I know what you *think* you know, counselor, but you don't know shit." I left it at that and returned my remarks to Doe. "Anyway, you're facing some pretty tough questions, Senator. You ready?"

"Shoot," he said, relaxed and confident in his chair.

"First," I said, "I had my doubts in the beginning about the amnesia thing. You were right when you said it'd be almost impossible to go twenty years without some kind of verbal slip up at the wrong time...but something you said in our last meeting got my attention. I considered it the slip up you'd avoided all these years, and Sam picked up on it too."

Doe's brow's knitted. "And what would that be?"

"I'll make this short and sweet," I said, watching for a reaction from Doe, but he maintained a solid poker-face. "That phrase sound familiar?"

"What? Short and sweet? Sure," he said, "a common colloquial saying, meaning don't linger, say what you've got to say and be done with it, or something along that line. Why?"

I shrugged. *Thanks for the definition.* "I'm a stickler for detail, John. When I hear the same phrase, common or not, said within a twenty-four hour period by three suspects in the same case...I get suspicious."

"Exactly what are you saying, Stumbaugh," Henshaw asked, accusingly.

I ignored him and kept my attention on the senator. "Yesterday, when Petrie called you for the money, I had the phones in the hotel lobby covered. Inside and outside lines. Separate phone banks, by the way. Petrie went to the outside lines first and made a call to someone before he called you. He was verifying that he was on site at the hotel and getting ready to give you a call. He used that same phrase, saying something to the effect of, '*Yeah, I know, keep it short and sweet*', while talking to his boss or whoever it was. My man heard him and noted it. The *second* time I heard it was with Sam, when we met together at *your* house. You used the same phrase, short and sweet. I don't remember the exact context, but you said it. Sam picked up on it, too. A coincidence?"

I shrugged for a visual effect. "Maybe. Then, one of the detectives I mentioned earlier, that's in this up to his corrupt neck, said the same thing in my office today. Five other people heard it this time." I shrugged again. "Now in my book, three times blows coincidence out of the water. Can you see where I'm coming from here?" I stopped and gave both men a look for confirmation, but they didn't seem impressed.

Henshaw gave a sarcastic guff and a dismissive wave. "Purely circumstantial, if that, even. Means absolutely nothing. I use the same phrase myself. Frequently."

"Then, maybe he was talking to you, counselor," I said with hidden glee. Henshaw made motions as though he was about to stand and object like he was in court trying a case.

Doe waved him down. "Stay quiet, Garland." Doe furrowed his brows, looking pensive, then shrugged. "Don't know what to tell, you Harry. I can't speak for the other two men, but like Garland, and you yourself said, it's a common phrase." His lips pursed together, "What can I say?"

"Nothing," advised Henshaw.

I re-crossed my legs, still trying to keep a maximum distance between me and the babe on the couch. "Nothing else to say about it?"

Doe just shook his head in the negative.

"Well, I guess we'll just have to agree to disagree on the importance of three people saying the same thing." I played up my point by checking off the item from my list with some physical exaggeration. It got a snicker out of Hedy, but the other two clowns didn't seem to be amused.

"Okay, next." This was the one where I had to leave Hedy Doe out of the picture. I pretended to think, perhaps questioning what to do next, but I knew damn well, of course. "A side note first, how many times did you talk to Petrie on the phone, John? About the extortion...or anything else for that matter?"

Hedy Doe casually readjusted her seating position.

Henshaw straightened up in his chair. "Now just a---"

"Sh-h-h," I sounded out, with my finger vertically crossing my lips. Then, I whispered, "Don't interrupt."

"Only once," Doe said, without any hesitation or forethought, "when he called me from the hotel for the money. And I only *saw* him once, when he initially came by my office before that."

"Okay," I said, making another check mark. "The first two were child's play, Senator, here's the biggy. I sent my people down to the courthouse to do some digging and..."

"About what?" Henshaw asked, doing his lawyer thing again.

I hesitated and took a deep breath for effect. Time to make an impression. I clicked the fountain pen, clipped it into my inside jacket pocket, and stood up, list in hand. "I'm done, Senator. I'd be glad to meet you and discuss this further without your mouthpiece and his interruptions. You can fill him in later." I tucked away my list and headed for the door. Doe popped out of his seat like a Jack-in-the-box.

He pointed at Henshaw. "Garland, you keep your God-damn mouth shut. You were warned, but evidently you can't refrain from trying to take center stage. This isn't a courtroom. If you persist, I'll ask *you* to leave the room, and I'll retract that fat retainer of mine from your law firm. You'll be chasing ambulances for clients by Friday, if you fuck this up in any way." Doe turned to me and pointed back at the sofa. "Harry, you sit down and ask your questions."

Interesting.

Henshaw adjusted the knot of his tie, which couldn't get any straighter, and then crossed his legs. Doe's outburst didn't ruffle him one bit. Hedy just smiled and took a sip of her martini. I went over and leaned against the bar, preferring to stand if I needed to make a quick exit, stage left. "I'm liking you better all the time, Senator. Okay…the records from the courthouse. It shows that in 1943 you defended one Robert Petrie in criminal court…*twice.* And this happened when you were an associate at the law firm of *Henshaw*, Dozier, and Epps."

I glanced at the attorney and let that little bombshell hang out in the breeze for a few seconds to see who picked up the pieces first. Hedy Doe's chin and composure dropped down to her well-developed breasts.

Finally broke down that sultry façade.

Henshaw didn't react. Which I found interesting. Doe's face turned the color of a pomegranate and I could see the explosion coming. Again. Two temper tantrums in thirty seconds. All directed at Henshaw. The attorney saw the writing on the wall too, but I had the feeling this was commonplace between the two men.

The senator took a step forward and jabbed a finger in Henshaw's direction. "You!" He yelled. "What did you do,

Garland?" Next, he spun around on me, like I was the one that mattered, which was true, in my opinion. Doe wasn't losing control or panicking. He was just plain ol' pissed off. I waited for the spit to start flying. "I never defended that son-of-a-bitch in '43 or any other year." He twisted around on Henshaw again. "But I *did* work for you, Garland."

This time, Henshaw snapped to his feet, hands poised to stop the verbal attack he was taking. "Whoa! Hold on just a minute. I don't know anything about this, but it'll be easy enough to check on." He nodded at Doe. "John, you know as well as I do, at a firm the size of ours, cases and attorneys can get switched around. One lawyer sloughs off a case and passes it on to another lawyer and paperwork gets screwed up. You know the kind of clients we defended back then. We were building our reps. We weren't all that picky about the cases we took, like we are now." He redirected his conversation to me. "Mr. Stumbaugh, I can assure you that if John says he didn't defend this Petrie character in court, he's telling the truth. He can probably tick off the name of every client he had back then with that photographic memory of his."

Didn't know Doe had a photographic memory. All kinds of good things were popping up.

Henshaw checked his watch, then strode with determination to the desk and snatched up the phone. "Matter of fact, I'll take care of this right now. My personal secretary is still in the office, I'm sure." He started dialing and waited for the answer at the other end. "Betty? This is Garland, I need you to do some leg work for me. What are you working on at the present time?" He listened for a second and waved his arm, as though shooing a fly. "Drop it; it can wait. First thing in the morning, I need you to go back to our file cases from 1943." He hesitated. "No, I'm not kidding. I need you to cross-reference the names of Robert Petrie and John Doe." There was another pause, and it was easy to see his irritation building. "Don't get smart, Betty…your job isn't that secure. *Senator* John Doe from when he worked with us." He listened for a second.

"Yes, I understand...it's an easy mistake to make...no, I don't want you to get any help, this is for your eyes only." He stared up at the ceiling, obviously getting more exasperated by Betty's questions. "Well, it's your damn filing system, so figure it out!" He hung up, plopping the receiver back into the cradle louder than necessary. "She's a great girl," he said, managing a weak smile and pointing at the phone, "but after twenty years of employment, it's hard to tell who's the boss anymore."

"She was then, and probably still is, Garland." Doe turned to me. "Harry? Satisfied?"

I shrugged. "I'll let you know when I see the files. The question is...are you?"

"All I know is the truth," he said. "I never met that little weasel until the day he walked into my office yesterday." His face flushed and he talked through gritted teeth. "I'm being set up, Harry. That's the bottom line."

"Mr. Stumbaugh," Henshaw said, diverting my attention back to him. "I believe I owe you an apology, sir. I'll admit, at the beginning of the meeting, I was intentionally adversarial, and I don't mind telling you, I wasn't pleased when John told me he'd hired you."

Now he's being all nice and everything. What's that all about?

"Hired an investigator or just *me*?"

"You," he said emphatically. "I'm aware that you do good work for Cameron Epperson and engage in high profile clientele, and that's all well and fine, but your past termination with the Dallas PD left a blight on your record, as far as I was concerned. True or not doesn't matter. Inference or even the slightest whisper of collusion with organized crime marks a man with a scarlet letter. As I said before, my sole duty in this room is to protect the interest of my client. And, I intend to do that regardless of whose feelings I may injure. That part of it is not my concern. But I'm attuned to the fact, and you've proven to me tonight that, as we say in Texas, you don't have dog in this fight...and I prefer that, to someone sugarcoating the facts to satisfy a client's particular need or worse, holding out for more money." He cleared his throat, which meant he wasn't done yet. "You must admit, not everyone in your profession has the same scruples and determination as yourself." He grinned as though he'd paid me the ultimate compliment.

"You're right, counselor…I guess I could say the same about your profession too."

That one got another giggle from Hedy. She was enjoying the show tonight, but I noticed that she'd been watching and observing and taking in every word, gesture, and tick of the three men in the room

"Touché. No offense intended," he countered with a smile.

My turn. "None taken, counselor, but since this is the second time you've brought it up, just to bring you up to speed on my departure from Dallas PD…you don't know shit about the blight on my record. Only what you heard from the courthouse rumor mill. I can count the number of people that know the real facts and the truth on one hand and still have fingers left over…and you're not one of them. And to be honest, I'm not interested in rehashing old times or justifying my actions to you or anybody else. Let's move on."

Henshaw held up a hand, nodding. "I concur and I misjudged you. Evidently, John was more intuitive in regards to your character and ethics than me. Your investigation and the questions you've raised have proven a unique talent for due diligence and detail. I'm impressed." He turned to Doe. "I suggest you keep this bulldog on the payroll, John. I like the fact that he's not biased in his research, and that fact alone will prove your innocence to the ninth degree."

Hedy set her drink on the table and stood. "That was never your decision to make to begin with, Garland. The question is…do *you* stay on the payroll."

His reaction wasn't what I expected. Instead of objecting or acting indignant, he just smiled. "That's your choice, Hedy, and

John's, of course. I'm here only to serve," he answered, bowing stiffly to the queen.

Hedy saddled up beside her husband and hooked her arm in his. "Are we done, John? I'm famished," she said.

Doe turned to me. "Harry? Anything else?"

"Yeah, I'd like a list of the attorneys that worked for the firm when you were there in '43."

This got a rise from Henshaw. "What for? The records will clarify the problem."

"Like you said, I'm thorough and I don't have a dog in this fight. I like to do my own research. Besides, what I discover, if anything, should just verify your own findings. There's not a problem, is there?" I asked, putting the shyster on the spot.

"No, of course not," he said, none too happy. "But I'm afraid in regards to the files themselves, client-attorney confidentiality prevents me from showing you the records from the cases you requested." He paused, "However, I will allow John to see them. Fair enough?"

Doe said, "I don't see any harm in that, Harry." Doe went to the desk and grabbed a pad of Adolphus Hotel stationery and a pen and started writing. When he was done, he tore off the top sheet and handed it to Henshaw. "Did I miss anybody?"

Henshaw checked over the list and handed it back to Doe, shaking his head. "I think that's everybody, but I'll double check my records in the morning."

Doe handed me the paper. "Five attorneys. They're the ones I worked with. Have at it."

"Two of them have departed," Henshaw said, as I glanced at the list. "Wellstone and McAllister, but they're still in town."

"Good," Doe said. "Then, we can get together and compare notes tomorrow, Harry. I've put a hold on all campaign appointments for the next twenty-four hours. I'd like to be hands-on in the investigation from now on. If you need *anything*, then let me know."

Great.

I snatched my hat from the coffee table and tugged it on at an angle, indicating I was done. "Good, then. You can call my office with your list as well, first thing in the morning, counselor. Any paralegals or aides would be helpful, too." I didn't want to forget about the little people. "They're the ones that really know what's going on in the office." No negative reaction from Henshaw.

"First thing, then," Henshaw responded. "The records will take a little more time, but Betty's good. If anything's irregular, she'll find it."

"Meanwhile, I've got more work to do," I said.

"It'd be difficult to top tonight's performance, Mr. Stumbaugh," Hedy said with a slow, musky drawl. "What do you have in mind?"

"Real answers," I said, letting myself out.

Chapter 21

A lot of things rambled through my head as I rode the elevator down to the lobby. I liked what I saw in Doe tonight. He was aggressive and scared shitless at the same time. His performance was even good enough to give me second thoughts about him being guilty as hell, which I believed he was from the beginning. But I wasn't about to turn down his ten g's over a little thing like guilt. I never bought the amnesia bullshit and figured all along that he was just very good at deception. I mean, after all, he *was* a politician. That being said, though, I still needed solid, cold, hard proof to totally eliminate him as a thief, cop-killer, and liar. That's quite a resume to carry around.

Now, Hedy Doe on the other hand…that babe was a real piece of work and hard to figure. She was as cool as a cucumber tonight, but when the facts came to light about Petrie being a former client of her old man, the surprise and shock on her face was genuine. She knows more than she lets on, but there could still be some surprises ahead for her. I also believed that she truly loved her husband. She was the one with the money, and Doe was definitely not some boy-toy to hang on her arm and showoff. But still…there was something about the two of them I just couldn't put my finger on…but I would, sooner or later.

Garland Henshaw was the reason the general public disliked lawyers so much, until they needed one, of course. Flashy, cocky, always thought he was right, and rich. What's not to dislike? But, very good at what he does. Rich and flashy doesn't win court cases, but being at the top of your game does. The relationship between Doe and Henshaw seemed more like a marriage than an attorney/client relationship. They'd evidently known and worked together for a long period of time and that played out in their back and forth with each other. We'd see how cooperative Henshaw was with the files and the rest of the attorney list in the morning. I was more interested in talking to the ones that *didn't* work for the firm anymore. If they were disgruntled employees, then that's even better. They wouldn't give a shit about any non-disclosure clauses that might've been part of the termination or voluntary release at the time. We'd see.

The elevator bottomed out on the first floor without any new passengers interrupting my ride or train of thought. A Budweiser was sounding real good about now, so I headed towards the French Room. I crossed by the grand piano and a young bellhop in a braided red jacket and a pillbox hat ran up to me.

"Mr. Harry Stumbaugh?"

"That's me, son."

"You've got some guests waiting for you in the French Room bar, and they wanted you to join them."

"Thanks kid," I said, peeling off a bill from my thinning wad of greenbacks, "here you go." I figured that if the kid had the gumption to run around a high class hotel in a monkey suit, he deserved a nice tip.

Curious about my *guests,* I rounded the corner and saw Sam, Epperson, Jenny, and Kate sitting at one of the large round tables in the center of the room. Sam saw me first and hoisted his glass in a salute to get my attention; Jenny and Kate followed suit when they spotted me, too. It wasn't until I got close to the table that I saw close-up the beating that Cochran and Megs had given Sam back at the police headquarters. He looked like shit. One eye was swollen and bruised and the opposite cheek sported stitches. He must've removed the patch, wanting to show off his badge of courage. "Just when I thought you couldn't get any uglier," I said, shaking his hand. "Good to see you up and about."

"I wear my scars well...and I've still got *two* good legs," he said.

I rapped one of his legs with my cane and reached over him and gave Kate's hand a squeeze. "How's it going, kiddo? Jenny took good care of you today?"

She gave me a toothy grin, "Of course she did. I could get into this detective stuff. It was fun." She scooted her chair over closer to Sam. "But, I'm looking forward to starting at Walgreen's tomorrow. Jenny took me by to meet Mr. Martin, my new boss. He's very nice."

"Good," I said, switching to Epperson. "Well, Cam, you've had a busy day, huh?"

He saluted me with a short tumbler, half-filled with Crown Royal, his usual drink. "It was great getting down in the pits again, Harry. Reminded me of the old days when I was fresh out of law school, scrounging for business and bustin' butts."

"Appreciate you taking care of Sam. Should probably put you on a retainer just to keep him out of trouble."

He took a sip of his drink and waved me off. "Today's Tuesday, right? That's pro bono day. This one's on me."

"No argument here. Sam's the one that should thank you; it was coming out of his percentage, anyway."

I finally sat down in the free chair between Sam and Jenny, leaned over and gave her a peck on the cheek. "Have fun today, Doll Face? Working in the field?"

"You know it big guy. Wanna know what Kate and I found out when we went to Santa Fe Railroad?" She smiled and winked at Kate. "You tell him, Katie, you're the one that got the personnel shmuck to open up."

I raised an eyebrow at Kate. "Really? Good job. Give me the short version." I spotted Michelle two tables over, got her attention with a wave, and motioned for a beer. "Go ahead."

"Okay," she said, taking a breath like she was about to be

interviewed for a job. "Abner Strong, remember him?"

"Kinda," I said. "Dead from what I remember. What about him?"

"He used to work for Santa Fe Railroad!" She paused. "He was an engineer on the trains. A boiler or something blew up. He wasn't on the train when it happened, but close by and he got hit by tons of shrapnel. He had extensive damage to his spine, and he was paralyzed from the waist down."

I could tell she was giddy with excitement. "And, when did this happen?"

Epperson did a drum roll on the table with his hands. "You're going to love this one, Harry."

I eyeballed Cam and back to Kate. "Well?"

Kate, with dramatic flair, swished back a stray hair from her face. "October 27th, 1930."

Epperson gave a second drum roll. "Ba-boom," he said, topping it off. "Two years before the heist, but same date. Anniversary of the heist. Anniversary of the extortion. And, ol' Abner bought the farm on the same date. Hell of a case!" He exclaimed. "I love it!"

Twelve to twenty-four hours ago, this would have gotten me excited, but all it did for me now was confirming how smart I was. When I found out Abner joined his wife and two boys in the underworld, I knew he had to be in on it. "Damn," I said, giving the girls their moment of triumph. "That little piece of information is the string that ties together all kinds of loose ends. Great work, girls."

Jenny reached over and patted my leg under the table. She knew I was blowing smoke, but Epperson didn't.

"Explain, if you don't mind," Epperson said. "I'll offer my services, whatever you need for this case, Harry. Let me in."

I liked it. "Okay, I need to fill in everybody, I guess." I pulled out my list and started at the beginning, when Doe first came to the office. We all needed to be on the same page if we were to work together. I ran it all down for them, events, questions, who did what to whom, and included the conversations with Doe, Hedy, and Henshaw I'd just had. I also gave them my personal observations about the trio. When I was done, I nodded at Kate. "So, you can see how it all ties together?"

"But, you already had it figured out, didn't you," Kate asked, with a tinge of disappointment.

I held up a hand. "Ah, but you *confirmed* it, kiddo. Speculation don't mean a damn thing if you can't verify it." I turned to Epperson. "Right?"

He nodded. "Never ask a question to a witness in court unless you already know the answer. Rule number one. Verify and confirm. He's right, Kate."

Michelle brought my beer to the table. "Hey, sweetie," she said with a soft pat on my shoulder. "Anybody want another drink? Want me to order you something from the kitchen?" I noticed half-empty drinks around the table and nodded. "Another round and some menus. Looks like it's going to be a working dinner tonight."

Michelle left with drink orders and I thought of a good way to get Cam in the middle of things since he wanted in. "Cam, what can you tell me about Garland Henshaw?"

"He's a smart cookie. Flamboyant, but a top-notch attorney. I'm glad he's not a prosecutor because I'd hate to go up against him in court."

"Is he honest? Assuming there's no such thing as an honest lawyer." I asked.

Cam smiled. "Point taken, but as far as I know he's straight up. I've never heard any bad scuttle-butt against him. We started out about the same time, but never worked for the same firm. He struggled in the beginning like we all did, but he must've caught some big cases along the line. I was still hustling, doing okay mind you, but the next thing I knew, he was on his own, big offices, and hand-tailored suits. It only takes one good case to open the right doors for you in this business, you know."

"Any idea what his deal breaker was?" Sam asked.

Epperson shook his head. "None. But, I know he defended a friend of yours, Harry, back in the day."

"Really? Who?" I asked.

"Giovanni Gamboa. I remember because it was in all the papers at the time. About ten years ago, I think. It was a simple assault case. Gamboa beat up some guy in his restaurant, but it didn't go anywhere, though. Just made a hero of a bad guy. Garland got him off without a problem. If I remember right, then the judge threw it out before it even went to trial."

Interesting.

"Did he ever defend any other wise-guys after that?"

"Nah, not that I remember. He didn't become a mob lawyer if that's what you're asking. I think it was a one-time deal."

I sipped the foam off my beer and fired up a Lucky. "Okay, let me ask you this. I told you about Doe being on the docket as Petrie's attorney. Doe's claiming foul and Henshaw says it's a paperwork snafu. How common is that?"

Epperson dipped a finger in his tumbler and stirred the brown liquid thoughtfully. Hedy Doe and her martini came to mind. "It could happen…once maybe. Twice…I'd have to see the file."

"Well, that'll never happen," I said. "He's going to show them to Doe, but I can't trust what he'll say. It's his neck on the line. Doe gave me a list of five attorneys he worked with back in '43, and Henshaw verified the names. Both thought it was the full list, but Henshaw said he'd compare it with his records in the morning and get back with me. I also told him I wanted the names of any paralegals, office personnel, and so on. I'll make headway with it tomorrow. That's what I'll be doing, chasing down lawyers."

Epperson took a sip of his drink. "Let me see the list."

I pulled the piece of Adolphus stationary from my inside pocket and gave it to him. "Know anybody on there?"

He nodded. "Oh, sure. All of them. It's a big city, but small world among the law business." He pointed at the list. "This one," he said. "I'd check with him first. He gives the term *shyster* a bad name. That's why Henshaw probably got rid of him. Randolf Wellstone. Start there. What've you got in mind, exactly?"

"See if I can find a disgruntled, former employee that might know something and be willing to talk about it," I said.

"Then, he's your man." He held up the list like an exhibit in the courtroom. "Three out of the five on this list are still at Henshaw, Dozier, and Epps, and I can tell you right now, nobody that's still with him will even talk to you, if they care anything about their job, that is. Anybody that left and went down the road could be equally hard to crack, if they'll even talk to you. Investigators aren't our profession's favorite animal, you know. Unless they're on the company's payroll."

Here came a good question. "Would they talk to you? Another lawyer?"

Epperson stared at his drink for a second before answering. "Depends on what you're fishing for, Harry."

"A dirty lawyer," injected Sam. "Somebody that was directed, under orders from the top, or on his own even, to put Doe's name on the case. Somebody that might not want their name on the same page as the brother of a cop killer."

"Took the words right out of my mouth, partner," I said.

Epperson frowned. "Man, I don't know, Harry. You're skating on thin ice. Even with Wellstone. You're talking about somebody ready to give up their ticket to practice law with that one."

I understood where he was coming from. "Who's the other guy on the list?"

Cam smiled. "We call him Fancy Pants McAllister. He makes Henshaw and me look like we shop down at the Salvation Army Store. Flashy, bright colored shirts and ties and wears a bowler. Walks with a cane, except he does it for show, not because he has to."

"Fancy Pants have a real name?" I asked.

"Edmund. Edmund McAllister."

"I've heard the name."

Cam said, "I doubt you'd even get in to see him, Harry. He's very high profile. Goes for the civil cases. If there's not a half million dollar fee in it for him, he doesn't even touch it."

"Well, I don't want to put you in the eye of the storm, Cam. I'd rather keep you in the background anyway. Maybe, we can get together in the morning and you can give me the right questions to ask, in the event I even get my foot in the front door."

"I like that better," the attorney said. "What else have you got planned?"

I finished off about half of the mug of beer before answering and turned to Sam. "You and your ugly mug ready to go back to work or do you need some more *convalescing* time?"

"I need to earn my keep. I get arrested when I hang around the office too much."

Kate reached into her purse, pulled out a Kleenex, and lightly dabbed the stitches on his cheek. "You need to keep your bandage on that, Sam. It's oozing."

Beauty and the Beast.

Jenny pressed her knee up against mine. At least she had a good sense not to gush on about how sweet it was. Sam gave me a wink.

Son-of-a-bitch, she's got him hook, line, and sinker.

"Think you could make it to Denton this time if I sent you again?" I asked him, sarcasm dripping from my tongue.

"Sure, last time I detoured, it got me this," he said, pointing to his face.

"And me," added Kate softly.

I think I'm going to be sick.

"Two errands," I said, trying to start a new momentum. "First to the hospital. I really need a look at Doe's medical records from his stay there in '32."

"I'm not much on medical jargon, Harry. What am I looking for?" Sam asked.

"Real simple," I said. "Even a leatherneck like you can figure it out. Doe's missing the first knuckle on his right-hand pinkie. When I first met him, he told me it *was* part of the accident that landed him in the hospital. Abner Strong told me that when he met Ralph Morris, prior to the heist, part of *his* right pinkie was missing."

"Holy shit," exclaimed Epperson. "You're really good, Harry. I may put *you* on a retainer."

I smiled. "It's just grunt work, counselor. We'll talk terms in the morning, though, if you like."

"It's more than that, Harry. Sorry, go ahead."

"It's obvious."

Jenny evidently couldn't control herself and jumped in to steal my money line. She clapped her hands like a child opening up the first Christmas present under the tree. "If he lost the pinkie in the hit and run…then he's innocent! He *couldn't* be Ralph Morris! According to Abner Strong, right?" She said, checking all the faces at the table for confirmation.

"Right you are, Doll Face," I said. "*That's* why I keep you around."

Epperson smiled and gave me a wink. There was way too much eye-blinking coming my way tonight.

"And, if it *wasn't* part of the accident?" Sam asked, throwing a bucket of water on Jenny's euphoric revelation. "What next?"

"Go to the Sheriff's office. Get with Roscoe. That old coot has been the sheriff there since the days of Wyatt Earp. If anybody remembers anything, he will." I had a second thought. "Matter of fact, no matter what the results are from the hospital, check with Roscoe. See what he's got to offer."

Michelle's timing was perfect. She came back for our food order and delivered a fresh round of drinks for everyone. Before, during, and after the meal, we scarfed down our food like ravenous wolves, and it was hard not to talk about anything else but the case. Kate expressed her sorrow about not being able to help any more, but Sam appointed her our official counter spy at Walgreen's and promised to keep her up to date. Jenny wanted a turn at the lawyers from Henshaw's firm, declaring she'd get things out of them I'd never be able to. I didn't doubt that she could, but thought it best to put her back on the phones. We were going to be scattered to the wind and somebody had to man the office and keep tabs on all of us.

After we finally finished our meal and decided to call it a night, we made our way out to the front drive to get our cars. Riley had every car jockey in the joint shagging ass to get our cars ahead of people already waiting on their drives. The man knew when a good tip was coming his way.

Epperson tapped my elbow to get my attention and pulled me to the side away from the girls, motioning for Sam to follow, too. He waited until we were out of earshot. "Listen, both of you. This case...and I may sound a bit over dramatic, but I have a feeling things are about to start busting wide open. Get nasty. We need to consider the girls," he said in a low tone, glancing at Jenny and Kate. "They're vulnerable pawns in this game being played by someone who doesn't mind killing. Two pawns are already dead and it appears to me that anybody that gets tagged isn't just *it*. They're dead. Do we agree?"

I didn't think Sam or I either one considered the girls being in any danger from this. It was just another job to me, but when Cam brought it up, I started looking at the case from a completely different perspective. I saw it in Sam's face, too.

Grim-faced, Sam nodded. "I agree. I'll follow the girls to Jenny's place and cover the apartment from the outside tonight," he said. He automatically touched the small of his back and felt the .45 back in its place.

"I'll get in touch with Benny Martin tonight and delay Kate

starting at Walgreen's in the morning. It won't be a problem," I added.

"Let's all meet at my office in the morning," Epperson added. "We can get the game plan going from there."

"Come on guys! The cars are coming," Jenny called, waving us on.

I waved back, "Coming, Doll Face." Our cars were pulling up in a caravan of four, one after the other. When they stopped, doors were opened and tips were dished out.

Jenny hooked her arm in mine before getting in, stretched up on her tiptoes and kissed my cheek. "I had so much fun today, Harry. I felt...like we were all a family tonight. I wish it could have gone on forever."

I cupped her face with both hands, bent down and kissed her forehead. "It will, Jenny. Nothing bad is going to happen. I promise."

Chapter 22

At three in the morning, I eased up behind Sam's Ford that was parked in front of Jenny's apartment complex, flashed my lights once, and parked. I killed the engine and walked to the driver's side of his car. I leaned against the Ford, my elbow resting on the roof, and pointed to the .45 lying on his lap. "So, you're taking Cam's paranoia to heart about the threats to the girls, I see."

Sam grunted and motioned for me to move so he could get out. "Never leave home without it," he answered.

I moved over and opened the door for him. "Thought I'd give you a break. Both of us might as well spend the day running on three cylinders."

"All's quiet here, appreciate it. A couple of hours of shut-eye will do me good."
He stepped out, stretched his arms, and yawned. "Yeah, and I think *we're* probably targets, too."

"Yeah, maybe," I answered.

"I sure could use my other piece. Think you could contact DeRita and see about getting our hardware back?"

"Yeah, I'll call him first thing once I get back to the office, and by the way, there's no need for you to come to the meeting this morning at Cam's place. Go home and grab a couple of hours of shut-eye and some breakfast before heading out to Denton. I've been thinking, just call me with whatever you get from the hospital before you go running to the sheriff's office. We'll see if there's a need at that time. No need running all over the place if we don't have to."

"Soon as I know something."

"Call the office first, that's where I'll be operating from. If I'm not there, then touch base with Jenny at Cam's and leave a message. She'll know how to reach me. Reverse the charges," I added. "He can afford it."

"Yeah, he's a good guy. Still might need him. Okay, later, then" Sam said, getting back in the car and firing up the engine, "I'll call as soon as I can."

I watched the taillights grow smaller as the Ford disappeared down the block and went back to my car and settled in for the rest of the morning. It was going to be an interesting day. I rolled down my window, placed my .38 on the console, grabbed the Styrofoam cup of hot coffee from on the Healey's dash, tossed a Bayer aspirin in my mouth, and took a sip. I needed to knock the edge off the earlier beer fest at the Adolphus Hotel. It was quiet and the early morning temperature was brisk, a slight chill in the air. It felt good. Sometimes, I'm a little slow on the uptake, but something Sam said before he took off puzzled me. I didn't catch it at first. What did he mean when he said, he might need Cam later?

The boy worries me.

Sitting in a sports car for hours was no way to conduct a stakeout, but it'd been a long time since I'd watched the sunrise. The dawn brought on a new day and I was ready for it. As soon as I saw Jen's kitchen light come on, I headed for the office for a quick clean-up and grabbed my notes for the meeting.

At Cam's office, the four of us sat around a fancy mahogany conference table that cost more than all the furniture in my humble little office. We sipped coffee from fancy cups with grapevine designs and nibbled on Danish and homemade cinnamon rolls that Jenny brought with her from home. I didn't even know she knew how to turn on a stove. I called her apartment last night, after I got to the office, to let her know the new plans for the morning meeting and told her to bring Kate along. She didn't ask any questions, and

I didn't offer an explanation. I'd also left a message with the night manager at Walgreen's to let Benny Martin know that there'd be a delay in Kate's start date. When I saw him this morning at breakfast, he'd relayed to me that he got the message and it wouldn't be a problem. So that took care of the minor details for the day.

My plan of execution, for the morning at least, was to field phone calls in my office while the girls set up office with Cam and Sam was in Denton. I'm not one for paranoia, but like Sam, Epperson got me to thinking that he might be onto something about this case and the sinister repercussions that could come down the pike, and he was right about another thing. The hammer was dropping on what I considered, the original planners of the heist in '32, and if new faces started dropping dead, then we were getting into a whole new level of things. We'd be dealing with somebody that didn't give a shit about a body count. Somebody that wanted to cover their ass at all costs. My idea was to focus on the money. Where was it? Who had it?

Find the money…it'll lead to the root of all the evil…guaranteed.

"You look like hell, Harry," Epperson said. He took a bite from his Danish and quickly wiped away a dribble of jelly clinging to his bottom lip.

"Thanks," I said. "At least I know how to eat a donut without getting it all over me."

"You should," he countered, "you're a cop. You've got more practice than me."

I liked Epperson, even if he was a lawyer. "Tu-shay," I said.

Jenny set down her coffee cup. "Well, he should, after sitting in his car in front of the apartment all night." Then she corrected herself. "Well, it was about three, I guess, when he took over for Sam." A single eyebrow raised over one eye, and I knew a question was on its way. "Would you like to explain what this is all about, Harry? You and Sam playing bodyguard and all of us meeting here this morning instead of our own office?"

"Don't need to explain it, Doll Face. We're just taking precautions," I said.

Epperson jumped in to save the day and changed the subject. He directed his attention to Kate first. "Kate, I've been thinking, since we met yesterday, and if you're agreeable, I'd like to offer you a secretarial position here in my offices. Hiring another person has been on our agenda for the past weeks, and besides, I think it's time for you to think about the future in long terms, not slinging hash for two-bits an hour at a drugstore."

Kate's eyes instantly welled with tears, and Jenny reached over and grasped her hand for assurance. "I-I…"

"You can start now," Epperson said in a businesslike tone, cutting off the mushy sentiment that was about to invade the room. "Why don't you go out to the front office and ask Marlene for a couple of writing pads and pens so you and Jenny can take notes of the meeting? I've already spoken to her and she's excited about having an extra hand around here. After we're done, we'll get you started with training. Okay?"

"Of course! Of course!" Kate exclaimed. "Oh, thank you so much. I promise I'll do good for you, Mr. Epperson."

"Okay, okay, now go get the pads," Epperson instructed.

After Kate left the room, Jenny said, "That was very sweet of you, Cameron."

Epperson just nodded. "We really do need the help and she seems like a nice kid that just needs a break. Besides, if she doesn't work out, I'll pawn her off on Harry. He can afford it." Kate returned, gave Jenny a pad and pencil of her own and sat down beside her, poised and ready to go. "Harry," Epperson said, "this is your show. What do you want to do?"

When I was on the beat, I didn't like the daily shift meetings we had, and I didn't care too much for this one either. As a one man operation all these years, I just did what I wanted without reporting to anyone, but I knew Cam could be helpful with the case, so if this was the way it was going to be, I'd rather take the lead.

Epperson seemed okay with it, too. "Okay, then. Sam's on his way to Denton to see what he can flesh out from the hospital stuff about Doe's injuries and then maybe to the sheriff's office to see what old Roscoe can offer. That'll depend on what he comes up with at the hospital. Didn't see a need for him to be here this morning. Waste of time. Like I told you last night, my little meeting with Doe and his cohorts gave me a small, very small, mind you, inkling that he might be on the up and up with his story. And the only way to prove it for a fact will come from the hospital."

"And me?" Epperson asked.

"You think you can dig up anything on Doe from when he was a defense attorney? The kind of cases he took? Associates?"

Epperson scribbled down some notes. "Maybe. A friend of mine used to be with the D. A.'s office back then. He's on the other side now, but he might know something. I'll see what I can do." He looked up from is notes. "And you?"

I checked my watch. "First, I'm going to check with DeRita about getting the guns back that Cochran confiscated, and see if he's got anything new for me. Then, I'll call Doe and make sure he's on top of getting those records from Henshaw. Later, depending on time and what Sam comes up with, I'll see if I can get in touch with Wellstone and McAllister. See if either one wants to confess to past sins. After that, I'll just wait."

"Wait?" Kate asked. "For what?"

"Whatever happens next, sweetheart. There doesn't seem to be a lack of bombshells dropping every other hour on this case. So, I'll just wait for the next one to drop.

Denton was located forty-five miles north of Dallas and forty miles south of the Oklahoma border, and the peaceful drive through the rolling hills of ranch country gave Sam's mind a chance to defrost. The Doe case had manifested emotions that had been buried deep inside him for years, and he wasn't sure if it was for the better or worse. Since the war, he just wanted to maintain. Stay busy. Don't think beyond the task at hand. Harry kept him busy with divorce cases and civil affairs; jobs that were dull and mundane, meant to keep his mind and body busy, but this was a new twist all together. And, they were nowhere near done, and he knew it. He felt alive again. Even the beating he took from Cochran and Megs didn't bother him. He'd already taken care of half of the problem. One down, one to go. Also, he intended on stopping to see Gamboa when he got back to Dallas. This was a meeting Harry didn't need to know anything about.

His mind drifted and unclouded even more when the image of Katie's face surfaced in his eyes and it made him smile. Two lost souls brought together by a violent circumstance of fate. Brief as the moments had been, he was at ease...at peace when they were together...even just the thought of her chipped away at the cold, dark crust that enveloped his soul. He was gentle, totally at ease in her company. Katie seemed oblivious to the scars on his face and the ones he carried inside; like the scars she had inside carried no weight with him, either. Maybe, there was a chance for them together, perhaps...but first, he had to make sure she was safe. That had started with him talking to Epperson about giving her a job. Something with a future, a career.

Rolling into town, Sam stopped at a Gulf filling station for gas and directions to the Denton Hospital. While the attendant filled up the Ford, Sam plugged a nickel into the soda machine and got a Nehi Grape. The sweet, frosty drink felt good to his throat, knocking the fur off his tongue from last night's beer and the four cups of coffee from this morning. "What do I owe you?" He asked, reaching into his pocket for some cash.

The attendant was finishing off cleaning the Ford's windshield, gave it one last swipe, and checked the numbers on the pump. "Two-fifty," he said.

Sam handed him three dollars. "Keep it and thanks for the directions."

"Anytime."

The attendant had given him excellent directions, and it took him less than ten minutes to find the hospital. The city of Denton was a rural town of less than twenty thousand people, but two popular colleges helped the city to afford more public amenities to its citizens, visitors, and rambunctious college students than an average town of its size. The two institutions of higher learning, Texas Women's College and North Texas State College, allowed plenty of fresh capital to flow into the city coffers. The town had the look and feel of a college town. Row after row of shops and saloons, fronted by wide sidewalks, parking meters, and a steady flow of foot traffic with college youths. It had a nice feel to it.

A good place to settle down in with a family. With Katie.

He pulled into the Denton Hospital parking lot and cruised along the lanes closest to the building, which was a long rectangular, two-story, red brick affair, and appeared to wear its age well. It was smaller than Sam expected, but twenty years ago it was probably considered state-of-the-art. He parked, walked up the steps to the front entrance, and entered through double glass doors.

The antiseptic smell of alcohol and disinfectant, common to hospitals, hit him instantly and full-force, with his first step inside. Bad memories and flashbacks of the white walls and gray floors from the hospital ship, the *Mercy*, stationed in the Pacific, jumped around crazily in his head. He stopped cold in his tracks, feeling dizzy, one hand holding onto the front door handle, steadying himself. Sometimes smells or sounds triggered flashbacks that crippled his mind. Like now.

Let it pass. Let it pass. Please.

Sam closed his eyes, trying to regain his equilibrium.

"Can I help you, sir?" A distant, assuring female voice asked him.

While lightening white darts danced erratically in his darkness, he heard soft soled shoes squeaking at a rapid clip against the sterilized tile floor and felt a hand gently grasp his forearm, doubling the support he gained from the door. His eyelids lifted slowly, gradually bringing the form of a young nurse dressed in a starched, white uniform and a tri-cornered cap resting on the crown of strawberry blonde curls. Sam smiled, reluctantly letting go of the door. "I'm fine," he said. "I just had a dizzy spell hit me all of a sudden." He pointed to his injured face. "I was in a car wreck a couple of days ago and kissed the windshield. He lifted his arms and shoulders slowly, "And cracked a couple of ribs, too. Is there somewhere I can sit for just a minute?"

"Of course," the nurse said, leading him to a row of chairs by the front information desk, guiding him by the arm. "Would you like some water? Something to drink?"

"That'd be nice," Sam said, taking a seat.

She returned in less than a minute, and sat down beside him, handing off a mid-size paper cup filled with ice cold water. He gulped it down quickly. "Are you here to see a doctor?" She leaned forward slightly and gently grazed the blood crusted stitches on his cheek with the tip of her finger.

He didn't jerk away, but allowed her to make the move. The strawberry blond curls accented hazel eyes and a small turned-up nose sprinkled with freckles. *Cute* immediately came to mind. She wore no makeup, but didn't need it. *Tomboy*.

"You need to keep those stitches covered so infection doesn't set in." She examined the wound closer. "Someone did a wonderful job with this; you'll barely have a scar if you take care of it properly."

Sam wasn't sure of how to respond to such words. "Yeah, wish I'd had him when they stitched up the other side," he said with a crooked grin.

She shifted around in her chair so she could face him and then gently angled his chin so she could see the old scar that dominated the left side of his face. "Army doctor. Am I right? He did good, whoever he was."

"Navy," Sam answered without hesitation. "Didn't have time to get a name, but I don't complain."

She smiled. "I know. Most men like you don't. Are you

here to see a doctor? Do you have an appointment? If you don't, I can..."

Sam held up a hand, stopping her mid-sentence. "No, not anything like that. I'm fine. Actually...*Think before you talk...Fate may be helping me out here...* "I just came by for some information about a former patient of the hospital's. I...I'm a detective, and I'm doing some background work." He hesitated for another second, thinking about what to say next. He didn't want to lie or mislead this little pixie of a girl. She'd been kind without asking for anything in return. Just a gut feeling that it was the right thing to do. "I'm the good guy" he said, "not a hack trying to dig up dirt on somebody. I'm here to help someone clear their name against false accusations, and this is the only place I can get it."

"A detective? With the police department or private?" She asked, not indicating a judgment either way.

"Private."

"M-m," she hummed, gave Sam a crooked, mischievous smirk, and then leaning forward and lowering her voice, she whispered "Who's the client?"

This wasn't what he expected. Sam thought he'd have to tear down stone wall barriers of resistance to even get a morsel of info. "Then, you'll help me?"

She frowned, as in thought, but not concern. "I can't show you another person's medical records; that could cost me my job if I get caught doing that, but maybe we can figure out another way." She reached up to his face again, her fingers cool and light to the touch. "You really need to let me clean and bandage those stitches. Then, we'll see if I can help you out. Sounds fun. I could use some excitement around here."

Sam shrugged. "Sure, I can live with that deal." He offered his hand. "Sam Wolfkill, Private Eye, at your service."

"Nice name, I like it. My friends call me, Max," she said, "and so can you."

"Max? I'm guessing...short for Maxine."

"Very good, *detective,* now who's the patient? Or *former* patient."

Sam balked at revealing the senator's name just yet. "Listen, there might be a way around the paperwork. Do you know anybody...nurse, doctor, any medical person that was here twenty years ago, in '32?"

"That far back? Wow, I..." Her brows knitted together. Then, she snapped her fingers. "Of course! Nurse Hugghins! I think she's been here since they built the hospital hundred years ago. She's a walking Library of Congress when it comes to this place and can probably rattle off the names of every patient and every child that's ever been born here. The two of you will get along famously, you'll see."

"Sounds like the one I need to talk to, then."

Max laughed with the same crooked, mischievous grin from before. "Oh you'll get to..."

Then, a coarse disciplined voice abruptly boomed and echoed through the empty hallway leading up to the front entrance. "*Do* we have a problem here and *why* aren't you at your station, Maxine?"

"Meet Nurse Hugghins," Max whispered, standing up at the same time. "No, Nurse Hugghins, I..."

Sam stood too.

Nurse Hugghins stepped forward between Sam and Max and stopped with her legs spread in a military at-ease stance, except her fists were planted on firm, wide hips, instead of behind the back. "Who is..." she stopped in mid-sentence when she stared up into Sam's face. Her firm military stance complimented the bulldog visage that exaggerated a wide white scar that began just above the right eyebrow, skipped the eye, and continued down her cheek to the corner of her mouth.

Sam knew a military nurse when he saw one. They were the heart and soul of the hospital ships and his respect for them ran deep. "Hell-o gorgeous," Sam said. His face was calm, expressionless, but his eyes spoke volumes. He stuck out a hand. "Sam Wolfkill, First Marine Division. I was assigned to the War Dogs attachment in the Pacific."

The pugnacious face melted and an unexpected, dimpled smile showed off perfectly white, aligned teeth, forming the white scar into an S shape. "I was assigned to the *Mercy*," Nurse Hugghins answered with pride. "Served her proudly for three years in the Pacific."

"I was there, too," said Sam, rubbing the scarred side of his face. "We were probably onboard at the same time."

She reached up to his face and traced the scar lightly with her finger, imitating Max's same gestures. "Looks like Dr. Sheffield's work. You were one of the lucky ones. Some of those doctors were just wam-bam, thank you ma'am docs that did their best to sew you up and move you down the assembly line. But not Sheffield."

"Never got his name," Sam said. "And you?"

Nurse Hugghins smiled. "What? This little thing?" She said, touching the scar on her face. "Let's just say I disobeyed orders and went somewhere I wasn't supposed to be and got caught up in a firefight."

"That was bad for the Japs, I bet."

"Well, I'm here and their spiritual beings are in the House of the Rising Sun, so to speak." She frowned and asked with some concern. "You okay, hon? You don't look so good." She reached for his wrist and said, "Sit down."

Sam knew better than to argue so he sat and let her read his pulse without making a fuss. "The smell got to me when I stepped inside. This is my first time inside a hospital since the war."

"What about those," Nurse Hugghins said, pointing to the stitches on his face. "Those are fresh and need to be cleaned."

"Doctor's office. It didn't bother me."

"Okay, but follow me so I can clean those stitches. Maxine, back to the desk."

Sam stood and offered a hand to Max. "Thanks for the rescue, Max. I'd be flat on the floor if you hadn't showed up."

Max shook his hand firmly. "My pleasure, Marine, you take care."

Nurse Hugghins took Sam back to a small examination room, instructed him to sit on the examination table, and started dabbing his wound with cotton swabs soaked in alcohol. "What do you need, Marine?" Nurse Hugghins asked. "I know you didn't come here to find a pretty face to match your own."

Sam smiled. "A little love. Somebody to kiss the boo-boo on my face. Information."

Chapter 23

I left Cam's office with a new legal pad I swiped off his conference table and two fresh cinnamon rolls. No need to let good food and a perfectly good writing pad, minus one page, go to waste. Back in the office of Stumbaugh Investigations, I put on a fresh pot of java and settled in behind my own desk, and laid out my original list of questions on the desk pad and my to-do list next to it. *DeRita, numero uno.* I dialed his number, using my private line, but there was no answer after several rings. *He must be at the donut shop.* Then, the office line rang.

And, so it begins.

"Stumbaugh Investigations."

"Harry…DeRita, here. You busy?"

DeRita's voice sounded funny. Shaken. "Uh, no. Matter of fact, I just tried to call you. I guess great minds think alike. What's up?"

"What were you calling about?" He asked, quickly.

"Just wanted to see if I could pick up our .38's from ballistics since there's no need for you guys to keep them. You okay, DeRita? You don't sound so hot."

"I'm on a call, Harry, and I think you should meet me here."

"Sure, like the old days. Wanna give me a heads up on what I'm walking into? I've had breakfast, you know."

Why call me?

"That probably wasn't a good idea. Meet me at 3131Carroll Avenue. Tell patrol to ask for me when you get here."

DeRita hung up abruptly, leaving me hanging with a phone in one hand and a half-eaten cinnamon roll in the other. I had a feeling another bombshell had just dropped. I chunked the last bite of the roll in the trash, turned off the coffee pot, and headed out the door. I didn't bother to tell the girls next door I was leaving.

The address wasn't familiar to me, but the place was easy to find once I got onto Carroll Avenue. It was the house that had six patrol cars with lights flashing silently, several unmarked vehicles, an ambulance, and the coroner's wagon in front of it. Shit, this must be *some-body.* It was a nice place with a manicured lawn and shrubs, two big pecan trees in the yard, and a cream colored brick home accented with dark green trim and fake shutters. I had no idea who it belonged to until I got to the mailbox and saw individual metallic letters spelling out the name, *COCHRAN.*

Son-of-a-bitch. Did he eat a bullet? Cochran didn't seem the type.

This one caught me way off the mark.

Wonder who does his yard? Can't imagine Moby Dick pushing a lawn mower.

That last cinnamon roll I had on the way here settled like a brick in the right-hand corner of my stomach.

Boom. Another bombshell.

Uniformed cops meandered around in the front yard and in the streets; one came out from the front door, his head hanging low and shaking in disbelief; another officer rushed from behind him and barely made it to the flowerbed before throwing up his breakfast; a collapsible gurney, manned by two men in white uniforms, raced towards the front door, ignoring the gagging patrolman who couldn't catch his breath.

What the hell is going on?

I stepped up on the porch, and a young patrolman I didn't recognize, raised an arm to stop me. "Sorry sir," he said, "unless you're law enforcement, I'm afraid you'll have to leave. Official personnel only."

I gave him his moment of glory, since he was probably a

rookie and just doing his job. "Name's Harry Stumbaugh. Detective DeRita asked me to meet him here."

"Just a minute, sir. I'll check." He went inside the house and in less than a minute returned. "Go on in, Mr. Stumbaugh. Detective DeRita is in the living room to your right when you go in." He held the door for me.

"Thanks," I said. Before stepping into the entryway, I glanced at the door jams, checking for any signs of forced entry. There were none.

Cochran let his murderer inside. He knew him.

"I don't think you'll be thanking me, sir," the young patrolman said over his shoulder.

The two mugs from the coroner's office stood impatiently to my left in the dining room beside their gurney like two vultures, anxious to haul off the road kill. I recognized Rick Lowry from Forensics talking to DeRita in the living room. We never cared that much for each other when I was on the job. And there were a couple of reasons for the mutual dislike. First, there were differences in our personalities. I had one and he didn't. Second, he believed the garbage about me being on the take when I retired from the force. Dirty like Cochran. In my humble opinion, he was a pompous prick, but I put all that aside for now. I made my approach and Lowry frowned, slamming his trap shut when he saw me coming towards DeRita and him. "Hi gents," I said.

"Hey, Harry," DeRita said, "you know Lowry, don't you? He's filling me in."

"What're you doing here, Stumbaugh?" Lowry growled, obviously not pleased with my intrusion.

I didn't see any reason to offer my hand for old time's sake. "Nice to see you too, Lowry. I was invited," I said, pointing to DeRita. "And you know, not everybody believes what they read on bathroom walls. It's time to move on, Rick."

"Like you did?"

I guess we aren't friends anymore.

Lowry returned his attention back to DeRita, acting like I wasn't in the room. "We done here? Me and you? I've got more work to do," he said, pulling some rubber gloves from his jacket pocket.

DeRita nodded. "Yeah, go ahead, but give me a minute before you go back to the bedroom, I want to take Harry back there first. I can see you two boys aren't going to play nice on the same playground." He took me by the elbow. "Come on…and prepare yourself."

Detective DeRita led me down a long narrow hallway, our heels clicking on the hardwoods, and then he pointed to an open door on the left. "In here," he said, stepping aside to let me go first.

I took a step inside, and I don't care how long a person has been on the job, there's no way to prepare for *that*. The naked, mutilated body of Detective Carl Cochran was spread-eagle across his bed like a beached whale. Wrists and ankles tied to the four-cornered bed posts and a bloody mass of mush between his legs, the lower half of the bed sheets almost completely soaked in red. But that wasn't the worst part. His eyes were bugged out like ping pong balls on the edge of busting out of his skull, and something very similar to a dick hung like a…well, a limp dick from the corner of his mouth. Since he evidently didn't have one between his legs anymore, I assumed it was his. "Rules out suicide, huh?"

"Not funny, Harry," DeRita said with a bite. "He's one of us, regardless of the history you two had in the past."

"He might've been one of *yours*, but there was never anything in common between the two of us, DeRita." Then a truly awful thought came to me. "Where's his old lady? He was married, wasn't he?" I was hoping she didn't have to witness what happened to Moby Dick. That would've been ugly.

"Yeah, and thank God. Neighbor said she was out of town visiting relatives, down in the hill country near Fredericksburg. We finally got hold of her and the family's bringing her home."

"Lucky for her, then. Any trace evidence? Prints? Hairs?

Anything?" I asked, stepping deeper into the scene, examining the bedroom as a whole. I wasn't too interested in dick-face on the bed, anymore.

"Not so far," DeRita answered grimly, "but we're nowhere near done, yet."

"I didn't see any marks around the door or the jam when I came in. Any busted windows anywhere, or signs of a break-in?"

"No. For now it looks like he let in whoever did this," DeRita said grimly, "and that worries me even more."

"I'm not trying to be cute when I ask this, Dan," I said, pre-empting him taking the question wrong, "but...cause of death?" I had a great one-liner follow-up, but decided not use it, yet.

"His death would've been a slow agonizing bleed out from the castration, but his balls were stuffed down his throat, too. He died from asphyxiation. He choked on his balls, Harry."

I worked hard to suppress a grin and giggle and exercised a tremendous amount of self-control in holding it in. DeRita invited me here as a courtesy, not as an opportunity to gloat. "I appreciate the heads up here, but why did you ask *me* to come by, Dan. You could have just as easily called, instead." But, I knew why I was here the second I saw Cochran smoking his own jewels.

"Yeah, I know. Let's step outside and turn the scene back over to Lowery so he can get this thing nailed down. Anything else you need to see?"

"Nah, I'm good," I said.

The fresh air gave me an immediate appreciation for the outdoors. The stink of death and blood and Cochran's fat ass was nauseating, and I didn't want to add my cinnamon roll to the patrolman's breakfast in the flowerbed. We left the porch and found a patrol unit at the curb and parked our butts side by side against the front fender. I fired up a Lucky and offered one to the detective."

"Nah, gave 'em up, remember?" He said, folding his arms across the chest.

"Alright...get it out of your system, Detective DeRita, just say what's on your mind. You didn't call me out here for a refresher course in crime scene investigation. We've known each other long enough not to mince words with each other and pout about it later."

DeRita kept his eyes focused on the front porch, avoiding eye contact. "So...speaking of crime scene investigation...what's your take on this, Harry? The whole nasty scene."

"Well," I said, taking a drag from the Lucky, "it's not Gamboa or a mob hit, if that's what you're thinking. I know it *looks* that way, but it's almost *too* obvious if you ask me. Which you are."

"Maybe, but they have a history that goes back a ways, you know. Perhaps Gamboa decided to take him down while Cochran was on the outs. You know, he and Megs were coming up on disciplinary charges, and worse probably for their actions against Wolfkill. And, I'm sure Gamboa knows what's going on here. He knows everything else that happens in this damn town."

"In the first place, Dan, this isn't Gamboa's style. He doesn't kill cops, dirty or otherwise. It's bad for business. He's sixty-five years old and doesn't have any desire to spend his retirement years in jail. It just doesn't figure. He's not Al Capone and this isn't Chicago. Hell, you remember earlier this year when that idiot Paul Roland Jones tried to bribe Sheriff Guthrie for a hundred-fifty K on the golf course to turn the tide and let the mob come to Dallas full hilt? He got his ass thrown in jail. We don't put up with the mob or unions here in Texas. You know that and so does Gamboa. Besides, Gamboa's not going to snuff out a cop over a six-year-old, misdemeanor shoplifting beef against his nephew. Especially when he was guilty. That'd be nuts."

"Yeah...maybe, if you say so...maybe."

I could tell DeRita was turning things around in his head, and I had to get him off the Gamboa track. "And another thing, if Gamboa *did* do this...we wouldn't even be having this conversation. He'd do it in a way that'd have you chasing trails in every direction but his."

His head made a half turn and faced me. "Sounds like you know him pretty good." It wasn't an accusation; he was just stating a fact.

"Yes, I do."

Switch gears.

"What time do you think old lard ass was killed?"

DeRita let out a heavy sigh and shot me a nasty look. "Somewhere between four and six this morning is the preliminary. We'll know more once we get him over to autopsy."

Turn the tide.

"Well, somebody's an early riser and likes the morning hours. Whoever did this, probably knew the old lady wasn't around or didn't really give a shit. He'll make a mistake, though. They always do."

DeRita's got more on his mind. Move him along.

"So, we're good? I can go? I can't see myself being any use around here."

"Yeah, and touch base with me later and you can pick up your pieces at HQ." Another audible sigh escaped his lips. "But, before you go, I gotta ask this Harry, so don't get all bent out of shape when I do."

Here we go.

"Shoot," I said, "I don't have anything to hide."

"Where were you between four and six A. M. this morning?"

I chuckled softly. "I'd have been disappointed if you hadn't asked, DeRita. I was parked in front of Jennie's apartment knocking back coffee and smoking cigarettes from three to about six-thirty." I waited for him to ask why.

He frowned. "For what purpose?"

Close enough.

"Well, to be honest, Cam Epperson expressed some concern about Jenny and Kate's safety. He's afraid that whoever's killing people might retaliate against me and Sam and anybody associated with us. If we get too close...which we will...anyway, Sam and I took turns watching their place last night."

"Sam? So…his whereabouts?"

"I relieved him at three."

Shit.

"What'd he do after that?"

"Went home and got some shuteye."

"M-m-m, and where is he now?"

"Denton," I said, "chasing down some background on Doe and his accident in '32."

He nodded. "You're not on a wild goose chase with this Doe thing, are you Harry?"

"Just doing the job I was hired to."

"So…you don't really know where Sam went after he left Jenny's, do you? There's a bit of history between him and Cochran, you know. More recent and more serious than a six-year-old misdemeanor rap, like you said. I like him and all, but there's some serious issues brewing inside that man. War does funny things to people once they get back into the world again."

Double Shit.

"No way," I said. "Look, Dan, whoever did this to Cochran is a sick psychopathic fuck. There's something here that goes a lot deeper than revenge. Does Sam have a few bolts missing from the framework since he came back? Yeah, he does, but who wouldn't. Would Sam find a way to get back at Cochran and Megs for what they did to him? Sure, wouldn't you? But not *this*. I know Sam. You're way off base if you like him for this. Trust me."

"Oh, I do trust you, Harry, you know that, but sometimes you can get close to somebody and it clouds your judgment. You can't always see the forest for the trees."

"Bullshit. I can see the trees and the forest perfectly fine." I shifted my weight to the other cheek and fired up another Lucky Strike. "Go with me here for a minute, Dan. Let's walk through this."

"Okay," he said. "I'm game."

"From the beginning. This all goes back to the heist in '32." I held up one finger. "First to buy the farm was Pete Strong, but we can't count him because he got caught and was sizzled like bacon in a frying pan by Old Sparky in Huntsville."

DeRita grunted, "Yeah, metaphorically speaking. Harry, anybody ever mentioned your obviously deep sympathetic feelings for your fellow man?"

"No. Now stay with me. Robert Petrie gets the shit beat out of him. I never saw any tox reports, but I'm betting he was drunker than a June bug, since he was found in the alley behind a titty bar in the early hours of morning. So the question is...what did he have in common with Pete?" I asked.

"Yeah, there was a fair amount of alcohol in his system." DeRita hesitated and said, "The heist...maybe Doe."

"Very good, and Sam had no motive and he had an alibi. Now, number two," I said, holding up two fingers. "Who's the next victim?"

He shrugged. "Abner Strong."

"Shot in the head with a .38. Another brutal take down. And, the connection?"

"The heist and Doe, maybe," DeRita sighed.

"Very good, you're on a roll. And, Sam..."

He nodded. "I know...no motive and an alibi."

"Right. And, the third victim," I said, holding up a third finger, "is the cock sucker inside. Connections?"

"Don't be disrespectful, I told you Harry, I don't like it." DeRita shifted his weight off the fender. "Give me one of those butts," he said, pointing to my pack of Lucky's. "Cochran...there's some kind of connection to the heist. He was on the scene, I'll give you that." He cupped his hands around the flame of my lighter and inhaled deeply on the Lucky. "I see where you're going with this, Harry...and if your theory is true...there's a psychopathic serial killer out there covering his ass. Jesus. Do you really think Doe could have any kind of involvement in this thing? That's pretty far out there in left field, don't you think?"

"Do I think he's *the* killer? Do I think he's involved in some way? Don't know yet, but I never rule anything out. But, deep down, in my opinion, he's like Gamboa. Both of them have more money than Clark Gable. The percentages don't add up."

"What about the money?"

"Oh, that's the key to solving the whole case, but I don't think it leads us to Gamboa, for sure. Doe...*maybe,* as you like to say when you can't think of anything else."

"Yeah...maybe," DeRita said, finally allowing a small grin to crack the mask of fatigue he'd been wearing ever since I got to Cochran's place. "There's going to be more body bags," he added with resignation. The detective pushed off the fender and eyeballed me hard. "Megs...I need to get to a phone and put some feet on the ground at his room. If Cochran's involved, so is Frank. And, your boy better have an alibi if anything happens to Detective Megs, Harry. He's not off the hook, yet. I want to talk to him. *Today*." DeRita refocused his attention back to the porch as the coroner twins wheeled out Cochran's mammoth corpse through the front door. "In the Pacific," he said, "you know what the Japs did to our boys after they killed them, don't you?"

I thought back to the confessional drunk-fest me and Sam pulled off at the Adolphus a year ago. "Yeah," I said quietly.

"Stuffed their dicks and balls down their throat," DeRita whispered.

Chapter 24

After leaving DeRita behind at the crime scene with a bad taste in my mouth, I decided to swing by the Adolphus and pay a visit to Doe. I figured the latest on Cochran would be of interest to him, and I wanted to see if he'd made any progress with Henshaw checking out his past employment list. As I passed the phone bank, I decided to check in at Cam's first. See if there was any news from Sam.

"Epperson, Freeman, and King," a familiar voice answered at the other end of the line.

"Well, hell-o, Katie, I see you've been put to work," I said with some lightness to my voice.

She was in a panic. "Where *are* you, Harry? You've got to get over here to Mr. Epperson's office *now*!" She exclaimed.

"Whoa! Hold the barn door for a second, Katie. What's..."

Her voice became distant as she held the phone away from her face. "Yes! It's Harry!" She said to someone.

I heard the phone piece being exchanged. "Hey Harry," Epperson said, calmly. "What cha' doing?"

"Hey Cam," I said with a chuckle. "I'm at the Adolphus. I came to drop in on Doe. What've you done to get my girl so excited there?"

"Don't bother with Doe. He's here with his mouthpiece, Henshaw."

"Really? What's that all about?"

"You remember those bombshells you mentioned earlier? Well, a big one just dropped."

"Then, that makes that *two*," I said. "I've got one of my own. You show me yours and I'll show you mine."

Epperson laughed. "Like two boys on the playground, huh? You show me yours first, Harry. Mine's bigger."

"Okay, I'll play. I just came from Carl Cochran's house. Somebody cut off his balls and stuffed them down his throat. He's gargling with the demons, as we speak. Now top that one, counselor."

"Not bad," said Epperson, "breaks my heart. Why were *you* there?"

"DeRita called me in, wanted me on the scene. He seems to think either Gamboa or Sam did it. I told him he was pissing in the wind. He was on a fishing expedition, that's all. Okay, I showed you mine, what've you got to play with?"

"I'm afraid I've got you beat, ol' buddy. You familiar with a reporter from the *Dallas Morning News* by the name of Tony Zucker?"

"Yeah," I answered, "I've known him for years. He's a dandy. Why? What's he got to do with anything?"

"Well, his byline just jumped to the front page. He called Doe this morning at the Adolphus and said he was face-to-face with the senator's ex-wife and son from Ardmore, Oklahoma. He wanted to know if he had any comment."

Chapter 25

The atmosphere in Cam's conference room was as heavy as a lead balloon. I noted the absence of Jenny and Kate; I guess they didn't want any notes taken. Senator and Hedy Doe looked like shit. Actually, Hedy looked good, as usual, but my highly-refined detective skills denoted some strain around the eyes that clued me into the fact that all was not hunky-dory in the Swiss Avenue Wonderland. Henshaw looked dapper and full of himself; I suppose if it's not your ass on the line and the hourly fees are racking up, you can afford to be calm. Cam looked to be enjoying himself, and I knew he looked forward to some tit-for-tat with Henshaw. Personally, I also figured he was waiting for the opportunity to *one-up* his adversary across the table.

I shook hands all around, and each responded with short, curt hello's. Across the table from the Does and Henshaw, I sat next to Cam. It seemed safer. "Anybody heard from Sam, yet?" I asked.

"Not yet," answered Cam. "But, I'm dying to know what he's found."

"Yeah, me too." The Does looked like they were too stunned to start things off and Henshaw looked like he was above it all. So, I got the party started. "Well, sounds like we've all had an eventful morning," I said. I'm sure Mr. Epperson here…," I nodded at Cam, "has filled you in on the demise of our beloved brother, Detective Carl Cochran." There were just nods from across the table. Evidently, the tears would come later after the full effect of his loss would hit them. Or not. "Okay, well…I guess we can look on the bright side, another one of the bad guys has taken a fall. So, if they keep dying at this pace, you may not have to pay a thing, John. Process of elimination." No reaction. No sense of humor with this group. Might as well move on. "Okay, fill me in, John. What's with Zucker and your extended family?"

Doe's eyes shifted quickly to Hedy, and then he grasped the hand in her lap. "First off, I might as well make it known that I'm going to drop out of the election. Whether what this lady says is true or not is irrelevant...as far as running is concerned. There's no way to overcome the damage from this."

Henshaw jumped in, "For the record, I've tried to dissuade John from being rash about this decision. And, I'd just like to say..."

Doe turned on his attorney like a pit-bull. "There *is* no Goddamn *record*, Garland, and to be frank, I never should have let you talk me into running for the Senate in the first place. Even you said I'd lose, but the name recognition alone would boost my run for governor in the next gubernatorial election. Hell, even *Harry* told me I didn't have a snowball's chance in hell in winning. I think this whole thing has come about *because* I'm running."

"John," Hedy whispered. "Now's not the time or place for this. Just tell Harry about the woman."

The voice of reason in the storm, but I filed Doe's little outburst in the back of my mind for future reference. Interesting.

Doe took a breath, collecting himself. "Okay...Zucker called me this morning about...oh, I don't know...nine or ten o'clock. The conversation only took a few minutes and he was short on details."

Epperson asked, "Did he let you talk to the woman?"

Good question.

I saw Henshaw's face turn grim. He evidently didn't like being pre-empted by another attorney.

"No, I asked him after he told me everything, but he wouldn't allow it. Supposedly, they were in the office with him while we were on the phone."

"He put you on a speaker?"

"No, and I didn't think anything about it in the beginning, of course. He said she claimed to be my wife. She said we got married in April of 1931 and had a son a year later."

About fifty questions tumbled around in my head and there was one thing I knew for sure, now. It was a scam. Somebody, whoever was pulling the strings, had saved this move as their coo-dee-ta. This was supposed to be the last nail in the coffin for Doe. The thing to put him over the edge so he'd cough up the money. "Let me stop you for a second, John, and ask a couple of questions before you go on with this amazing narrative. Did she give a name?" I already knew what the answer would be.

"Mrs. Ralph Morris, *of course,*" he hissed, like a rattler before it struck.

"Yeah, of course. And, she said she was from Ardmore, Oklahoma?"

"Yes."

"Any of that ring a bell to you?"

"No. Because it's not true."

I nodded. "I'm beginning to believe you, John. But, why did she go to Zucker? Why not just come straight to you?"

"I asked Zucker the same thing and he gave some bullshit answer that she wanted the protection of the press. In other words, dodging the question. Bullshit."

"Like a good politician," I said. "Sorry, couldn't pass up the opening, John." Cam was the only one who gave a light snicker. Still no sense of humor in the crowd.

Henshaw finally spoke. "Protection my ass. He's a reporter, he's supposed..."

Doe cut off his mouthpiece. "Then, you believe me, Harry? You don't think I'm this Ralph Morris character?"

I gave him an encouraging smile. "Well, you may find this a little strange, but I think the fact that this woman has come forward in the manner that she has, *confirms* it, John. This is a setup if there ever was one. Doesn't it strike anyone at this table, especially our esteemed counselors-at-law, as mighty coincidental with the timing of all this?" I pointed at Doe. "John, here, gets blackmailed because he's an easy target. He's got the whole amnesia thing going for him, which is indefensible; he's married to a wealthy, beautiful woman; he's a dashing, charismatic public figure who bravely charges into an election nobody believes he can win, but declares he's doing it for the democratic process of a choice on the ballot." I gave Doe a nod. "Have I got the spin about right on the election thing, John?"

The senator finally smiled. "On the money, Harry. But, do you think that whoever is behind this crazy scheme, actually believes I'm going to pay up? A half million dollars? If they do, no matter what slander and libel they throw at me, I'm not paying a dime. They can kiss my ass on a Tuesday morning in the middle of Main Street, for all I'm concerned."

"Tomorrow's actually Wednesday...but, that's neither here nor there," I added for cleverness.

He's got the fire in the belly thing going again. Good.

I watched for the reactions of the others at the table, during Doe's triad. Hedy watched her husband with the same intensity as his delivery. I thought the *damn the torpedoes* speech worked better on her than it did me. This chick is in love. Henshaw's face remained stoic, not really showing any emotion either way, and Doe's reprimands didn't seem to bother him.

Are they that close in their relationship?

Epperson scribbled something on his legal pad and passed it to me. It said, *I'm w/ you on this. I've got an idea but maybe you should take the lead. ATTACK! TAKE THE OFFENSE!* I eased the pad back to him without a reaction, but I agreed with him. Henshaw's eyes followed the pad.

Time to get back on track.

"Okay, John, but let's get back to Zucker and the chic from Ardmore. Nice speech by the way." Still no reaction from anybody. Humor has evidently fallen to the wayside. "Okay, what exactly is her story? Did Zucker give you any details? Or was he just gonna leave you hanging in the wind."

"Both. She claims that I told her I was a farm equipment salesman when we got married, and that's why I was gone and on the road all the time, servicing my territory. She said I took off on a sales trip in mid-September, and she never heard from me again. That would've been the month before the '32 heist."

"And, the kid?" I asked. "What's the Ardmore Mama got to say about him?"

Doe shrugged. "He was a baby when I supposedly left. Five months old or so. And before you ask, his name is Ralph Morris, Jr. Of course."

"Of course, it is," I said. "And, she wants money?"

"No. That's the strange thing about this whole affair. She claims she never divorced me. We're still married, and she wants me back! Can you believe it?"

"Nice touch," I said.

Henshaw laughed. "Can you imagine the nerve of this...this *woman*? She and her twenty-something bumpkin kid come to the big city and just want to take daddy home...back to the farm? Just drop everything, wife, career, reputation...and follow Thelma Lou back to Oklahoma?" He turned to Doe. "I'm going to make a personal call to Jake Armbrooster, the owner of that shameful rag of a paper, and threaten him with libel, slander, and everything else I can think of, on your behalf, John. If he prints one word of this tomorrow or any other day, I'll sue his ass!" No one, including Doe, reacted to his predictable rant.

Epperson raised a hand, indicating a question, and I reached over and took the legal pad and pen from in front of him and scribbled a note to myself. The memory fades now and then. I looked up and spotted Henshaw eyeballing me. I smiled and covered the pad with my hand like a schoolboy covering his homework so nobody could cheat off of him. He returned a tight smile and looked away.

Prick.

"Senator Doe," Epperson said, "something you said strikes me as odd...or more odd than the rest. You said she didn't want money, well if that's the case---"

"Somebody's *paying* her to do this," I threw in. "How else would she know to go to a sleaze-bucket like Zucker? Somebody had to point her in that direction. Hell, if she's for real, they had to know about her, and if they dug her up, they just got dealt aces and queens to a gut-straight." I took a breath, letting everyone soak-in my words of wisdom. "And, third...she's just another hard-luck mama pulled off the street that wanted to make some quick dough."

"Exactly," Cam stated, "and I think it's the latter. Does she want to meet with you, Senator? I'm curious about that, too."

It was obvious from the look on Henshaw's face that he wasn't enjoying Epperson out score him with intelligent questions and observations. I rather enjoyed it.

"Call me John, and nothing was mentioned about that...at least yet. Remember, Zucker wouldn't even let me talk to her on the phone, so meeting her face-to-face was probably out of the question. That's the *protection* he was talking about. He pretty much told me he believed her story and planned to put it in tomorrow's paper. He said he was just giving me the courtesy of knowing what was to come. He said he didn't want to blindside me. Can you believe that shit?"

"Anybody think Zucker's in on the deal, or is he just a dupe?" Henshaw threw the question out to no one in particular.

Doe nor Hedy offered an opinion. I shrugged. "Don't know, but I doubt he's involved. Probably being used and manipulated like everyone else on this deal," I said.

Epperson stayed quiet, but I saw him glance at my note and smile. Henshaw saw it too.

"Well," Henshaw said, standing up, straightening an already perfectly tied knot of his tie, "I know what I'm going to do. I'm going back to the office and get Armbrooster on the phone and stop this in its tracks, right now, before this goes any further."

Doe reached up, grabbing his arm. "Just a minute, Garland. I want to hear more from the other side of the table, first. I'm not sure that's the right thing to do...just yet, anyway." The senator motioned for his attorney to sit down. "Gentlemen?"

I definitely had a plan, but before I could speak, there was a soft knock on the conference room door. "Come in," Epperson responded.

Katie appeared through the open door, smiling, her eyes big and bright. "Sam's here," she said, working hard to contain her excitement.

"Send him in, Katie," Epperson said, getting up from his seat. He moved over one space, leaving the chair by me empty.

I tried to read Sam's face when he stepped in, but it didn't reveal success or failure, but I could damn sure tell he knew he was the man of the hour.

"Howdy," he said, casually, stepping up to the table and wrapping both hands over the back of the vacant chair. His eyes gazed across everyone's face. "I've missed something, haven't I?"

"Sit your ass down, Sam," I said, lightly. "We need some good news."

"I'm okay, I'll stand." He turned his attention to Senator Doe. "Senator, would you hold up your right hand for me, please sir?"

Doe didn't ask why, but instead immediately raised his hand, as though he was taking an oath.

"Very good, sir," Sam said, keeping his eyes on Senator Doe and his wife. "Well...I've got verification, sir, that your little finger was mangled in the hit and run accident." He let that declaration settle for a second. Hedy Doe reached over and grabbed her husband's hand. She was beaming. "The emergency room nurse distinctly remembers seeing the tip of the finger hanging by the skin. There was no way it could have been saved. *And*...there's more. You'll be glad to know your name is not Morris. Or Doe, for that matter."

Sam knew how to deliver the punch lines; I had to give him that. The silence in the conference room, to use an old cliché, was deafening, and Sam's very words sucked the air from the room like a vacuum as we all unconsciously inhaled a deep breath, waiting for the other shoe to drop. Doe's brow furrowed, as though confused. Hedy Doe's eyes instantly filled with tears, as if on command, and her bottom lip trembled. Henshaw looked genuinely surprised. Shocked, actually. I just smiled.

Sam gloated for a millisecond and continued. "I'd like to introduce everyone to someone I brought along, if you'll bear with me a second," Sam said. He turned back to the door. "Would you please come in now, Nurse Hugghins?"

I turned around in my seat to see a stout woman dressed in a heavily starched nurse's uniform, and tucked tight under her arm was an old shoe box that looked half squashed. She had a distinctive scar that started above the eyebrow and dropped down to the corner of her mouth like a jagged bolt of lightning. Sam and her could've passed as brother and sister, sporting twin scars. The sturdy nurse stood beside Sam and carefully took in the face of everyone at the table. When she got to Senator Doe, a hand flew up to her mouth, as though shocked and pleasantly surprised at the same time. Her eyes watered, which was contradictory to her no-nonsense stature.

I was afraid the women were going to start flooding the place. I shifted in my seat to sneak a look at the senator. First, he exhibited confusion. I don't think he'd recovered from Sam's entrance and verification of who he *wasn't*. His face reddened. He blinked his eyes in quick succession. He stood up, holding on to the back of his chair for support, staring at the nurse across the table from him.

"Ma-Maggie? Nurse Maggie? Is that really you?" Senator Doe croaked, his voice catching in sob.

Chapter 26

While everybody in the room *ou'd-and-ah'd* about Nurse Maggie, I was more curious about the battered shoebox held snug under her arm. The fact that Doe recognized a nurse that took care of him *after* he lost his memory didn't impress me. I also knew Sam well enough to know that he wouldn't bring this drill sergeant of a nurse all the way to Dallas just for a family reunion.

Senator Doe weaved through chairs and around the end of the conference table to get to Nurse Maggie like a halfback dancing through the line with a nose for the goal posts. "Maggie, I can't believe it!" Doe slowed down to a steady walk when he got within a few feet of the nurse then whispered, "Maggie, so good to see you."

Maggie Hugghins smiled and reached out with her free arm and wrapped it around the senator's neck when he stepped closer. "Senator," she said. Doe gently put his arms around her and held her quietly for a few seconds. Then, she stepped back, went through the motions of straightening out the front of her uniform, as if it really needed it, and quickly retained a staunch, military glare at Doe, and brought her shoulders square again. "You're such a big shot now that you're too damn busy to keep in touch over the past twenty years, *Senator*?" She took a step back, glancing across the table at Hedy Doe. "And, I see my affections have been replaced by another pretty face."

Doe smiled. "You always were the jealous type." He reached up to her face and softly outlined the new scar down her cheek. "Maggie...what happened?"

"World War II happened, honey," she said.

During this love-fest of a reunion, which was getting on my nerves, I noticed a couple of things. For one, Nurse Maggie held on to that shoebox like it was the family jewels, and two, she kept referring to Doe as *Senator.* Not John, or Mr. Doe. It was time to move things along. The lovebirds could chew over old times later. "Uh...," I stood up, "*Miss* Hugghins, is it?" I asked, assuming the old broad wasn't married. "My name is Harry Stumbaugh." I stuck out my hand.

She took it immediately and gave me a firm grip like a man. "Sam told me all about you, Mr. Stumbaugh. Nice to meet you, sir. And, *Miss* is correct," she said. "What about you?"

That one caught me off guard. "Uh...single, if that's what you mean." Hell, I didn't know what else to say. I damn sure wasn't going to lie to her. I wasn't *that* stupid.

Cam stood up beside me and offered his own hand, obviously seeing an opportunity for a good time. "Cameron Epperson, attorney-at-law, Miss Hugghins. I'm one of the good guys and yes...I'm available," he quipped with a wink.

"Hard to believe that...pretty boy like you," she said with a straight face.

Thankfully for me, Doe finally came to his senses and our rescue. "Uh, Maggie," he said, pointing across the table, "I'd like you to meet my wife, Hedy."

Hugghins looked me up and down first, then Epperson, returning the wink. "Don't worry, boys. You're both free to play the field. I'm more into ex-Marines like Sam over here. You're not my type."

Sam grinned like a shit-eating raccoon. He was enjoying himself *way* too much. I, on the other hand, didn't know whether to be relieved or pissed, but I decided to stay with relieved. Cam bowed and said, "My loss, Ma'am." After that little show, I figured silence was the best response, so Cam and I retreated to our seats to get out of the line of fire. We'd bought favor and that was all I was interested in.

Hedy came around the table and greeted the nurse with a genuine, heart-felt hug and said, "I can't believe it. I'd hoped that one day I'd get to meet the famous Nurse Maggie that brought John back to health so long ago. He has spoken so often and fondly of you over the years."

That was one woman I just couldn't put a finger on. One minute she comes on like a sultry cabaret singer, dipping her finger in a martini glass like Marlene Dietrich in *Blue Angel*, and the next minute she's more wholesome than Harriet is to Ozzie. All this warm and fuzzy was getting on my nerves, and we weren't getting anywhere with all this huggy stuff. To make matters worse, I spotted Jenny and Katie standing in the doorway, both grinning and teary-eyed. *Great.* I looked at Sam, raising my eyebrows, and gave him a, *Let's move along* look.

He nodded and stepped up to the huggy-huggy trio and took the nurse by the elbow, moving in. "Senator Doe…Mrs. Doe, if you would…have a seat, please. Maggie has some things to tell us, which I think will bring some closure…to the last twenty years."

Way to go, Sam. That got their attention. Nice lead-in.

Doe and Hedy returned to their seats. I noticed that the mouthpiece, Henshaw, and I were the only ones who weren't glowing in the moment. Jenny and Katie were still standing in the doorway, and I jerked my head towards the outer office, indicating it was time to go back to work. Baby Doll pouted her lips, evidently dissatisfied with yet another episode of rudeness on my part, and took Katie by the arm, closing the door behind them.

Sam watched the girls leave and started once the door closed. "Okay," Sam said, "as all of you know, I went to Denton this morning to see if I could find out anything about Senator Doe's stay at the hospital in 1932, after his accident. The primary purpose was to see about the famous pinkie. Did he loose it before or after the accident? Well, I found the answer…and more. In a…"

Henshaw evidently didn't want to hear the prologue to the book and wasn't moved by all the gushy emotion in the room, any more than me. "Could we move this speech along and get to the facts, please...Mr....Wolfkill, is it? The clock is ticking, I might add. The senator's reputation and good name are about to be slandered and maligned across the headlines of one of the biggest and most read papers in the state and...and you're going through introductions."

Sam didn't miss a beat. "Well...*Mr. Henshaw,* is it? I assume that *Senator Doe* is paying for *your* time...so why don't you just relax."

Oh, that went over real well.

"Now, where was I? Anyway, in a roundabout way, that I won't go into right now...to save time, I met Maggie Hugghins at the hospital and hit the jackpot." Sam turned to the nurse, "It's all yours, Maggie," and sat down beside me.

It was one of those Nick and Nora Charles moments from *The Thin Man,* when all the suspects were seated at the dining room table and the murderer was about to be exposed, except I didn't think we had one in the room at this time.

Nurse Maggie Hugghins stepped forward and glanced at Henshaw and gave him a tight smile. "Sir, I don't know who you are because you didn't have the courtesy to introduce yourself, but if you interrupt *me* the way you did Mr. Wolfkill, I may end up being *your* nurse, too. From the looks of you, I'm sure you spent the war behind your own desk somewhere." She sniffed the air as if there was a bad odor somewhere. "I was on Guadalcanal, by the way."

I was beginning to like this old girl more and more by the second. As much, I'd say, as Henshaw disliked her, but he kept his mouth shut. He was another man who knew when it was best to be invisible in the room. Sam coughed. The senator and Hedy must've caught something in their throats too and had to clear them several times.

"It's true," Maggie continued, "I was the senator's nurse at Denton Hospital. Actually, I was on duty in the emergency room when he was brought in and continued on by his side every day until his recovery. He ended up staying with us for almost six weeks, since his injuries were quite extensive. During this time, his recovery involved the healing of a broken leg with compound fractures; a dislocated shoulder; multiple lacerations, including the loss of the first knuckle of his fifth digital; and of course a severe concussion, resulting in amnesia. He was subject to, not only physical, but extensive psychological rehabilitation. Now…any questions up to this point?" She gazed around the room, with Henshaw being last in line and earning a raised eyebrow. It looked like a dare, to me. Everybody passed on the offered opening to speak up, remaining quiet and focused on her.

She continued. "Shortly after the senator was released from the hospital, I felt compelled to join the Army WAC's Nursing Corp. I felt I could do more there, and over the years I was moved from one military base hospital to the other. Then, during the war, I was assigned to the *Mercy* hospital ship. It wasn't until this year that my twenty-year hitch came to an end, and I retired from the military. Upon retirement, I returned to Denton Hospital. Any questions?"

No one dared, but it was obvious Henshaw was getting impatient. I sure as hell wasn't about to say anything. The old girl hadn't wavered one inch from her original stance of spread feet, one arm still gripping the shoebox, and the other locked behind her back. Hell, I couldn't even tell if she was breathing or not.

"Okay," she said, "now for the part you've been waiting for. When Sam told me what he was looking for…well, I was shocked. Twenty years in the past suddenly came to life again." She directed her attention to Doe. "Many times, I've wondered about you, Senator, but you can understand that since I've been gone, globe-trotting around the world on Uncle Sam's dime, I had no way of knowing whatever became of you." She nodded at Sam. "Sam's inquiry, needless to say, was only by the grace of God, in my opinion. What are the odds of two veterans, wounded on the same island, being on the same hospital ship, and landing in Denton, Texas in search of the same thing? Fate, maybe. Call it whatever you want, but I'm here to tell you God's hand is right in the middle of this affair."

She paused, and then her tone darkened, her brow furrowed. "Sam and I went down to the basement where the archives of records from the past fifty years are kept. All the records were there...except for the patients who were admitted in October of 1932. The entire file is gone. Missing." She finally shifted her weight. "I know the person that keeps those records, and he's been there for forty years. This had nothing to do with him. Someone removed them, for whatever reason."

The moans and facial expressions from the senator and Hedy magnified their disappointment. Epperson smiled, though. We were on the same page. Henshaw smiled, but I don't think it was for the same reason. I raised my hand, like a kid in school trying to get the teacher's attention.

"Yes, Mr. Stumbaugh?" She asked, turning in my direction.

I wanted to be the teacher's pet. "But, that's just the *bad* news isn't it, Nurse Hugghins? You have *good* news, too. Right?" I did this for the Doe's benefit.

She almost smiled. "You go to the head of the class, Mr. Stumbaugh."

Could the old broad read my mind?

She set the shoebox on the conference table. "But Sam, actually, found this...sitting alone on the shelf above the place where the missing records were *supposed* to be. Whoever took the records wasted a trip. After looking inside this old battered shoebox, I knew that the missing box records were inconsequential." She removed the lid, put it on the table, and then tilted the contents from the box, slowly emptying them randomly for everyone to see. A well-worn brown leather wallet that looked as though it had rode the hip pocket of a man's pants for many years; a gold pocket watch, bob, and chain with faded initials *J S* engraved on it; a dark yellow, four-inch switchblade knife; some dollar bills and change; a silver dollar; and a man's comb were scattered across the table.

Nobody said a word. We stared at the pile of miscellaneous items like they were gold nuggets. I was betting they were more valuable than gold to John and Hedy Doe, though. But to me, they were everyday items that any man carried in his pockets.

"Those are your belongings, Senator," Nurse Hugghins said. "Whoever it is that emptied your pockets when you were brought into the emergency room that night must have dropped them in that box. It is highly unusual, and I have no explanation for it. I had never seen that box or the things in it, until this morning when Sam and I opened it together." She nodded at the shaken man across the table from her. The handsome, chiseled face of Senator John Doe was drawn. The ruddy cheeks slightly pale.

"That's your wallet, Senator," she said. "Go ahead and open it."

Now this was a *real* Nick and Nora Charles moment. Senator Doe reached across the table. His hand had a slight tremble to it as he reached for the wallet. The hand remained poised over it momentarily, then he turned to his wife. "You do it, Hedy," he said with a nervous laugh. "I'm too damn nervous."

Hedy Doe gave her husband a quick smile and nodded. She stood, reached across the table without any hesitation, picked up the wallet, and opened it. Inside were plastic sleeves for pictures. She flipped through them quickly and found something that immediately caught her attention. A knowing smile crossed her lips. She focused on whatever it was for a brief moment and flipped through one more sleeve.

I had to admit, the woman knew how to hold her composure and leave the rest of the room biting their nails. It was a great show.

"Well...I have a driver's license for a...six-foot-two-inch...my, you seemed to have gained some weight since you got your driver's license...Jeffrey. Senator Jeffrey Allan Shockley!"

A few minutes later, after choruses of *Oh my's* and *This is unbelieveable's*, Doe or Shockley, or whatever the hell his name was now, started going over every scrap of paper in the wallet with Hedy practically sitting in his lap.

Very touching.

He kept saying over and over, *I can't believe this!* Maggie Hugghins took a seat beside the senator and began going over the items with them, too. Evidently, Jenny, Katie, and Cam's secretary heard all the commotion from their desks in the outer office and felt the need to join the melee.

Henshaw bolted to his feet, grinning like a Cheshire Cat. "Cameron, would you mind asking one of your girls there to contact Armbrooster at the *News* for me? I need to get that hack on the phone and cut off Zucker's story before it gets printed. The son-of-a-bitch will owe me big-time for this one." Then, he put one hand on the senator's shoulder and stuck out the other to shake his hand. "John…er, Jeff…hell, I'll never get used to that one…anyway, I'm thrilled for you, buddy. And, as much as I'd like to pop a cork with you, I've got to get busy. This brings an end to this extortion business, the whole ball of wax. I need to arrange interviews, pictures, radio, even television to get this out to the public. Hell, I'll have you on Dave Garroway's show before the end of the week!"

Doe just gave him a glance with a weak smile. It was obvious that publicity was the last thing on his mind. I had a feeling that his political career was the last thing on his mind at the moment.

Henshaw ignored the look and kept rambling. "Just let somebody call for a half-million now in extortion money, now. The bastards. And, forget that business about dropping out of the race, too. Price Daniels better watch his ass, buddy-o. With this in our pocket, there could be a Republican U. S. Senator in Washington, D. C. in January!"

"Becky," Epperson said to his secretary calmly, not getting caught up in the attorney's fervor, "would you assist Mr. Henshaw with his phone call?" Then, Cam leaned towards Sam and lowered his voice, whispering, "I don't know about you boys, but I'm not as optimistic as Counselor Henshaw. I don't think this damn affair is anywhere near finished, yet. We've still got dead bodies everywhere, and I doubt the kingpin of this operation is going to just drop it after going to all this trouble. Do you, Harry? Sam?"

"Nope," I said. "It's not about Doe. It's all about the *money*."

"I agree," Sam said, and added with grin, "not by a long shot, buddy-o."

After all the secretaries went back to their jobs and Henshaw was finally out of our hair, Epperson, Sam, and I moved away from the reunion to the other end of the conference table so we could talk privately for a few minutes before making our own exit.

"Sam, what else was in the wallet?" I asked. "That driver's license could belong to anybody. There's no damn picture on it for identification."

"Oh, it's him alright, Harry, I'm sure of it. Maggie and I went through every piece of paper and picture we could find in there. I think the first thing Mrs. Doe stopped on when she was flipping through it was a picture of Doe and another man. It was a picture from one of those photography booths at the train station for a dime. It was Doe alright. On the back of it were two names and a date. Jeff and Teddy. July 10, 1930. They both looked to be in their early twenties."

"Was there a picture of Doe, just him? Anything better to nail it down? I asked.

"Yeah, a picture of him and a dame. More names and dates on the back. Jeff and Amelia. Dated August of 1929. It looked like it was taken in a nightclub somewhere. I assumed he was the Jeff, not Amelia."

"Very funny. Well, let me ask you guys this. Do either of you two movie stars carry pictures of yourself in your wallet?" I asked.

"Harry," Sam said. "Look at this face. Would you carry a

picture of *this* in *your* wallet?"

"Since when did you develop a sense of humor, Wolfkill? Anything else?"

"Yeah." Sam answered.

I watched him glance at the happy trio, then he reached to his inside jacket pocket and pulled out a folded piece of paper that probably used to be white, but had yellowed with age. From the looks of it, it could've come from Doe's wallet.

"This," he said, sliding it over to me. "I found this in the wallet and nicked it out before Maggie saw me. It's a list of names and phone numbers."

"Really," Epperson said. "Any familiar names on it?"

"Just one."

"Shit," I said. "Why do I have a bad feeling about this?" A heavy sigh escaped my lips, and I crossed my arms. "Okay, Sam, who is it?"

"Giovanni Gamboa," Sam stated.

"Son-of-a-bitch," Epperson stated.

"Shit," I said.

Chapter 27

Frank Megs was miserable. He was stuck in bed with a thick plaster body cast that started mid-chest high and angled to his left shoulder, enclosing the left arm down to the wrist. The damn thing was so heavy. An aluminum bracket was required to stabilize the fractured arm, keeping it board straight at a ninety degree angle from his body. Pain shots were scheduled every six hours, but the Demerol wore off in four.

Another thirty minutes to go before the next shot.

He was imprisoned in the hospital with no release date in sight, couldn't get out of bed or take a piss on his own, and worst of all, he was cut off from Cochran and the others and had no clue of what was going on in the outside world.

How was the deal going down?

But, one man kept the fire burning inside him, and his jaws clenched together tight just thinking about him. The one that did this to *him*. Sam Wolfkill was a dead man walking. He knew that the pleasure of killing Wolfkill would have to go to someone else, but he'd be there to watch it happen. The fantasy danced in his head…watching…hearing the bones snap. Only for Wolfkill, it would be worse than his own personal torture…not just one bone, but all of them. Slowly. One at a time. The thought of it excited him. It gave him purpose.

It was all he could think of…and the money, too. With the elimination of Petrie and old man Strong, everybody took a bigger cut…over fifty grand each. Only four of them left to divide the money, once Doe paid up. And, the son-of-a-bitch would, there was no doubt about that. Before it was all done, he'd have no choice…if he loved that pretty little rich bitch wife as much as he claimed.

Ah yes, the money…Megs closed his eyes…dreaming, imagining himself on a Mexican beach with a tall, cool drink in one hand and the other wrapped around a tall, cool senorita…nursing him back to health…every night. Whispering in his ear. He smiled to himself, silently mouthing her words.

"Having a wet dream, Frank?" A voice interrupted calmly.

Megs's eyes flashed open, the unexpected intrusion from the voice and the words scared the shit out of him, reflexive impulses caused his body to jerk, spasms shot excruciating, shearing pain through the joint of his broken elbow, crashing into the shoulder like a lightning bolt. "Arg-g!" He moaned, his good arm automatically reaching across to the cast. "What the fu…"

"Sh-h-h," the man said, closing the hospital room door behind him. "Relax Frank, I just came by to talk and see how you're doing. You okay?" He strode quietly up to the bed, and gently touched Megs's cast. "That's got to hurt, huh?"

Megs winced, resettling, trying to get comfortable. The pain was even worse now.

Shit! How much longer? I need a shot now!

Sweat beaded his forehead like a rash; he finally managed to gather his thoughts, but the words came slow. "Like…like a mother-fucker. How'd…how'd you…get in here? DeRita posted a patrolman at the door. Right? Nobody's supposed to…" Then, he noticed the uniform. "Hey…where'd you…"

"Sh-h-h, it's okay, Frank. Officer Berkey went to get some coffee. Nice guy. No problem." The man held his arms out from his body. "You like the uniform? I always wanted to wear a badge. What do you think?" He asked, turning in a circle. "I look good in blues, huh?"

"Are you crazy, fucking coming here? Wearing *that*? You could---"

"What Frank? Nobody knows who I am. I'm just another cop that's come up to see his old buddy. We all look the same, right? Isn't that what you say about the coloreds?"

Frank Megs licked dry cracking lips. No matter how often he swabbed them down with Chap Stick or lotion, they never stayed moist. His mouth was suddenly dry, no spit, and his tongue felt like it was growing thicker. Sand paper. "Say, could you get me some water? There's a pitcher and glass by the sink. The fucking nurses always leave it out of reach. Masochists, every one of them. Do you mind?"

The man said evenly, "Not at all." First, he wheeled over a portable stand by Megs's bed and adjusted the height so it was level with the mattress. Then he strode to the sink, wrapped a napkin around the glass, poured the water, and brought it over to Megs, a slight grin on his face. He left the pitcher at the sink. "Here you go." He set the glass of water on the table. "You look uncomfortable, Frank."

Frank Megs grabbed the glass and thirstily drank the water, sloshing some of it around to let it saturate the inside of his mouth before swallowing. "There *is* no fucking *comfortable* with this fucking thing," he complained, nodding at the cast. "You ever tried to sit on a crapper, take a shit, and wipe your ass with one hand without being able to bend over? It can't be done, and all the nurses around here look and act like Attila the Hun. No fucking sympathy anywhere around here. I even think they're watering down the pain shots. Fucking things never seem to last long."

He downed the rest of the water and licked his lips again. "But, that's okay. I've got one man on my mind that keeps me going. I'm gonna kill that fucking Wolfkill…no, let me rephrase that. *You're* gonna kill that fucking Wolfkill, while I watch you break every fucking bone in his body, then cut his throat. I'll watch him bleed out and enjoy every fucking minute of it."

The man smiled. "If that's what you want, Frank. Consider it a done deal." He took Megs's empty glass, set it on the table, rolled it away from the bed and moved in closer. "Let me move your pillow around here for you, Frank. It's all scrunched up under you here. That might help you be more comfortable."

"No, I'm---*Shit! Not me! No! Please---*"

The man ignored Megs' pleas and slipped the pillow out from underneath his shoulders, then quickly flipped it over the detective's head, gripping either end of the pillow, and then he mashed it over Frank Megs' face with the full force of his weight.

Megs struggled as best he could, but his mobility and ability to fight back was limited.

No! This can't be happening to me! I've been in on it from the beginning!

His right fist floundered uselessly against the arm and shoulder of his attacker. His legs kicked. He bucked his hips up and down, but nothing kept the pressure off his face. The pillow muted his muffled screams.

Damn the pain! Have to live! Too many pain shots. Too weak. Oh God, can't breathe! Can't breathe! C-can't...

When the kicking finally stopped, the man lifted the pillow slowly and stared into a face with an expression masked with pure fear. Eyes bulging from their sockets and the mouth gaping wide open. The body lay still and relaxed, and the man noted that the detective's resistance had been rather weak and disappointing. Placid almost. Mostly just a lot of kicking and flailing. He rearranged the pillow under the dead man's head, then closed the jaw shut and with two fingers lowered the eyelids. He laid the right arm across the stomach, thus returning Megs to a peaceful appearance of taking a nap. He straightened and rearranged the sheets and blanket, covering Megs up to the cast.

"Sleep tight, Frank. Now, only two more to go," he noted as he walked out of the room.

Officer Berkey had returned to his post, and the man told him not to disturb the sleeping Frank Megs, as he closed the door behind him.

"It's done," said the man, speaking from a phone booth two blocks from the hospital. "I actually enjoyed this one. Megs was a pig. Even gave cops a bad name."

"Very good," said the voice at the other end of the line. "No problems, I assume."

"None. The uniform worked out perfect. In and out in less than five minutes. Can I keep the uniform?"

"I don't care. Go ahead, it may be useful down the line."

"Good," said the man. "Now, once Cochran is finally taken care of, it'll be time to make our move on Doe. I was thinking about tomorrow. I've..."

"Actually...that's been taken care of already. Someone saved us the trouble," said the voice. "It occurred this morning and whoever it was, went to the trouble of removing his penis and testicles and asphyxiating him with them. Very gruesome, but effective, I suppose."

"What? What're you talking about, *somebody else*? Somebody's trying to horn in on our action?"

"I'm not sure, but I think for now, the best thing to do is absolutely *nothing*. Finish that other little job I gave you. Today if you can. Then, your work is done for the time being. Let's allow things to develop on their own for a day or two. We have the time. Frank Megs's death and the one today will more than likely put the competition and the local authorities in a tailspin. Those two detectives have enlisted the services of an attorney, Cameron Epperson, so now there is actually a functional brain to interact between the two of them. I'll see how things progress before determining if any or all need to be eliminated," said the voice.

"Okay, but the way Cochran died isn't good. It concerns me," said the man.

"And, why is that? What does it matter how another pig like Cochran is killed? It's good riddance."

"It has *mob* written all over it, that's why. That's how they deal with people they don't like in a special way. I just don't like it, that's all."

"Not to worry. I can take care of whatever arises," said the voice.

"And, another thing," the man said, "just something for your own benefit. It would be a big mistake on your part to underestimate Harry Stumbaugh, my friend. I've known him a long time, and the prisons in Huntsville are full of men who made the same mistake…and I also know of five men, that are on the books at least, who are six feet under for the same reason. All of them underestimated that wily old gumshoe. He's very dangerous and protective of his friends."

"You should know, but not to worry. I don't make mistakes."

Chapter 28

The boys and I decided to let the love-fest in Cam's conference room continue without us, as we retired to my humble abode next door. I also grabbed Jenny to answer the phone since I figured we had enough firepower between me and Sam to prevent any skullduggery. While Cam and Sam settled into the chairs across from my desk, I grabbed a fresh bottle of Jack and three reasonably clean glasses from the filing cabinet. That's what they're for, right? I poured a couple of inches in each glass and passed them around.

Cam raised his glass. "Hell of a job, boys. I'm beginning to think I went into the wrong line of work. Guns, murder, blackmail, booze, and dames. I think we're halfway home, gentlemen." He raised the glass higher in a salute and knocked back the whiskey in one quick, liquid move, grimaced a bit, smacked his lips, and then replaced the glass on the desk. "Hell of way to start lunch. What's next?"

Sam sipped from his glass. "You know, Cam, *real* private eyes just sip their whiskey in the afternoon. We don't really start slamming them down until after dinner."

"Then, you should be an attorney, Sam. We knock 'em back in the daytime and sip *after* dinner, for appearances."

Cam was alright and fitting in just fine. "Okay boys, let's get down to brass tacks." I replenished Cam's drink with two more fingers worth. "Sip this time."

"Got it," he said. "What've you got in mind?"

"The floor's yours, Cam. Your note said we needed to take the offensive. What'd you have in mind?" I wanted to see if his ideas jibed with mine.

Cameron Epperson loosened his tie, crossed his legs, and relaxed his arms in his lap. "The money. It's all about the money, like you said. We've been chasing the bad guys all along. They do something, and we chase it down. They're always one step ahead of us, knocking off every potential witness before we can get to them. The body count is stacking up quick, so…it's time to let them come to us. They, whoever the hell *they* are, want the money…so let's give it to them."

I liked it. "Go ahead, I think we're on the same page."

He sipped from his glass this time. "Feel free to jump in any time. I'm just winging it here. Okay…Zucker, the reporter guy, just got the shit kicked out of his story on Doe because there's no mystery about who the senator is anymore. He wouldn't dare run it after he knows what we do. That'd be editorial suicide. I'm willing to bet he'd play ball with us. Redeem his standing at the paper. We make a big splash about finding the money. You and Sam get your picture taken---"

"Whoa partner, no pictures of this mug," Sam interrupted, "I think you're on the right track, but how 'bout this? We should use the little prick, sure, but if we go in big time with this, then we'll have to get Santa Fe Railroad involved, the newspaper, even the cops maybe. That's too many loose tongues and we could get burned. Literally. Word could get out to the wrong guys and we'd get added to the body count." He took another sip and contemplated for second. "I think you're right about Tony Zucker, though…he just got his ass handed to him on a platter, but think about this. *Somebody* from the inside got to him and fed him the story about the old girl from Oklahoma. *That's* our link. What if we…"

"Inside of what, Sam?" I asked.

He shrugged. "Hell, I don't know. The paper. Henshaw's

firm maybe...the cops. Do we assume Cochran and Megs are the only dirty cops involved? To be honest, I think we know him. We've seen him. Hell, probably been in the same room with him. Talked to him on the phone maybe. We just don't know *who* it is."

"That's scary," I said. "That could be how they stay ahead of us, though. You could be on to something there, Sam." I gave my two associates a hard look. "From now on, whatever is said in this room or any other place stays with us. The Doe's, maybe, at the right time, definitely not Henshaw or DeRita. We can't even tell Jenny what's going on...unless she gets in on the action somehow. Agreed?"

"Agreed," they said in unison.

"Okay Sam, Go ahead, finish your thought," I said with a nod and took a well-deserved drink of Jack myself.

"Well, I was going to say, somehow or other, we get the word to him, Zucker that is, that we've found the money, the loot from the Santa Fe heist. Tell him we'll give him an exclusive about the whole blackmailing scam and..."

It was my turn. "Right...except we don't *tell* him about the money. We let it *slip*. We're giving him the lowdown on the whole Doe extortion scheme, how we discovered his identity, the whole la-dee-da. Gives him redemption like Cam said, and makes us heroes. Then, one of us starts to say something about the dough and the other cuts him off. Give each other go to hell looks or something, like a major screw up. Then, cut it short. Make it convincing. Let him think he's learned something he's not supposed to. I guarantee that little weasel will run straight to whoever set him up with the dame from Ardmore in a heartbeat. We sit on him, wait for him to make a move, then badda-bing, badda-boom...we nail the bastards." Proud of myself, I took another sip of Jack and leaned back in my swivel chair, waiting for the applause and adulation from my peers. But, of course, Jenny, with the uncanny timing she possesses, knocked once and blessed us with her presence.

"Phone call," she said, "Captain DeRita's on line one."

"Hold that thought," I said to the boys as I glanced over at the phone and a saw the single blinking light. "We only have one line, Jenny."

"I know *that,*" she said.

Dames.

"How'd he sound?"

"Depressed. He said he needed to talk to you *now.* And, he wanted to know who was with you." She wrinkled her nose and cocked a hip. "I felt like I was being interrogated or something. He wanted to know how long you've been here, who you're with, that kind of stuff…that's why I came in instead of ringing you."

"Good girl. What'd you tell him?" I inquired.

"Harry, I'm surprised at you…I didn't tell him anything except, *hold please.*"

I smiled. "That's my girl, Doll Face. I'll take it in a second, let him sweat a few."

Jen winked and gave me a little extra hip action as she twirled around and went back to her *PhotoPlay* magazine. She knows how to impress me.

"What's *his* deal?" Sam asked. "You talk to him about our pieces?"

"Yeah, but last time I said something about guns, Cochran turned into a eunuch. Let's see what he's got on his plate, now." I grabbed the receiver, but before I punched the blinking button I said, "Don't forget our master plan, we pick up on it after I talk to DeRita." I jabbed at the button. "Harry Stumbaugh, Private Eye Ex-straw-doe-nair, speaking." I figured that'd piss him off.

"At what?" DeRita asked dryly.

"Wild women, Jack Daniels, and keeping people on hold. How 'bout you, DeRita?" I said, throwing it back at him. Thought I'd see if I could knock some of that sharp edge off his attitude.

"Where have you and Sam been since I saw you this morning? Is he back from Denton yet? I tried to call earlier and there was no answer."

Straight to the point. So much for the sharp edge maneuver.

I wasn't going to give in that easily, though. Time for little indignation. "What? No small talk, Dan? No heavy petting first?"

"Not in the mood, Harry."

"So you want me to just bend over and grab my ankles right off the bat, huh? Okay...but I wasn't aware I needed to start accounting for my time with you, *Captain.* Is there something else we're being accused of? One murder a day is enough for me."

"Cut the shit, Harry. I need to know. They found Megs dead this morning...in his room at the hospital. I need solid alibis so I can take both of you off my list of suspects and put stars by your names as good boys. And Sam, by the way, isn't off the hook on Cochran's murder either. Is he there with you?"

"Gee, that's too bad, sorry to hear that," I said, still dodging his questions. "I thought you were putting a guard on his door, after we talked this morning."

"I did."

No elaboration, huh?

"Somebody fed his dick to him like they did Cochran?" I covered the phone and mouthed, *Megs,* to the boys and sliced the phone across my throat for their benefit. They were surprised, but I could tell they were as broke up about his demise as me.

"No, Harry," DeRita answered, "He was suffocated. Not sure yet, but it looks like somebody smothered him with his pillow. But, you didn't know that already. Right?"

Now he was pissing me off. "How do you kill a guy with a pillow and not alert the guard outside, Dan? I'd figure Megs for a screamer, squealing like a teenage girl at the prom."

"Can't go into that, but you still haven't answered any of my questions, Harry."

"Sounds like somebody screwed the pooch to me, Dan. And, to answer your question, no DeRita, I didn't know Megs got what he deserved. And, if you have to know, Sam and I have been in a meeting with two upstanding Dallas attorneys, three good-looking secretaries, and a Senator, along with his wife all morning. I keep pretty sophisticated company these days, don't you think?"

"Right."

"What time did the blessed event happen, if I can ask?"

"About an hour ago. I'm still at the hospital. Would you like to join me?"

"No, that's okay. Too much happiness in one day makes me giddy and breaks my concentration. Know what I mean?"

"Not really."

"You're up against a shit storm, aren't you DeRita, with two crooked cops dead by lunch. The papers are going to have a field day with this story. Wouldn't want to be in your shoes, buddy." I let the silence drop like a lead balloon, but he didn't bite, so I decided to dig a little more. "Any leads on the babysitter that gave Megs a bedtime story?"

"Nothing I can release to anybody. So...how'd Sam's trip to Denton go? Did he find whatever it was he was looking for?" DeRita probed back.

"Suddenly, you're interested in my case, huh? Well...sure, I'll feed you an exclusive. Just a little thing. We discovered Doe's real identity. He's off the hook for the Santa Fe heist, and he's not Ralph Morris, so the blackmailers have lost their leverage. Now, we're back to the wait and see game. Let them make the next move."

"Damn, Harry, congratulations. That's one hell of a blockbuster. The man who found John Doe. Sounds like headlines."

"Nah, two dead cops sounds like headlines, to me, Dan. Doe will take second banana and not mind a bit."

"So, you think the extortionist will give up? Now that Doe can claim justification." DeRita asked.

I shrugged, as though he could see me through the phone lines. "Don't know. Like I said, wait and see. May not be anybody left with Megs out of the way."

There was a moment of silence, then, "Yeah, maybe…"

Something was bugging DeRita, I could hear it in his voice. "What's up, Dan? Something's bugging you. Something besides two dead cops and reams of bad publicity that's about to fly up your ass. What's up?"

"You don't think that's enough on my plate to worry about?"

"I can tell there's more," I said.

"Things just aren't adding up…I…listen, I still need to talk to Sam about Cochran. I've got to cover my ass on this before it hits the fan and the newspapers. I've got to at least interview an unnamed suspect."

"A fall guy, huh? Fine, but his alibis are solid and you know it."

"Yeah, sure.'

This appointment will never happen.

"I'll send him down with Epperson." I pointed at both of them and then, at the phone. Cam nodded and Sam shrugged indifferently. "Ya'll are all good friends now, and, after you cut him loose, you can release the custody of our pieces and give them to Sam or Epperson or whoever, just so we can get them back."

"That'll look good. Interrogate him for one crime and return his weapons from an earlier crime. Wait till the press gets hold of that one."

"That was a false arrest, if I remember right. Don't think you want to reopen that can of worms, Dan. Anyway, they won't know unless you're the one that tells them. Hey, by the way, did you get a chance to talk to Megs before he went bye-bye? You know, he was the last known link that was still breathing who could tell us the truth about everything. Who was in on the heist. Who was the real Ralph Morris. Why Doe was targeted. Little things like that." I was ready for a blow-off answer.

There was a moment of hesitation before DeRita responded. "No, Harry, I didn't, and I'm telling you this out of professional courtesy…after you left, I had a patrolman put on Meg's door.

Hospital security was posted there until the officer arrived, and in the meantime, I was at Cochran's the rest of the morning. I planned on visiting Megs later in the day because he sure as hell wasn't going anywhere. And to be honest, until I get some hard facts and evidence in front of me, I'm not totally convinced Cochran and Megs were involved in your wild theories of armored truck heists and extortion. You and I both know they weren't the sharpest knives in the drawer, and the scenario you've put together takes a higher intelligence. I don't know a cop, honest or dirty, that has the brains to pull off the kind of operation you're talking about."

Interesting.

I rolled my eyes during the sermon, letting the guys know I was getting jerked around. "I didn't say they were the brains, Dan. Shaking down greasy spoons, hash houses, and mom and pop grocery stores was about as high on the social ladder those two mugs could handle. But, they make excellent button men to take care of the dirty work when it's needed. Like Abner Strong and Robert Petrie. Wave big bucks in their faces, and they'd kill the Pope if you asked them. And you know it."

"If you say so. I still want to see Sam before the end of the day…and that's not a *request*."

"You're chasing up the wrong tree, but I'll make sure he's there. Anything else?"

"Yeah, how 'bout a beer later tonight. I need some relief. You game?"

Interesting.

"Yeah…sure, Dan. We can hook up," I said. "Keep in touch."

DeRita hung up first, without a goodbye or even a kiss on the cheek. I hung up and looked across the desk at my two *compadres*. "We're friends again, and he wants to grab a drink later." I contemplated our evening date. "You know, DeRita and I have been friends for a long time, and he was one of the few that stuck by me when I was railroaded off the force. But you know, I can count the times we've drank beer together after hours on one hand."

"Really?" Cam inquired. "Interesting. Remember, if somebody asks something of you, there's always a motive behind it."

I shrugged. "We'll see. Something's bugging him. Bugging him bad, I can tell. Anyway, Megs is dead. Somehow, somebody got by the patrolman on duty and suffocated him."

Sam added, "Well, at least he got off better than Cochran did, and like you said, there goes the last known connection we had to the whole operation."

"And, another thing," I said, "you know, when I told DeRita about Doe, he didn't even asked who he really was. Just congratulated me."

Epperson shrugged and finished off the last of his Jack Daniels and slid the glass to the side, indicating he was done. "How'd the killer get past the cop on duty, anyway?"

"He wouldn't say."

"You'd think that the guard would have to know who he was before letting him in. He wouldn't just admit somebody off the street," added Sam.

Cam said, "Think about who he *would* allow to go inside…if *you* were the guard."

"A cop or a doctor or nurse, maybe. Well…we can probably eliminate the nurse. A guy in a dress would be pretty easy to spot," I said, adding some humor.

"A doc could get in easy enough," Sam said. "A street cop, especially one that just got assigned to the job wouldn't know one from the other. Fake or legit."

"Harry, if you were the one on guard, would you let a cop in to see Megs if you didn't know him?" Cam asked.

I shrugged and pointed at Cam. "Good question. If it was a plain clothes cop, like a detective, I'd ask for ID. If it was a patrolman in blues, I'd probably glance at the badge and name tag maybe, if that even. He could claim orders or just visiting an old friend. I wouldn't give it a second thought, probably."

"Whoever's behind, this is *very* good," Sam said.

"Looks like they've got unlimited resources, too," Cam added.

"And, they don't mind killing people to cover their tracks," I said.

I had some calls to make before we put together a definite plan for the Zucker scam. Cam claimed to have some lawyer stuff to do and returned to his office until it was showtime; Sam decided to take advantage of the down time and left to take Katie and Nurse Maggie to lunch at the French room, promising to stay in touch; and while they were having fun, I jotted down three names. Doe/Shockley, Randolf Wellstone, and Giovanni.

That was the order I planned to approach them in; so I told, or shall I say *asked,* Jenny to go next door and see if the Does were still there. If not, find out where they were. I needed to talk to them ASAP.

I poured myself a refresher of Jack and waited for her return while I thought about the Giovanni call I had to make. As always, my wording and inferences had to be exact.

Light laughter from the hallway and the office door opening let me know that the Does were still around. I was glad that Sam took Nurse Maggie with him, making one less person to get rid of so I could talk to them in private. My door was open so I decided to cut them off at the pass before another love-fest took place around my desk, and besides...the Jack was running low. I greeted everybody with open arms, kinda. "Senator, I appreciate you coming over. I needed to speak to two of you alone before you got away." I pointed to the only two empty seats in my office. "If you'll have a seat, I'll be right with you."

Gently now.

I patted Jenny on the small of the back and guided her back to the front office, closing the door behind me. I could tell she wanted to stay with the Does. "Jen, listen, I need you to do something important. I need you to make two calls for me."

She took her seat behind the desk and moved her magazine to the side, grabbing her pad and pen. "Okay, Harry. Who?"

She was pouting, but I was about to make her day. "Okay Doll Face, if you wanted to hide...get out of town for a few days...where nobody could find you or think to look, where would you go?"

"Your apartment," she said, sarcasm dripping from her words like ice melting from a cherry snow cone on a hot August afternoon.

I decided to go for the guilt maneuver. "Cute, Jenny, but I'm talking about getting the Doe's out of town. Their lives could be in danger, and I'm drawing blanks on where to send them."

Oh...that worked perfectly, I saw it in her face. The mouth dropping slightly open, now here goes the eyebrows...up, up. I felt kinda guilty for the way I tricked her...several seconds worth.

"The same place you took me four summers ago. That private lake in Oklahoma with the cabins. Remember those quaint cabins we stayed in, just off the lake? *Re-mem-ber* Harry?" She finished off her suggestion with that quirky, mischievous little grin of hers.

She played me a lot better than I could ever play her. "Y-yeah, I remember you little vixen, near Oklahoma City. You still got the number of the place?"

"Sure, Harry, saved it thinking we'd go back one day." Her fingers walked through the rolodex and went right to it. "Are they really in danger, Harry? I mean why? Isn't this over for them now?"

I put my hand on her shoulder, leaning over to read the card with the name and phone number. "Not really, Doll Face, but I'm going to take care of it...and soon." The card read, Pine Cone Resorts, Oklahoma. "Call them and make reservations under the name of...L. B. Johnson, that's the ticket. Shouldn't be that busy in the fall. If they're full up, buzz me in the office."

Jen jotted down her notes. "When will they arrive?"

"Tonight. Now, as soon as you're done with that, find the number for Randolf Wellstone, he's an attorney. Tell him it's imperative that I see him *today*. Not tomorrow, not tonight, but today. I want you to talk directly to him, Doll Face, not the secretary. If he balks, go ahead and tell him I'm working for the senator. Got it?"

"Gotcha. Want me to buzz you after I talk to him?"

"Yeah, confirm the Oklahoma reservations and the time for Wellstone." I gave her a peck on top of the head. "You're the best, Doll Face."

"I know *that*," she said, picking up the phone.

I let Jenny do her thing and entered my office in order to deal with the lovebirds.

"So…do I call you John or Jeff? Senator Doe or Senator Shockley?" I said, getting things started.

They looked like two newlyweds sitting across the desk from me, glowing from his newly found identity. The senator smiled. "I'm sticking with John Doe. I see no reason to start changing things. I've always worn that name around my neck as a reminder…a reminder of the blank wall that encircled my memory bank. But now…I see it as a symbol of a new beginning. And Harry, Hedy and I can't thank you enough. You really came through for us. I never believed it would end this way, but I always had hope. Even when you gave me a hard time and questioned my motives." He scooted forward in his seat. "And, I don't care what it costs, Harry…I want you and Sam to find out who Jeffery Shockley is. Where I'm from…family, the whole ball of wax."

I nodded. "I understand, Senator, and I'd be glad to do that, but for now, I'm afraid I'm gonna have to rain on your parade a little bit."

"You're always raining on our parade, Harry," Hedy chided, good heartedly.

"You're welcome. Anyway, we're not out of the woods yet.

After coming back to the office, I got a call from Captain DeRita from Dallas PD, and there's been another murder. Detective Frank Megs was killed in his hospital room about an hour ago. I'm afraid the trail of bodies is growing."

"Oh my God," exclaimed Hedy.

Doe leaned sideways and wrapped an arm around her. "I'm so tired of this, Harry. Where...when is it going to stop?"

"Well, I'm still on the payroll, as far as I'm concerned, and there's a plan being put together to bring this all to an end. But, I need some cooperation from you and Hedy. Do you trust me?"

"Of course!" The Does chimed in two-part harmony.

"Then, from this point on---" The phone buzzed. "Just a minute," I said, "that's Jenny." I picked up the line and listened to her report, all the time keeping my eyes on the Does. The glow and euphoria was replaced with concern. "Okay, okay Jen...that's good, thanks Doll Face."

"What's going on, Harry?" Doe asked. "Why do you want to know if we trust you? That should be a given, especially after what's taken place today."

I put on my best, *this is serious business*, face. "Has Henshaw gotten in touch with Tony Zucker, at the paper, yet...to give him the story?"

Doe checked his watch. "Not yet, but matter of fact, I'm supposed to meet Zucker, along with Garland, at my suite at the Adolphus in about thirty minutes. I'm going to give him a statement and show him the proof of who I am." He glanced over at Hedy, who'd been unusually quiet during the meeting. "I still plan to withdraw from the race and not only that...at the end of this term, I'm resigning from the State Senate. No more politics. I've had enough. It's time to start enjoying my new life...with Hedy. No more being apart for days and weeks on end."

I dropped the serious grimace from my face and put on the "fo-pah" happy face. It hurt for just a second. "I think that's a hell of a deal, Senator. I'm really glad for you." And I was.

"We're excited about being private citizens, out of the public limelight," added Hedy.

"Cookouts on the patio, touch football games..."

Hedy Doe smiled. "You got it, Harry."

I directed my attention back to the senator so I could erase the visual of Hedy Doe in a pair of jeans and a tee shirt chunking a football down field. "Then, let's make it happen. First, you and Hedy need to talk to Zucker alone. No Garland Henshaw in the room. Focus only on the identity thing and don't say a word about the heist, the extortion, the money from the heist, the murders...any of it. Just say I was hired to find your identity and nothing else. If he brings any of that other stuff up, which he might but I doubt he knows anything about it, just tell him it's under investigation and you can't comment on it. That's your answer for anything he asks outside of what you tell him. Got it?"

"Got it." He answered with a grin. "A non-answer, answer. Typical politician reply. No problem."

I continued, "And for now, I'd leave out Nurse Maggie, by name at least. You can give credit to her later, if you like, but I doubt she wants the scrutiny anyway."

"She's already threatened to shoot me if I mention her name...and I believe her," Doe said with a light chuckle.

Hedy frowned. "What's the deal with Henshaw, Harry? Is there something you're not telling us?"

"No," I said, "let's just call it keeping you safe for the time being. Every time we make a move, mention a name...they end up dead. Sam and I think it might be somebody close to us. I'll be honest, though, that I have no reason to suspect Henshaw of anything. It's just that we're going to keep things close to the chest at this point."

"I understand," said Doe. "What do you have in mind after that?"

"I want you and Hedy to leave town. I want you completely out of sight. Let the paper do its thing. Do you two like to fish?"

"Of course," Hedy answered.

"Good, because I've secured a nice little place in the country for you. How does Oklahoma sound to you?"

"Different," Hedy answered again. "Why?"

I tried to think of some good Indian jokes, but none came to mind. "I want you two completely isolated from public scrutiny, the bad guys…the world in general for a couple of days. This is a safe place I've found, and no one but us, Jenny and Sam will know where you are. Got a truck or station wagon?"

"We've got a Woody," Doe said.

"Of course you do. You got maids or butlers, or something like that at your Swiss Avenue digs?"

"There's a married couple, that's the only staff we have. Why?"

"Call them from here, have them load up the Woody with enough food, clothes, fishing gear, whatever for two or three days' worth. Tell them to meet you in the parking garage at the Baker Hotel after your interview with Zucker. You might even tell him you're headed back to Austin. They can't know where you're going either."

"We can tell them we're going to our cabin in Fredericksburg. That wouldn't draw any suspicion from them," Hedy said.

Suddenly, a brilliant idea flashed through my brain. "Good, do that. Now John, let me ask you a question. What would you think about telling Zucker about your plans for dropping out of the race and retiring from the senate? Is it sooner than what you had planned?"

Doe didn't answer immediately. His brows furrowed together and he rubbed his jaw, thinking. "Well, I really wanted to inform my staff first and my campaign manager, of course. Why? What's the rush?"

"Just strategy. It might accelerate another plan I've got in the works to bring this all to an end. What do you think?"

Doe glanced at his watch. "I'm scheduled to meet Zucker in about fifteen minutes. I might have time to at least speak briefly with my manager before I go into the interview."

"John," said Hedy quietly, "if it will bring this awful business to an end any quicker…I think you should consider it. The sooner this is over the sooner---"

"I'll do it," Doe said definitively, "but we need to go now so I can talk to Byron, my manager, first."

"Good," I said. "I'll make sure either Sam, Jenny, or somebody from Epperson's office will be there to help at the Baker and tell you where you're going. Just walk over to the hotel, hand in hand together, just like you're going to lunch. Someone from here or Epperson's will meet you. *Do not* go with anyone else, regardless of what kind of story they might tell you. If we're not there, get something to eat, go to the bar, anything as long as you stay in the open at the hotel. After you get off, I'll get in touch when it's time to come home. Got it?"

Hedy said, "My God, Harry, you're serious about all this, aren't you? You really think *we're* in danger?"

"Better safe than sorry, Hedy," John said, reaching over, grasping her arm. "When was the last time it was just you and me? Nobody calling, stopping by. How many times have the interruptions ruined any private time we ever had. Me shuttling back and forth from Austin? You going from one social function to another?"

"Where you're going, I promise, there will be no interruptions. Just bugs, wildlife, and fish."

Doe gave me a firm nod. "Okay, Harry, we do it your way. I'll call Freeman at the house and have him get things together." He checked his watch again. "Hedy and I need to get back to the Adolphus. Zucker will be showing up soon, and I need to make an excuse to get rid of Henshaw."

I stood and reached across the desk to shake their hands. Hedy Doe stood, came around the desk, and went up on her tiptoes to give me a kiss on the cheek.

"Thank you, Harry," she said.

"Better not let Jenny catch you doing that. I'm not real fond of cat fights in the office."

Since I considered myself the chief executive of the three-man brain trust, I'd made an executive decision about Doe moving up the date concerning his retirement announcement. Not only would it justify a quick, unannounced trip back to Austin as a cover story, but I figured it would force the hand of the powers-that-be to make a move quicker than they planned. Make a rush to judgment that could be fatal. Might even get somebody killed, but that was a risk I was willing to take, as long as it wasn't me or any of my associates. Jen's call during the Doe conference was to let me know that reservations had been made for the Oklahoma trip, and that Wellstone said he would meet me for a drink at the French Room in thirty minutes. I had twenty minutes to spare to make it on time, and this was one appointment I planned to be prompt for.

Against my better judgment, I called out for Jenny from my desk, "Hey Doll Face, would you get The French Room on the line? I need to talk to Sam if he's still there." Then, I dialed Epperson's number from my private line as fast as I could, attempting to head off the tongue lashing I was about to endure.

"Yes," I said quickly, as Jen materialized in my doorway, frowning, fists planted on her hips with a wide stance, and I might say, none too happy. Actually, the phone was still ringing, but I knew I didn't have time to waste. "Could you…what? I can't…" Thank God, somebody finally picked up at the other end. "Yes, lost you there for a minute, let me speak to Counselor Epperson, please." I covered the mouth piece with my hand. "Sorry about that, Jen. Things are moving too fast. I need Sam on the line now, Doll Face. *Please*."

The extra emphasis on *please*, helped, I thought. At least, she didn't yell at me. When Cam got to the phone, I filled him in on the Doe deal. The interview with Zucker and the Oklahoma thing. He liked it, of course, and volunteered to meet the Doe's and the butler guy in the lobby and take them down to the garage, give them directions to their cozy getaway cabin, and said he'd even arrange to have one of his guys follow them to the lake. Sounded like a plan and I felt good letting him take care of the details. One less thing for me.

After I hung up, Jenny yelled from her desk so that the insurance company on the top floor could hear her, "Sam's on line one!"

We were even-Steven. Next I filled Sam in on the goings on. Epperson and the Doe's, the interview, and heading across the Red River into Indian Territory. He liked it, too. I told him to dump the dames and wait for me at the restaurant because I wanted him with me when I met with Wellstone. Two heads were always better than one when dealing with an attorney, who was obviously well thought of…in his own mind. He liked that plan, too. I grabbed my fedora off the rack, told Doll Face to lock up the office and go to the next door, gave her a conciliatory peck on the cheek, and headed for the Adolphus. The call to Giovanni would have to wait.

Randolf Wellstone was fifteen minutes late.

"You know what this pecker-wood looks like?" Sam asked as we eyeballed the lobby from our table, searching for someone that looked and acted like a rich lawyer.

"Probably more like a peacock than a pecker-wood. I wish he'd hurry up because this place is about to look like Grand Central Station soon. Everybody's in the house. I'm sure Henshaw's around, sulking somewhere after Doe told him he wanted to interview Zucker alone, and he's going to shit a brick when he finds out second hand that his client isn't running for the senate. The Does will be heading to the Baker soon, and then if Wellstone shows up, we'll have quite the little reunion in the lobby. They'll all hit at the same time, just watch and see."

This was a love-fest I didn't want to see take place. I should have thought this out better.

"Probably got hung up at the office," Sam said nonchalantly and took a sip of iced tea. "Lawyer stuff. Being fashionably late."

"Or cold feet. How's Katie doing?" I asked, just to kill time.

"Good."

That didn't go far.

I spotted a bellboy in the red monkey-suit, bee-lining for our table. "I think we just got stood-up," I said, already reaching in my pocket for some cash to pay the kid off.

Sam spotted him, too. "Probably."

"Mr. Stumbaugh," the kid said, "a message from the front desk for you, sir." He handed me a slip of paper and waited. They train 'em young here.

"Thanks kid," I said, snatching a dollar bill from my roll and waited for him to leave before reading the note.

"Thank *you*, sir! Mr. Stumbaugh!"

I was going to need another retainer from Doe at this pace. I checked around the lounge, from force of habit, checking to see if anybody looked suspicious or was keeping an eye on us, before I unfolded the message. It read: *Sorry I missed you. Could you come up to my suite and we can meet here? Room 1200.* It was signed, *Randolf Wellstone.*

I slid it over for Sam to read. "We've got to get a suite and set up office here, I guess. Everybody else does, evidently. I'm surprised they have any rooms left for the guests."

Sam tossed a couple of bucks on the table for the tea. Two bucks for fifty cents worth of drinks. His twenty-five percent share was draining as quickly as mine...but was definitely fun while it lasted. "Let's go," I said.

We managed to cross the lobby and get to the elevators without running into anyone we knew. I punched the up button and stood there with Sam like a couple of jerks with our hands in our pockets, watching an ornate needle above the elevator doors slowly descend, one floor at a time. What else do you do when you're waiting for an elevator? The doors opened and sure enough, somebody we knew was getting off.

"Eddy?" Sam and I said in unison. We were surprised, but not as much as him.

Giovanni's body guard had been staring down at his feet when the door opened. No doubt our unified greeting shocked the hell out of him. "H-harry! Sam! W-what are you guys doing here?"

That was a funny thing to say since he knew better than anybody that I spent more time at the Adolphus than my office. "The usual," I said, stepping aside and letting him out as the people around us shuffled in and commandeered the elevator. We'd catch the next one. "Giovanni here, or are you alone?" I didn't want to sound like I was trying to interrogate him, but I was.

"Uh, no he's---"

Sam gave the body guard a light, friendly slap on the arm. "We're about to have a drink in a minute, at the French Room," he injected quickly. "We're dropping something off for a client and then we'll be back in about five, if you'd like to join us."

Nice save.

"Yeah, about five minutes. Why don't you hang around? Boss man won't mind, I'm sure," I added.

Eddy nervously straightened his tie and smoothed his jacket lapels; then, his composure returned. "Hey…love to guys, but I've got to get back to the restaurant…place falls apart without me, you know. Rain check, though?"

"You bet," I said, "tell the old man hello for us and the best to Eddy Junior, you hear? Okay?"

"Yeah, yeah, sure will." Eddy gave me a departing pat on the arm and pointed his finger affectionately at Sam. "Later guys," he said, heading for the entrance revolving doors.

"Now, that was weird," Sam said, watching the body guard scoot through the hotel lobby.

I shrugged. "Who knows. Those guys live in another world all to itself."

We caught the next elevator up to the twelfth floor lobby

and found the right direction for Suite 1200. The room was at the end of a long winding hallway, announcing its presence with double doors, gold plated numbers, and tucked away in a large alcove. If you weren't looking for it, you'd never find it. Sam and I stopped in our tracks simultaneously when we reached the double doors. One was slightly ajar.

Sam looked at me, eyebrows raised.

I shook my head in the negative, indicating it was probably in our best interest to stay outside. "Wellstone?" I shouted for kicks, leaning in towards the narrow opening, but being careful not to touch anything. "Wellstone? You there?" No response. It was too damn quiet.

"Shit," I said. "I smell a setup. Let's get the hell out of here."

Sam reached out and stopped me. "You know as well as I do that we've got to check inside."

I hate it when he's right. I checked back around the alcove corner into the hallway to see if any unexpected guests were coming to join us. "Shit. Okay, you stay here and warn me if somebody's coming. I'm just gonna have a quick look-see. Okay?"

"Okay, but make it quick. I'm expecting a squad of cops to come charging down the hall any minute now. This smells *re-al* bad."

"I'm with you." I nudged the door open with the tip of my cane, again careful not to touch anything that could leave my prints. That was *all* I needed, leaving physical evidence where it didn't need to be…which was what I was afraid of here. When the door swung back, giving me a clear view of the den area, I recognized the same layout as Doe's suite, except everything was bass-ackwards and more grand. But, I didn't even have to go inside to size-up the situation. A body, which I assumed was Wellstone, was in the floor, sitting up with his back propped up against a small sofa, his head cocked to one side, resting on his left shoulder; his legs were sprawled in a V under the coffee table, his feet sticking out of the other side facing me; his arms were limp by his sides; and his face was a dark purple, which actually matched the necktie tied around his neck, and I'm not talking about a Winsor knot, more like a square knot and the obvious source of the purple coloring factor; a fat, swollen tongue lolled to the side of his mouth, and his eyes bugged out like someone had just cut off his dick. That's when I realized it wasn't his tongue hanging out of his mouth. That's also when I noticed a fresh pool of blood forming underneath the coffee table. This killing had happened less than thirty minutes ago, by my estimation. Sam and I were sipping iced tea in the French Room, and Wellstone was getting castrated.

"It's Cochran's twin," I said with a small laugh. I turned around with a grin, ready to share my findings and another fresh, smart-ass remark with Sam.

His back was to me as he watched the hallway. "Then, I don't need to see it, Harry. Already had my share of that...in the Pacific. Let's get the hell out of here before we get busted."

I didn't have to be told twice. "Let's take the stairs down a couple of flights before we catch the elevator. Don't want to meet somebody like DeRita getting off as we're getting on. Know what I mean?"

"You think it was Eddy?" Sam said as he fast-walked down the deserted hallway.

"Don't know," I said, step-caning my best behind him to keep up.

Giovanni...what have you done, my friend?

Chapter 29

When Sam and I got back down to the lobby, undetected I might add, we decided it'd be a good idea to touch base with DeRita. After all, we didn't want him to miss out on all the fun. And besides, there was a paper trail leading us to Wellstone's room, so there was no way to claim innocence about the situation.

Sam went back to the bar and got a table for us, where I'd join him after tying up a few loose ends. Before calling Dallas PD, I decided to inform the front desk about the cleanup needed in Suite 1200. I figured this was a situation fit for management since they were going to need more than a mop and bucket of water for the mess on the twelfth floor. They sent a bell boy for the head honcho of the hotel, Mr. Jeremy Posey, and I greeted him in the lobby by the grand piano intended for the *Titanic*. It seemed appropriate for the situation. I informed him of the situation and suggested putting their security man, an ex-cop, up there until the police arrived. He'd know how to keep the scene secure until the real cops arrived. Needless to say, Posey was a little unnerved when I told him about the dead lawyer, the lollipop he was sucking on, and the discount he might offer to the next guests for the room. I could see his brain twizzling in circles, and he started buzzing around like somebody had stuck a hornet's nest in his bonnet.

With that nasty bit if work out of the way, I strolled over to the phone banks to let Dallas's finest know they had another murder on their hands. I called Homicide, expecting DeRita to be back in the office, but a voice and a name I didn't recognize answered instead.

"Detective Rick Ford, Homicide. How may I help you?"

"Yeah, I need to speak to Captain DeRita. This is Harry Stumbaugh calling." There was a slight hesitation before he responded, evidently he knew *my* name.

"Uh, yeah, Mr. Stumbaugh…well, he's not here right now. He got a call about fifteen minutes ago on a possible homicide, so he'll be out of touch for a bit. Can I help you with something?"

Fifteen minutes ago? I left the scene less than ten minutes ago. Interesting.

"No, that's fine, I have a feeling I'm about to see him, anyway. Did he by chance go to the Adolphus Hotel?" This young detective I didn't know from Adam, was about to plug in an important piece of the puzzle to the crime of the century and didn't even know it.

"Well, I'm not at liberty to say, Mr. Stumbaugh…why do you ask?"

That wasn't a casual question, Detective Ford.

"Well Detective, I'm asking because I'm calling to report a homicide that occurred at the Adolphus, and if he's on his way here, you can save me a dime for another phone call just by letting me know."

"Really? Are you there now? At the Adolphus?"

That answered my question.

"Yup. Standing in the lobby."

"Then I suggest you wait for him, Mr. Stumbaugh. I'm sure he'll be interested in talking to you. As a matter of fact, I believe he uttered your name as he was leaving."

"Fondly, I'm sure."

"Not exactly. As I said, I suggest you wait, he'll probably be walking through the door any moment."

I heard a commotion behind me and turned to see a harried DeRita and an entourage following in his footsteps, including street patrol, forensic personnel, and the same two vultures from the coroner's office that had worked Cochran's place this morning pushing their gurney my way.

Busy boys.

They crested the stairs at the entrance like an army that'd been rode hard and put up wet. Tired little puppies. Three homicides in one day will do that for you. They were in for a surprise when they got up to Suite 1200.

"Bingo. I see 'em now, Detective," I said, "thanks for the help, and I'll tell him what a fine job you did not revealing any vital information to a stranger on the phone." I hung up and made my way to meet the fun bunch from downtown.

When DeRita spotted me, he lost a step in his stride and his chin dropped down to his chest. I guess he wasn't happy to see me. I smiled and gimped my way towards him. My leg was getting a little achy, chasing down dead bodies all over town. "Busy day, eh, Captain?" I was right, he wasn't happy to see me.

He ignored me and said something to my best friend, Rick from Forensics, evidently giving some instructions on how to push the button going up, as he pointed at the elevator. Then, still in an unhappy state, he angled in my direction. He definitely needed to smile more when he greeted old friends.

"What the hell are *you* doing here, Harry?"

"My civic duty, Dan. You know me. I stumbled onto a dead man and thought I should call it in. Spoke to a fine young detective on the phone. Ford. You know him?"

DeRita looked at me suspiciously. "When did you talk to him?"

"Just hung up as you walked in the door."

Fatigue was all over DeRita's face like a hot towel before one of those good barber shop shaves, which he needed, by the way. "The vic is Randolf Wellstone and you're not gonna like this part of it either...he was chewing on a dick last time I saw him. His own, I'm pretty sure."

The detective's head dropped. "Shit, this one's even more

high profile. What can you tell me, Harry?"

I shrugged. "I've got a lot to tell you if you're ready to listen. What do you say, you go work your crime scene, and I'll wait for you in the bar?" That was the best suggestion I could think of for the minute.

"Okay," he said, "just let me scope things out and get everything started upstairs. I'll get down here as quick as I can." His face turned grim, "I don't want to get jerked around with any double talk or theories, Harry. I think you know a lot more than you've been up front about, and I need facts...not bullshit. City Hall is breathing down my neck as it is, with two dead cops. And after this, with Wellstone, they're gonna be jumping straight up my ass. I don't need this shit. Retirement is looking *real* good about now." He jabbed a finger at me and then tapped his own chest. "We on the same page?"

Now that sounded more like my old boss.

"That's what I intended, Dan. I've already got a table reserved for just the two of us at the bar. You still drink on duty, don't you?"

"I am today," he quipped, heading to the elevators.

Sam had an ice cold Budweiser waiting for me. "You were right, you know."

"About what?" I asked taking a seat.

"Wellstone. He was a peckerwood, not a peacock." He grinned and pointed to the beer. Since it's mid-afternoon, I figured you were ready for more than tea. I also ordered some steaks...on your tab."

"I like the way you're always taking care of me," I said, "and your new sense of humor is enlightening. Katie brings out the best in you."

He didn't bite and ignored my subtle inquiry. "How'd DeRita take it? He didn't look too happy."

"He's not a happy camper, for sure. He's going to get the boys in the band started upstairs, then he wants to talk." I downed about half of the Bud and was glad he'd ordered steaks. The rest of the day was going to get very busy.

"What's he want to know? How I killed Cochran?"

"I'll pretend I didn't hear that."

I hope he's joking.

"But no, I think he's beyond that. He wants it all, and I think I'm going to enlighten him. He's…" Over Sam's shoulder, I spotted another pissed-off acquaintance that was bee-lining straight for our table. "Uh, I think we've angered more than one person."

Sam looked up and smiled. "Can I handle this one, or is this one for upper management?"

I had to talk fast before our guest landed. It looked like everyone being here at the same time was going to work out after all. "I've got this one, but I need you to go call Doe upstairs in his suite and tell him to get the hell out of town. Meet him at the elevators and escort him to the Baker if Epperson's man isn't here by then. Hold on to Zucker too, out of sight, and bring him to the table after Henshaw's left. You figure out the details. I'll hold off the prick until they're out of the hotel. Go!" Smiling, I stood up to greet Garland Henshaw, and Sam threw a dollar on the table for show, saying goodbye as though he didn't even see the lawyer steam rolling our way.

"Later," he added loudly.

I didn't think Henshaw was coming for drinks, and I damn sure wasn't going to keep my seat and look up at him while he tried to scold me like a child. If I'd had my own way, I would've punched out his lights, but the better part of valor and common sense prevented my hastiness, unfortunately. I was sure he was a lawsuit-happy kind of guy.

Henshaw's five-hundred dollar suit was perfect; his quaffed silver hair-do was perfect; and his two-hundred dollar shoes had a shine like the emperor's mirror; the snarling mouth, though contrary to his clothes, complimented the beet-red complexion and fire in his eyes. I waited for him to get closer and waited for the greeting that I was sure would have something to do with my heritage and my mother, God bless her soul.

"Stumbaugh, you son-of-a-bit---"

That was my opening. Timing it just right, I brought my cane up to his chest and stopped him dead in his tracks. "I can shove this up your ass, Counselor…if you like, or you can tone it down a notch. Your choice. It's never a good idea to show aggression towards someone you know can mash you like a bug."

His eyes narrowed and I allowed him to lower the cane from his chest. "Who the hell do you think you are, Stumbaugh? First, you squeezed me out of the interview with Zucker and deprived John of my counsel, *and* you advised him to announce his retirement, for Christ sakes!"

I pointed at the table. "Protecting *my* client, Counselor. That's all. Why don't you have a seat…there's a few things I'd like to discuss with you. Things that will put all this deep-seeded, unhealthily animosity you're holding inside to rest and lower your blood pressure to boot. What do you say?" I gave him my best, *let's be friends* look.

His shoulders relaxed a bit and the snarl disseminated to a look of grim distaste instead. At least, it was an improvement. I took my seat and offered him one where his back would be to the lobby. "Sam'll be back shortly," I said.

He sat down, smoothed his jacket, and adjusted his cuffs, briefly fingering the diamond cufflinks for my benefit. Then, that self-confident smirk returned and his color faded back to normal. "Okay, Stumbaugh, take your best shot. Massage my ego, unruffled my feathers…you think you're the master." He raised an arm and snapped his fingers twice at one of the waitresses two tables over.

"I always said that money and class didn't necessarily go together."

"What would you know about having class, Stumbaugh?" He returned.

Michelle showed up, rolled her eyes, and wrinkled her nose

at me, indicating her own disgust at my new guest. "Can I help you?" She asked, her voice disguising her true feelings about the attorney. After all, this *was* the Adolphus Hotel.

"Crown and water," Henshaw answered, without giving her a glance, "and I'm in a hurry. I won't be here long. I have a party to prepare for tonight."

"Yes sir." She turned to me. "Harry?"

"I'm good, darling," I said. She left with Henshaw's order. "Party? Can I come?"

"Hardly. Not quite your social order of clientele." The attorney folded his arms over his chest. "Where'd your pit-bull go, Stumbaugh? You send him off to chew on somebody's leg?"

I gave him a short laugh. "You mean, Wolfkill? Nah, he's really just a quiet, little pussycat, you know. He does his own bidding. I think he's more particular about the company he keeps than me."

Henshaw grinned. "Okay, what's this all about? I know you didn't ask me to sit down to chew over old times and demonstrate our dislike for each other. That we can agree on as a given. I've got things to do, so shoot. What's on your mind?"

I decided to take a wild stab in the dark at something that'd been bothering me, and I had nothing to lose by it. "Something I just figured out, Henshaw. About you and it's all come together. And, since you're so kind to come over for a visit…"

He smiled, and it wasn't a happy one either. So I continued. "I just thought I'd let you know that your little game is up. I know you're the one that's been pulling the strings on this whole scam. Mister Big, if you like." His reaction was exactly what I expected. He remained cool, nondescript, and unrevealing.

This time his grin was sly and a bit of a snarl creased his lips, before he addressed my accusation. "I'm afraid I don't know what you're talking about, Harry. But, amuse me. Why don't you lay it out for me?"

I shrugged. "Sure, I don't see any harm in that." I took a

quick glance at the lobby behind Henshaw's shoulder and spotted Epperson and one of his boys escorting the Doe's through the revolving doors onto Commerce Street, and Sam was strong arming Zucker towards Walgreen's.

I love it when a plan comes together.

"There's still a few gaping holes in my story, but I'm sure they'll come together with time. So, I'll just give you the short version. I know you're a man in a hurry."

"Please do," he said, checking his watch, letting me know I was right again.

You ready to bolt, Mr. Attorney? I would if I was sitting in your seat.

"It's all about the money...and power, of course," I began. "The power of being a buddy of a senator...a future governor, even. The power to eliminate loose strings."

"Go on. I like it so far. It's beginning to sound like a sweet fairy tale."

"From the top then. Let's begin with Robert Petrie. You knew him from the early days when your office defended him in court."

He interrupted. "That's no big secret. John defended him, actually, not me. It's all in the docket records. What else do you have to offer?"

Nice move.

"Yeah, that's probably one of the reasons Randolf Wellstone isn't with us any longer."

"Really? I didn't know that," Henshaw quipped innocently. "Sorry to hear that."

I ignored him. "Somehow or other, after all these years, Petrie contacts you and spills a story about a million dollar heist in '32. He knows the original players. Pete and Abner Strong, Detectives Cochran and Megs, himself, and of course, the elusive Ralph Morris."

The grin again. "Ah, the elusive Mr. Morris, yes.

Interesting. Fantasy, but interesting. Continue."

"Petrie probably knew that you weren't the upstanding pillar of the community that you pretended to be and hit you with a proposition. And Senator Doe, your buddy, was the perfect target. He was married to the daughter of Daddy Warbucks, who has more money than God, and Doe doesn't know his past from Shinola and can be made to believe whoever *you* wanted him to be. Your close relationship to him was the kicker. That's why Petrie came to *you*. The idea was to convince Doe he was a cop killer, a thief, and then absconded with the dough. You squeeze him for a half-mill and split the proceeds. You're the knight in shining armor and cover the mess from the public and advance his career. He eventually makes it to the mansion in Austin and you've got the goods over him...and the ear of the governor. You've got your very own puppet as the Head of State for the great state of Texas. A sweet deal."

The grin again. "I don't have the slightest idea of what you're talking about, but continue. It's very amusing."

I took a sip of beer and returned his grin. "All the players were in place and ready to act out their parts. Petrie was the front man to get things started with Doe. You probably suggested for Doe to get a private dick, instead of the police, since you didn't want any kind of official investigation to get started on this." I lit up a Lucky and paused for some extra drama. "I'm curious, did you give him my name or was that his idea?"

He shrugged. "As I said, I haven't a clue of what you're talking about."

"I'm thinking you gave him my name. Retired cop with a black cloud hanging over his professional career. Forced off the force. Possible connections to the mob boss of North Texas. Loser. It sounded perfect. Then, there was Cochran. He was the only guy on the force that would know anything about something that happened as far back as '32. You knew we had a history. I should've been suspicious when the prick was so agreeable. The way he threw out Abner Strong's name. He was the clincher.

Bringing up Ralph Morris. Hearing him on the radio. The missing pinkie finger. All that bullshit. I'll admit, he had me going hook, line, and sinker. Played me like a fiddler. Any of this sound familiar, yet?"

He checked his watch again. "You're doing fine. I can't wait to get to the ending. Soon I hope."

"The wheels were in motion. You either decided this week, or planned on eliminating the fodder all along. You had a man on the side none of the others knew about, and you started eliminating the losers, possible loose tongues in the gang...one by one. Petrie, Strong, Cochran, Megs, and most recently, Randolf Wellstone. Somebody, you or your button man, came upon the idea to make the hits look like a mob connection. A red herring for the cops. And me. Send the boys in blue chasing their asses in a circle. Maybe even pin a couple of hits on me and Wolfkill. Was that the idea?"

Michelle finally showed up with Henshaw's drink and set it on the table in front of him. "There you go," she said. "You still okay, Harry?" She said, turning my way.

"I'm fine, darlin', I need to keep my wits about myself today," I said.

"Add this to Mr. Stumbaugh's tab," Henshaw said and stirred the drink with his finger and flicked the moisture to the side.

I gave her a nod confirming it was okay. "Everybody else does."

Henshaw waited for her to leave before speaking. "You know...someone told me recently not to underestimate you, Stumbaugh. Guys in the pen. Blood on your hands. I didn't believe him at first...I took you for another has-been dirty cop, turned gumshoe. Taking dirty pictures of wives cheating on their pathetic husbands." He shrugged innocently. "Perhaps they were right."

Interesting.

"I'll take that as a compliment, coming from you. Who was it? Must be someone I know."

And I'm sure it was.

He waved me off with a smile and stood, smoothing down his jacket and tie, adjusting his cuffs, briefly fingering the cufflinks again. "I'm afraid I'm going to have to cut your little narrative short, Harry. This has all been very entertaining, but as I said, it's all fantasy in that alcohol soaked mind of yours."

"Need time to cover your ass, huh? You don't want to hear the part about you killing Wellstone and calling the cops? Hoping I'd get caught in the room when they showed up?" I hesitated for effect. "I'm afraid your timing was a bit off on that one. Oh wait...or were you trying to set up the button man you hired to do your killing for you? No, that wouldn't work...you don't leave any live bodies around to talk, do you?"

One last tug on the cuffs. "How *do* you come up with all this...this fantasy, Harry? It *is* amazing, but---"

"It's easy when you're up against an inferior mind."

The smile. "Yes, I'm sure, but as I was saying, none of these fantasies, based on what you've said here today, have any validity. Where is your proof? Hard facts? Pure speculation all of it, and I might add, grounds for suspension of your license to practice as a *private eye*," he said with a laugh. "Possible lawsuits for libel, slander, or whatever I'm sure I can manufacture...financial ruin."

I knew he was the suing kind of lawyer.

"I'll crush whatever scraps of a reputation you may have remaining, if you even attempt to go public with any of this. Who's going to take you seriously, anyway? No one with any credibility, for sure." Now he gave me the, *let's be friends smile* I gave him earlier. "Maybe, you can occupy the same alley where you found your friend, Mr. Wolfkill. The possibilities are unlimited! Downtown will still be your kingdom!" He exclaimed laughing.

"I'm shaking in my boots, Henshaw," I said with as much sarcasm as I could muster.

"Time for me to go, *Gumshoe*. Remember what I said." He turned to leave.

Let's see what kind of poker player you are, Henshaw.

I kept my seat, giving him the moment of looking down on me. "Want to know where your mistake was, Counselor?

He stopped. "There were *no* mistakes, Harry."

"Just one, my friend."

"Enlighten me, then."

"The poor country girl you sent to Zucker with the pathetic story about being married to Doe."

He shrugged. "Don't know what you're talking about."

The subtle eye twitch and repeated tugging on his cuffs told me different. "You used her name in the meeting this morning as stereotyping a poor country hick from Oklahoma. '*This Thelma Lou won't get away with this,*' I believe were your very words. That caught me as curious at the time. So, I checked with Tony Zucker this morning before his interview with Doe and asked him about her name. He wouldn't give it up, but I pressed him. He coughed it up. *Thelma Lou.* A slip of the tongue brought down the whole house of cards, Counselor." I was pretty damn proud of myself.

"Never happened," he said. Then snarled, "Be careful for your friends, Stumbaugh. Collateral damage can be a bitch."

I snarled back. "*You* be careful, Henshaw. My pit-bull is a lot worse than yours. Trust me. You go after family, you'll be dead before the sun sets…chewing on your dick just like the others."

He smiled and nodded at the table, "…thanks for the drink, you can have it." He turned away and headed for the revolving doors leading out to Commerce Street, but before he was out of earshot I yelled, "Hey Henshaw! All this was for nothing! The power…the money is gone! You'll never get a dime out of Doe! Nothing Henshaw! Nothing! It was all for nothing!"

Garland Henshaw's pace increased as he hit the doors.

I sat down and finished my beer.

Where's that steak?

Chapter 30

I was halfway through my steak when Sam returned to the table with the reporter, Tony Zucker. I considered him a *Dandy* if you know what I mean. He'd been the lead writer and editor for the entertainment and social events circuit for the *The News* ever since I could remember. He knew who was screwing who, who got knocked-up by who, and every other piece of rumor-mill gossip that circled the drain among the rich and famous of Dallas. And, he kept his mouth shut…as long as it suited him.

Physically, Zucker reminded me a bit of Petrie. He was short, maybe five-six or seven, thin, but unlike the gangster, he dressed to the T's. Black pin-striped suit, black dress shirt with a black and red stripped tie with a gold stick pin and a matching silk handkerchief prominently poised in the breast pocket of his jacket. And don't forget the black, tasseled loafers. His manner of dressing was his trademark. The problem was that ridiculous *fold-over* hair-do he sported. He was as bald as a cue ball on his crown with that semi-circle of hair thing going around his head, and a part above the ear on one side that folded over a length of hair a foot long to the other side of his head. A weak attempt to give the appearance of a full head of hair, if you ask me.

Idiot.

Zucker stood over me, hands on his hips, and I assumed a scowl on his face, observing me as I cut off another healthy chunk of a well-done T-bone steak. I dipped it in a pool of catsup for effect.

He wasn't happy. "Harry Stumbaugh, I want you to know

that I resent being manhandled by this...this *goon*," he said, pointing at Sam, who had silently started into his own steak.

I kept my eyes focused on my plate while his rant continued. "He dragged me into *Walgreen's* for God's sake! I just hope no one of importance saw me in there, with...*those* people." He checked the room for familiar faces.

"You should've tried their ham and egg omelets while you were over there, Tony," I said, digging into my baked potato. "Really good and the biscuits taste homemade."

"I'm sure they do," he said, wrinkling his nose." Then he stared down at my plate. "You're not *really* doing that are you? Eating an overdone steak and sloshing it around in a puddle of *catsup*! My God, Stumbaugh, don't you have *any* class? This is the *Adolphus*!"

I forked the last piece of steak into my mouth, lips smacking as I chowed down. "That's the second time I've heard that today, Tony," I said in between chomps. "Speaking of class, wanna compare haircuts?"

He sniffed and inhaled with an open mouth. "Really, Harry." He took a seat beside me and craned his neck, searching for a waitress. "The service here can be atrocious sometimes," he complained. "Why *am* I here, Harry? As you well know, I've got a story to file. *The* story of the year, I might add."

"When you get their attention, would you order me a beer?" Sam threw in between bites. "And some French Dressing?"

Zucker's nose wrinkled again and he stared at Sam like he was something he needed to scrap off his shoe. "Oh-my-God, I'm surrounded by..." He stopped and grinned. "Oh, I see, what's going on here...this is a big show...you two are doing this on purpose. To get my...goat, as you would say." He waggled a finger at me. "You two," he admonished playfully.

If he kept on I was going to lose my lunch.

"Okay, now that you've had your fun, will you please tell me what this is all about? Scooting me away fresh off the elevator like

I'm some sort of common criminal. I mean, I've never been treated so rudely before. I swear," he whined, removing a white linen handkerchief from his inside pocket, dabbing his forehead. "I just never---"

"Relax and sit down, Tony," I ordered, finishing off my salad. He took a seat, but wouldn't shut-up.

"I really need to get this story filed, Harry. Please. You know how big it is...and thank you by the way, I know this is your doing. But think about it, Harry! To be able to scoop those uppity investigative reporters in the news room, cub reporters really, with their big headlines...oh Harry, it's going to be so wonderful!"

As I pushed back my plate and took a sip of tea, I waved to our waitress to get her attention. "You want something to eat, Tony? The catsup here is exceptional."

He did the nose-wrinkling thing again. "Club Soda with a lemon twist, please. I've lost my appetite," he said, frowning at me and glaring at Sam. "So? Can we get on with it? Whatever *it*, is?"

He's a dandy.

"We're here to save your life, Tony."

"Really?" He checked the room with an amusing grin on his face. "Appears to be reasonably safe to me."

"You want to tell him, Sam? Since the two of you bonded so well at Walgreen's?" Michelle appeared and Sam ordered his beer and French Dressing, the dandy ordered his Club Soda with a lemon twist, and I got some more tea.

"Go ahead," Sam answered, getting back to his steak. "I'm still eating. You lead and I'll clean-up with the blood and gore part."

Zucker's head bounced back and forth between us like a spectator at a ping-pong match. "What's this all about, Harry?"

"The woman from Ardmore," I said, firing up a Lucky. "And don't give me any of that constitutional bullshit about confidentiality and protecting your sources crap. It doesn't apply since she was lying through her teeth. I probably know better than you do how she arrived on your doorstep, to start with." Sam finally looked up from his food after that little piece of information. I had his attention, too.

"Harry, I..."

I interrupted the dandy with the palm of my hand. "Ol' Sam and I saved your editorial bacon by killing the first Morris story before you went to press with it...and we're the ones that dropped the Doe identity and retirement story into your lap. Right?"

"Right," he said softly. "And I've already offered my gratitude, Harry."

I continued. "Our business is just like yours, Tony. One hand washes the other." I let the statement stand for a second. "I just want to know one thing. She gave you the name Thelma Lou Morris, claimed she was from Ardmore Oklahoma, and claimed to be John Doe's wife. Right?"

"Well, that's three things actually, but the answer is *yes* to all three. Now, could we please get to the part about saving my life? That's the part I'm most interested in, of course."

Gotcha, Henshaw.

I decided to keep pushing. "I'm getting to that. She came to you of her own accord, right?"

The dandy's nose wrinkled again. "You should be a reporter, Harry. That's correct. She didn't mention anyone else's name, except her son's, of course. Ralph, Junior. Anything else while I'm sitting here with a supposed death sentence hanging over my head?" His eyes checked around the room for lurking assassins.

The table went silent when Michelle returned with the drinks and French Dressing. Our silence at her arrival and her own experience as a waitress alerted her to the fact we wanted privacy; she left immediately without asking if we needed anything else.

Sam finally pushed back his plate and took a swig of beer. "Yeah, I've got a question. Why would she go to you instead of one of those investigative pups you talked about? Seems like that's who'd she go to, to me. The front-page boys."

I thought Sam's question ruffled his feathers a bit. "Well...I...I suppose she might have known of me, perhaps. I *do* have a reputation. You know, many people, far and wide, read my columns," he answered indignantly.

"Yeah," I said, "I'm sure most of the people in Ardmore are dying to know about which debutant the Dallas Cowboy quarterback screwed this week. Good point."

Verification of Thelma Lou's name was the main thing I needed from Zucker, and I got it. But I wasn't done yet. The dandy stood up, evidently I bruised his pride and ego about his far-reaching readership.

"If you're not going to tell me anything, I must return..."

It was time to get serious with the reporter. "Sit down, Tony. Your life really is in danger, and we're here to help you."

I think the tone of my statement got his attention for good this time, and he dropped in his seat like a sack of potatoes. "My God, what have..."

"You were set up, as I'm sure you've figured out after your interview with John and Hedy, earlier. The Ardmore woman, Tony...she was *sent* to you. She didn't just drop in on your doorstep because you can rattle off the name of every rich person in Dallas."

Zucker was genuinely shocked by this piece of news. "By whom? Who would do that to *me*?"

"You're just one piece of a larger puzzle, Tony. A very complex puzzle. You were set up by somebody, who, in the last forty-eight hours, is responsible for the deaths of a mobster, a crippled old man, two cops, and a prominent Dallas attorney...and there's a good possibility that you could be next on his hit list."

Zucker's face paled. "You...you mean those two detectives that were murdered this morning?" He frowned. "But, what have I done? I haven't done anything wrong!" He exclaimed. "I'm a social reporter for God's sake!"

"The woman from Ardmore. You talked to a link to the

killer. He's eliminating *links*," Sam said.

"But, I don't know who *he* is!"

"Doesn't matter," I added. "In his mind…you're expendable."

"*Ex-pen-da-ble*? Who on this Earth is an expendable human being, I ask you?"

In my opinion, Tony needed to get off the social circuit and experience a little of the real world. "Tony, there's no time to debate this."

With trembling hands, the reporter retrieved his handkerchief again and started dabbing beads of sweat from his forehead. His nose wrinkled and eyebrows lifted. "What prominent attorney were you talking about? I haven't heard anything about another murder."

"Randolf Wellstone," Sam answered. "The cops are up in his suite upstairs right now, canvassing the crime scene. It happened less than an hour ago."

Zucker's face grew even paler, if that was possible. "He was murdered while I was having coffee and joking around with John and Hedy? Oh my God, no-o! No, not Randy! I…I just spoke to him this morning. We were making plans to meet at a gala function tonight at the Magnolia Petroleum Building."

"You knew him?" Sam said, asking the obvious.

Zucker was having a hard time collecting himself. "Yes…we were…close friends. We'd known each other for years."

Sam and I let *that* statement stand without any further inquiry. "Yeah, well…sorry for your loss there, Tony." I needed to give Zucker some hope. I couldn't let him fall apart on me at this stage of the game. "We were supposed to meet him…he was a brave man, Tony. He was going to give us important information about the mastermind behind this whole affair. He was well aware of the dangers in what he was doing." I pointed at Sam. "We're the ones that found him and called the police. We probably missed the killer by minutes."

"How did he die?"

This was the sticky part. "A knife wound," Sam injected quickly.

"But *why*? What's this all about? Why would anybody want to kill such a...a kind person?"

"Same reason he might come after you, but Randolf had information against him and knew it. Unlike you."

"Information? What kind of information?"

Here we go.

"A million bucks, blackmail, power, and---"

Sam held up a hand to muzzle me. "Uh...I think you better stop right there, partner." He shook his head. "We don't want to say too much."

I nodded and took a sip of tea. "You're right."

"Wait! You can't stop there! Are you talking about John and Hedy Doe? What money? What blackmail?"

I looked across the table at Sam, as though asking for confirmation to speak. He paused a second and nodded approval. Zucker's head was back into the ping-pong action again. Back and forth he went.

"Tony, my friend," I said, "those are the reasons your life is in danger. The reason all those men were murdered. But, I can tell you this, soon, and I mean within the next twenty-four hours, those front page reporters at *The News* will be bowing to you in homage every time you walk through the office...that is, after we give you an exclusive on a story that will bring down one of the most renowned members of Dallas's social circle. We're talking national, baby." Then, something Henshaw had said earlier popped into my head and gave me another one of my brilliant ideas. "But, we may need your help."

The bait was cast. Now, it was time to reel him in.

It was easy to see that Zucker was still shaken by the death threat on his own life and even more by the murder of a friend, but the possibility of having a story picked up by the likes of the

Washington Post or the *New York Times* was easing his pain. "Will I be able to get any kind of vindication? Retribution for Randy's death?"

"Complete," I said.

"How can I help? Anything, just ask."

"Who's going to be at this shindig at the Magnolia tonight?"

"*Everybody*, of course," he answered matter-of-factly.

"Meaning everybody who's anybody in this town, I assume," I said, stating the obvious.

"Of course," Zucker answered.

"What's the occasion?" I asked.

"Well, as a matter of fact, Hedy Doe's father, Joseph Davis, was throwing a fund raiser as a last minute push for his son-in-law's bid for the United States Senate. Every oil man and anybody connected with the oil industry will be there…from Texas, Oklahoma, Louisiana, all over. But now…with him dropping out of the race…well, it's going to be an interesting evening, as you can imagine."

My partner's eyes and mine met in the middle of the table. "Think you can get me and Sam…" I stopped and decided to put on my best manners. "Excuse me, do you think it would be possible for you to appropriate an invitation for my associate and partner, Mr. Sam Wolfkill and me to the gala tonight? Of course, each of us will be escorting a beautiful woman on our arms."

Zucker's eyes narrowed. "My God-in-Heaven, what have I gotten myself into?" An audible sigh escaped his lips. "It is a black tie affair, you realize that, don't you?"

"I've got a black tie," I said.

Zucker's chin dropped to his chest. He lifted his head slowly, glaring at the two of us. "I'm afraid to ask, but do either of you two…*gentlemen*, even own a tuxedo?" He asked dryly.

"Several," Sam answered. "What color do you want me to wear? I have several to choose from," he added and finished off his beer.

"My God," moaned Zucker.

"I like him," Sam said, unexpectedly, after Zucker left to make arrangements for our invitations to the gala at the Magnolia. "Hope we can protect him."

"Yeah, he's a dandy, for sure," I said absentmindedly, checking out the scene over his shoulder. "Hey watch," I told Sam, motioning for his attention as Tony Zucker strutted across the lobby.

Sam twisted around in his seat for a look and spotted the reporter just as he flew through the revolving doors onto street like a man on a mission. "I've seen people navigate revolving doors before, Harry. What's your point?"

"Just keep watching, smart ass," I said. "There," I said, pointing him in the right direction, "heading towards the doors behind him. See her?"

"Very nice," Sam said, as he watched a gray-headed woman in a pillbox hat and a loud, flowered dress with a mink wrap follow the reporter outside. "Excellent."

"Thank you, I thought it was a good idea, too." I said. "She'll call from the newspaper if she spots anybody on his tail."

"What about DeRita? You going to wait for him?"

"Not if he doesn't get down here before Jenny calls. He'll have to wait."

"He won't like it, you know."

I shrugged. "We've got a party to get ready for."

Chapter 31

Garland Henshaw flew through the revolving doors at the Adolphus and walked one block to his offices at the Davis Building, the home of Republic National Bank, and coincidently next door to the Praetorian Building where the offices of Stumbaugh Investigations were housed. He made it through the lobby, stepped into the elevator, without having to acknowledge a soul, and got off on the eleventh floor. As he greeted the secretary posted in the waiting area, he told her to hold his calls and entered his office. He had one call to make before executing his departure plans. He dialed the number and waited through five excruciating rings before the other end picked up.

"Yes," answered the voice.

"I'm going to be out of pocket for a few days," said Henshaw. "You can begin with the others. I want that son-of-a-bitch, Stumbaugh, gone before midnight, and I want his dick and balls stuffed down his throat. The others...use your own judgment. Time isn't a factor. Are we clear?"

"Sure. When the money's in the account, you can consider it a done deal."

"Thirty minutes," Henshaw stated and hung up.

Henshaw leaned back in his chair and looked around his office, reflecting.

It's been a great run.

Leaving his briefcase on the desk, he grabbed only his car keys and left. On the way out, he instructed his secretary to cancel all his appointments for the day. He told her he'd work from the house, and he'd be at the Magnolia Petroleum party the rest of the evening.

From his office, he went downstairs to the bank, transferred ten thousand dollars into Gamboa's account, and cashed another check for five thousand; he retrieved his car from the parking garage behind the bank and headed to his home in north Dallas. As he drove, the wheels of his Mercedes coupe turned and so did the gears in his head.

Stumbaugh, that son-of-a-bitch, ruined everything. How did he figure everything out? Was he that good or just lucky?

It had been a mistake suggesting him to Doe. He *did* misjudge him. The gumshoe had nailed him good, but he wasn't one to dwell on spilled milk. What was done was done. And besides, he'd be long gone before the shit hits the fan. And it would. Hard. Garland Henshaw had a contingency plan, though. All his life he had managed, planned, and disciplined himself to stay ten steps ahead of the game at play. And now wasn't any different. After the meeting with that interfering gumshoe, he knew it was time to leave the game all together.

There wasn't any baggage in his life. No wife or kids, and he'd been planning for a day like this for years. Funneling cash to a bank in Mexico City. The plan was simple, and he rewound it mentally as he cruised down the highway. He'd go home, pack a few things, and head for Albuquerque, New Mexico, where he'd catch the first of several flights that would eventually land him in L. A. Then, a pleasant drive along the coast to San Diego. He'd already made an appointment with a discreet plastic surgeon there, where he'd change his looks, maybe grow a beard, and let his hair grow. He smiled thinking about the image. He'd spend some time in the city recovering, and finally slip across the border into Mexico.

Poof! Gone! And, as a symbolic gesture of his new found freedom, he planned to throw away his watch when he crossed into Mexico, never to worry about time again. Living the life of an expatriot. He had a little villa already squared away in Acapulco, Mexico, a quaint little village on the coast that hadn't been completely marred by commercialism and tourism. It was an out of the way playground for the rich and famous. He'd be sipping Crown and water on the beach while Stumbaugh, Wolfkill, Epperson...and, of course John and Hedy Doe would be food for the worms...six feet under.

He pulled into his driveway, but didn't bother parking in the garage. He didn't plan on being home long enough to deal with it. Henshaw ticked of his 'to-do' list in his head: Change from his suit, which he never planned to wear again, into boots, jeans, leather jacket, and a Red Sox baseball cap; leave behind his wallet and any identity papers linking him to the name of Garland Henshaw and grab the birth certificate, driver's license, social security card, and passport for his new identity, Wyatt Norton; grab the battered old duffle bag with a few clothes and necessities already packed, and hit the road. Thirty minutes max. He had a two-year-old Chevy stashed at the long-term parking lot of the airport, where he'd exchange it with the Mercedes; then, he was Albuquerque bound.

Henshaw walked through the front door loosening his tie and tossed the keys to the Mercedes on a small table by the door.

"You're home early, aren't you, Garland?" Eddy said, sitting on the couch with his legs crossed, lighting a Chesterfield, then exhaling a stream of smoke.

The sudden and unexpected intrusion of the voice caused Garland Henshaw's body to jerk reflexively and his head twisted to his right. His heart tried to shake itself free from his chest. "Shit!" he screamed. "What? How'd you g..."

Eddy lifted a crystal tumbler full of brown liquid in salute. "I like your taste in liquor, Counselor. Care to join me?"

After his nerves ceased coursing electrical shocks through his veins, and when he realized who the intruder was, he took a breath and flopped down in the closest chair. "What the hell are you doing in my home?" He said, in an effort to regain some of his dignity.

"Insurance," Eddy answered.

"Insurance? What the hell are you talking about?"

Eddy stood up. "Let's go into the den so you can fix yourself a drink, then we'll retire to that nice office you have next to your bedroom."

"You've been going through my house? Who do..."

Eddy held up a hand to stop him. "Don't say something you might regret, Counselor. Fix yourself a drink. Relax."

Henshaw did as he was told, going behind the wet bar in the den, grabbing the crystal dispenser of Crown Royal and the shot glass waiting for him on the bar. He splashed in at least two fingers of the fine bourbon and decided to forego the water.

Eddy stood a few feet away, staring through the plate-glass sliding door that led out to the backyard. "I really love what you've done with the place. The patio. The pool. You need to cut back your banana trees. All very nice, though. I'd like a place like this one day."

"Yeah, someday. Now, what the hell do you want?" Henshaw said, taking a sip from the tumbler. He had to keep his wits, and he wasn't about to let some Neanderthal thug that played gopher for Gamboa push him around. "I've got things to do if you don't mind."

Eddy turned his gaze back to the lawyer and shrugged. "I don't mind." He waved his arm down low as an invitation to proceed ahead of him. "To your office, then. I've got everything waiting for you."

Henshaw came out from behind the bar. "Son-of-a-bitch, I can't believe you invaded my house and made yourself at home."

"Well, I didn't think you'd come to my place if I invited you, so I decided to come here."

Eddy followed the lawyer into his office and directed him to sit behind the desk. A legal pad and a pen were laid out neatly on a leather desk pad. Gamboa's man looked around the room admiringly. "I'd like to have an office like this one day. Very professional. Is that mahogany paneling on the walls? I like it." He pointed at the numerous framed items that adorned the walls. "Kind of a Garland Henshaw shrine, huh? Diplomas, awards, pictures with the rich and famous. Nice."

Henshaw took a seat, checking the desk to see if anything was missing. "Well fuck, Eddy, since you like everything so much, why don't you just buy the place. I'll make you an offer you can't refuse."

Eddy nodded. "Might take you up on that. Take the pen and write what I tell you."

Henshaw frowned and mumbled something unintelligible, then said, "Fine, what do you want? The deed to the house? The convertible in the driveway? Let's just get this done."

Eddy started, "I, Garland Henshaw, do hereby confess that I am responsible and ordered the deaths of Robert Petrie, Abner Strong…"

Henshaw stopped writing after he wrote *I,* and started laughing. "Are you fucking *crazy*? I'm not writing…"

Eddy shrugged. "What? It didn't sound proper? I thought that's how it would be worded to make it sound legal and all. You can reword it in your own terms if you like. I really don't care, just as long as you state the facts as I recite them." He pointed at the writing pad on the desk. "And by the way, I found copies of your handwriting and signature in the desk, so there's no need to get cute. Now…one way or another, before I leave, I'm going to have your confession and signature signed and dated at the bottom of that paper. That way…I know we'll be buddies for a long, long time."

How do I play this? Hell, the cat's out of the bag anyway. Give him what he wants. I'll be in Mexico in a week. Get this Gum-bah out of here…but don't give in too easily.

Garland Henshaw reached down, tore the top sheet off the pad, wadded it up in a ball, and threw it at the mobster's chest. It bounced off. "No fucking way. And, if you try to strong-arm me, I've got an envelope just waiting to be mailed to the right person in the event something happens to me. Now get out. I've got a party to get ready for."

"The Magnolia Petroleum shindig? Should be fun." Eddy smiled and withdrew a .38 revolver with a silencer attached to the barrel from his waistband and pointed directly between the eyes of the man across the desk from him. "Let's try this one more time. I, Garland Henshaw..."

Chapter 32

After Jenny hit the street, I went up to the front desk and told them I was expecting a phone call, and that I'd be in the French Room bar, as if they didn't already know. I filled Sam in about nailing Henshaw to the wall, and, of course, he was amazed at my intuitive, deductive reasoning powers. But, we still had to come up with the proof against him and find the shooter. Sam commented that the targets on our backs just got bigger now that Henshaw knew we were on to him. The conversation gradually drifted into tuxedos for us and dresses for the girls when a bell boy came running up to let me know there was a message waiting for me.

"That was quick. Tip the young man, Sam," I said getting up. "If I'm springing for the tuxes, you get the tips. Give him a fiver, he's been a busy man today." I left lickity-split to get the phone so I wouldn't have to deal with Sam's blow-back. I knew it'd come sooner than later, at any rate.

I had a little surprise waiting for me at the phone bank when I picked up the line. "Hey, Doll Face, give me what cha' got," I said in my best seductive voice.

"I'm not sure I'm your type," an Italian accented voice answered. "Sex on the telephone, huh? I can see some possibilities with that, Harry," Gamboa said with a small laugh. "I must look into it."

Shit. Never lose face to this man.

"You never know till you try, my Italian friend." A hearty laugh exploded at the other end of the line.

"Only you, Harry Stumbaugh, can get away with such a thing." Then, he got straight to the point. "I would like to visit with you."

"Okay, when?" As if I didn't have enough on my plate already. DeRita, Jenny, tuxedos.

"Now, would be a good time, if you can spare it. I know you have a lot of things going on right now, Harry, but this will be to your best interest, I believe."

I'm sure it will.

"On my way, see you in ten or fifteen."

That was a change of plans I hadn't counted on. I informed the desk that Sam would take any calls meant for me. Then, I covered the bases and told Sam where I'd be. I told him to relay to DeRita that I had a hair appointment, and I'd call him later. That done, I had Riley bring up my car, and I was on the road.

When I entered the restaurant, I spotted Gamboa at his usual table, and he waved me forward. I glanced at the bar. Eddy wasn't at his usual spot, but there was another one of Gamboa's soldiers at the post. He gave me a nod, confirming it was okay to approach the boss. All very subtle. Moves that no one but me would have noticed.

"Have a seat, my friend," Gamboa said affectionately, pushing out a chair next to him. "How are you? And Sam? By the way, give him my blessings. I understand he has taken up with the lovely Kate Culpepper. I believe they will be good for each other. So many dark secrets between the two of them that need to be eradicated."

There's some kind of bond thing going on between Sam and Giovanni that I've missed, somehow. "I'll do that, and pass my regards, but I'm having trouble picturing you as Cupid, Giovanni."

He shrugged. "We all play different roles as time passes, my friend. And you?"

"No new roles for me and I'm tired as hell. I'm getting too old for this shit, Giovanni. I never thought a divorce case could look so good. And your family?"

He smiled. "The girls and wife are good, and yes, we all are growing tired, I believe. But I suspect divorce cases will be a thing of the past for you after this, my friend. Would you like something to eat? To drink?"

"I'm fine. I just ate, and I've already drank too much today. I need to save it for tonight."

He nodded. "Ah, yes, the big gala at the Magnolia Building."

The man never ceased to amaze me, but I'd never ask how he knew so much. I didn't want to know. "Yeah, you don't have an extra tuxedo in your closet, do you?"

A short laugh. "I'm afraid not, but I dare say, it might be a size or two too big for even you."

Our eyes met on a direct line. "New man at the bar. You didn't have me searched. New policy?"

Giovanni shook another cigarette from the pack on the table and lit it from the butt of the one he'd just finished. "It is all about trust, you know that, Harry. If I cannot trust you…then it doesn't exist for me." He stubbed out the smoldering butt into an overflowing ashtray, and his facial features drew a shade darker.

I was about to find out why I was summoned. Yes, summoned.

"I have a favor to ask of you, Harry. A difficult one."

I had a pretty good idea of what he was going to ask of me and had to come up with an answer that wouldn't offend him when I turned him down. "All you need to do is ask, Giovanni, but this could be a first for me."

His face questioned me. "A first?"

"Yes. You've never asked me for a favor in all the years I've known you. And now…I'm afraid I may have to turn you down."

He smiled and nodded knowingly. "I understand. And that's very bold of you to say so. Then, I will not embarrass either one of us by asking for an answer." He took a deep drag from his cigarette, squinting as some of the smoke drifted up into his eyes, but the mutual eye contact never broke. "Perhaps we can...talk, then."

"I'd like that."

"You plan to take down Henshaw tonight, I assume."

I smiled this time. "You *are* an old fox, my friend. Nothing gets by you, does it?" I didn't expect or get an answer. I shrugged. "There's not exactly a *plan* in place, but it is what I have in mind, yes."

Gamboa dropped a long ash into the ashtray and stared at the finger tapping it in. "And the button man? You've plans for him?"

This was the touchy part. How do I breach the idea that his own man is the assassin? "*That,* I can't honestly say." I decided to toss the ball back in his court.

He smiled. "You're getting much better at this game, Harry. Then...the favor...as it is, is this. This has become a...*family* matter, now. And, as I'm sure you understand...if this were to become public knowledge...even *rumor,* for that fact...it could be very embarrassing for me. I must be...proactive, you understand."

I nodded. "Yes, it would be embarrassing. You're right."

Giovanni continued, not dwelling on that subject or my response. "My wish is to take care of the situation *within* the family. There should be no *official* knowledge or interference. Your success in this case has been...extraordinary, Harry. And, my hat goes off to you...but now...I'm asking you to stand down. Henshaw is yours, as he well should be. But, the button man is mine."

I glanced to the post at the bar where Eddy normally conducted business. His eyes followed mine, and I noticed a crooked, mischievous grin crease his lips.

Am I getting snookered here?

"Do you..."

He waved me off. "Harry, this would have happened with or without you, Doe, or any of the other principals. There is no one to fault, except for the one who decided to shoulder the eventual and inevitable consequences on his own."

"I know."

He nodded and smiled. "No…you just *think* you know."

That was a strange thing to say, which wasn't unusual for the old man.

He continued. "The last two days have been good, no? A hanger-on who wanted to be a made-man is out of *my* hair. Two dirty cops, who were a pain in the ass for both of us, have finally met justice."

"What about Abner Strong and Wellstone?" I asked.

"Strong was a bitter old man who was consumed with misguided revenge and was simply put out of his misery."

Giovanni Gamboa spoke of another man's death as though he were talking about stepping on a roach. No emotion. No remorse.

Old man, have I misjudged you all these years?

"And Wellstone?"

He shrugged. "I did not agree with his lifestyle and have little tolerance for such men, but it was unfortunate. Unnecessary, in my opinion, knowing what I do. As you know, I do not put a price on a man's value to society. I price his value to me…or the harm he can do." He shrugged again. "This man was neither." He reached across the table and grasped my hand. The meeting was abruptly adjourned. He'd made his request. "I've enjoyed our time together, Harry. And, I will do my best to protect you…you know that."

Shit. I knew exactly what that meant.

"I know." I checked my watch and stood. "Tuxedos and evening gowns to buy."

Giovanni lit another cigarette from the previous butt. "I suggest Neiman-Marcus, of course."

"With your pocketbook, I'm sure you do. I'm just a poor gumshoe getting by one day at a time."

A short laugh. "Bullshitting a bullshitter, Harry? Only you, my friend."

"Yes. And we *are* friends, Giovanni. Right?"

Another small grin. "Harry…a…sweetener for you. To confirm our everlasting friendship."

"A sweetener?"

"Cochran…it was a rogue killing. It had nothing to do with my family."

Chapter 33

Gamboa had given me a lot to chew on, and I didn't like the taste left in my mouth. Why couldn't he just come out and *tell* me what was on his mind. Two things he said stuck in my head like a piece of gum on the sole of my Wingtips. One, he indicated that I didn't know as much as I thought I did. Well, that was obvious. But, it was that crooked little grin of his when he said it...that's what bothered me. Second, the old man said he would *do his best to protect me.* Henshaw's threat, during our earlier little conversation, about watching out for my friends, pretty much told me we were targets; I knew that much.

So hell, if Gamboa knows who the hit man is, why doesn't he just take care of it, instead of letting him go after me and the others? Why all the games?

As far as Henhaw was concerned, the shyster was right when he said there were no hard facts that actually pinned him to the wall involving the conspiracy. I had no clue of how to pull it off...unless I got to the killer, first. That being the case, all I had to do was figure out a way to do a trap and nab plan without killing him first.

Nothing to it.

Before I left, I called Sam at the hotel from a phone booth at Gamboa's place to see if he'd heard anything from Jenny. He had, and, as far as she could tell, Zucker hadn't been followed. That was good, at least. Jenny headed back to the Adolphus to meet him and on to Epperson's office to collect Katie. I told Sam to take the girls to Neiman Marcus to check out gowns for the party at the Magnolia Building and to see if he could find a tux that wasn't the wrong size or color. He answered by referring some unique things I could do with a dildo.

Before hanging up, I gave him a brief rundown on the conversation I had with Giovanni and the circles I had running around in my head and his blessing from the old man. No comment was forthcoming from him on that matter. So…I left out Gamboa's *sweetener* comment about Cochran's killing not being connected to the others. I was holding on to that juicy morsel for now. I wanted to talk to him face-to-face about that little item.

Then, I gave him the hard facts. "We're on the hit parade list, too, buddy. In round about ways, that's been confirmed by Henshaw and Gamboa. And, I don't have to tell you that this guy's a professional, not some Joe off the street. The only way we'll get to Henshaw, as far as I can figure, is to get his button man before he gets to us."

"I agree. You got something in mind?" Sam asked.

"He wants a target…let's give him one."

"I'm game, let's play," Sam answered immediately. "When?"

"Tonight. But in the meantime, you stick with the girls like glue, and I'll meet you at the Magnolia after I get my tux and make some calls from the office." I hung up, knowing the girls were in safe hands.

Next, I headed for Epperson's office. I needed an update on the Doe's situation and needed to get in touch with DeRita before he had a coronary. Epperson was sitting behind the receptionist's desk, picking at his nails, when I walked in the front door.

"You been demoted?" I quipped.

He leaned back in the chair and propped his feet on the desk. "I'm an empty-nester, evidently. Sam and Jenny came by and picked up Katie. Something about a party and a new dress. Everybody else in the office has already hit the road for the day."

A row of four chairs were lined up against the opposite wall from the receptionist's desk, intended for waiting clients. I never had that problem. I took the first one next to the end table with an ashtray, stretched my legs out straight, and lit up a Lucky. "How're John and Hedy doing?"

He smiled. "Like newlyweds. I've never seen so much hand-holding and cooing back and forth in all my life. It looks like John's new identity has given both of them a new lease on life. It's like they've been reintroduced to each other. Kevin called me from Oklahoma after they arrived and said they loved the place. Hedy's already talking about making an offer to buy it lock, stock, and barrel. Oh, and I took the initiative on something else. A friend of mine is a Captain with the Oklahoma PD, and I told him I needed a good protection detail for a few days. He gave me the name of a reputable private agency in town. I contacted the owner of the company, and he sent a couple of his best operatives out to the cabins to babysit the honeymooners." He laughed. "I doubt the lovebirds will get much fishing done, like they talked about. They'll probably never come out of the bedroom. Anyway, I set the detail up in a cabin close by so they could keep an eye on things. I figured the happy couple could afford it. Probably won't even know the agency men are there."

I was impressed. "Wow. I'm impressed, Cam. Good work."

At that point, I needed a good sounding board; so, I shared the conversations I had with Henshaw and Gamboa to see if a fresh pair of ears and an actual working brain could read anything different than my own conclusions.

The Henshaw thing floored him. And, pissed him off, evidently. He planned on going to the Bar Association to file a professional misconduct or unethical practice charges, or some garbage like that, against him. He admitted it didn't mean much in the scope of things, of blackmail and murder, but it would get the ball rolling to start putting his butt under the microscope. And based on the evidence, I gave him about the son-of-a-bitch, he confirmed what I already knew. That we'd need a hardcore witness with first-hand knowledge on the entire conspiracy in order to go to the grand jury and get an indictment filed against him. In short order…we needed the button man. The man that took the orders directly from Garland Henshaw. That was the way it had to be.

"What's the party the girls were talking about? Sounded fancy," Epperson asked, after we'd exhausted alternate theories and possible solutions of the case out the kazoo.

"Magnolia Petroleum's annual shindig."

"Really? I've been to a couple of those." Epperson interlocked his fingers behind his head and grinned. "Went with some of my oil clients. Quite the extravaganza. Opulence out the ass. More food and booze in one place than I've ever seen before. And the women…big hair, big tits, lots of cleavage, and big egos for the yahoos that escort them, in their Tony Lama boots and Stetsons."

"Really? And I was afraid I wouldn't fit in. You doing anything tonight?"

Epperson sat up straight in his chair, anticipating my next words. "Not really. Why?"

"Do you have a tux that fits?"

The process of buying a tuxedo at Neiman-Marcus was an experience, to say the least. I'd rather get cracked over the head with a pool cue than do it again. Carlo, my personal salesman, took care of me. We didn't get off to a good start. I told him what I wanted and my sizes, but he insisted on measuring every part of my body before even showing me what he had on the rack. He poked, prodded, and measured arms, legs, neck, and fingers; but when he started measuring my inseam and stuck that measuring tape in places I'd never let anyone but a woman get near, I thought I was going to have to take out my gun and shoot him dead on the spot. That was the first time I thought about shooting him. And, he knew damn well I was packing because he definitely noticed the .38 holstered snug in its shoulder harness and the .25 caliber secured on my ankle. He didn't ask any questions, and I didn't offer any answers.

Evidently, purchasing a plain black tuxedo at Neiman's is unheard of. There was nothing plain or simple to choose from. A lot of satin and velvet. Puffy shit. But, I finally settled on one I could live with, and the fact that it fit like a glove and made me look like a million bucks didn't hurt either. When I refused to put on the cummerbund or purchase a pair of black patent sissy shoes, Carlo got his panties all twisted out of place. I thought he was going to shit himself when I said I could wear the same belt I'd been wearing for the past five years, and my Wingtips would shine up just fine, thank you very much. That was the second time I wanted to just shoot him and get it over with; but lucky for him, a good-looking broad with blonde hair, a disarming smile, and deep cleavage stepped in, refereed a peace treaty, and saved the day and Carlo's life.

Leaving the high-end department store, I hit the streets and thought about how much I loved downtown and the Big D. The Adolphus, the Baker, the Magnolia Petroleum Building, and Neiman's were all located at the corners of Commerce and Akard. The cop shop was three blocks east and the *Dallas Morning News* was six blocks west. The Healey had covered parking and everything I needed was here. This was my world.

When I passed by the Magnolia Building and observed some of the early arrivals for the big gala, there were limos, Caddies, Lincolns, Mercedes, and just about anything that costs over ten grand lined up at the curb, waiting for young studs in tuxedos to open car doors with one hand and open palms with the other. Cam was right. The babes were gorgeous. Long dresses, big diamonds, big…everything. This was the perfect place for this kind of shindig. Texas style. The Magnolia Building was owned by a home grown oil company, so of course, they built the tallest and fanciest monstrosity in the state. But that wasn't enough. The oil barons added a unique feature unlike anything in the country. Outlined in red neon, a giant figure of Pegasus, the winged horse of mythology, rotated in a circle on top of the twenty-fifth floor. You could damn near see the thing from Fort Worth.

Only in Texas.

After seeing the line of cars at the curb, I decided it'd be a good idea to throw back the rag top on the Healey and make my own grand entrance at the Magnolia with Doll Face on my arm, instead of walking from the Adolphus.

Jenny makes the rest of those painted up broads look like poodles in need of a good grooming.

Why not? I'd had a pretty good run at it the last couple of days, and I was feeling full of myself, as I strolled back to the office at a leisurely pace. I'd cracked open and solved a case that'd been dormant for twenty years and got a state senator his identity back; two crooked cops, that'd been my nemesis for almost twenty years, were buried six feet in the ground; and I had a wad of cash in my pocket, not to mention a new tuxedo, cummerbund, and new black patent shoes slung over my shoulder. Life was good.

When I got to the office, I hung up my new duds that were snug in their genuine plastic hanging bag with the Neiman-Marcus name emblazed on it, on the hat rack and tossed the box of patent leathers on the floor. After propping Old Hickory against the desk and throwing the fedora on one of the wingbacks, I settled into my swivel chair to make one more call before I took a shower and got ready for the party.

Time to face DeRita.

It was a little after seven, and I wasn't sure he'd be in the office, but I could at least leave a message and cover myself if he wasn't in. I dialed the number and the son-of-a-bitch picked up on the first ring.

Doesn't he ever go home?

"Captain DeRita, Homicide," he answered, fatigue all over his voice.

"Have you had any of those today?" I asked, trying to be funny and begin the conversation with a little humor.

"You stood me up."

"I got called away, couldn't help it."

"How was your hair appointment?'

"I'm beautiful again. You should try it."

"Okay, we've made nice. What have you got for me, Harry? I'm dead tired and want to go home and get some sleep before somebody else drops dead from a gunshot to the head or a new smile carved into their throat."

"Garland Henshaw, the big shot attorney, is behind the murders. Strong, Petrie,... Cochran," I decided to throw that one in for grins, "Megs, and Wellstone. The whole package."

"Oh, for crying out loud, Harry. Can you tell me why and how you came up with him?"

"He didn't want to share his toys with the other kids, and he didn't want anybody around that could talk about it. Same old story...greed and power."

"Got any proof?"

"Nope."

"Then you don't have shit, Harry."

"But I'm going to a party tonight. Wanna go? Henshaw will be there. We can rattle his cage a little bit. Let him know that *we* know."

"You rattle. I'm going to roll in bed. I'm so tired I can't think straight right now. I'm sure this will sound more exciting and feasible tomorrow after I've had some sleep. In the meantime, stay out of trouble. Can you do that for me? Huh, Harry?"

"Fine, I'll..." I heard the front door in the reception area open, figuring it was probably Cam. "Just a sec, Dan, somebody's at..."

A young man, who looked to be in his early twenties with dark features, dressed in a black suit and shirt open at the collar, suddenly appeared in my office doorway. He was a handsome young man, with almost Greek, godlike features, and his hair was cut short and laid naturally over his scalp. But, it was the .45 automatic pointed at my chest that caught my attention first. He waved it sideways, back and forth. "Hang up the phone," he said, almost in a whisper.

I held up my free hand, as though it would stop any bullets flying my way. "Okay fella, just take it easy with that heater," I said cautiously, setting the receiver down on the cradle. I dropped my hands to my lap, my right easing to my .38, holstered under my jacket.

This could be interesting.

"Hands face down on the desk," he said, pointing the automatic at my waistline.

I did as he said and stared at the intruder harder…there was something familiar about the face, then it hit me. "Alexis Gamboa," I said. "I see you've graduated from shoplifting cigarettes from the five and dime stores to bigger things…like murder."

"So you remember me?"

My eyes bored in on his. If he was going to shoot, the eyes would be the first signal, not the hands. "I should. It ended up costing me my job." *Keep him talking.* "The boys in the penthouse offices decided I was double-dealing with your Uncle Giovanni. Evidently, the mayor is narrow-minded and frowns on doing supposed favors for the kingpin of organized crime in North Texas."

"That's too bad," Alexis said with no remorse. "Now, with your left hand, reach over and remove the .38 from underneath your jacket with your forefinger and thumb, remove it very slowly from the holster and place it on the desk."

"So…you going to shoot me or what?" I asked, not following his instructions just yet, my hands still flat on the desk. "Henshaw gave you a new list of people to kill?" I could tell the mention of Henshaw's name alarmed him, but only for a split second. A movement of the eyes and quickly raised eyebrows told me that.

The young hood extended his gun arm, as though he was about to shoot, and said, "Do it…now. Or I blow your ass away where you sit."

I held up both hands. "Okay, fine. No big deal." I did as he said and placed my piece on the desk. Getting to the .25 was going to be a problem.

The hit man edged closer, took my .38, shoved it in his waistband, and moved backwards a couple of steps, keeping a distance between himself and target. Me being the target, of course. "Keep both hands on the desk." He shrugged. "And, as far as Henshaw, it doesn't matter. Money's already in the bank. I don't care if he gets caught or not. He just wanted me to make sure *you* were dead by midnight. The others...whenever the timing is right for me. I'll fulfill my obligations whether he's sitting in a six-by-twelve cell or not. I have a rep, now. You hire me to do a job...I follow through."

"Very professional of you."

I can take this kid if I can just get up from behind this desk.

"So, he offered you a piece of the deal? The blackmail money? Looks like you might get short-changed, kid. Not a very good beginning to your chosen profession."

He smiled. "He offered, but I turned him down. His first offer was one grand a hit. I'm getting two. All up front. I'm no fool."

Yeah, I can tell, that's why you're shooting off your mouth instead of the gun.

"And, does your uncle approve of your new professional endeavor?"

Keep him talking.

He laughed with contempt. "*That* old man? He's getting soft. He tried to teach and lecture me about the evils of the family business after I got busted for shoplifting. He said I should thank you for saving me from a life of crime. He even said he'd get out of the business himself, if he wasn't in it so deep. But, as I'm sure you know, once you're a made man, you're in for life. The only way out is to swim with the fish or sing with the angels."

"So, he kept you from becoming a made man? Is that what this is all about? Your pride?"

Oops, that hit a nerve.

Alexis angrily jabbed the .45 like he was poking me in the ribs or something. "I've proven I don't need that old man. Like I said…he's soft. He doesn't have the stomach for what it takes to get things done anymore."

"Right," I said. "So, he didn't know what you've been up to the past couple of days? Killing cops, lawyers, things like that."

The contemptible laugh again. "He's not as smart as you think he is. Actually, it was Eddy, his faithful lapdog, was the one that found out. But, he's been a step behind me the whole time. He's not as smart as he thinks *he* is, either. After I'm done with you, I'm splitting from town for a while. Let things cool down." He waved the gun at me again. "Enough talk. Stand up," he ordered, motioning the automatic to his right, simultaneously sidestepping to his left. "Into the other office."

I stood, keeping my hands up and out to my sides, showing no resistance, but staying close to the desk. Not moving.

Seeing that I wasn't following his orders, he stepped up so we were in a direct line with each other, and with his free hand, he pointed to the side office again. "Get your ass in there, we're wasting time."

I sized up my opponent. I had him by height and size, maybe twenty pounds, but I could tell he was bulked up under the suit jacket.

I can take this little prick.

He was also twenty-five to thirty years younger than me and quicker, no doubt. But, this wasn't my first rodeo. I'd been handling punks like him all my professional career. I didn't glance down, but I knew old hickory was propped against the desk in front of me.

There's my distraction.

I just needed to get him to blink once. One bad move.

I decided to prod some more. "You know I'm not going to make this easy for you…don't you, punk? I'm not going to negotiate, beg, moan, piss myself, or cry for mercy offering you the world not to kill me like the others probably did. I'm going to make this hard for you. You're going to have to *earn* your money on this hit." I moved up a half-step.

"Fuck you, old man. You'll be chewing on your balls in two minutes. Now move."

I kept my hands out and to the side for balance and took another half-step to my left, this time away from the desk. I shrugged and gave him what I hoped was a disarming smile. "Then as I see it, you only have two choices to make."

"And what would that be, old man?"

"Do you want me to shove that pop gun up your ass or down your throat before I pull the trigger on it?

Blink.

That was my moment. I kicked the cane just below its center point and it lifted end over end in the air. Bending at the waist, I charged low at the young Gamboa. His initial reflex was to raise the gun at the first thing coming at him…the cane.

His recovery was quick, but not before I had time to crash my body into his with all the force I could muster, driving his back hard into the opposite wall. I grabbed the hand with the gun, and slammed it twice against the wall, but I misjudged his strength and moves. After the second slam, his resistance was even stronger.

Strong little fucker.

My left kept his gun arm pinned high against the wall and my right forearm was jammed against his throat. I pressed arm and body against him as he squirmed around to get repositioned and air in his lungs. He gained a half step and tried to knee me in the balls. But, my inner thigh took the full blow instead. It felt like I'd been frogged. The combination of pain and reflexes made me bend over just enough to ease the force against his throat and for him to get some leverage. He grabbed my shirt at the chest with his left hand and attempted to twist me around and free himself, but I still held on firm to his wrist, keeping the gun high overhead.

This was where old tricks and age came into play. I didn't resist the move to twist me around and rolled with it, but I still needed more leverage and momentum. My right hand free, and I crashed a haymaker down on his temple. It stunned him temporarily, but his grip on the .45 was like a vice, and he still wouldn't let go of it.

The fist upside the head gave me the split second I needed, though. I grabbed his jacket by the lapels, pivoted with my left leg and swung Gamboa with everything I had, released my grips, and watched him fly across the room and over the desk. A fistful of my shirt went with him. He slid across the top and disappeared on the other side.

He's still got the fucking gun!

I was in mid-crouch to get my .25, and, once again, his recovery was quick and unexpected as he came up from behind the desk, his right hand extended, the .45 pointed at my chest.

"You're one dead fucker, Stumbaugh!" He screamed, spit flying with every word.

We were no more than six feet apart and there was no way I'd get to the .25 before getting blown away.

I'm a dead man.

But, instead of firing and taking the kill shot, his eyes shifted a fraction to the right, widening, his gun making the same adjustment as his eyes, and then I heard the sound of a single puff of compressed air.

A silencer. Who the hell is that?

Alexis Gamboa jerked back and sideways as a bullet crashed into his right shoulder, finally forcing him to drop the .45, as he fell back behind the desk. I heard him screaming like a little boy that'd fallen off his bike and skinned a knee on the sidewalk. I gripped the .25, ready to blow away somebody's kneecaps, when, to my left, Eddy Valachi stepped into the doorway; his right arm extended straight, a snub-nosed .38 with a silencer extending from the barrel balancing nicely in his hand. I relaxed for a split second, but still withdrew the small revolver from its holster, prepared for anything, even though Giovanni's bodyguard just saved my life.

Without a word, he moved into the room, gave me a silent nod, and went behind the desk to check on Gamboa. After kicking the .45 across the room, he grabbed the kid by the collar of his shirt and shoved him into my chair, retrieving my .38 from his waistband, and tossing it on the desk. Alexis gripped his wounded shoulder, trying to stop the staunch of blood, moaning. "Get me a doctor! I've been hit!" Blood seeped through his shirt and began to ooze through his fingers. "Get me to a hospital, asshole!"

Eddy backhanded the punk across the jaw, starting a new flow of blood from the kid's busted lip. "You've disgraced your family and your uncle's name, Alexis. For this, you will pay dearly." He turned to me. "You okay, Harry? You hit anywhere?"

Before I could even answer, the front door crashed open and Captain DeRita charged in, his own gun sweeping the room, with two patrolmen, guns drawn, on his tail. His revolver stopped, directed at Eddy's chest. He recognized the mob goon immediately. "Freeze! Gun on the ground! Hands behind your head!"

That was probably the first time DeRita had drawn a gun from his belt in twenty years. As he was so focused on Eddy, he didn't even see me standing to his right. It was all a little late and anti-climactic after the body guard had saved my bacon, but I appreciated the effort of my old friend.

Eddy immediately tossed his gun to the floor, locked his fingers behind his head, and turned around, his back to DeRita without being told. "Okay, okay," he said calmly. "I know the drill."

DeRita spotted the bleeding man in my chair and turned to one of his patrolmen and pointed at the reception area. "Use the phone in there and call an ambulance. Tell them it's a gunshot wound." He pointed at Eddy, holstering his weapon. "Frisk him," he told the second patrolman, "and cuff him." He stepped back, came over my way, and looked me over. "You okay?"

"Yeah, for somebody who almost got put down by a twenty-something-year-old punk. I turned around and saw my door hanging by the hinges. "Hope that didn't hurt too much, 'cause you're going to pay for it, you know."

"Too dramatic, you think?"

"Nah, it was perfect, Dan. Just like the old days."

"Good thing you didn't hang up the phone, Harry," he said, then returned to my desk and picked up the receiver and spoke. "We made it on time, Joe. Did you get everything?" He waited for his answer. "That right? Even better. Get everything typed up, official like. Send a couple of patrolmen over to Parkland. There'll be a gunshot wound to the shoulder on his way. Stay with him at all times. What? Just a minute." DeRita stuck the phone up to Alexis Gamboa's face. "Repeat your name for the fine detective at the other end. We'd like your name to match the one on the tape."

"Fuck your mama," spewed Alexis. He watched DeRita drop the receiver back to its cradle and frowned. "Son-of-a-bitch. Type what up? What're you talking about?"

I answered for him. "Old dog, old trick, kid. You've still got a lot to learn. I never hung up the phone, shithead. From where you were standing, it just looked that way."

"I was on the other end, kid. A room full of cops got your whole confession. About ten of Dallas's finest heard everything you said. And I'm sure the D. A. will line them up one after the other on the witness stand at your trial."

"Fuck you, copper."

I smiled. "You like Cagney, kid? Can you say, *Old Sparky*?"

DeRita nodded at the patrolman that had cuffed Eddy and pointed at Alexis. "Cuff this piece of shit too, and take him down stairs and let the ambulance pick him up there. When they take him, stick to him like glue."

The patrolman grabbed Alexis underneath the armpits and hoisted him out of the chair like a ragdoll, standing him up on his feet.

"Hey! Watch it flatfoot! I'm hurt!"

"He watches too many old movies," I said, watching him being dragged through my busted front door.

"Lucky for you, I didn't fall asleep during your Q & A session," DeRita said.

"Yeah, glad you stayed awake." I needed to do some cleanup work and motioned at Eddy. "You've got the wrong man, DeRita. I shot the kid, not him."

Eddy's head twisted around and his eyes met mine.

The old man protected me…now it was my turn to pay him back.

DeRita directed some nasty looking, cold, steely eyes my way, and the stare told me that he wasn't in the mood to play games. "You're full of shit, Harry. You didn't shoot him, and I know it. I was on the phone, listening. Joe told me that when I was on my way here, the two of you two crashed around the office like two bulls in a china shop. He didn't say a damn thing about Valachi. He came in after the fact and blew the kid away."

"Really? How much did you hear?"

"Enough, but I had to haul-ass over here to save your sorry butt. I didn't need the extra paper work. I had Joe Ballou take over. He put it on the speaker phone and nine more cops heard the whole thing. I'll know everything that happened, Harry, so be careful what you say."

"Good. Then, you're going to have some interesting notes to read. I just wrapped up your five homicides in a nice little package for you, and the penthouse boys are going to love you. You're going to be their new boy wonder, Dan. They'll be kissing *your* ass, for a change."

DeRita walked over and picked up Gamboa's .45 and the .38 with the silencer from the floor, then held up the .38 between his finger and thumb. "Are you saying this is yours? Since when did you keep a .38 with a silencer in your office?" He spotted my .38 on the desk. "There's yours," he said, pointing.

I shrugged. "Eddy came in for a meeting we set up earlier,

and he heard what was going on." I pointed to where the whine-baby had been sitting in my chair. "The kid already had the drop on me with that .45, and then Eddy came charging in like the 7th Calvary. He's a man of few words as you can tell. He surprised the hell out of the punk that bled all over my chair, and they started two-stepping around the room like ballroom dancers. They were the two bulls in the china shop your boys heard. Eddy here, lost his gun in the melee, but the kid held on to his. I grabbed Eddy's .38 off the floor and shot the little fucker. You know I'm a good shot, Dan. That's why I hit him in the shoulder. I wanted him alive. For you. I could've killed him and you know it." My shoulder was sore from slamming into the wall, so I rotated it, thinking it would be better, but it wasn't. I was also stalling to figure out if I should expand on my lies or stop while I thought I was still ahead. Stopping seemed like the best route to take. "Your man can confirm it, I'm sure."

DeRita's eyes narrowed. "You're so full of shit, and that's the lamest story I've ever heard, even coming from you. None of it will hold water and you know it. *Valachi* was holding the .38 with the silencer when I busted in. Not you, Harry."

Wow. Caught me on that one. "Really? Then, I gave it back to him at some point. It's his gun, after all."

DeRita shook his head with disgust. "Really. That's your story, huh? I'm not sure about why you're doing this..." Then, his eyes zeroed in on Eddy's back, "then maybe I do. Shit."

I shrugged. "Does it really matter, Dan? Who shot the little punk? I mean, there's no doubt that it was self-defense, regardless of who shot him. Right? Think about this. It's mine and Eddy's word against a guy that's murdered five people; two of them cops, and two with their dicks stuffed down their mouths after cutting their throats. If he denies it, then who's the jury going to believe, anyway?"

DeRita just shook his head. "You're so full of shit, Harry. What are their choices? The jury gets to choose between the testimony of the nephew of a mobster against the mobster's bodyguard and a former Dallas detective that was drummed out of the force for consorting with the same mobster. Shit."

"See…it could be worse."

"Explain how it could get worse."

I shrugged. "I don't know, but anything's possible."

DeRita walked over and turned Eddy around by the elbow. "And what do you have to say about all this?"

"Nothing."

"That's what I figured. You and Captain America over here…shit."

Eddy turned completely around to face DeRita. "However…Captain," he said, "if you'll look in my inside jacket pocket, there's an envelope in it. I'm pretty sure it will confirm what you need to know about the hits, plus what you got on the phone."

"So, now the mobsters are helping out the cops?" DeRita asked incredulously, moving towards the cuffed man.

"We had nothing to do with this," Eddy said.

DeRita took the envelope from Eddy's pocket. "What is it?" DeRita asked, skeptically.

"A written confession by Garland Henshaw, detailing everything. Setting up Senator Doe. The extortion. The killings. The money. Even the details of the Santa Fe heist in '32, according to Cochran and Megs."

"See?" I said. "All tied up in a bow for you."

"Shit," DeRita said. "And where's Henshaw? Is he chewing on his dick too, by chance?"

"No, he's alive and well…and I can tell you where to find him," said Eddy Valachi.

Chapter 34

DeRita invited me to come down to HQ and give a statement about what went down at the office, but when I told him I was sticking to my story, he just told me to think about it some more and we'd talk about it tomorrow. He took Eddy Valachi with him, but removed his cuffs before leaving the office, which was a good sign. Maybe, he wasn't going to book him after all. He sure as hell wasn't going to get him to talk about anything, except where he could find Garland Henshaw. That was his get out of jail free ticket, I bet.

I also told him I had a party to go to and things to take care of quick-like. I called the building maintenance guy and told him I had a little front door issue he needed to take of tonight. I also told him to check the top drawer of the filing cabinet where he'd find a bottle of Jack. He's known to take a nip now and then, and I figured the bottle should ease his pain some.

Next on the agenda was Sam, Katie, and Jenny. I was supposed to meet them at the Adolphus and then all of us walk to the Magnolia together, but that whole shootout at the OK Corral thing in my office threw off my timetable. I left a message for Sam for us all to meet a Jenny's, and I'd be there in about forty-five minutes and we'd leave together.

I had another change of plans in mind, too. On my way out the door, what was left of it, I grabbed the genuine plastic Neiman Marcus bag with the monkey suit inside and the plastic patent shoes and headed for my apartment. Once there, I took a long, hot shower washing off the day's dirt and grime from my body and mind and even brushed my teeth. Henshaw was going to be substituting his tuxedo for pin stripes and sleeping with some of his former clients, *and* Alexis Gamboa, the pretty boy, would end up being Queen for the Day in the suite next to him. Therefore, tonight was a night to put the case behind us and celebrate the evening. Kick up some dust. Boot-scoot across the floor with a beautiful babe on my arm.

After I dried off and slicked back my hair, I grabbed the clothes bag and dumped everything onto the bed. I got dressed in the tuxedo and white pleaded shirt with that little bent collar thing, added the black studs and cuff links, and then tossed the bow tie, cummerbund, and plastic patent shoes back inside the bag. In my closet, I found my turquoise bolo, Tony Lama black alligator boots and belt with the turquoise studded buckle, and added them to the tuxedo attire. I was pretty proud with what I saw in the mirror, except one thing was missing. I went back to the closet and got the black felt Stetson cowboy hat from its box. Checked the mirror again and smiled. *That's what I'm talkin' about.* I decided to ditch the shoulder holster because it hampers my moves on the dance floor, so I clipped the .38's holster to my belt, leaving my jacket unbuttoned so it'd be noticed that I was packing heat. After all, this was Texas and the Big D, not some mamsy-pamsy get-together in Iowa. I headed out the door for Jenny's place.

When I got to her apartment, I knocked on the door once and she opened it up immediately. Standing in front of me, framed by the open doorway, was the most beautiful angel I'd ever seen. Her blonde hair fell to her shoulders in loose curls, her lips were ruby red, and the long black evening gown clung to her body like a glove. The gown was cut tastefully low and showed just enough cleavage to make a man want to look harder to see where it was all coming from.

"My...my God, Jenny...you're beautiful..." was about all I could manage to mumble through my teeth.

"I know," she said softly. "And you, you'll be the handsomest cowboy of all. She hooked her arm in mine and led me back inside her place. You and Sam will be the only *real* men there tonight, you know."

Suddenly, I cared about how I looked. "You don't think the hat and the boots are too much, do you?"

"No, Harry. A bow tie and patent leather shoes...on you, that would have been too much, Sugar Doll."

Sam and Katie were the second best looking pair I'd ever seen. Katie's hair was piled high on her head, bringing out the natural beauty of her young face, and her dress was also a long black satin affair, showing off a fine figure that I didn't know was there. Sam's tux was double-breasted, and he too chose to dump the cummerbund and bowtie, deciding to forego a tie all together, and went for the open-collared look. I glanced at his feet and grinned. Black alligator boots. When the back-slapping, huggy-kissy thing was done, we headed for the Magnolia Building.

As we strolled out the door, I told Sam, "Great minds think alike, buddy."

"Always," he said.

Chapter 35

After the Magnolia Petroleum Gala two weeks ago, things have been like a rapid succession of West Texas dust devils ripping across the plains, and it all started at the Magnolia shindig. The fact that John and Hedy weren't there for their own campaign fundraiser never put a damper on the occasion. Evidently, Zucker couldn't keep a lid on his own exclusive about Doe's newly-found identity, his dropping out of the U. S. Senate run, and another tidbit of a bombshell, his upcoming resignation from the State Senate. So the theme changed from a money raiser for a losing campaign to a celebration of Doe finding out his real name. Any excuse to party. The reporter was also kind enough to mention to everyone that Stumbaugh Investigations and Cameron Epperson were the driving forces behind the discovery of Jeff Shockley, aka John Doe, and he promised more bombshells to follow.

Our little foursome, of course, were the belles and beaus of the ball. The rich and famous love to mingle with the little people, especially when they're going to be headline news and heroes at the same time. Sam and I may not have been the most handsome ones attending the ball, in the unimportant opinions of the other guests, but we damn-well cut-a-rug across the dance floor and two-stepped across the hardwoods with our beautiful partners better than any of the other yahoos trying their hands. I can still scoot across a floor with one good leg better than anybody with two. Epperson, on the other hand, worked the room like a barker at the carnival, talking up our names for future business and enjoying his own elevated standing among the rich and famous.

Afterwards, the office phones rang off the wall for missing person cases, mysterious deaths in the family cases, and we even had the mayor's wife call about her missing Cocker Spaniel. We passed on that one. It was nice to be able to pick and choose our clients for a change, but, for the time being, Sam and I had been playing the stall game. We wanted some breather room and made excuses to be out of the office, but Jenny wasn't having any of it. She's been so busy these last few days taking messages and separating the kooks from the real thing; she hasn't had a chance to read her new *Photoplay* magazine. And, if she couldn't play, neither could we. She started setting appointments for the following week.

Later in the week after the lovey-dovey couple returned from their romp in Oklahoma, John and Hedy Doe announced that they would soon be off on a cruise around the world to spend some quality time together and stay away from the limelight, reporters, and cameras that were sure to follow them at every step in order to avoid the expected onslaught of publicity that was bound to come their way. Sounded like a good idea to me.

On the lighter side, in the November 4th elections, Price Daniels became the new United States Senator for the State of Texas, which is a pretty easy thing to do when you're the only one on the ballot. And Ike, the old general, took eighty percent of the vote, just like Doe said, in a blowout against that wimp Adlai, to become our new President of the United States. I should have made that bet Doe suggested.

The even bigger news was the arrest and indictments against Garland Henshaw and Alexis Gamboa for their collusion in the deaths of five men and the extortion of John and Hedy Doe. The Dallas District Attorney doubted the signed confession by Henshaw, implicating himself in the three day killing spree, would hold any water since Eddy Valachi held a gun to his head when he signed it. A minor point in my opinion, but then again, I don't have to follow the rules anymore. But, the impromptu confession overhead by me and ten other detectives while Gamboa held a .45 to my head would hold solid. Henshaw was keeping his mouth shut, like a good attorney, and Gamboa was singing like a bird in an effort to get the death penalty taken off the table. The full confession on his part in the affair, at Henshaw's direction of course, and him cutting a deal to avoid a trial, I'm sure, were at the *urging* of his famous uncle. My guess is, Giovanni assured his wayward nephew that he'd be protected during his lifetime residence in the Big House and wouldn't have to worry about a homemade pig-sticker in the back or a pecker up his ass if he went away quietly. Henshaw, on the other hand, could be assured of both. The shyster becoming a queen for the day on Huntsville's Death Row facility brings a smile to my lips every time I think about it. But, there was one thing they both squawked to the rooftops about...they denied having anything to do with the killing Detective Carl Cochran.

Eddy must have made a pretty good deal for himself with the coppers. He was cut loose after he said his piece about Henshaw's confession, and his name was never mentioned in the papers. He was referred to as a *material witness,* and that was it. Gee, I wonder how that came about? Sam found out, through Giovanni, that when we ran into Eddy at the elevators, he was chasing down Alexis and discovered Wellstone's body. How he knew the attorney was the next target, I'll probably never find out. And, Sam's coziness with Gamboa...that was a bigger mystery than Doe's identity.

And, that brings me to where I am now. There're some things I need to get wrapped up to really bring this case to an end, for my own peace of mind. There's only one person that can do it. Giovanni Gamboa. It's going to be tricky, though. I need some straight answers to things he might not want to discuss. But after all, what do I have to lose? Just a valued friend, an irreplaceable source, and the creation of an enemy. No big deal.

When I stepped into the Cairo Room, one of the waitresses sent me to the bar, instead of Gamboa's table. The old man and I made eye contact, but he didn't motion me over. No direct path to his table this time. Eddy was back at his usual spot and gave me the heads-up nod and a smile, indicating he was expecting me. We shook hands. I got the pat down. He had a cold Budweiser waiting for me.

"Thanks for the beer," I said, "I usually don't drink before ten-thirty in the morning, but I can make today an exception to the rule." I wasn't about to turn it down, so I took a deep swallow of the golden liquid and it went down smoothly.

"Good to see you, Harry," Eddy said.

"You too, Eddy. How's that material witness thing going for you?"

"Much better than the alternative."

I gave him a light pat on the arm. "I bet. Say, I want to thank you for saving my bacon the other day. Haven't had a chance before now. That little bastard had me dead-to-rights in his sights, and I just knew I was a dead man. Thanks buddy."

He shrugged. "It's what I was instructed to do…but for you, Harry, I'd have done it anyway." He gave a short laugh and I reciprocated, for my own health. "And you too, Harry, for standing up for me that way. Mr. Gamboa was deeply moved by what you did." Then, he added in a whisper, "That should go well for you…in your favor today." After turning to face the mirror behind the bar and glancing at the old man's reflection behind him, he said softly, "You're not his first visitor today."

What the hell is that all about?

Still staring into the mirror, he saw the signal from Gamboa and said, "You can go now. Good to see you, Harry." There was no parting handshake or glad-handing. *Just go to your meeting.*

Gamboa stood when I reached the table, and he greeted me with a big bear hug. "Harry, my friend, I was wondering when you'd get time to come and see your old friend. As you know, I don't get out much these days, and I know things have been busy for you. Something to eat? Some breakfast, perhaps? Coffee to wash away that beer Eddy forced on you?"

"No, thank you, Giovanni. I've already eaten, I'm fine." He sat down and I followed suit. "Thank you for seeing me this morning."

His hand waved across his face as though swatting away an annoying fly. "Anytime for you, Harry. I'm glad you're here so I can thank you personally for what you did for Eddy. I know it has put you in an uncomfortable position with your friend, Captain DeRita. But, I know that it was me you were thinking of when you offered yourself as the shooter. That puts our friendship at a much deeper and affectionate place, Harry. You were unselfish...in the risk you took. Thank you." He lit another cigarette from a smoldering butt. "Now...what can I do for *you*?"

Without a word, I reached into my inside pocket and pulled out the yellowing, folded sheet of paper that Sam stole from John Doe's wallet. The one that had five names written on it...one of which was Giovanni Gamboa's. I slid it across the table. "Sam found this in Ralph Morris's wallet. It's been laying in a box in a store room at the Denton Hospital for the past twenty years." I searched for a reaction in his face, but it was blank. The man was very good at checking his emotions at the door.

When Gamboa unfolded the paper, a strange unexpected thing happened. It was in his eyes and the faint smile that appeared out of nowhere. The best way I can describe it is...it was one of those looks you get when you hear a song on the radio that sparks a fond memory from the past. The old man was reminiscing!

No denial, no question to the Ralph Morris reference.

"These names...certainly do take me back to another time, Harry."

I watched him tick them off mentally, one at a time.

"Of the five, I am the only one still around. The others are...well, gone." He gave a deep sigh and returned to the present time. He refolded the paper and replaced it in the middle of the table.

Neutral ground.

I pushed it back and said. "That is yours." He nodded and left it on the table. "Giovanni...I'd like to clear the air, if I can...with some things that..." I was having trouble wording my thoughts.

"Do you mean, you want to *cleanse the soul* instead of *clear the air*, my friend?"

"Let me put it this way, as far this last *case*, for lack of a better term...I don't want any secrets. I'd like to be on the same playing field as you. After all...you know all *my* sins."

Giovanni nodded and took a drag from his cigarette. "Indeed I do...and I agree, Harry. It is the least I can do for you, after what you did for our friend, Eddy. I like the idea of a level playing field. I will do this for you...this time."

This will make us even, is what you're saying, you old fox.

"You are a fan of poker, I assume?"

"I am," I said. *More games.*

"How would you like to play it?" Giovanni asked.

"Straight up, for a change."

He nodded. "Only you, Harry. Your open, then."

I had to pick my questions well because I knew they would be few and far between; so, I decided to go for the jugular. "John Doe and Ralph Morris is the same person." It was a statement, not a question.

He smiled. "You are leading with aces, I see, but only confirming what you already know. You burned an ace, my friend." He tapped the long ash, barely hanging on to life from the end of his cigarette, and smiled. "Your perceptions have always amazed me, Harry. Your next open?"

Well, shit.

"October 1932."

Another smile, reminiscing. "Ah, a wonderful time in my life, Harry...but you know, when men are young and choose their life's path...they believe they are immortal and are willing to dance with the Devil to attain their dreams..." He let the last words drift away.

"Was Cochran the devil?" I asked.

He laughed at me as though it was an irrelevant question. "No, Harry. *Morris* was the devil. Unlike anyone I'd ever seen. Ralph Morris made Clyde and Buck Barrow look like choirboys."

"Then, the whole amnesia thing...it's bullshit," I said.

Giovanni shrugged. "That, my friend, is something we shall both have to find out in our own due time. But, let me answer your question with a question."

Of course.

"Do you think that a young amnesic man in his early twenties could leave the hospital with no job, no name, no money and could afford to go to a top rated college like the University of Texas, then on to law school at SMU with a blank past and only charm in his pocket? And then, land at a thriving law firm with a top notch defense attorney in Dallas fresh out of school? Do you think such a man could find the affections of one of the most available and richest women in Texas without *resources*? Old man Davis has always been very protective of his young Hedy."

Holy shit. No wonder he wants to take a trip around the world.

"So, he *did* have the money. And the rest of the shares?"

"Share, you mean." The smile. "Another question. How do you think a young soldier in the family moved up so quickly through the ranks? By hustling prostitution and gambling rings? In Texas? Really?"

I decided to go out on a limb. "And the other four names on the list? They were part of it too? You obviously knew them."

He shrugged. "When the devil came to me to sell my soul, he had the plan and the manpower, but not the funds to pull off such an operation. I personally couldn't bankroll the proposition, but I knew who could. Unfortunately for them, their fates were sealed when I brought them in. As I told you, I had dreams, too."

You're a chameleon, old man. A ruthless killer with a

grandfather's demeanor.

"Then, the shakedown on Doe was legitimate." I was talking more to myself than asking a question. I could see in his eyes that our time was coming to a close.

Stall.

"Things seem to have worked out well for Eddy. I'm glad."

The smile again. "You play the game well, Harry. Yes, it did. Still a few minor details left to be taken care of...but they won't be a problem. You see, I'm not as out of touch as some like to think. I can still stick my fingers into a bowl of icing and stir things up a bit."

I did the nodding this time. "You have been very generous, Giovanni, but if I may...one more question."

He smiled. "Sometimes...you can be very predictable...like a pit bull." He lit up another cigarette and nodded.

"Cochran. Who killed him?"

The smile was tighter this time. He snubbed out the old butt. "You and I...we are smart men. Men of the world. We can read and judge other men. Their strengths and weaknesses. But others, some never learn that it is a bad idea to poke a stick at a sleeping bear...especially when her cubs are threatened. Do you know of a sleeping bear who has been...disturbed by a fool?"

Yes I do.

I was about to be dismissed, but I wanted to swing for the bases with one more question. "And speaking of Sam, how has he come into your confidences so quickly? You'd think the two of you were related or something," I added with a light laugh.

This brought a full blown laugh from the old man. "Ah, Harry, your bluff just cost you the game, my friend!" Giovanni stood and opened his arms.

I stood, received his hug, and returned it. He leaned back and gave me an affectionate pat on the cheek. "I look forward to our next adventure together, my friend. Which now, I suspect, will start up soon. I'd say you have one week left before the ship leaves."

Epilogue

I hit the office in full stride and full of piss and vinegar, but I did slow down just long enough to admire my brand new door and new fancy print on the frosted glass window, identifying the offices of Stumbaugh Investigations, Inc. I added the *Inc.* to make it more official sounding and chipped in a couple of extra bucks to put mine and Sam's name at the bottom. Mine was on top, of course. As soon as I stepped inside, I got all riled up again, knowing what I was about to do. Nobody plays me for a fall guy and sails away into the sunset.

"Doll Face, please get Mr. Doe on the line for me. Try him at his hotel suite first, Room 1449," I said, back to full stride and heading to my office.

"You want me to call his direct line instead?" Jenny asked, trying to get the full sentence out as I whizzed by her desk.

I stopped, knowing it was the polite thing to do. "No, go through the hotel switchboard." I figured he'd answer that line before the personal one. "Buzz me in the office." Even Doll Face couldn't calm me down. I was fuming. And the more I thought about it...the more I wanted to shoot somebody.

I had just enough time to park my hat on the rack and my butt in my chair before Doll Face stood in the doorway, that concerned, pouty look on her face. "Harry? You okay? Your face is all red and you've got that little snarly thing going on your top lip." She tried to imitate my lip as she described it.

A perceptive babe.

I smiled as best I could. "I'll be okay…any luck with Doe?" I asked, deflecting the subject of my snarling lip.

"He's checked out, Harry! They don't have the suite anymore. I guess…maybe he doesn't need it anymore since he's not a senator. You think, Harry?"

Why keep a room when you don't plan to come back?

"You're probably right on that one, Doll Face. Call the house on Swiss. The butler's name is Freeman. See if you have any luck there." While I waited for her, I spotted my as-of-now-still-unread novel, *The One-Eyed Witness*, still sitting on the corner of my desk.

Only ten pages to go...

After a few minutes, Jenny rushed in like she'd just accomplished something big. "Harry, he's on the line! Mr. Doe, I mean…not Freeman…he's on hold…for you," she said, stammering her way through the sentence.

"Thanks, Doll Face. Now, see if you can find Sam. Tell him our work isn't done yet, and to get his ass out of the bar and in the office."

Jenny smiled, turned, and headed for her office, before stopping in the doorway. "You know, I love it when you talk that way, Harry…and that little snarly lip thing you do," giving me a little extra hip action on the way out.

Now, I was feeling good. Back on the job. I propped my feet on the desk, leaned back in my swivel, and picked up the line…with a smile on my face. "Hello?"

Doe answered with mock enthusiasm, "Hello, Harry! Sorry we've missed each other lately. I understand the Magnolia party was a hit. Glad you got to go. What can I do for you?"

"You must be a very happy man by now, John. Sitting on top of the world."

"And I have you to thank for that, Harry. Is there something I can do for you? Hedy and I are in kind of a hurry, preparing for our cruise."

"Well, Ralph, you might want to keep the thank you and

cancel the cruise." And as expected, there was a pregnant pause at the other end of the line. Actually, just heavy breathing, so I decided to fill in the void. "So, Ralph, let me ask you one thing before I let you go. How much did you have to pay Nurse Hugghins to switch out the hospital records for the old battered shoebox?" I thought I'd let him chew on that for a second or two, while I played the strong silent type.

"I'm not sure I understand what you're saying here, Harry," Doe responded matter-of-factly, "why are you turning on me like this?"

I sighed. "Playing games with each other is over, Ralph. I know who you are. Either you or your nurse-babe-friend got sloppy. Sam found a piece of paper with a list of interesting names on it. He lifted it right under her nose, by the way."

More silence, then, "I see," Doe finally said, "I suspect you've been talking to our mutual friend who owns the Italian restaurant on Mockingbird, then. That's too bad. You know how I dislike loose ends. If I may ask, what are your future plans in this regards, Harry? Expose me as a fraud to the world? At the word of a known criminal? You really think that'll hold water with the public? I can shoot that down myself without the aid of a hundred-dollar an hour mouthpiece. Besides, if you expose me, then that will automatically put your friend, Giovanni, on the hook for his part in the robbery... and yes, don't forget about the two dead police officers. Capital crime. Old Sparky, as you're so fond of saying. You ready to see him go to the chair as well? Perhaps, it's your own future you should be concerned about instead of worrying yourself so much about mine."

I smiled to myself, since there was no one else in the room. "Who me? I don't plan on doing anything with what I know. Absolutely nothing. I'm as free as a bird on this one, Ralph. The John Doe Caper is officially closed."

"Well, that's mighty nice of you, Harry, but hard to believe. I know you better than that. Loose ends are a passion for you, though. Not a vendetta."

"Oh, you can believe it, alright, Ralph. And I'm keeping the shoebox that Sam and Nurse Hugghins brought to the gala at Epperson's office yesterday. That was all a little over-dramatic for my taste, by the way. All the huggy-kissy stuff. But, once you make a mistake and one domino falls…the rest follows behind."

"Really?"

"Yeah…really. It's all falling down around you as we speak and you don't even know it."

Doe actually gave a small laugh at that one. "I knew hiring you was a mistake, Harry. Well, I must go. Watch your back, my friend."

"Don't have to, Ralph. Giovanni doesn't like loose ends either…and he is a man that definitely believes in vendettas. You might start letting the hired help start your cars for you. Know what I mean, buddy?" That seemed like a good closing line so I hung up and snatched Perry Mason off the desk. Only ten pages to go, and I was dying to know whodunit.

About the Author

Buz Sawyers resides in Rowlett, Texas and teaches Creative Writing and Composition courses at Argosy University and the Art Institute of Dallas. *John Doe* is his sixth novel and once again he has crossed into a totally different genre from any of his previous writings. Currently, he is working on a sequel to *John Doe.* Also, Buz is working on the memoirs of Major James Capers who served during the Vietnam War and was finally nominated for the Congressional Medal of Honor in 2007. Buz can be contacted at his website & email:

www.bsawyers.com
buzsawyers@tx.rr.com

www.ingramcontent.com/pod-product-compliance
Lightning Source LLC
Chambersburg PA
CBHW051236260626
47162CB00002B/456
* 9 7 8 0 9 8 9 5 1 9 1 2 0 *